ONCE A YEAR

Felicity Hayes-McCoy, author of the best-selling Finfarran series, was born in Dublin, Ireland. She studied literature at UCD before moving to England in the 1970s to train as an actress. Her work as a writer ranges from TV and radio drama and documentary, to screenplays, music theatre, memoir and children's books. Her Finfarran novels are widely read on both sides of the Atlantic, and in Australia, and have been translated into nine languages.

She and her husband, opera director Wilf Judd, live in the West Kerry Gaeltacht and in Bermondsey, London. She blogs about life in both places on her website www.felicityhayesmccoy.co.uk and you can follow her on Bluesky @fhayesmccoy.bsky.social, on Facebook at Felicity Hayes-McCoy Author and on Instagram as Felicity Hayes-McCoy.

ALSO BY FELICITY HAYES-MCOY

The Finfarran series
The Library at the Edge of the World
Summer at the Garden Café
The Mistletoe Matchmaker
The Month of Borrowed Dreams
The Transatlantic Book Club
The Heart of Summer
The Year of Lost and Found
The Bookseller's Gift

Standalone fiction
The Keepsake Quilters

Non-fiction
The House on an Irish Hillside
Enough is Plenty
A Woven Silence

ONCE A YEAR

Felicity Hayes-McCoy

HACHETTE
BOOKS
IRELAND

First published in Ireland in 2025 by HACHETTE BOOKS IRELAND

1

Cataloguing in Publication Data is available from the British Library.

ISBN 9781399743792

Typeset in Adobe Caslon Pro by Bookends Publishing Services, Dublin
Printed and bound in Great Britain by Clays Ltd, Elcograf S.p.A.

Hachette Books Ireland policy is to use papers that are natural, renewable
and recyclable products and made from wood grown in sustainable forests.
The logging and manufacturing processes are expected to conform to the
environmental regulations of the country of origin.

MIX
Paper | Supporting
responsible forestry
FSC® C104740

Hachette Books Ireland
8 Castlecourt Centre
Castleknock
Dublin 15, Ireland

A division of Hachette UK Ltd
Carmelite House, 50 Victoria Embankment, London EC4Y 0DZ
www.hachettebooksireland.ie

For Marcella

Invitations

A cardboard box stood on the console table just inside Nora Sullivan's door. She noticed that, as usual, it had been neatly addressed by hand, and earlier, from her bedroom window, she'd seen a lad get out of Cassidy's van at the hotel entrance and climb the steps carrying the box with care. Proper order too, she thought, given how much work Cassidy's Print Place has had from me for nigh on sixty years.

Finding a pair of scissors, she slit the tape with a bit of effort, opened the box and revealed its contents. The design of her cards hardly changed from one Christmas to another: urns of bright-berried holly flanking the open door, and above, picked out in glitter, the words 'Castlehill Hotel'. This year's photo had been taken from the bottom step, leading the viewer's eye to the welcoming entrance. Last year's, though charming, hadn't been quite so inviting. Examining the difference this slight change made, Nora smiled. No one could say she'd lost her touch when it came to detail; and the hand-delivered box demonstrated that, though she'd decided it was time to make way for a new generation, she retained her status in the town.

On top of the tightly packed cards and envelopes was a small folder. Opening it, Nora looked with satisfaction at four embossed invitations. *You are cordially invited to the annual Sullivan Girls' Get-together* … a different font this time, and a new border, but the same words she'd drafted every year for decades, with the dates below and space for the personal greetings she always added in blue biro. She'd never believed in leaving a job to the last minute so, taking the invitations and four cards, she got on with this one. In past years, she'd sometimes written at least a dozen invitations, and sometimes so few that she'd considered dropping her tradition. Still, *I've stuck with it*, she thought, *and it's been the right thing to do.*

Ten minutes later, she lined up the envelopes on the console table and read each name under her breath to herself. Sheila. Máire. Barbara. Henrietta. *My girls*, thought Nora, with a satisfied nod. *I wouldn't say they'll all be over the moon at the thought of coming. But I do know for certain that they'll come.*

Chapter 1

Henrietta looked doubtfully at the chicken. She had bought organic regardless of cost and roasted it with sage and apricot stuffing but the fact remained that she was serving it cold. She peered out of the kitchen window hoping to see a break in the clouds beyond the streaming raindrops. Stuart's plane was due to land at seven and the forecast had said no rain before midnight, so chicken salad had made sense this morning when she'd gone shopping. Now she frowned. If he came in wet and tired, he wasn't going to be thrilled by cold cuts, but last time he'd flown home from a conference he'd stopped at the airport for a drink with a colleague, and the leg of lamb she'd cooked for dinner had ended up tough as old boots. Not that Stuart had been bothered. He'd gone and rummaged in the kitchen, and they'd eaten tuna mayo and rocket instead. Which was partly why Henrietta had opted for salad this time. Though she'd also been carried away by the butcher's rapture over the chicken, which, apparently, had lived a life of sybaritic luxury, wandering about nibbling wildflowers and being checked by vets.

Turning, she found Jane had come in behind her and was looking sceptically at the large oval platter. But sceptical silence was Jane's default mode, so that didn't reveal much. Henrietta went to the table and did things with watercress till, eventually, the silence unnerved her.

'What d'you think?'

'About what?'

'This is dinner. D'you think your dad will like it? Should we have soup as well?'

Jane raised an indifferent shoulder. 'Whatever.'

'Soup would be warming. Look at the weather. I mean, salad just before Christmas is probably dumb.'

Jane took a dried apricot and licked it tentatively. 'Are these in the stuffing?'

'Don't you like them?'

'They're okay. When will Dad be home?'

'The plane should touch down in ten minutes. I've been tracking it on my phone.'

'I'm going back up to my room.'

'Okay. I'll have a quick shower and change.'

Jane gave her an appraising look, disconcerting in a twelve year old, and disappeared through the kitchen door.

In the en-suite bathroom, her hair twisted up in a towel, Henrietta was struck by doubt again as she dried between her toes. Was it daft to have bought chicken when, only a week from now, they'd be wading through the huge bronze turkey she'd ordered for Christmas Day? That in itself had been an iffy purchase. She'd known as soon as she'd tapped her credit card and seen the total that letting the plausible butcher advise her on size had been a mistake: she was going to be disguising turkey for weeks in pies and fricassées. And, possibly, desserts. So, of all things, why decide to serve chicken tonight? Shaking out her hair, she stared at the mirror, her features distorted by anxiety. Leaning closer, she wondered if she ought to buy age-defying cream. It seemed too early to start when she was only twenty-six, but the guy who did her hair claimed stress was a major factor in ageing and, what with buying Christmas presents, keeping house, and trying to handle Jane, she already felt half a step away from becoming a withered crone. But, once she'd stopped frowning, the mirror showed nothing but radiant skin and dimples so she reached for her usual moisturiser, telling herself to chill.

It was silly to get worked up about things that Stuart would call trivial. Household panics just made him hug her and laugh. Suddenly, the thought of his dark, teasing eyes made her body tingle, and the fact that he was on his way home became the only thing that mattered. Everything in life was simple to Stuart, whose bank balance matched his self-assurance. He powered through life brushing aside problems, and considered recrimination a waste of time. It was she who fussed about value for money and forward-planning and what people might think. Stuart, who was twice her age, was different. If the turkey got boring, he wouldn't make a big deal of it. He'd ruffle Jane's hair with his powerful, manicured fingers and suggest a trip to a restaurant for artisan fish and chips.

Henrietta had lifted her mascara brush to her lashes when the thought of fish nearly made her poke her eye out. Seafood. That was what she should have chosen if she was going to serve a salad. Lobster was Stuart's favourite. It even made Jane crack a smile. Lobster mayonnaise with micro leaves and, to cover all bases, something warming for afters. It would have been so easy to get a lobster, she thought crossly, blinking away excruciating tears. There was always a tank of them in the fancy fishmonger's window next to the plausible butcher's on her suburban village street. Admittedly, taped-up claws and waving antennae freaked her out. Still, if only she'd planned better, she could have left the freezer-and-boiling-water bit to Annaliese, the au-pair. But she'd given Annaliese the day off and allowed herself to be talked into clover-fed chicken, so, dabbing her streaming eye with the towel, she told herself firmly that chicken would have to do.

Stuart arrived in time for dinner, shaking a dripping umbrella, with sodden leaves caught in the wheels of the suitcase he'd trundled from the garage to the porch. As Henrietta let him in, Jane appeared, in a fluffy pink jumper worn over white leggings. She charged down the stairs and threw herself into his arms. Earlier, she'd been wearing jeans and an old grey sweatshirt so, like Henrietta's turquoise dress, which was Stuart's favourite, her new outfit demonstrated the importance of the occasion. 'Here's my princess!' Kissing the top of Jane's head, Stuart held out his free arm to Henrietta. 'Come here, gorgeous girl. God, it's good to be home!' Gathered into the hug,

Henrietta buried her face in his shoulder, smelling damp cashmere and feeling herself relax. Wriggling free, Jane asked about Stuart's flight. 'What kind of plane was it, Dad? One of the new ones?'

'Haven't a clue. I just found my seat and slept.'

Henrietta looked up at him. 'Oh, no, darling! Was the conference exhausting?'

'Not a bit. I just took a power nap. Look, I'm going up to grab a shower. Is that okay with you, dinner-wise?'

The question was rhetorical, as he'd already made for the stairs, but Henrietta felt a glow of satisfaction. 'Fine. Take your time. It's only salad.' Pausing on the staircase, Stuart looked down and smiled at her, then, taking the steps two at a time, he called over his shoulder, 'Have a rummage in my bag. You too, Princess. See what you think.'

In the dining room, as she finished laying the table, Henrietta admired the gift she'd found in his briefcase. It was a silver chain bracelet hung with green gemstones, the perfect accessory for the turquoise dress that matched her eyes. Jane had disappeared upstairs with a giant, gold-wrapped Toblerone, which would ruin her appetite for dinner. Straightening the platter of chicken, Henrietta went to the fridge to check the temperature of the wine. The cut-crystal glasses she'd just set out weren't really to her taste: given a choice, she'd have gone for something modern. Actually, the same applied to the dining-room furniture. And the living-room curtains. But, as everyone in her family had cheerfully assured her, this was par for the course when you were somebody's second wife. Her granny, an outspoken woman, had put it more forcefully than the others. 'Don't go mistaking his house for yours, Hen. You'll only end up frustrated.

It's the dead wife's first and the child's next, with you in the ha'penny place a long way after them.'

At the time, Henrietta hadn't paid much attention but, in the two years she'd been married, she'd come to see that her family had been right. Not that it mattered, she thought, as she put the wine bottle into a terracotta cooler. The house, on the southern outskirts of Dublin, was charming and comfortable, and she'd no intention of pitting her own preferences against Stuart's daughter's emotional needs. After all, she'd told her family, when your dad brings home a stepmum, you don't want to feel your own mum's been forgotten. You want your familiar surroundings to stay the same while you adjust.

A bedroom door slammed and, moments later, Jane came into the kitchen.

'There you are. I hope you haven't eaten all that chocolate.'

'Nope.' Jane leaned on the worktop. She was small for her age and had her father's narrow gem-bright eyes. Along with the Toblerone, Stuart had brought her a sparkly hairband, which now held back her straight dark hair. Henrietta never questioned what Jane chose to wear, but she sometimes wondered if, given that she'd be thirteen in a few months, she'd passed the stage of wanting to look like a little princess. The wardrobe in her pretty bedroom was full to bursting with outfits that only came out when her dad was home. They ranged from things like tonight's pink jumper and leggings to expensive frilly dresses that, when she'd grown out of them, often went to the charity shop hardly worn. But, as Stuart's doting mother always bought more of the same sort of thing, and Jane always seemed happy to wear them on family occasions, Henrietta never interfered.

8

The youngest of three, she'd always been treated as the baby of her own family, so overriding other people's decisions wasn't her thing.

Dinner was a success. Stuart came downstairs wrapped in a towelling dressing-gown and they sat around laughing and chatting over their plates of chicken salad. Elbows on the table, Jane reeled off her latest school results. 'Exceptional in Chemistry, Dad. That's the second time running. And Oisín, Suzy and me came up with a thing for Applied Technology. We designed a feeder that portions out food so, when people are away, they can leave seven days' worth of seed for the birds in their garden. We built a prototype and ran a trial.'

'Impressive.'

Happy to see them so relaxed together, Henrietta sat back and watched the interaction. When she was newly married, she'd hoped Jane would see her as a kind of big sister, to have fun with and turn to for advice. Stuart had talked about it the night he'd proposed.

'Seriously, Hen, this is a big undertaking,' he'd said. 'I mean, there's my age ...'

'Your age is just a number. It doesn't matter.'

'Not now, maybe, but when you're in your forties, I'll be drawing my pension.'

'Doesn't matter.'

He'd kissed her, then pulled away, saying, 'And there's Jane.'

'Jane's a sweetie.'

'Yes, she is. She's also a huge responsibility.'

Henrietta had tried to laugh him out of it. 'What's this? Are you withdrawing your offer?'

'God, no, of course not. I love you. I want you to marry me. I just need you to think about what you're taking on. It's not just me, it's also a child who's lost her mum.'

'Stuart, I know I can't replace her.'

'Darling, I want you for yourself, not to act as a replacement.'

'Good. Because I couldn't be Jane's mum. I wouldn't know how. What I do know is that you and I were meant to find each other. I promise you won't regret this. You won't forget your past, and I don't want you to, but you, Jane and I will be starting a new life together. And Jane adores you, so she and I will begin with the most important thing in common.'

It had been a sudden proposal after a whirlwind romance, but Henrietta had had no regrets, no reason to doubt that he loved her, and she'd understood the need for what Stuart's mother had called 'a period of transition'. All the same, it had been daunting to return from her honeymoon to a big house, a taciturn child and a tight-lipped nanny. Stuart had had to go abroad on a work trip almost at once. His farewell to Jane was casual, but when he kissed Henrietta he muttered, 'I hate this. I always have. It gives me nightmares. This time, at least, I know she's safe with you.' Having had charge of Jane for years, the nanny was bristling under a month's notice and, far from making things easier, had made them worse. Things had improved when she left, but the relationship with Jane never became what Henrietta had hoped for. She'd imagined shopping trips, girl-talk at home, making cupcakes and painting their nails together. Instead, she found herself living with a reserved, obedient child who seemed never to need help or advice and was quietly self-sufficient.

When Stuart was home, they had great family times together but, as the months went by, Henrietta had concluded that, if she were to disappear in the morning, Stuart would be devastated but it wouldn't matter to Jane.

After dinner, when Jane went to bed, Stuart and Henrietta sat by the living-room fire with a couple of brandies. The previous day, with Annaliese's help, Henrietta had decorated the Christmas tree. Now, leaning against Stuart's knees as she sat cross-legged on the hearthrug, she admired the firelight dancing on gold baubles and silver bells. Stuart was lying back in his armchair, swirling the drink in his glass. Twisting a strand of her hair round his finger, he tugged it gently. 'What are you thinking about?'

'Nothing. Just that it's lovely to have you home.' With her elbow on his knee, she turned and asked what he thought of her decorations.

Stuart looked from the sparkling tree to the holly wreaths and evergreens tied with ribbon. 'Haven't you gone a bit over the top?'

'Oh, darling, it's Christmas!'

'But, surely, you've doubled up since last year?'

'That's what people do at Christmas. It's traditional. Every year you add something else. It's how you build up memories.'

'Exponentially?'

Henrietta giggled. 'There's no need to be a Grinch.'

'Actually, I like it. Who sent the cards you've put on the mantelpiece?'

'My granny. Obviously. And the reindeer one's from your mother.' Henrietta stood up and fetched the cards, to show him. 'Not many people send cards any more. I think they're nice, though. Very retro.

11

Here's the obligatory shot of the family business.' She held out her granny's card to show him the hotel's welcoming door. Silver specks had stuck to her hand when she'd lifted the card from the mantelpiece and, turning to replace it, she flicked them off with a grin. 'I suspect the glitter is a huge environmental no-no, but it's traditional too, and you won't get Granny to drop it.'

'Fancy a second brandy?'

'No, thanks. I'm half-cut already.' She stood on tiptoe to put the cards back on the high mantelpiece without disturbing the pine cones and evergreen garland. 'I'd say that when I'm in Castlehill this year you and Jane might still be eating turkey. I got conned into buying a monster. It'll probably last till Easter.'

'When do you go?'

Henrietta was struggling to find the flat surface under a garland of gilded pine cones. 'Same as usual, first weekend after the New Year. Driving down Friday, coming home on Monday.'

'Can't be done, darling. I've a meeting in Turin that weekend.'

Still holding her grandmother's card, Henrietta swung round and looked at him blankly. 'But I have to go. You know I do. It's the Sullivan Girls' Get-together.'

'Oh, sweetheart, you can't always be at your gran's beck and call.'

This was so unjust that Henrietta was astonished. 'I'm not. I never have been. It's once a year, Stuart. Once a year, in Granny's hotel. You know we've always done it.'

'I'm sorry. It's not possible. Can't you ask Nora to change the date?'

'What? No, of course I can't. Not at this stage. She's eighty-four. It's a big family thing. She's probably been arranging it since September.'

'Well, we can't leave Jane alone while you take off to the midlands.'

'She won't be alone. Annaliese will be here.'

'Don't be ridiculous, Hen.'

'Ridiculous? Why would you say that?'

'Annaliese is seventeen.'

'Eighteen.'

'She's not a responsible adult. That's the point.' Stuart got to his feet and poured himself another brandy. 'Sure you don't want more of this?'

'No. I mean, yes, I'm sure.' She did her best to speak reasonably. 'I don't want a drink. I want you to listen. I can't just not turn up. They're my family.' Then, seeing a strange look cross his face, she instinctively took a step towards him. 'What?'

'Nothing. Just that I thought Jane and I were your family.'

'Oh, Stuart.'

She reached out a hand but he'd turned away with the bottle, saying, 'Sorry, it can't be done. Nora will change the date if you explain that I've got a meeting. She and your granddad were businesspeople. She's sure to understand.'

'But there's everyone else to consider. Máire. Barbara. My mum.'

'It's only a girls' get-together, Hen. There's plenty of time to reschedule. Don't fuss.'

Sitting down on the hearthrug again, Henrietta stared at her brandy glass. It seemed that, whatever she did, she was going to upset someone. And it's not fair, she thought. I understand Stuart's obsessive concern for Jane. In fact, I probably understand it better than anyone else does. But I also know how much the get-together means to Granny. I can't ask her to change the dates, and I don't intend to miss it. So what on earth am I going to do now?

Chapter 2

At a table in her junior suite at the front of the hotel, Nora finished a full Irish breakfast. Only a few years ago, upstairs in the family's flat, she'd have cooked it herself and prepared a tray for Martin, who'd always enjoyed breakfast in bed. But after Martin's death, she'd ceded the flat to their granddaughter, Máire, and given her the management of the hotel. The truth is, she thought, that I miss running the place more than I miss Martin. Still, there's one thing you learn when you're raised on a farm, and that's to step back from jobs you haven't the strength for. It's just as well I learned it too, or I'd be clinging to power and looking over poor Máire's shoulder. The bottom line is that I'm not getting any younger and, given all the work I've put into Castlehill Hotel, what matters now is to secure its future.

Breakfast in bed had been typical of Martin, who'd then read the paper and wander down for a chat with the guests and locals in the bar. Usually, his day would continue with a stroll around Killmoy, the little midlands riverside town ten miles from Athlone, where his family had lived for generations, and where he knew everybody and they knew him. Well-respected and always willing to chair a local committee, he was a fanatical angler, a generous host, and had no interest in work. It was Nora who'd built on the hotel's success, having married into the business. Martin, who'd inherited it from hardworking parents, had been happy to sit back and let her get on.

Squaring up her cutlery, Nora stood up from the table. There was a tap at the door and a girl from Housekeeping looked in. 'Good morning, Mrs Sullivan. Will I take the tray?'

'Thank you, Ursula. That was very acceptable.'

'I'm glad you liked it. I'll tell the kitchen.'

'The pea-shoot garnish on the eggs is new.'

'We're growing pea shoots now, in the polytunnel. The guests seem to like them.'

'Well, thank the kitchen for me, will you?'

The girl had lifted the tray when Nora stopped her. 'Just a moment. Is Máire upstairs, do you know?'

'I'm not sure. I can find out.'

'Don't bother. Take this envelope up to the flat for me. If she's not there, just step into the hall and leave it on the stand.'

'Yes, Mrs Sullivan.'

'Thank you, dear.'

When the door closed, Nora sat down abruptly, struck by how much she missed her mahogany hallstand. Little losses like that had seemed to hit her lately, making her doubt decisions she'd known had to be made. Taking a deep breath, she focused on analysing the issue. Her suite had the console table just inside the door, so she didn't lack somewhere for staff to leave messages and post. No, the fact was that the hallstand, with its mirror, drawers and umbrella hooks, had a dignity that had lent weight to her own. Losing it, plus the loss of her private entrance hall, disconcerted her: she'd never get used to staff being able to pop their heads round her door. Still, the move down to the junior suite had been at her own insistence.

When she'd told them she'd be giving the flat to Máire, the family had wanted her to move to the penthouse above the new spa. But the penthouse, which was the height of luxury and had views down to the river, had been featured in several upmarket travel magazines, so losing potential revenue from it had made no sense to Nora. And what would an eighty-four-year-old woman want with a television that shot up from the foot of a queen-size bed?

They'd laughed, talked about watching the All-Ireland Final in luxury and assured her she'd love the modular kitchen and bar area in the penthouse. But, in her opinion, that was arrant foolishness as well. If she wanted to eat, she could take the lift down to the hotel dining room, and if she fancied watching a match, she'd be happiest with a toastie and a half of lager under Martin's portrait in the bar. Besides, she preferred the handsome proportions of the original building: the big spa now tacked on at the back was impressive, but steel girding and huge plate-glass windows weren't her style. That said, Máire had been right to push through plans to replace the dated leisure centre. Opened not much more than a year ago, the state-of-the-art spa was already in profit and proving to be a magnet for locals as well as the hotel's guests. Having calmly considered the matter, Nora stood up smiling, pleased she could still analyse a list of pros and cons. All things considered, moving to the junior suite had been sensible and, though handing over the flat to Máire and Raymond had been a wrench, it had definitely been the right thing to do.

Upstairs in the flat, Raymond came into the kitchen wearing a tracksuit, trainers and a GAA beanie. Máire looked up from her laptop. 'How was your run?'

'Bracing. I took the riverside path to the boathouse and back.'

'There's coffee in the pot, if you'd like some.'

'I'd better not stop. I've a man coming at ten about a loan.'

'Just before Christmas? I bet he's sweating.'

'Ah, he'll be grand. The bank's done business with him for donkey's years.' Raymond came round the kitchen island to hug her and, laughing, Máire pushed him away.

'Talk about sweating! You're sodden. No, back off, Ray, they're waiting for me downstairs.'

He hugged her anyway, and handed her an envelope. 'Here, I picked this up from the hallstand on my way in.'

Máire opened it. 'Granny's Christmas card, regular as clockwork. You know, I offered to set her up a template for e-cards, but she's still using Cassidy's Print Place in town.'

'Fair play to Nora, she's always shopped local.'

'And has never wasted money on an unnecessary stamp.' Máire flipped open the glittery card, holding it well away from her dark business suit. 'Yep, same as ever. Season's Greetings, Happy New Year, and the invitation for the Sullivan Girls' Get-together, all printed in festive green ink.'

Ever-sensitive, Raymond cocked his head. 'What's the matter?'

'Nothing.'

'Yes, there is. Tell me.'

As always, she was both touched and annoyed by how well he knew her. 'You don't have to analyse every look that happens to cross my face. It's irritating.'

'Stop waving the card, you're getting glitter in your coffee. Sit down a minute and tell me what's wrong.'

With a gesture of resignation, Máire allowed herself to be steered to a stool by the island. Raymond sat opposite her and waited. Pushing her hand through her dark curly hair, she shrugged. 'Okay. If you must know, I feel like Granny's get-together is just one more thing to crowbar on to my vast to-do list. I was so on top of stuff when I got out of bed this morning. Spa bookings dealt with. A hundred per cent room occupancy right across Christmas. Staff rotas sorted. Everything under control, and business booming. Then this turns up, and I know exactly what's going to follow. A list of instructions twice as long as her arm.'

'But, love, it's just a family thing. It's meant to be relaxing.'

'It would be if we weren't relaxing in a hotel that I manage. I know she thinks she schedules it for after the Christmas rush, but that's the problem. Christmas is always massive and, this year, I've pulled out all the stops. Plus we've extended the New Year events programme. By the time that lot's over, I'll feel like lying in a darkened room for a week. Not taking part in a knees-up I'll have to organise and run.'

'Did you talk about this? Nora might have changed the dates if you'd asked her.'

'Oh, Ray, I couldn't. You know yourself she's felt disempowered since Granddad died. This is the one time of the year when she can still be certain that, when she clicks her fingers, we'll dance to her tune.'

'That's a grim way of putting it.'

'Yes, it is. I don't mean it, not really. Getting together with Mum and the girls is fun. But, Granny keeps adding bells and whistles. This year, it looks like she wants us all cavorting around in the spa.' Máire groaned. 'I love my work but, oh, God, Ray, the logistics that weekend are going to be brutal. I've so many spa groups booked in already. Hair appointments, afternoon tea by the pool, dancing at dinner. One of them's a crowd that calls itself the Second Chance Club.'

Distracted by the name, Raymond asked, 'What's that?'

'God knows. Usually, that kind of thing seems to be just an excuse to party.'

'Your team will cope.'

'And there's this Investing in Futures thing in Reception.'

'You're going into financial services?'

'Ha, ha. Very funny. It's an organic-gardening exhibition, run by Seedsavers. They're going to have a stall and offer advice and information.'

'So what's the problem?'

'It's something we haven't tried before. I'd planned to be on call myself.'

'Well, you can be.'

'I can't be in two places at once, can I?'

'Calm down, you'll manage. I have perfect faith in you.'

She gave him a tremulous smile and caught sight of the clock behind him. 'Ray! Look at the time! You're not even showered.'

'Shit, I'd better get moving.' He was halfway across the room when he turned back to take her by the elbows, his voice showing the concern he'd tried to hide. 'You really have been working too hard, love. Getting the spa up and running was a huge undertaking and, this past year, you've been driven by the need to make it pay for itself. You're exhausted, and you'll be working flat-out through Christmas.'

'Raymond, we both need to get on. I've got staff waiting.'

'I'm just saying you might do well to give yourself a break.'

Máire hugged him. 'I'll be fine. Go away. Oh, damn, that's my phone. Seriously, go. I'll have to take this. It's Henrietta.'

'But think about what I said, yeah?'

'You should be thinking about that poor guy waiting for you at your bank.'

Outside in the corridor, laptop under her arm, Máire moved at speed with her phone jammed between shoulder and ear. 'Hen. Sorry, yes, I'm here. Anything the matter?'

'No. Well, not really. It's just that I need a favour.'

'Not a great time. I'm on my way to the lift.'

'It won't take a minute. Truly. It's important.'

Máire pushed through double doors to the lift lobby, and found a group of guests looking up at the digital display. The lift doors opened with a ping, revealing several occupants. Concealing frustration, she waved the guests in and went through to the stairs. No one was coming up or down, so she sat on the top step, switching her phone from one ear to the other. 'Okay, shoot. But make it quick.'

'I've had Granny's invitation.'

'And?'

'And the thing is, Máire, it's awful timing for me.'

'Yeah? Join the club.'

Henrietta rushed on nervously: 'No, you see, Stuart's abroad that weekend. At a meeting in Turin.'

'So what? It's Sullivan girls, not Sullivan girls plus spouses. Or, in Barbara's case, Sullivan girls plus latest significant other.'

The barbed joke seemed to go over Henrietta's head. 'Stuart only told me about it last night, and there's a problem. He doesn't want Jane home alone.'

'What's happened to your au pair?'

'Nothing. She could be here. That's what I told him. But he's dug his heels in.'

'Oh, for feck's sake!'

'No, in fairness, I do understand.'

'He's just being Stuart.'

'And you're being dense.'

'Henrietta, you do know Stuart walks all over you?'

'Oh, get off your high horse and have a bit of empathy. Jane was alone in her cot for hours when her mother had the heart attack.

Stuart was abroad. She was only found when a neighbour came knocking.'

Máire swapped the phone back to the other ear. 'Okay. Yes. I'd forgotten that. But Jane wouldn't have known, would she? I mean she was still a baby. It's not like she was lying there knowing her mum had died.'

'But I'd say Stuart is still traumatised.'

'He also walks all over you.'

'Yeah, well, that's your opinion, but it's not the point here, is it? Annaliese is great, but she's only eighteen. What if something happened and she couldn't cope? And could you stop arguing, Máire? I'm looking for help here, not marriage counselling.'

Máire was uncomfortably aware that she'd sounded unfeeling. 'All right, fair enough, I get it. What d'you want?'

Having reached the crux of the matter, Henrietta veered away from it. 'Getting us all together once a year is a huge thing for Granny. I said that to Stuart. And, for all we know, this could be the last time we do it. I mean, let's face it, she's not getting any younger.'

Máire's voice softened. 'I know. The timing's doing my head in too, as it happens. I haven't the heart to tell her, though.'

'Really? What's the problem?'

'Nothing I can't handle. What's the favour?'

Henrietta took a deep breath. 'Can I bring Jane?'

'Here?'

'Stuart couldn't object, and I can't see Granny complaining. Mum used to bring us along when we were kids.'

'Teenagers.'

'Not true. I remember being brought when I was eleven. You and Barbara were teenagers, but I got to tag along. Oh, come on, Máire. I don't want to upset Granny. Jane's practically a teenager. You know that. And if I can't bring her, I'll have to stay home.'

'What about Stuart's mother?'

'Stuart says she wouldn't be up to coping in a crisis. Stop *arguing*, Máire. What's the problem, anyway? Jane can share my room.'

Máire shook herself. 'You're right. I'm sorry. There isn't a problem. I'm just dealing with too many moving goalposts down here. Do bring her. It'll be grand. I'll give you one of the family rooms, so you won't be on top of each other.'

'You're a star! Thank you.'

'Think nothing of it. I notice there's no suggestion that Stuart might be the one to stay home and babysit. I bet he didn't even consider the option.'

'No, he didn't. Would you, if you had a big meeting to go to?'

Máire pushed herself to her feet as the lift swished back up to the lobby. 'Probably not. That's why I don't have kids.'

Chapter 3

Barbara stood at the huge window of her Dublin apartment looking down at the lights reflected in the Liffey below. She'd been lucky to find it, given the rental market, but her top civil-service post had impressed the agency, as had the years she'd spent abroad as an environmental scientist working for a Norwegian corporation. In Oslo she'd lived with a colleague who'd since been headhunted for a job in the US. He'd been like every boyfriend she'd had since college – intelligent, honest, fun and, most importantly, undemanding. Now, sipping coffee, Barbara imagined him in his own high-rise apartment with Manhattan's Christmas lights like a twinkling carpet below. She wished him nothing but happiness in his new life there. Relocating to the States hadn't been on her bucket list, so they'd parted more than a year ago and, seeing her present job advertised, she'd decided to apply. Returning to live in Ireland hadn't been on her bucket list either, but her qualifications had made her a perfect candidate for the post and, anyway, she'd always enjoyed the thrill of acting on instinct.

The lights below her blurred in a drizzle of soft rain. Night was falling and she'd gone to turn on the news when her phone rang.

'Baba! How are you? Is this a good time?'

'There's never a good time to call me Baba, Mum.'

Sheila laughed. 'Sorry, darling. I know you hate it.' Her voice changed slightly. 'Look, I'd hoped you and I might chat before we all meet up after Christmas.'

Barbara, who'd joined in the laugh, sat in the compact armchair that faced the TV. 'Okay. Why?'

'I have some news.'

'What's happened?'

'There's no need to sound apprehensive. It's good news. In fact, it's great. I've divorced your dad.'

Barbara shot upright in amazement. 'Wait. Say that again. You're doing what?'

'I'm not doing anything. It's a done deal. I've divorced him.'

'Seriously?'

'Absolutely. It's taken months and far too much money, but he's gone.'

'I can't believe it. Really, Mum? Why now, after all you've put up with?'

'Straws and camels' backs, Barbara.'

'So, tell me what happened.'

'I hadn't seen him for ages. He was on tour – well, a hanger-on with one of the bands he used to play for. Actually, I wasn't aware of that. He hadn't been in touch, but I knew he'd reappear at some point. Well, he always had. Then, out of the blue, he turned up on my doorstep with a floozy.'

'A floozy?'

'That's not what they call them now, but you know what I mean.'

Barbara's voice was grim. 'Oh, I know what you mean. I've seen Dad's floozies.'

'She was only about nineteen. Called Afric. Totally smitten by him. She'd fallen for the ageing-rock-star glam.'

Barbara snorted. 'Dad was never a rock star.'

'Don't I know it? Rock stars' wives don't have to work all hours to pay the mortgage. But, presumably, he looked the part when Afric met him. She was starry-eyed at the thought of him hanging out with Elton John.'

'Oh, God, that old line. And the poor girl believed it?'

'Apparently the old lines are still the best.'

'Hang on, though. Why did he turn up with her on your doorstep?'

'Because he honestly imagined he could just move her in. He was broke. I have an income, empty bedrooms and a full fridge.'

'Christ, Mum. That's outrageous.'

'In fairness, I'd taken so much crap from him over the years that he probably thought it wasn't a big ask.'

'So what happened?'

'I lost my cool. Off the scale. Poor little Afric's going to be in therapy for life.'

Surprised, Barbara said, 'I've never seen you do that.'

'No, well, it's not my style, is it? Sullivan girls don't raise their voices. Especially not when they've run off and made a stupid, unsuitable marriage. They keep up a front, get on with things, and avoid having furious meltdowns in front of the children.'

'We sort of knew, though.'

'Of course you did. Well, Hen tries to fool herself, but she was besotted by your dad. You and Máire saw straight through him.'

Barbara took a gulp of cold coffee. 'If I'm honest, I was never sure. Not when I was a child. He was away so much that when he came home it always felt like a fabulous party. I've wondered since, though. Was he really touring all that time?'

'Some of it. He worked as a session musician too, but not half as much as he pretended. I've always suspected there was another semi-permanent home somewhere.'

'Oh, Mum.'

'I think I spent so long holding everything together that it just didn't occur to me to move on when you girls grew up. But now I have.'

'Well, congratulations.'

'I'm not sure what Hen and Máire are going to say. Or your granny. Look, will you be driving to the get-together? Because, if so, and you're coming through Athlone, could you give me a lift?'

'No problem.'

'I'd rather not arrive on my own. I could do with some moral support.'

'It's your life, Mum, you're not answerable to the rest of us.'

'I know that. But breaking the news is going to be complicated.'

Shocked by the unaccustomed wobble she'd heard in her mum's

voice, Barbara tried to find something to reassure her. 'Have you heard that Hen's bringing Jane along? With luck, that might distract Granny.'

'I hadn't heard, but you're right, that's great. It should knock me out of the spotlight. Your granny's been longing for a new Sullivan girl to join the knees-up.'

'Bit of a stretch to call Stuart's daughter a Sullivan girl.'

'As far as your granny's concerned, if you're female and family you make the list. And you girls aren't technically Sullivans, are you? I took your dad's name when I married.'

Barbara laughed. 'Maybe you can be formally reinstated at the get-together. We could gather for an official renaming ceremony.'

'Don't even think about it! I wish I could get away without saying a word about the divorce.'

'That would be weird, when we're all going to be there.'

'Which is why I'm going to bite the bullet. But, like I said, I'll need a little support.'

When the conversation ended, Barbara lay back in the armchair wondering what she'd just let herself in for. Obviously, she couldn't ignore her mum's request for support, but she wasn't crazy about the idea of being a human shield. Fond of her family, and especially of her granny, she turned up faithfully once a year when summoned to Castlehill. This year was shaping up to be seriously stressful, though.

She had made more coffee and returned to her armchair when Henrietta phoned.

'Máire's in a flap. She's got a big festive programme planned, and it sounds like Granny's dates are clashing with it.'

'Given that Granny's been throwing this bash for decades, it sounds more like Máire's dates are clashing with hers.'

'That's what I thought. I kept my mouth shut, though. You know what Máire's like. If you ask me, she's overworked. I bet Raymond's worried about her.'

'Sounds like we're in for a fascinating weekend.'

Intent on her own concern, Henrietta plunged on. 'I haven't told Jane about it yet. I'm praying she won't complicate things.'

'She doesn't know she's coming? When do you plan to mention it?'

'Not until after New Year's Eve. Stuart wants me to throw a Christmas drinks party for the neighbours, and then have them all round again to sing "Auld Lang Syne".'

'I can see why you want to pace yourself.'

'I am so looking forward to winding down in the new spa. Máire's even put in a rasul chamber. Basically, it's fabulous communal therapy. You detox your emotions as well as your body.'

'Well, I hope it's optional, because I'm not sure I fancy it.'

'I think it might be sweet. Life-enhancing. You know? Four generations together, all covered in mud.' Suddenly, Henrietta's voice became anxious. 'But, like I said, I haven't a clue how Jane will react to the thought of coming with me to Castlehill. I've decided to hit her with the luxury spa weekend to begin with, and slip in the get-together bit by degrees.'

Barbara laughed. 'Good luck with that.'

'Oh, don't, Barbara!' Sounding unconvinced by her own argument, Henrietta said she didn't know why she was fussing. 'Jane's sure to enjoy it. There'll just be the spa treatments, and the pool, and hanging out together and catching up over drinks and meals and stuff. Just a fun family tradition we've kept up for yonks.'

'I'm sure you're right. It'll be fine. And, if I were you, I wouldn't worry about Máire or Raymond. It sounds like you've got more than enough on your plate at home.'

When the call ended, Barbara went to the window with her macchiato. She'd always believed that independence should matter more to a woman than any relationship with a man. That's certainly made me the odd one out in the family, she thought wryly. But I've never really felt I belong, so I guess it just amounts to fulfilling my role.

Sipping her coffee, she studied her reflection in the darkened windowpane. Nearly five years older than Henrietta and four years younger than Máire, she had freckled skin and auburn hair that made her look like the portrait of her late granddad that hung above his favourite seat in the hotel bar. Taller than both her siblings, she'd felt ungainly in her teens, and instead of accepting her proper place between Máire and Henrietta in family photos, she'd tended to shuffle to the side. These days, when she bothered to think about her appearance, she took the pragmatic view that it was an asset. Height, and the ability to wear clothes well, had turned out to be useful in a career that required her to be both authoritative and convincing.

Which is just as well, she thought, since I started out with no real idea of where I was going.

None of her family had shown much interest in her ambition to study environmental science but, as Máire had evidently been in line to take over the hotel, and Henrietta, even as a child, had been hell-bent on marriage, it had been felt that Barbara might as well go to university. This had been fine by her, though the lack of interest had stung, as had the apparent assumption that she had had nothing to offer that might be of value at Castlehill. Her first Dublin flat was shared with three other students from the midlands. Smiling, she recalled the dingy basement, its draughts and mousetraps, and her constant, irrational fear of getting lost in the crowded streets. Back then, she wouldn't have believed that, one day, she'd stand in a linen kimono surveying that intimidating cityscape from above.

By the time she'd achieved her degree, her horizons had broadened and, though Ireland had offered its own opportunities, life abroad had seemed to offer more. Her sisters and her mum had seemed surprised by that, but her granny had slipped her a bulging envelope full of banknotes. 'You'll get nowhere in life without taking risks, Barbara, but risk-taking's a fool's game if you've nothing to fall back on. Keep your wits about you and don't let anyone put you down.'

Beyond her own reflection in the window Barbara could see patterns of light thrown up by traffic on the quays. When she'd applied for her current job she'd been tipped for promotion in Oslo, so choosing to leave had seemed counterintuitive to her friends.

Plus, they'd been baffled by the thought of going from the private to the public sector. 'Honestly, Barbara, the civil service? You'll spend your days filling in forms and hacking through red tape - well, green, given the department's remit, and the fact it's in Ireland.' No one had asked about money, because that would have been unacceptable, but beneath the jokes, Barbara had felt them wondering, and drawing conclusions about the options she must have weighed up. In fact, she'd taken the Irish job without knowing how much she might have been offered had she stayed in Oslo, and had consciously not looked back to find out. An easy-going, satisfactory relationship had been over and, embracing her granny's view that God never closed a door without opening a window, she'd followed her instinct. And, as usual, she thought happily, acting on instinct hasn't failed me. It never does.

Yawning, Barbara stretched her arms widely, thinking about her phone conversations with Sheila and Henrietta. She hadn't revealed to either that she had her own pressing reason to feel apprehensive about returning to Castlehill. She didn't want their advice. If things worked out as she hoped, they'd be astonished; if not, to echo another of her granny's favourite phrases, it would be a case of least said, soonest mended. I've lived with it for a year, she thought, and, if nothing else, this visit will bring closure. In the meantime, I'm not letting anything spoil my plans for a full-on urban Christmas. She loved how the city emptied out when people went home for the holiday, leaving uncrowded streets where you could stop and admire your surroundings without being jostled by workers in a hurry. She'd organised her annual leave so's to be free for the get-together at

Castlehill, which this year was set to run from a Friday to a Monday. Until then her time was her own and she was determined to enjoy it. The weather forecast was good, so she planned to bundle up and drink coffee outside pavement cafés, take a bus to the seaside and go for hikes in the Wicklow hills, and she and a group of colleagues had decided to join forces to cook and eat dinner together on Christmas Day. It was a carefully worked-out schedule, intended, like every other arrangement she'd made in the past twelve months, to fill every waking hour and leave her too exhausted by bedtime to think about her impending return to Castlehill.

Taking her empty cup, she washed it in the sink and upended it on the drainer. Her studio was at its best at night, when its large windows seemed to allow the outside in, making the little space feel part of the dark panorama beyond. Securing it had added to her conviction that each time she allowed herself to be guided by her instincts, they led her to something better than logical planning ever could. She went through to the shower room, brushed her teeth, hung up her kimono and, coming back, turned down the bed. Slipping under the duvet, she reached to switch off the lamp and settled back against her pillows, drowsy after a long day, and feeling at one with the night.

She was half asleep when her eyes opened and she sat up abruptly. It had suddenly struck her that she'd been happily acting on instinct when she'd made the worst mistake of her life, down at Castlehill last year.

Chapter 4

'Happy Christmas! Have I interrupted your breakfast?'

'Not at all. I've just finished. Come in and sit down.'

Raymond obeyed, and gave Nora a peck on the cheek. 'Máire should be along shortly. She's organising something in Reception.' Thinning hair rumpled and long legs outstretched, he slouched comfortably in a chair opposite Nora's, having showered and changed after his Christmas-morning run. Except for the hairline, he didn't look very different from the loose-limbed schoolboy he'd been when he'd fallen for Máire, and Nora, who'd approved of him then, hadn't changed her mind since. He was steady, personable, and content to live out his life in Killmoy, which, from her point of view, made him the perfect choice for her favourite granddaughter. She folded her napkin and crossed her legs at the ankles. 'I hear we have two lunch sittings this year, both booked out.'

Raymond grinned. 'It's all fixed to run like clockwork. After their main course, the first lot get ushered through to the bar for prosecco and carols with their pudding. Then it's the same again with the second crowd, so the staff can reset for dinner. And if people hang on for a pint or two in the bar, that's all to the good. The fizz and the carol concert are freebies, and the ushering's done by Santa, so Máire tells me only a Scrooge could complain.'

'A few glasses of free fizz never fail.'

'Personally, I like to eat Christmas pudding on a sofa with my shoes off.'

Nora, whose thoughts were elsewhere, gave him an absent smile. Throughout his long courtship of Máire, she'd felt as if she'd been holding her breath but, having made the mistake of speaking her mind about her daughter's love life, she wasn't one to make the same mistake with her granddaughter. Unlike Sheila, Máire had taken to hotel work in her teens. She'd begun by doing shifts as a cleaner, progressed to waitressing and bar work and, when she'd left school, had gone off to do a hotel-management course, apparently uninterested in Raymond's interest in her. He'd never seemed discouraged by the boyfriends she'd brought with her when she'd come back to work at Castlehill in the holidays. Instead, he'd accepted them when they arrived, and stood by as a friendly shoulder to cry on when things went wrong. Though Nora had found it hard, she'd listened to Martin, who'd said Raymond needed time to reel the girl in. 'Don't be interfering, love. Remember what happened before.' So Nora had watched from the sidelines with her fingers crossed. By the time Máire was thirty, she was working in Castlehill at management level, and Raymond, who was two years older, had progressed through the ranks to become a bank manager in Killmoy. Then, having refused to commit for so long it had almost become a joke, Máire had turned up one day wearing a sapphire engagement ring, and announced she and Raymond were planning a spring wedding. That night in bed, Nora had felt the weight of the world lifting from her shoulders. Máire would marry a grand local lad, settle into the business and, unlike Sheila, wouldn't be left to battle alone among strangers.

Whatever way you looked at it, Sheila's marriage had been a disaster. Nora still couldn't understand how a child of hers could have been so lacking in common sense. It had been clear as day that the fellow she'd fallen for was a chancer, but saying so had made matters worse. Sheila had argued, shouted and, finally, disappeared without warning, leaving the town agog and her parents distraught. After that, there'd been months of wakeful nights and anxious days, before she called to say she'd had a baby, and was moving back to Killmoy, but not coming home. 'Finbar's in the States. I've decided to take a job while he's touring. Sitting at home with Máire would be a bore.' Nora had known immediately that this was about saving face. Wherever Finbar the chancer had fecked off to, it was evident that he wasn't sending home money. But that was one of many things that mustn't be said out loud, either on the phone or when Sheila rolled up later in a clapped-out car, with Máire strapped into a baby seat and an attitude that suggested the wrong question might drive her away. It had turned out that one of her school friends, who'd opened a dental surgery, had offered her a job as his receptionist. Once again, the town was agog and her family embarrassed: if she'd wanted that kind of work, she could have had it at Castlehill, and a comfortable place to live with her child besides. Instead, she'd rented a poky flat in town and insisted on going her own way. But, given a second chance by God, Nora hadn't interfered. And, throughout the years when Máire remained apparently blind to Raymond's quiet devotion, that hard-learned lesson from the past, combined with Martin's warning, had kept Nora's mouth shut and allowed the affair to take its own course.

'Penny for your thoughts?'

'Sorry, love. I was reminiscing. That's what age does for you.' Nora bent forward and pushed a basket of pastries across the table to Raymond. 'Have one of those if you've just come in from the cold. I never eat them myself, but they're always there on the breakfast tray. It's dreadful waste. I've been meaning to tell Máire.'

Raymond took a croissant, broke it in half and dusted away flakes of pastry. 'Ah, leave it to me. I'll tell her and save you the bother.'

Nora gave him a shrewd look. 'You know, people used to say you'd be lucky to get her. I've always thought she was the lucky one.'

'Sure, it's all worked out in the end.'

'If I'd allowed that kind of food waste in my day, there'd have been no money to spend on a luxury spa.'

Gently, Raymond said, 'I know that. So does Máire. She's just up to her eyes over Christmas.'

Reminding herself of past lessons learned, Nora suppressed the flash of irritation she always felt at any suggestion her judgement might be at fault. The door opened and Máire came in, focused on the phone in her hand. Pushing it into her pocket, she bent and kissed Nora. 'Morning, Granny. How was your breakfast?'

'Happy Christmas, dear. It was grand.' Nora's eyes flicked sideways. 'In fact, I just said so to Raymond.'

Máire saw the wicker basket. 'Oh, for Heaven's sake, have they sent you pastries again? I've told them not to. They come down uneaten every time, and it's an awful waste.' This time she caught their exchange of amused glances. 'What have I said?'

'Nothing at all. Your granny was also telling me how great you are at your job, weren't you, Nora?'

Máire laughed. 'Good. Because it feels like, this Christmas, I'm running to stand still. Look, I've got to get back. I just came up to ask about dinner, Granny. How are you feeling today? If you think you'll want an early night, I can have your dinner sent up to you. Chances are, Raymond and I won't be eating till late.'

'Sure, what have I got to do but potter around and put my feet up? I'll take a bit of a walk in the grounds this morning and, maybe, watch an afternoon film on the telly. You can let me know when you want to have dinner, and I'll come up to the flat.'

'Okay. We can do that.'

'If I won't be in your way.'

'Don't be daft. Of course not.'

'Perfect. And we can talk about the get-together. It'll be on us before we know it, and there's details to be finalised, so we really ought to get organised and make a proper list.'

About an hour's drive away, Sheila was eating smoked salmon and scrambled eggs. Now that the girls had grown up and left home, she was used to spending Christmas alone in her comfortable house. Máire had been nearly ten and Barbara five when she'd left her job in the dental surgery. A friend with a small, terraced house to rent had opened a shop in Athlone, and offered her work and accommodation. Though it had felt like a leap of faith, Sheila had taken it. She'd be working in fashion, which interested her, and her girls would no longer have to share a bedroom. The last thing she'd expected was that less than a year later she'd find herself pregnant with Henrietta but, with another mouth to feed and a job that offered a career path, she'd felt that, in more ways than one, the move had been the right decision. The older girls, who had friends in Killmoy, had travelled there each day on the school bus. At seventeen Henrietta, who'd gone to school in Athlone within walking distance of home, had been the last to fly the nest. To begin with, the house had felt empty but now, with her divorce completed, Sheila felt newly liberated. The boutique she'd helped to set up had done well and, as the years had passed, she'd bought into her friend's business and managed to take a mortgage on the house. Now, mortgage-free, with a decent pension fund, and having sold her share of the business at a profit, she could think about a new future, and face it on her own terms.

Her phone rang and, swallowing the last forkful of salmon, she picked it up and heard Henrietta's voice. 'Happy Christmas, Mum! What's the weather doing there?'

'It's nice. Sparkly and frosty, but not freezing. What's it like in Dublin?'

'Jane's been hoping for snow but I don't think it's going to happen.'

'How's your day going? I can hardly hear you over the music.'

'I know, sorry, the neighbours are here for drinks. Stuart claims my decorations are way over the top, but he's the one who's playing carols at max.'

'I'm looking forward to seeing you at Castlehill.'

'Me too. Oops, got to go, there's the doorbell. I just wanted to say happy Christmas.'

'Thanks, Hen. It's always great to hear your voice. Love to Jane and Stuart.'

She'd known the caller was sure to be Henrietta. Barbara would get round to calling later, and Máire would probably be too busy, but Hen was a worrier who'd never liked the thought of their mum sitting alone at Christmas. In recent years, when urged to spend the day with her and Stuart, Sheila had prevaricated. 'Your dad might be free to come home this year. I'm not certain.'

'Mum, you do know you'd both be welcome here any time?'

'Well, thank you, darling. That'd be lovely. But the way it is with your dad's schedules, I can't really pin things down for Christmas at present.'

Since this had been the norm in Henrietta's childhood, she'd always backed off, leaving Sheila feeling guilty when, as was usually the case, she'd had no idea whether or when Finbar would reappear. For years, that uncertainty and the need to save face by fibbing had combined to make her reclusive. But from now on, she thought, I can do whatever I fancy. Find new work that interests me, visit the girls, relax here alone, or take off on a cruise. I can be like those single women who book Christmas at Castlehill, stroll in the grounds, do yoga in the spa and sit in the velvet armchairs with a glass of wine and the latest bestselling novel.

It was lunchtime when a text arrived from Máire. **Happy Xmas. Granny and R send love.** Pinging back a smiley face in a Santa hat, Sheila remembered the chilly day, more than thirty years ago, when she'd driven home to Killmoy with Máire in a baby seat in the back of a clapped-out Micra. Finbar had gone on tour while she was pregnant and had hardly been in touch for several months but, right up to when she'd gone into labour, Sheila had been certain that, somehow, he'd turn up at the hospital to support her. Instead, once she'd been moved to a ward and was having tea and toast, she'd had to send a text to tell him she'd given birth to Máire. At the time, she'd been living in Limerick, where the band had rehearsed, and nothing about the flat Finbar had rented there was baby-friendly. After three months of struggling up four flights of narrow stairs with a buggy, and days and nights in tears because she had no one nearby to help her, she'd given up, gritted her teeth and called Nora.

It hadn't been an easy conversation and, looking back, Sheila could see that both she and her mum had been profoundly shocked by what had happened. Which wasn't surprising. It was hard to believe even now, all these years later, that her twenty-two-year-old self had simply walked out on her parents and disappeared. But I wasn't callous, she thought. I was stupid. I just went along with Finbar's bullshit, and followed wherever he led; and, even when it was plain who he was, I clung to my illusions. The bottom line was that if I was wrong my parents had to be right, and I couldn't accept that. And then, when I came back to Killmoy, I didn't behave any better. Mum and Dad would have taken me in. I know that. I knew it then but, rather than face the truth about Finbar, I chose to make a show of myself and them in front of the town. No wonder they didn't argue when I moved here to Athlone. God knows what people in Killmoy said when they saw me renting a place the size of a cupboard, and sitting behind the desk in the local dentist's. There must have been plenty who'd thought Mum and Dad had shut the door on me, and plenty of theories about why Finbar never came home for more than ten minutes. Though, to be fair to Mum, she's never thrown that up at me, not at the time and never since.

It was afternoon, and Sheila had gone for a walk to stretch her legs, when the phone rang again and this time it was Barbara. 'Happy Christmas, Mum.'

'Same to you, darling. How's your day going?'

'I had lunch with friends. Actually, we're still lazing about watching telly. I'm in the hall. I just slipped away to call you.'

'Ah, lovely. Enjoy yourself. I talked to Hen this morning.'

'Was she hosting half her neighbourhood?'

'It did sound like it.'

'That's Stuart, pulling out all the stops. She'll be ready for a spa break.'

Sheila's voice was thoughtful. 'You know, when I said goodbye, I sent my love to Jane and Stuart. And I realised afterwards that I've hardly met them.'

'Well, Stuart's abroad a lot for work.'

'And I've been way too focused on getting rid of your father. It'll be good to have time to get to know Jane.'

'I've had dinner at theirs now and then. Stuart's a bit sure of himself, but he and Hen are obviously happy. I haven't seen Jane since the wedding. Lots of pink ribbons and a bridesmaid's dress complete with panniers.'

Sheila laughed. 'Oh, I've vivid memories of the dress, and the matching marabou headpiece. Apparently, they were chosen by Stuart's mother. Poor Hen had to carry pink roses to coordinate.'

'Well, if Jane's terribly girly she'll probably love a spa weekend. Hen hasn't told her she's coming yet, you know.'

'Why not?'

'Scared she'll act up, I suppose.'

'That's just silly.'

'Says the woman who's in a state about telling her daughters about her divorce.'

'And that's a low blow.'

'True, though.'

Sheila pulled a face. 'I'm not worried about how Máire will take it. I dare say she'll wonder why I've left it this long. But family means a lot to Henrietta.'

'You've always fussed over her.'

'Well, by the time she came along, your dad was hardly around. Oh, he dropped in and out, like always, but I suppose I feel I raised her as a single mum.'

'Look, Mum, I'm sorry, I ought to get back.'

'Of course. Don't let me keep you. You're still okay for picking me up on your way to the get-together?'

'Stop twitching, I've told you it's no problem. Enjoy the rest of your day.'

Sheila put away her phone and continued on her walk, leaning into a wind that whipped litter along the pavement. Pulling her scarf closely around her face, she glanced up and saw that the light was fading. She'd been lost in thought and had walked further than she'd intended so, drawn by the prospect of tea by the fire, she made for home.

The previous day, when she'd done the last of her Christmas shopping in town, she'd bought herself a slice of Black Forest gateau from a deli. The thought of it, and the conversation she'd just had with Barbara, reminded her of her first Christmas with Máire when, determined to cope alone, she'd refused an invitation to dinner at Castlehill. She'd been struggling to heat a bottle while Máire screamed in her cot in the corner, when Nora had knocked on the door and come in. 'Look, I know you don't want to see me, but I'm not here to judge or pass comment, and your father has no idea I've come, so you needn't be thinking he sent me. You've made it plain that you won't sit down with us tonight in the restaurant, but it's Christmas Day, Sheila. Would you not have a cup of tea with us? I've a chocolate cake made in the flat. We could go up and have it now, by the fire. Martin would love a chance to see the baby. We'd both like to see you too, for the matter of that.' Máire's screams had been piercing by then, and the thought of her mother's chocolate cake had overcome Sheila's resolution.

Up in the hotel, the flat was warm and smelt of baking, and her dad's beaming smile when she appeared with the baby had made her blink away tears. Nora had produced the fir-cone tea service kept for special occasions – such as Christmas and the return of a prodigal daughter – and, with Máire bouncing on Martin's knee, they'd restored a semblance of family life over tea by the fire and slices of chocolate cake.

It had been rapprochement, not reconciliation. But, though Sheila remained wary and kept her distance, Máire, and later Barbara and Henrietta, got used to thinking of Castlehill as a second home. It was also the start of Máire's interest in the family business, and the reason she'd been working there when Martin had died unexpectedly four years ago. There and then, Nora had made Máire the hotel's General Manager, handing over the flat along with the role.

Darkness had fallen by the time Sheila sat down by the wood-burner with her slice of Black Forest gateau and a pot of Assam tea. She ate lazily, with her feet up, savouring the sharp cherry jam and chocolate ganache along with the thought that this was the first Christmas in nearly forty years when her ears weren't pricked for the sound of a key in the door. Finbar had never really done Christmas. Or birthdays. Or school prize-givings. At least, not reliably. 'Other people have diaries, chickadees. I have schedules. But our family celebrations are special, aren't they? Not knowing when they're going to happen makes them extra-super!' At the least convenient moments, he'd sweep in unannounced, overexcite the children and expect everyone to party. There weren't many presents, but lots of talk about what he'd intended to bring them.

'A bear cub! Really? A live one? Dad! Where is he? Why isn't he here?'

'Import and export shit. Customs are crazy. I'll take you to see him sometime. He belongs to a friend of mine.'

'In Canada? When? Really? When will you take us?'

'One of these days.'

Sheila would have been happy if he'd even brought them teddy bears. Or remembered to send cards. Or noticed that it cost money to keep them in food and clothing. She'd convinced herself she'd put up with him because her girls needed a father, but the fact is, she thought, I remained susceptible to his dubious charm for far too long. Not any more, though. He's gone, I've changed the lock, and Finbar is history. All I need to do now is break the news when I get to Castlehill.

Chapter 5

Jane hadn't said a word since the car left the motorway. As they bowled along roads between winter-bleached hedges, checking out TikTok felt more interesting than conversation. She didn't find silence awkward, although other people seemed to, Henrietta more than most. But, as Henrietta was casting increasingly covert glances at her from the driving seat, she felt she'd better say something to put her at ease.

'Is there far to go?'

Henrietta's shoulders relaxed. 'Not far. About another half-hour. Say twenty minutes. Are you tired?'

'No.'

'Hungry? We could stop for a bite.'

Only a couple of hours ago, they'd eaten a vast turkey salad for lunch. Jane shook her head. 'I'm good. Unless you want something.'

'No, I'm okay. There's sure to be coffee waiting when we arrive.'

That seemed to be that, so they stopped talking. And now, thought Jane, we've got an awkward silence, when what we had before was just a couple of people not talking. Returning to TikTok, she told herself she ought to have known better. The best way to deal with grown-ups was to ignore them as much as possible, and if they made a suggestion, to agree to it at once. Obviously you couldn't stick to this as a hard and fast rule but, as a general plan, it kept life uncomplicated. The trouble was that Henrietta got flustered when ignored, and then compounded the problem by trying to hide it. This was something Jane hadn't met before in an adult. The various nannies who'd come and gone before her dad remarried hadn't been desperately eager to be her friend. Her dad's mum, who was the kind of person who never stopped talking, required no more than a nod now and then. But at times Henrietta seemed close to desperate, like the boy at Jane's school who was always sidling up with a bag of Percy Pigs and hanging about in the hope that someone would want one. It wasn't hard to ignore him but the look you got when you did made you feel like you'd squashed a beetle or kicked a kitten.

Jane smothered a sigh. The stupid thing was that Henrietta was quite fun to be with, and definitely super-good for Dad. At the start, everyone seemed to worry that Jane mightn't like her but, actually, there was nothing to dislike. Admittedly, she'd felt a bit uncertain before they'd been introduced. When she'd been little, her dad's mum had had a collection of old Disney videos. She'd always said, 'Sit here on Gan-Gan's knee, and we'll watch the pretty princesses,' but what had captured Jane's imagination had been the wicked stepmothers, with their long, curving nails, scarlet lips and croaky voices. Somewhere at the back of her mind she must have feared she'd find herself handed over to one. But that had been when she was only a baby. And, anyway, Henrietta simply didn't fit the wicked-stepmother role.

Dad hadn't talked much about Henrietta before saying he'd like them to meet. Gan-Gan had alternately gushed and fussed. When the day had come, Jane had sat waiting in her bedroom, wearing a pale green and lavender dress that channelled Elsa in *Frozen*. As soon as she'd heard the gravel crunch, she'd gone downstairs to let them in, and seen Henrietta get out of the car, shake back her hair and take a deep breath. They'd had tea in the conservatory, with cakes provided by Gan-Gan who, having laid the table, had discreetly slipped away. Henrietta had brought a tin of biscuits. 'They're M&S chocolate shortbreads. Your dad said they're your favourite.' In fact, Jane hadn't had that kind before, but she was cool with all kinds of chocolate, so she'd said thanks and taken one. In the silence that followed she'd bitten into the biscuit, feeling the chocolate crack and the shortbread crunch. Then, seeing her dad looking like a hopeful spaniel, she'd risen to the occasion and found things to chatter about.

Next day, at school, she'd told Oisín and Suzy. 'She's just ordinary. Blonde. Blue eyes. Looks a bit like Barbie.' Oisín had suggested the Barbie look was a onesie that could be zipped off to reveal a hideous witch inside. But that was just Oisín. He could never resist trying to wind people up. Suzy had asked how she felt, and Jane had shrugged her shoulders. The bottom line was that

Dad had found someone who made him happy, and that was good enough for her

At the time, she'd quite liked the Elsa-ish dress, which was more sophisticated than the Disney-branded outfits Gan-Gan had bought for her when she was little. She hadn't minded Gan-Gan's choice of bridesmaid dress either because, back then, she'd rather liked pink. Now, two years later, she wondered if Henrietta would have preferred to design her own wedding or, at least, stick to the norm, which, according to Suzy, was that the bride's mum got involved, not the groom's. 'I wouldn't want my mother-in-law choosing the flowers for my bouquet. And a bridesmaid's dress is supposed to match the bride's, not the other way round.' But Henrietta hadn't objected to carrying pink roses, and Sheila, who'd been quiet and seemed friendly, had stayed in the background at the wedding, apparently happy to give Gan-Gan her head. So, up to then, everything had gone off pretty smoothly.

Bored with TikTok now, Jane stared out of the car window, thinking it might have been good to have had more time with Henrietta before the wedding. But Dad had been abroad a lot, and nobody had suggested that she and Henrietta might do stuff without him. Then, after the honeymoon, he'd gone off and left them together, with Una, her nanny, behaving like a cow and Gan-Gan pointedly keeping her distance while calling ten times a day. It had all felt too complicated for Jane, who'd reacted by retreating to her bedroom. All she'd wanted was a bit of space, but it seemed to have made matters worse. Because, after that, Henrietta had got increasingly needy and nervous and, eventually, gone full Percy Pig.

It didn't help that this spa break, which was supposed to be relaxing, had started with a row between Henrietta and Dad. Jane hadn't let them know she'd overheard, but it interested her to hear Henrietta trying to dial down the emotion when Dad had started laying down the law. This was impressive strategy. The only emotional scenes Dad could handle were the ones he'd devised himself, in which everybody was laughing, happy and huggy. Anything else just made him dismissive, at which point the battle was lost. And, in this case, winning had seemed to matter a lot to Henrietta so, when it turned out that she'd found a workable compromise, Jane had decided on cautious cooperation.

Henrietta had said they could hang out together. 'Do stuff, you know? We've never really had a chance to bond.'

This had felt very Percy Pig, so Jane had said nothing.

'It's a luxury spa with all the bells and whistles.'

'Sounds great.'

'We'll have a bedroom for me, with another one off it for you, and we'll share a bathroom.'

'Cool.'

'Will I tell your dad you're up for it?'

'Sure. Why not?'

Later, Dad had asked, 'Do you really want to go, sweetheart?'

Remembering the tension in their arguing voices, Jane had hugged him. 'Of course I do. When you come back, you'll hardly recognise me. Henrietta says they do gel nail art and glitter acrylic tips.'

Now Henrietta swung the wheel and the car passed a sign for

Killmoy. The town was pretty, with winding streets clustered in a flat landscape on either side of a broad river. There were traffic lights at the bridge and, as they waited for green, Jane checked out the shops. Coloured lights were still up in the street, and cut-outs of 'The Twelve Days of Christmas' pranced in the window of a print place. She had counted ten lords a-leaping when Henrietta's voice interrupted her. 'So, it's going to be you and me, my mum, my gran and my two sisters.'

'I know. You said.' This came out more abruptly than Jane had intended. To make amends, she waved her hand at the view. 'Is this the river that runs through the hotel grounds?'

'That's it. Lots of the guests are anglers. The hotel has a mile or so of river and acres of ground all around.'

'So, what happens? People go out fishing and come back to get their nails done?'

'Don't worry, we won't be standing in freezing water, trying to put worms on hooks.'

'If you're fishing in rivers, don't you use flies?'

Henrietta laughed. 'I haven't a clue, to be honest. I've never bothered to ask.'

As they crossed the bridge, Jane leaned forward to peer through the windscreen. 'Where's the hill?'

'There isn't one, really. The hotel's built on a kind of mound by the river.'

'But it is a castle?'

Henrietta drove through a set of iron gates and along a curving drive that gave glimpses of the building ahead. 'Nope. See for yourself.

I think the main house was built at the end of the nineteenth century. You'll have to ask Granny or Máire.'

Jane looked at the square house, which had steps flanked by stone urns where holly was under-planted with cyclamen. It was recognisable from the Christmas card Henrietta had had on the mantelpiece, but as you approached you could see new wings, on either side, and a big steel-and-glass extension at the back. It wasn't on a hill, but the grounds sloped gently down in a series of broad terraces to the river. The grass was closely mown and there were no flowerbeds. Henrietta stopped the car in front of the sweeping steps. 'The parking's round the back, but we can take our bags in this way. It's easier.'

As Jane opened the passenger door, a guy strolled up and went round to the driver's side. Henrietta lowered her window and he leaned on the car roof. 'Hi. You're back again. Nice to see you.'

'You too. How have you been?'

He opened her door and she got out, smiling at him and beckoning to Jane. 'Come and meet Luke. He looks after the grounds here. Luke, this is my stepdaughter Jane.' Luke held out his hand, shook Jane's, and returned Henrietta's smile. He was taller than Jane's dad, and a lot younger. Closer to Henrietta's age, thought Jane, shooting a look at him from under lowered lashes. His grip was very firm and he was tanned and fit, like someone who spent most of his life in the open. As he let go of Jane's hand, Henrietta put an arm around her. 'He looks after the anglers too, don't you, Luke? He'd be the one to tell you about worms and flies and fishing stuff.'

Luke raised an eyebrow at Jane. 'Are you interested in angling?'

'Not really. I just said I thought people used flies when they fished in rivers.'

'They do. It's called game fishing. The season hasn't started this year. There's boats guests can go out in, though. Do you row?'

'I think we're supposed to be doing spa stuff.'

Henrietta squeezed Jane's shoulder. 'We're not supposed to do anything. We're here to have fun.' She smiled again at Luke. 'Thanks for the offer. I'll send her down to you if she fancies a boat trip.'

Jane wasn't sure what she felt about a boat trip, so she said nothing.

'Will I take in your bags for you?'

'They're not heavy.'

He strolled round, opened the boot and lifted the bags as if they weighed nothing. Henrietta made a grab for hers, then gave up, laughing, as he thrust out an elbow to hold her off. Turning, she linked Jane instead, and made for the steps to the door. It struck Jane that, for the first time since they'd left home, she looked completely relaxed and happy.

Barbara arrived in Athlone and pulled in to the kerb. Sheila was watching for her at a window. Moments later, she came out and set her case on the pavement. 'Hang on a minute while I lock the door.'

'There's no rush. Anyway, I'm early. I'll stick your case here on the back seat for you.'

They had joined the stream of Friday-afternoon traffic leaving town when Barbara asked lightly, 'Is that a new Chubb lock you've got on the front door?'

'It is. I've had the back one secured too.'

'Wow. When you told me you'd changed the lock I thought it was metaphorical. You know, Gloria Gaynor 'I Will Survive' stuff.'

'There's a reason that song appeals to angry women.'

'I didn't know you were angry. I mean, I know Dad was useless but …'

'… but I put up with it.'

'Well, yes.'

Sheila turned away and adjusted her seatbelt. 'I'm not angry any more. Not now I'm shut of him.'

'But you did change the lock.'

'Like Gloria said, I should've made him leave his key.'

'Really, Mum? You think he'll turn up again?'

'I've no idea. I just know that I wouldn't be going away for a long weekend if I thought I might come back and find him sprawled in front of my telly.'

Unaccustomed to this kind of conversation with her mother, Barbara said, 'I had a text from Hen. She'll probably get to Castlehill before us.'

'Well, as far as I'm concerned, there's no need for you to hurry.'

Barbara laughed. 'You've never been crazy about Castlehill, have you? When we were kids, we treated it like we owned it.'

'As kids, you girls could run in and out when you wanted to. When I was growing up, I was stuck there.'

'Was that how you felt? I knew you and Granny didn't see eye to eye when you married Dad. I didn't realise you'd had problems at home before that.'

Sheila seemed to search for a reply before making a dismissive gesture. 'My dad loved being a hotelier, but he wasn't a fanatic. Being raised by Nora was like being strapped to a juggernaut.'

'She's certainly a born organiser! When did she start the Sullivan Girls' Get-togethers?'

'You know, I'm not sure. They've been going on as long as I can remember. I missed a few years when you girls were small, and I think that at one stage they dwindled to herself, my dad's sister and a few cousins. She's always kept up the tradition, though, as well as working all hours to grow the business.'

Barbara grinned. 'Granddad was very sweet but I can't say much for his work ethic. I imagine the place would have sunk like a stone without Granny.'

'The problem was that I wouldn't have cared if it did. The hotel didn't interest me. I was the Big Disappointment.'

Barbara shot her a surprised glance. 'They actually said that?'

'Not in so many words, but I got the message. If I hadn't, I probably wouldn't have run off with your father.' Pulling at her seatbelt again, Sheila shook her head. 'I'm not saying they forced me out. That was entirely my own idiocy. I just … Well, it never felt like a home. It was always a business.'

'According to Hen, Máire's doing the juggernaut thing at the moment.'

'I hope she doesn't overdo it. No one knows better than I do how that place can take over your life.'

Barbara, who'd pulled out to pass a lorry, waited until she was back in her lane before speaking again. 'D'you reckon Máire and Raymond enjoy living in the flat?'

Sheila looked startled. 'Why? Do you think they don't?'

'Well, they'd bought that lovely house in the town when they married, and Máire had just put the finishing touches to it when Granddad died. I do see the logic of living on-site now she's the hotel's general manager, but the plan to rent out their own place and move to the flat wasn't theirs, was it? It was Granny's.'

'I can't believe that never crossed my mind. Has Máire talked about it?'

'Not to me. I wouldn't expect her to, though. She and I don't go in for cosy chats.'

'Máire doesn't go in for cosy chats with anyone. That's what makes it so hard to help her.'

Barbara laughed. 'It's not like cosy chats are a Sullivan thing, though, are they? Granny's never been one for letting her hair down and, whatever life's thrown at you, you've always just soldiered on and coped.'

Frowning, Sheila said, 'God, I've been far too focused on this bloody divorce from your father. I wonder what Raymond thought about moving from their house to the flat.'

'Oh, you know Raymond. He'll go along with whatever makes Máire happy.'

'But you think she isn't?'

'Mum, don't! I didn't say that. I told you I've no way of knowing.

Anyway, Máire's never been known to please anyone but herself. She made the move, which probably means she wanted to.'

Sheila turned her head and looked out of the window. 'It was your granddad's parents' flat, you know. He grew up there. His parents moved out of the hotel when he married, so he and your granny could move in and run the place. When your granny arrived she modernised and extended the hotel, but the family flat was hardly touched. I suppose my father liked it. Maybe she did too. I loathed it. I remember people I was in school with calling it groovy and retro. All I could see was mahogany with a touch of bamboo and wicker, and a lot of yellowing lace antimacassars.'

Surprised by this intensity, Barbara said, 'Well, at least, they're gone. And the kitchen is state-of-the-art.'

'Oh, even in my day, the kitchen was fine, and I'm not sure the antimacassars were ever there. Not really. But it was boring. Especially when my mother was bringing the hotel up to date by leaps and bounds.'

'Poor you.'

'Don't laugh. I know it sounds silly but, honestly, I've got such dreary memories of my bedroom there. I'd need years of major therapy to recover.'

Barbara had changed lanes to turn at the sign up ahead for Killmoy. 'I wonder if Máire and Raymond have made any changes to the flat. Last year, it was pretty much as Granny left it.'

'My goodness, I hope they've done something to make it their own.'

Taking the turn-off, Barbara said, 'Chances are Máire hasn't had time. She's redone all the hotel bedrooms at the back since the spa opened. The website calls them "A refuge from life's strains and stresses".' Seeing Sheila's expression, she added, 'Oh, Mum! She's a grown-up. We all are. You don't have to worry about us now.'

'Mums never get out of the habit of worrying about their babies.'

Barbara threw her a laughing glance. 'Was Granny like this with you?'

'Your granny and I had a complicated relationship.'

Something in the tone of her voice had shut the door firmly on the subject. So Barbara asked no more questions and drove on.

When they arrived at Castlehill, Henrietta met them at Reception. She kissed them both before hustling them into a corner. 'Look, I'm really sorry, but there's an issue with our accommodation. It's my fault, for bringing Jane. I thought it was going to be grand. Máire told me so on the phone. But now it's turned out that someone's messed up, well, not messed up, really. There's been a late addition to a group booking. And now all that's left is one twin room and a single.'

'So?'

'Jane has to be with me. So, that's the twin room gone.'

'Obviously.'

'But the thing is, it'll all be fine. We'll manage.' Henrietta looked pleadingly from Barbara to Sheila. 'It's just that one of you will be in the single.'

Realisation dawned on Barbara's face. 'And the other gets the spare room in the flat. That's what you're saying.'

'Yes. Máire's up in the flat now, making the bed. I told her I'd come down and tell you.' With a winning smile, Henrietta turned to Sheila. 'Actually, Mum, we thought you'd be the one who'd like to have it. It's the bedroom you grew up in, so that'd be nice.'

Chapter 6

On the way up in the lift they all avoided each other's eyes. At the second floor, Henrietta got out apologetically, saying she needed to check on Jane. Barbara and Sheila continued upwards in silence, then walked down a corridor, reading door numbers. When they reached the room, Barbara touched the keycard on the lock and stood back to let Sheila in first. Inside, they stood in silent appreciation. The single bedroom was one of those that had recently been redecorated. Its curtains and bedspread were a rich golden yellow edged in grey, the walls were a paler grey and the plain wall-to-wall carpet was relieved by a creamy-white sheepskin rug. Though the room was small, light streamed through a tall window, where an armchair was placed to take in a view of the curving river. On a small table beside the chair, a wicker welcome basket contained fruit, wine, a corkscrew and a box of chocolates. Barbara opened the door to the little bathroom, which had gleaming wall-to-ceiling tiles, a shower and a compact loo. 'Gosh, Mum, this is all lovely.'

'Isn't it? You must have it.'

'Don't be silly.'

Sheila shook her head. 'I'll be fine in the flat.'

'Don't be daft. The last place you'll want to retreat to is a bedroom you say you hate.'

'That was never going to happen anyway. Your granny schedules something for practically every hour of the day.'

'Oh, Mum! She's not going to force you to have a massage or a mud bath. You can always slip away, and this room is the perfect bolthole.'

'But what about you?'

'I'm not the one creeped out by your childhood bedroom.'

'Oh, Barbara, I don't know.'

'I do. You're having this room, and there's an end to it.'

Her resolution seeming to weaken, Sheila sat on the side of the bed. 'It would be so nice to have somewhere to slope off to. Once I break the news about your father, I'll be like the skeleton at the family feast.'

'I still think you're making way too much of that.' Barbara set the keycard on a shelf by the bed. 'Anyway, I'll leave you to settle. Enjoy it. I'm going up to the flat to unpack my case.'

Sheila came to the door with her and gave her a quick hug. 'I dare say you're right about my news, and I won't need a refuge at all. But thank you, darling. It's lovely, and so relaxing.'

As Barbara walked back down the corridor she didn't regret her decision, even though she was acutely aware that, on this particular weekend, she too might feel the need for a bolthole. If you're staying in somebody's home, she thought, you can't hide away in your bedroom: it's not only rude, but people are likely to want to know what's the matter, which can be hell if you're not inclined to talk. Still, I had no option. Leaving aside how Mum already feels about the flat, she evidently needs peace and quiet to sort her head out and, given her state of mind and Máire's current stress levels, there'd have been no chance of that if Mum had had to sleep up there. I don't know why she's in such a state about breaking her news but, at least, this is a practical way to help without being nosy. As for me, I'll just have to hope that I won't need to escape and that, if I do, Máire will have too much on her mind to notice.

In her junior suite, Nora was wondering what to wear at dinner. Selecting two possible outfits, she laid them out on the bed. Her built-in wardrobe, which had sliding doors, and shelves as well as hanging space, was one of the things she liked about her new accommodation. It was wide rather than tall, so there was no need to stretch and rummage, unlike the wardrobe she'd lived with throughout her marriage. In the 1960s, when she'd begun to remodel the hotel, she'd imagined that she'd redesign the flat as well. But soon she'd realised that Martin liked it as it was and, once she'd put her foot down about the need for a proper kitchen, she'd decided it would be wasteful to throw out his parents' well-made furniture.

Disapproval of waste was deeply ingrained in Nora. She'd learned it on the farm where her own hardworking parents had had to struggle to make ends meet. The youngest of five sisters and three brothers, she'd always thought that, like them, she'd emigrate before she was twenty with little to give her a proper start in life. But then she'd met Martin who, despite his family's disapproval, had fallen headlong in love with her and proposed. He wasn't the sharpest knife in the box, but he was gentle and generous, and the future he'd offered Nora had been dazzling, even though her mam and dad had been slow to welcome it. Her father had been particularly resistant. The Sullivans had begun making their money in the nineteenth century, by taking over rents in lean years when people failed to make payments. There were stories of how they'd moved onto land from which their own neighbours had been evicted and, to Nora's dad, no passage of time could wipe out that mortal sin. Her mother had been more troubled by the thought that Martin's family might think she wasn't good enough for him. 'Isn't he the only son and couldn't he have any girl he wanted? What would he do with a child of ours, that was reared picking stones in a field?' Ironically, it was this that had changed Nora's father's mind. She could see him now, with his back to the fire, bristling at her mother's question, and declaring that Mr Martin Bloody Sullivan would be damn lucky to get a daughter of theirs. 'She's a hard worker from a decent, upstanding family, which is more than most of his crowd can say of their own. Half of them were gombeen men and the other half lazy feckers. It's just as well he has money in the bank, I can tell you that for nothing. She'll never see that fella turn his hand to a decent day's work.' I didn't, of course, thought Nora now, but that was what gave me freedom. I was happy to take on the business from the day we married, and

I knew that if Martin had been a different man he wouldn't have let me.

Cocking her head, she looked at the blue dress she'd laid on the bed. It was nice enough in its way, but perhaps too dressy. She liked an informal start to a get-together: it relaxed everyone and set the tone for the weekend. The green silk was plainer and more casual, and it buttoned down the front which made it easier to slip into. And that, though she hated the thought of it, was important. Since Martin's death she'd discovered how often she'd asked him to zip up a dress for her, or remind her of things, or get something down from a shelf. Her widowed mother, left alone on the farm, had been the same way, frustrated by rheumatic pain, and shocked by the prospect of losing her independence, having worked every day of her long life.

Returning the blue dress to its rail, she went through to check the dining-table. Máire had sent two of the lads to set it up for her, and lay it with white damask, shining silver and bowls of flowers. They'd carried up six chairs as well, and stood them around it, removing her little round table and chair when they went away. She'd particularly asked for the cut-glass bowls to be small, and the flowers a mixture of evergreens and chrysanthemums. You couldn't expect people to chat across tall vases and, at Castlehill, she'd always taken pride in using flowers that were in season. It was sheer waste to do anything else and, besides, they looked better, just as seasonal food, which tasted the best, was always the best buy.

When she'd first arrived at Castlehill, she'd found the hotel still dealt with suppliers used by the family they'd bought the house from a generation before. By sitting down with a pencil and an account book, Nora had shown they'd been filling the pockets of shopkeepers in Athlone who'd doubtless been laughing behind the Sullivans' backs for years. She'd got rid of the chef, who'd been hand in glove with the worst of them, and had pointed out to Martin that time had moved on. No one, she told him, would ask for imports from England, like Fortnum & Mason's jams or Gentleman's Relish or potted beef. Not if you offered them food prepared and cooked in the hotel's kitchen, made with produce picked from the hedgerows, caught in the river or bought from a local farmer. Of course food like that wasn't fashionable in those days either but, armed with the figures, Nora had stood her ground. It was then that she'd realised Martin wouldn't care what she did to the hotel, so long as the guests kept coming and he could play genial host in the bar.

Straightening a napkin on the dining-table, Nora recalled her conversation with Raymond on Christmas Day. All I did, she thought crossly, was remind myself to mention those pastries to Máire, and Ray leaped in as if I'd threatened to add the last straw to a camel's back. Not wanting to pick a fight, she hadn't defended herself but, looking at it now in retrospect, his attitude galled her: when she'd managed Castlehill herself, she'd never had a Christmas when she wasn't up to her eyes in work. She half wished that she'd told Raymond Máire was damn lucky to have a recognised title at work, all the respect that came with it, and a seat on the town's business consortium. In the past, no woman could go to a bank with a plan she'd come up with and costed down to the last brass farthing, without bringing her husband along to pretend it was his idea, not hers. No bank back then would even consider employing a married woman; the story was they'd be taking away men's work. Raymond would have no idea of what she'd been up against at Máire's age because there was hardly anyone left who remembered. In fact, Nora was willing to lay good money that none of her family knew that, for years, she'd had no legal share in Castlehill. Martin could have sold the place over her head, on a whim, without even telling her. That had been the law in those days, and not a penny would have been hers, regardless of all she'd done to build the business. I should have told Raymond that, she thought, twitching the napkin again. He's a nice enough lad, and I'm fond of him, but he'd no business suggesting that I lean too hard on Máire or ask too much. The truth is she's got it easy and, while I don't begrudge it to her, I won't be put in my place by her husband.

Taken aback by this vehemence, which had seemed to come from nowhere, Nora went and stood by the window, telling herself she'd do well to calm down for the sake of her blood pressure. Raymond was a good lad, and had always been a good friend to her. Indeed, if Martin had been half as ready to stand up for me, she thought, I would have had a better husband and a happier marriage. And the fact is that Máire had already dealt with the pastry issue. You couldn't fault her arrangements for this weekend either. Everything had been printed up in a special souvenir programme, including the menu for tonight's meal. Consommé to start with, followed by venison stew with carrots and parsnips, and apple cake for pudding. None of these was on the restaurant menu, but all were staples on the first night of a Sullivan Girls' Get-together. Admittedly, it was a heavier meal than Nora had been used to eating lately, but that didn't matter so long as the others enjoyed it. Feeling her breathing get steadier, she smiled and thought of Jane. Apple cake had always gone down well with Sheila's children and, though girls these days seemed to spend half their time glued to their phones, no doubt they hadn't lost their appreciation of a good pudding served with whipped cream.

It was dusk outside and, glancing down, Nora saw Raymond approach the front door. He ran up the steps and disappeared under the portico that jutted out below her bedroom window. That meant it was nearly six, so she ought to get herself ready. She returned to the bed and looked again at the green dress, wondering if, after all, she might stick with the pin-tucked blouse and fine wool skirt she was wearing. Because it wasn't just a question of zips versus buttons. The truth was that, recently, the effort involved in dressing and undressing herself had grown tiring. Nora frowned. Though this physical aspect of ageing annoyed her, it hadn't come as a surprise. She'd seen it in her mother, and was resigned to it. The trouble was that it brought a disturbing loss of her sense of self which echoed the way she felt about the loss of her ebony hallstand. Hesitating, she assured herself that the outfit she was wearing was both stylish and informal enough for what would just be a family occasion. No one had been up to see her yet, so they'd never know that she hadn't changed for dinner. She had gone to the wardrobe and reached to hang up the green dress again when she turned back, sat on the bed, and began to unbutton her blouse.

To hell with feeling tired, she'd go for the dress and wear matching heels. The girls always made an effort on the first night of a get-together, and she wouldn't want to let them down.

When Raymond came into the kitchen, Barbara was leaning against the table, waiting for the kettle to boil. He stopped in surprise, then hastily tried to cover his reaction. 'Oh, hi. I didn't expect to see you here. I mean, I thought no one was in.'

'Brace yourself. I'm your houseguest.'

Putting down his briefcase, Raymond hugged her. 'Are you? That's nice. How come, though?'

'Last-minute accommodation issues.'

'Oh, Lord.'

'Máire had to redistribute us and I've ended up here.' Barbara reached to turn off the whistling kettle. 'She left me to do my unpacking and make a cup of tea for myself. D'you fancy one?'

'Go on. Why not? I've an hour before I'm due at the club to coach my under-twelves.'

'You're still doing that?'

'Ah, I had great coaching when I was playing at their age. It's good to be able to give something back.'

'How many evenings a week?'

'A fair few, most of the year round. Out in the field and down in the club for wet-weather sessions. It gets me out from under Máire's feet.' As Barbara poured the tea, he went to a cupboard for biscuits. 'Have an individually packaged cookie? They seem to migrate from the Housekeeping trolleys.'

'None for me, thanks. I know the size of the first-night dinner ahead of me. Máire says we're summoned for seven o'clock, which sounds kind of early.'

Raymond tore the wrapper off a cookie. 'It was Nora's idea. She said Jane would be tired after the journey.'

'It's only a few hours.'

Raymond laughed. 'I know. I'd say that was a cover story. Lately, Nora's been taking to the bed pretty early herself.'

This was news to Barbara. 'But she's okay? I mean, she's well?'

'Not a bother on her. She is slowing down a bit, though, and she doesn't care to admit it.'

In her twin room on the second floor, Henrietta hovered outside the bathroom listening to the sound of a rainforest shower running at full blast. Having anticipated that Jane would have her own space off the main bedroom, it was unnerving to find they'd been put in a smaller room than expected, with an upright chair on either side of a small round table, and beds separated by no more than the width of a locker. When Jane had been ushered in, she'd made no comment but, appalled by the room's dimensions, Henrietta had started to babble. 'Well, this is a lovely colour scheme, isn't it? Lemon and lime, I suppose you'd call it. It works really well with the pale wood. It's a shame our rooms had to be changed round at the last moment. Managing hotel accommodation's a nightmare. I don't envy Máire her job, do you?'

Jane had carried her bag to the window and set it on the floor. Joining her, Henrietta had found herself wittering on. 'Oh, look. We've got a river view. There's the boathouse, see, down there past the trees? Did I tell you this was a country retreat built for an English family that lived in London? They sold up and left during the War of Independence. Or earlier, maybe. Or later. I'm not sure. Anyway, they built it so they could come here for the fishing. And, look, Jane, there's Luke. We met him on our way in, remember? He's got a cottage in the grounds. You can't see it because of the trees.'

Jane had watched impassively as Luke, who'd emerged from the boathouse, was lost from sight among the cluster of leafless oaks. Getting a grip on herself, Henrietta had looked again at the bedroom, which, on second inspection, had seemed even smaller than before. Behind her, Jane had asked, 'Is there a bathroom?'

'What? Of course there is. Look here's the door. It's a whirlpool bath, there's the control panel, and, see, we've got a rainforest showerhead as well as an ordinary one.'

'That's cool.'

'I'm going to take a shower before dinner. Will you have one too?'

'Sure.'

'Well, you go first, and I'll put my things away. I'll leave you these two drawers. Look, there's masses of room in the wardrobe. And a shelf with coffee and tea things. And a safe.'

'Okay.'

Jane had disappeared into the bathroom fully clothed and, by now, the shower had been running for twenty minutes. Still hovering, Henrietta wondered if she should knock and call out to her. Might she be having difficulty with the controls? As she hesitated, the deluge stopped and Jane came out enveloped in a bath sheet, her clothes under one arm and a smaller towel round her head. 'Is there a hair-drier?'

'In the top drawer.'

Jane sat at the dressing-table, towelling her hair. She seemed completely composed. Following her lead, Henrietta undressed in the bathroom before taking her shower. When she came out wearing a hotel towelling dressing gown, she realised that by opening one of the wardrobe doors she could screen the space outside the bathroom from the rest of the room. Hastily wriggling into the outfit she'd chosen to wear at dinner, she closed the wardrobe and found Jane sitting on the end of one of the twin beds. She'd blow-dried her hair, changed into a pale lilac dress, and was bending forward to fasten a chain around her neck. Henrietta, who'd just put on a necklace, went to the dressing-table and looked in the mirror. The silver filigree, set with marcasite, looked well against her grey shirt, which she'd teamed with tapered black velvet trousers. Throwing back her hair, Jane said, 'You look nice.'

'Thanks. Your dad gave me the necklace last Christmas.'

Jane held up the little gold heart that dangled from the chain.
'He gave me this too. When I was five or something.'

'It's lovely.'

'Yeah, thanks. I like it. It was my mum's.'

Chapter 7

Though Barbara had known the flat since childhood, this was the first time she'd looked at it through her mum's eyes. The entryway, which had parquet flooring, was dominated by the ebony hallstand. A door led to a large, square living room, where a leather chesterfield sofa, flanked by a pair of button-backed armchairs, stood in front of a flatscreen TV. No one had been home when she came in, so she'd carried her suitcase through to her mum's old bedroom. At some point, its walls had been papered in a floral design, and there was a small, tiled fireplace, which had not seen a fire for decades. The room was comfortably furnished with a wardrobe and dressing-table, a tall chest of drawers and a brass bed. There was a duck-down duvet with matching pillows under the candlewick counterpane, but everything else felt light years away from the décor in the hotel bedrooms.

Máire arrived while Barbara was having tea with Raymond. 'You found the teabags. Good. I hope you'll be okay in the bedroom.'

'I'll be grand and, honestly, Máire, you didn't need to make the bed up. I could have managed that myself.'

'It was no bother. I would have had one of the staff do it, but I'm a bit short-handed. We had to work from midnight to get the Christmas stuff down before the first breakfasts – and, when you bump up the numbers on a night shift, there's a negative knock-on effect the next day.'

'Well, now that I'm settled, forget I'm here. I'll try not to be in the way.'

'I'm hardly up here myself, am I, Ray?'

Raymond moved to the sink to wash the tea mugs. 'Oh, I'm a grass widower most of the time. It's lucky I've plenty to do.'

'Don't be an eejit.' Máire gave him a cheerful push. 'And, Barbara, listen, I've cleared the shower room for you. We'll use the main bathroom while you're here.'

'Don't let me put you out of your shower.'

'You won't. I never use it.' Máire followed the push with a kiss and, linking Raymond, smiled at Barbara. 'Mind you, I'll have to suffer this fella coming in soaking or splashed with mud, but I'm pretty sure that's what I signed up for when I married him.'

Having showered and changed into a dark linen dress, Barbara emerged from her bedroom just before seven. In the kitchen, Máire had her phone to her ear and was shrugging on a fuchsia-pink jacket. She finished the call as Barbara came in, and turned to face her. 'Do you think I'll pass muster with Granny?'

'You look great.'

'That's probably overstating it. I like your dress.'

'I got packing down to a fine art when I lived in Oslo.'

Máire tapped a text into her phone and hit Send. Though her eyes were on the screen, she continued the conversation with Barbara. 'Scandinavian designers are fantastic. I sourced a lot for the spa from a guy in Sweden.'

'Judging by what I saw on the website, you've gone for state-of-the-art.'

'Well, I've always loved interiors.'

Barbara decided not to mention the house Máire and Raymond had bought when they'd announced their engagement. Built on the edge of town and surrounded by a mature garden, its interior had been the focus of intense discussion. Henrietta, then in a flat share and working at a jeweller's in Dublin, had chipped in enthusiastically. Barbara had contributed comments from a distance. There'd been consultations on colour and fabrics and kitchen appliances, and trips to Dublin to look at furniture seen online. It was hard to believe that, after such obsessive effort, letting the house had been easy for Máire. She and Raymond had been married only a few months when Martin died, and afterwards, Nora had moved at breakneck speed. Most of her decisions had been uncontroversial. Máire had already been on the management team at Castlehill, so it was no surprise when the general manager's job went to her. What had seemed odd to Barbara was her apparently willing acceptance of the move from her perfect house. By the look of things, Máire had done nothing to make the flat her own, though, as Sheila had said, she'd probably had no time for that.

Now, as if she could tell where Barbara's thoughts had strayed, and didn't like it, Máire picked up her handbag and said they'd be late if they didn't hurry. 'We're starting with canapés, and dinner's ordered for seven thirty. It's definitely not *cuisine minceur,* so I hope you're hungry.'

'I'll cope, I've been dieting in advance. And you look like you haven't sat down to a proper meal for ages.'

'Hoteliers don't sit down to eat. They graze.'

'Oh, please! When we were kids, Granny used to sit with us around this table, eating bacon and cabbage she'd cooked herself.'

'I'm far too busy.'

'The point is that Granny knew about work-life balance.'

'Granny was an amateur, Barbara. The point is that she's bright enough to know it. It takes a professional to run a twenty-first-century business. Why do you think she handed the reins to me?'

When Máire and Barbara got down to the suite, Nora was sitting on the sofa, a small, upright figure in green silk, with white hair tinted ash blonde. Jane was beside her holding a platter of canapés on her knees. Moments later, they were joined by Sheila, who held back until Barbara linked her arm. Nora could be heard urging Jane not to call her 'Granny'. 'If anything, I'm your great-grandmother, but that's not right either, is it? So you call me Nora, child, and we'll leave it at that. You've a grand name yourself, short and plain. I like it.'

Henrietta, who was pouring drinks, crossed the room to hug the arrivals and introduce them. 'Jane, this is my mum, and here's Máire and Barbara. You met at the wedding, remember?'

Before Jane had time to answer, Nora laughed. 'You can't expect the poor child to know one of us from another. People never look like themselves at weddings and, anyway, it was two years ago. I wouldn't have recognised her myself, with the long legs on her. What age will you be on your next birthday, Jane?'

'Thirteen. It's in April.'

'Ah, you're practically grown-up. At your age, I had a job in a shop.'

'Did you not go to school?'

'I did two hours in a bakery before school began, and another in the afternoon, carrying trays and cleaning up. I used to get given the crusty rolls that hadn't sold by dinnertime, and sometimes a seedy loaf, to take home to my mother.'

'Weren't you paid?'

'You can be sure of it. My father wouldn't have let me work for a handout. It was good bread, though. There was nothing to beat the smell of it on a cold morning.'

Henrietta leaned over the back of the sofa. 'I'll pass those canapés round, if you two are just going to sit there chatting.'

'Leave us be. We're getting acquainted, aren't we, Jane? And send your mother here to me, Hen. I haven't seen her in a twelvemonth.'

Henrietta went and offered a glass of wine to Sheila, who

summoned a smile and crossed to sit on the sofa. Watching her body language, Barbara felt a stab of sympathy. It would be odd to announce the news of her divorce with Jane in the room, but it was evident that she was longing to get the revelation over with. Jane held out the platter and Sheila took a canapé. 'These look delicious. What's in them, Mam?'

'According to Máire, they're all the rage these days. That one's a pea and mint fritter and the others are crispy gnocchi. What do you think of them, Jane?'

'They're good.'

Nora called over her shoulder to Henrietta. 'She doesn't say much, does she, Hen? No harm in that, mind. It's the onlooker sees most of the game. I'd say she'll soon have the measure of the lot of us.'

The conversation flowed on and, standing by the drinks tray, Henrietta lowered her voice to speak to Barbara. 'I wish Granny hadn't said that. Jane mightn't have liked it.'

'She doesn't seem bothered.'

'I know. But she's hard to fathom.'

'Well, Granny's clearly delighted with her.'

Getting no sympathy, Henrietta edged over to Máire. 'Isn't it time to sit down?'

'What's the matter? Are you hungry?'

'I'm worried that Jane's feeling cornered.'

'Well, go and rescue her.'

'That might make matters worse.'

'Oh, for Heaven's sake, Hen, stop *fussing*. As far as I can see, she and Granny are getting on like a house on fire.'

Outnumbered, Henrietta drifted back towards the sofa, hoping to overhear what was being said. Sheila wasn't contributing much to the conversation, but Nora seemed to be giving Jane the history of the hotel.

'We had twenty guest bedrooms when I arrived. It's a hundred and fifty now.'

'Wow.'

'The staff was mainly local then. Now we have them from all different countries. And the management team's expanded with the hotel. General and Deputy General Manager. HR. Finance. Sales and Marketing. Reservations. Reception.'

'And the guy who looks after the anglers and the grounds.'

'That's right. How do you know?'

'He carried our bags in when we arrived. Henrietta told me he's in charge of the grounds and the fish.'

'Well, you're right. He took over a few years ago when the previous man retired. Luke Something … What's his name, Máire?'

Máire came and perched on the arm of the sofa. 'Whose name?'

'The fellow you have working in the grounds these days. The one who took over from Matty.'

'Luke Ryan.'

'Where did you find him?'

'I advertised the job. He's highly qualified.'

'Ah, you're all highly qualified these days.'

'We're getting good value for money from him, Granny, I promise you that.' Máire held out her hand, offering to refill Nora's glass, but Nora shook her head. 'No, love, I won't have any more before I eat. The child might like a Coke, though.'

At the drinks tray, Barbara was dabbing with a napkin at a splash that had suddenly leaped from her glass. She glanced up as Máire reached for the ice-scoop. 'So Luke Ryan's still here?'

'Yep.' Máire began to pour Jane's drink. 'I didn't know you knew him.'

Barbara was concentrating on keeping her voice level. 'I don't. Well, hardly. I met him when we were here at last year's get-together.'

'Actually, I spent most of the rest of last year expecting his resignation.'

Though the splash had been absorbed by the paper napkin, Barbara kept dabbing. 'Did you? Why?'

'A number of reasons.' Apparently feeling this reply was too blunt to be gracious, Máire elaborated: 'He's over-qualified for the job and, contrary to Granny's suspicions, I've neither the budget nor the inclination to give him a raise. So I couldn't see why he'd hang around here with better options elsewhere.'

Certain the whole room could hear the pounding of her heart, Barbara said casually, 'But he did.'

'And didn't even try for more money. I can't think why not.' Hearing a knock at the door, Máire handed the Coke to Barbara.

'That'll be the food. Give this to Jane, will you, and start getting people to the table.'

Barbara held the cold glass tightly and made a stab at levity. 'Maybe he's running from something, and this is where he's gone to ground.'

'Who? Oh, you mean Luke. Don't be daft.'

'That was a joke.'

'Oh? Right. Well, could you get on now, and get people moving? You know how Granny complains if the consommé's cold.'

From under her eyelashes, Jane observed Nora across the table. She liked the old lady's straightforward way of talking, which meant there was no need to work out what she actually wanted to say. She liked her country accent too, and how Nora had called her an onlooker. It was how Jane saw herself, and something that no one before this had seemed to notice. The others were nice enough too, and less Percy Pig than Henrietta, though Máire was a bit snappy, and Barbara, who'd smiled and been friendly to start with, now seemed to have something on her mind. Their mum had introduced herself as Sheila but, since then, had hardly said a word. Jane, who remembered them all perfectly from the wedding, recalled that it had been just the same then: Henrietta's mum had kept quiet and out of the way, while Gan-Gan had spent the day rushing about organising things. Now she looked sideways at Sheila, who caught her eye, smiled and asked if she was enjoying the venison.

'It's good.'

Henrietta joined in from the far side of the table. 'I'd say the poor child is delighted it isn't turkey. I went for an absolute monster this year, and we've been eating it since!'

The kind of laughter this produced made Jane feel the need to say something supportive. 'I like Christmas food. It was nice turkey. Dad liked it too. We had sandwiches and salads and things. And a stew, like this one.' Realising they were all looking at her, she stopped, then staunchly repeated, 'It was nice.'

Nora threw Henrietta a smile. 'Fair play to you, Hen. And a good turkey makes a fine stock if you slow boil the bones.'

Jane looked down at her plate, remembering the stripped carcass Henrietta had dumped in the bin that morning before they'd left home. To her relief, Henrietta didn't succumb to conscience and confess. Instead, she said, 'You used to raise turkeys at one stage, didn't you, Granny?'

'Back on the farm we did, before I married. My mother would fatten them up for Christmas and sell them in Athlone.' Nora smiled. 'You know, if I had my time again I'd make proper use of the land round this hotel. Never mind your few polytunnels, I'd raise pigs and fowl and turn the grounds into grazing. You could grow enough food out there to save a fortune in the kitchen.'

Barbara, who seemed to have tuned in again, said, 'There's plenty of potential.'

Máire's expression darkened. 'Thanks, Baba, I know the potential. There's also the matter of prioritisation.'

Barbara stiffened and, unexpectedly, Sheila interrupted. 'Don't, Máire. You know she hates being called Baba.'

Máire closed her lips in a straight line, and Nora laughed. 'Ah, for God's sake! You'd think they were still in the school playground.'

Eager to paper over the crack, Henrietta smiled at Jane. 'They called her Baba before I was born because, back then, she was the baby of the family. By rights, the name should've come to me, but you don't hear me complaining.' Sheila laughed but, as Barbara and Máire didn't, the moment of tension hung in the air.

Pushing away her plate, Jane looked at Henrietta. 'Is there really apple cake and cream for afters?' Immediately, relieved responses fluttered around her like a flock of birds.

'There is, isn't there, Máire?'

'Is everyone ready for pudding?'

'It's always been a Sullivan Girls' Get-together thing, hasn't it, Granny?'

'It's Granny's own recipe, Jane, you're going to love it.'

'Here, let me help to clear. No, Máire, stay where you are, we'll do it.'

Sheila had got to her feet and Barbara and Henrietta were stacking plates. Ignoring the instruction to stay put, Máire went to the trolley to get the pudding. Amid the clatter of cutlery, and scraping back of chairs, Jane saw Nora, upright and neat in her green silk dress, suddenly looking old and tired.

Chapter 8

Sheila woke early on Saturday morning, stretched luxuriously and immediately felt a spasm of guilt. Perhaps when she'd given in and accepted her hotel room, she should have remembered Barbara's remark about not going in for cosy chats with Máire. The two girls hadn't been close as children and last night's dinner had shown the relationship hadn't improved much with time. It was strange how tension had seemed to bubble up without warning: one moment there'd been general conversation about raising turkeys, and the next, when Barbara had said something fairly innocuous, Máire had turned on her and snapped. At which point, thought Sheila, I went and stuck my oar in … but, to do me justice, Máire knows Barbara hates being called Baba. Using the name was playground stuff, pure provocation, and unforgivable in front of a child who hadn't a clue what was going on.

Getting out of bed, she reached for her hotel dressing-gown and, shrugging her arms into the sleeves, went to switch on the kettle.

It was nice to have the day's first cup of tea in an armchair by a window, with no one around and no need to make conversation. She wondered if Barbara, too, had woken early, and was now stuck in her bedroom with no chance of a cup of tea unless she went and made it in Máire's kitchen. Might she be lying in bed longing for one? Peering round her door, hoping the coast was clear? Or was this concern foolish? After all, by the end of last night's dinner, they'd all sat chatting as if nothing had happened. That was reassuring but, as the kettle boiled, Sheila realised it was wishful thinking. If Barbara *was* being the perfect houseguest and Máire the perfect hostess, it wouldn't necessarily mean things were fine in the flat: it was just as likely, given how fond they both were of Nora, that each was making an active effort to make the weekend go well.

Taking her tea to the window, Sheila sat down and looked at the view. Her room faced east and, as the winter sun rose behind clouds, the sky was tinged with pink, like mother-of-pearl. It was ten to seven. Mist floated above the river, and the close-cut terraced lawns were grey with dew. She was enjoying the warmth of the cup in her hands when she remembered how Jane had intervened to defuse the previous night's tension. Henrietta had tried to lighten things with her joke about Barbara's name, but it was Jane's childish question that had caused the diversion. Which was strange because, earlier, Jane hadn't been childish. She hadn't seemed fazed by being part of what was essentially an adult occasion. Though reserved, she'd held her own in her conversation with Nora and, when they'd sat down to eat, she'd needed no special attention. Yet the way she'd pushed back her plate and the voice she'd used when she'd asked about pudding had made her seem even younger than she'd appeared at Henrietta's wedding. Sipping tea, Sheila stared out of the window, trying to catch an elusive connection. Then it struck her. When Henrietta was growing up, she'd often behaved in exactly the same way.

Having recognised the comparison, Sheila couldn't unsee it. Her tea forgotten, she sat in the armchair, thinking. By the time they'd moved to Athlone, Máire and Barbara had begun to recognise Finbar's failings. They might still have been swept up in the excitement of his arrivals, which had always created an upbeat mood. But they'd also known broken promises and disappointments, and had lived in cramped rooms when she'd worked at the dentist's surgery in Killmoy. Born in a house with more space and a garden, and raised by a mum who was better off and less neurotic, Henrietta had had fewer reasons to question her dad's behaviour. And Finbar had fallen heavily for the new baby, loving the fact that, like him, she was blonde and fair-skinned, with striking blue eyes. The father-daughter love affair had been mutual from the beginning. When Máire and Barbara were sceptical adolescents, Henrietta was still a child who'd sit on Finbar's lap and listen to stories of record deals and arena concerts. He'd called her his golden girl and she'd never failed to charm him. That became her role in the family, thought Sheila. If I got irritated, or Barbara or Máire got stroppy with Finbar, Hen would cut the tension by being extra-childish, even when she was practically in her teens. I don't know if it was conscious, but I can see now that she did it, just as Jane did at dinner last night.

Henrietta and Jane had arranged to meet Barbara for breakfast in the conservatory. It was reached by walking through the bar, a very different place from what it had been in the days when guests had arrived with fishing gear piled in the back of their Morris Minors or walked from the station behind a porter who trundled their luggage along in a hand-barrow. The walls were now covered with photos and news cuttings from the years when Nora's shrewdness had elevated the business. As you entered from Reception, they stretched from the dado rail to the cornice, closely spaced and gilt-framed. A 1960s dance at which the band was a Beatles tribute act, and the younger guests did the twist in miniskirts. Bridge club meetings, charity events, First Communions and weddings. GAA whist drives. A Hollywood star, who'd stayed during nearby filming, caught at a table feeding steak tartare to a fluffy dog. Fewer priests and nuns in evidence as the decades passed. Swanky cars in the heady Celtic Tiger years, and politicians' wives in Paris fashions. Photos of international anglers who'd arrived incognito and, before leaving, had posed with good grace for a shot on the steps with Martin. Jane had lagged back to look, and now she stopped in front of one of the framed photos, a black-and-white image of Nora and Martin on the hotel steps. Henrietta asked, 'Would you recognise Granny?'

'Well, she's way older now but her eyes look the same.'

'I suppose that's right. I hadn't noticed.'

'In that photo she looks a bit like Máire looks now.' Jane switched her attention to one of the many shots of Martin holding a trout. 'You must have eaten an awful lot of fish when you were growing up.'

'Fly-fishers throw them back when they catch them. They just do it for sport.'

'Poor fish.'

Barbara, who'd come in behind them, laughed. 'Think of the Instagram accounts anglers must have, Jane. Like online versions of the walls of this bar.'

'Gross. Are there old photos of you and Máire and Henrietta here too?'

Henrietta shook her head. 'I don't think so. We didn't live here, you see. We just visited a lot.'

Jane moved to another photo, in which Nora, Martin and Sheila were sitting stiffly at a table, raising champagne glasses in a toast. Barbara came to stand next to her. 'That was our mum's eighteenth birthday, I think. Wasn't it, Hen?'

'I think so. Doesn't poor Mum look cross?'

'It looks as if it was shot by a professional photographer. She probably had to pose and didn't like it.'

Henrietta grinned. 'You always hated posing for photos too.'

'And you always loved it. Hen was the poster-girl of the family, Jane.'

'No, I wasn't!'

'Don't you remember when Dad came home one year with an expensive camera? It was his favourite toy that summer – he'd got it in the States. He spent hours taking photos of you looking winsome.'

Henrietta gave Barbara a cheerful shove. 'If he did, it was only because you and Máire refused to cooperate. Now, are we going to have breakfast or not? I'm starving.'

The menu promised a feast for the eye as well as the tastebuds and, when their food arrived, Henrietta reached for her phone. 'Hang on, Jane. Let me take a shot of you for your dad before you start eating.' As Jane posed obediently with her untouched plate, Barbara, who was buttering toast, shot her a comradely glance. 'For goodness' sake, Hen! Let the poor child eat her breakfast.'

Henrietta went into WhatsApp and hit Send. 'It's a gorgeous shot. See, Jane? I've sent it to Gan-Gan too.'

Barbara pulled a face. 'At least, as kids, you and I weren't endlessly uploaded to WhatsApp.'

Jane had cut into a waffle. 'Did your dad travel a lot?'

Henrietta, who was smiling at the response on her screen from Stuart, answered absently, 'He's a musician.'

'Cool.'

'He toured a good deal, when we were younger. He still does, doesn't he, Barbara?' Barbara said she hadn't been in touch with him for a while.

Jane looked at Henrietta. 'Was he touring when you and Dad got married?'

Putting down her phone, Henrietta reached for the cafetière. 'He was working. Did you want coffee, Barbara? You said you didn't have tea earlier. We could order a pot now, if you'd prefer it.'

'No, this is fine. What time do we gather at the spa?'

'Ten. Granny's coming down and Máire's going to give us all a walk-through. When we've seen everything, we can each decide what treatments we'd like to have.'

'Won't it be complicated if guests are wanting to book as well?'

'I wondered about that. But Máire's terribly organised, and she'd got today, all day tomorrow, and Monday morning to play with. Granny's ordered Bucks Fizz by the splash pool. After we've seen what's on offer, we're going to hang out there for an hour and decide on our treatments. I'm thinking hand massage and luxury manicure, for starters. Jane might join me.'

Barbara asked, 'Have you been to a spa before, Jane?'

'No. It sounds good.'

Sipping coffee, Barbara said, 'I might give the treatments a miss. Touchy-feely stuff isn't really my thing.'

Jane threw an uncertain glance at Henrietta. 'I'd kind of like to have a look around outside.'

Raising her eyebrows, Barbara said, 'I don't see why you shouldn't. There's plenty of time and plenty of grounds to wander.'

Henrietta's face puckered in anxiety. 'Honestly, Jane, it's like I said when we were talking to Luke. We can do whatever you like. You're here to have fun.'

'Okay. A manicure might be fun, though.'

'Well, let's wait till we see what's on offer. I've had my eye on a full-body Frangipani Salt Scrub, or maybe a Lotus Flower Detox Wrap.'

They gathered at ten at the spa's glass door, which was etched with a design that recalled the sinuous shape of the river. As Barbara arrived, Henrietta and Jane were already waiting, and Máire and Nora emerged from the lift. Minutes later, Sheila hurried down the corridor, casually dressed like the others and looking determined to enjoy herself. Máire opened the door and ushered them through to a low-lit room with a minimalist reception desk. There was a gentle sound of falling water and a faint, spicy scent in the warm air. Máire introduced them to a girl behind the desk. 'This is Shawna, our spa director. Shawna, these are my sisters and my mother. And this is Jane, who hasn't been to a Sullivan Girls' Get-together before.' Shawna murmured that they were all very welcome and, instinctively, everyone lowered their voices to reply. Máire moved to the front of the group. 'It'll take us about twenty minutes to look at everything. Then we'll go through to the pool.'

Sheila said, 'Lovely,' slightly too loudly and drifted to the rear as they followed Máire through the reception area to changing rooms and lines of lockers.

'They're secured with reprogrammable cards like your room keys. There are showers in the changing rooms, and we provide robes, towels and flip-flops. And, obviously, products. All organic and all for sale should people want to buy some to take home. We also have complimentary hair-ties, to keep long hair out of the way during treatments, and, if you follow me down here, I'll give you a look at the various treatment rooms.'

Feeling as if they were in a tour group being towed by a guide, Barbara trooped with the others down a corridor of doors, which Máire opened to reveal a facial salon, a dry-heat chamber, a steam room, and bowls of fruit and candles set out around a sunken bath.

Nora said she understood that the bath experience went down well with honeymooners. 'Those drapes around it are silk so fine you can draw them through a wedding ring. But wait till you girls see the rasul chamber. That's big enough for a group, isn't it, Máire? Mind, I haven't tried it myself but I'd say the rest of you would love it. Self-administered black soap detox and exfoliation, and a face and body mask of Moroccan clay. And argan-oil moisturiser, and God knows what. The feedback on the website says that groups have a whale of a time.'

No one spoke until Henrietta said they could probably work up to it. 'Start with a facial, or something less exotic. It's all amazing, though, Máire. I saw it on the website, but the photos don't do it justice. Well, they couldn't, could they? It's not just the place, it's the atmosphere as well.'

'Thanks. That's nice to hear.' Dropping her tour-guide manner, Máire suddenly looked younger. 'It was a huge undertaking, but it's worked out okay.'

'You should be proud.'

'I am. I hope you'll enjoy it.'

The soothing ambience seemed to enfold them and, to everyone's surprise, they found themselves in a clumsy group hug, half in and half out of the bathroom.

Upbeat music was playing at the poolside, where huge windows framed in steel overlooked a sloping green terrace, and pale gold tiling gleamed in the winter sunshine. Beside the tray of Buck's Fizz there was a luscious peach smoothie for Jane. As Henrietta helped with the drinks, Sheila sat and watched her, wondering how she was going to take the news of the divorce. This morning's realisation had been a troubling reminder of the intensity of Henrietta's relationship with Finbar. It seemed silly to worry about her now that she had a husband and stepdaughter to focus on but, in the run-up to her wedding, Henrietta had gone into full-scale panic about her father. 'I want him to be there, Mum, and I don't know where to send his invitation.'

Unsure of where he was and not having heard from him for months, Sheila had said, 'Send it to me, darling. I'll find out where to forward it.'

'Hasn't he been in touch?'

'You know how it is when he's on tour.'

'You told him about my engagement, though? I tried to phone at the time but the number wasn't in service.'

'Oh, you know your dad. He's probably got a new phone and didn't transfer the number. Look, I must rush. Don't worry, darling, I'll see he gets the invitation.'

'I really want him there, Mum.'

'I know, darling. Look, you've masses of other things to think about. Leave this to me. I'll sort it.'

She'd spent ages trying to track down Finbar through old friends and DMs on social media and, eventually, found an address to which she'd sent the invitation. There was no response so, when she couldn't stall any longer, she'd braced herself and lied to Henrietta, saying Finbar was touring in Australia and couldn't get home in time. 'He's devastated, sweetheart, but there's no help for it. You know he'll be thinking of you on the day.' To make the story convincing, she'd ordered flowers to be delivered to the wedding reception, and told the florist to include a card saying, 'Love and congratulations to my Golden Girl, from Dad'.

On the day of the wedding, she'd arrived to find Barbara, who'd got there before her, shoving the bouquet of lilies into a bin in a corridor.

'What on earth are you doing?'

'Keep your voice down. These are from you, I assume.'

'What? Yes, but what are you *doing*?'

'Henrietta's in there glowing because Dad has sent her flowers.'

'Then, what ...?'

'Not these flowers, Mum. Flowers *actually* sent by Dad. It's just as well I happened to be here when your florist's bloke arrived.'

Aghast, Sheila had opened her mouth to explain, but Barbara had stopped her. 'You don't need tell me why you did this. I know. It's typical Dad. Total bloody silence, so you try to make things better, then he steps in, steals the limelight, and nearly causes chaos.'

'Oh, my God, what if Hen had seen mine?'

'She didn't and she won't, so pull yourself together. You can't walk in looking like that.'

Shaking, Sheila had found a loo and dabbed her face with water. Then, straightening her hat, she'd made her way to where Henrietta was pinning a sprig of forget-me-nots to her dress. 'Aren't these gorgeous? Dad sent them to me, with rosemary for remembrance. That's what the card says. 'Never forget me, always remember.' I love it. But he's not in Australia, Mum. He's in Hawaii.'

'Really? They must have added a new date to the touring schedule.'

Briefly, Henrietta had looked confused. Then she'd turned to Stuart. 'See, darling? Aren't these lovely? I wish he could have been here for the wedding, but it's not his fault. He's a work-horse, just like you are. And you can see that he's always thinking of me.'

Now, watching Henrietta offering drinks to Máire and Barbara, Sheila sighed. Barbara's perfectly right, she thought. My girls are grown-up. Hen's even got her own little girl to worry about. She's a mother. But, where Finbar's concerned, she's never been like the others, so I still don't know how to tell her about the divorce.

When everyone had been served a drink and was lounging by the pool, Máire handed out brochures illustrating the spa's treatments. 'Just tick whatever you'd like and I'll manage the bookings. I may have to fit you around slots already booked by guests, but I'll let you know your appointment times before lunch.' By this stage, Barbara was chafing to slip away. After a cursory glance at the options, she ticked a few arbitrary boxes, and sat back trying not to show her impatience. Nora announced that she fancied a hand and arm massage. 'I've had it before. It's very good, Sheila, you should try it. There's seaweed in it, isn't there, Máire? Good for the joints. See, here's a picture.'

As the others discussed choices and swapped suggestions, she reminded them that, on Sunday, they were all having a champagne brunch. 'But don't think we'll spend the weekend breathing down each other's necks. It's about each of us taking time to wind down individually, as well as all of us spending time together.' Sneaking a glance at her watch, Barbara told herself that, with luck, she should be able to get out to the grounds before lunch. Sheila, who'd scooted her rattan chair closer, asked her what she thought about foil wraps. 'I've never had one. Have you?'

The last thing on Barbara's mind was spa treatments. 'Me? No. I don't really go for hands-on stuff.'

'But you've ticked a body scrub and a massage.'

'Have I? Yes, I have. Well, you've got to break your own rules sometimes. Push the boundaries.'

Sheila laughed. 'I suppose so. Okay, what the hell? I'll do the foil wrap.' She ticked it and recklessly added an ultrasonic face peel. 'Heaven knows what that is but, you're right, why not go for it?' Closing her brochure, she asked if Barbara had plans for the rest of the morning. 'I'm undecided myself. I thought I might corner Máire and break the news about your dad, but it looks like she's running on overdrive at the moment.'

At the opposite side of the circle of chairs, Máire was holding a drink and apparently being helpful to Jane and Henrietta. She was smiling, but sitting bolt upright, and one of her feet was tapping nervously on the poolside tiles. Sighing, Sheila shook her head. 'She won't have time for a chat, that's certain. Maybe I'll slope off to my room after this, and read a book.'

Barbara edged her sleeve up again to check her watch. 'I think I'll go stretch my legs in the grounds.'

'Oh, Barbara! You want to keep out of the flat! Is it awful? Should we swap back?'

Kind though this was, Barbara was in no emotional state to revisit the argument. 'Not at all. I practically have the whole place to myself. Máire's charging around doing stuff, and Raymond's out today.' Standing up, she hitched her bag on to her shoulder. 'I'm going to slip away when I've given her my choices. Let's meet for lunch in the bar, okay? You could ask if the others will join us.' She edged round the circle of chairs and laid the brochure by Máire, then, dropping a kiss on Nora's head, she walked away, pausing at the entrance to summon a cheerful smile and wave.

Outside the spa's glass door, she stopped, took a deep breath, and made her way to the ladies' room in Reception. In the mirror, her face looked back at her, taut and anxious. Crossly, she dug out her makeup bag, touched up her eyes and brushed some blusher across her cheeks. She was wearing joggers, boots and a hoodie she'd bought in Oslo so, before going outdoors, she zipped the hoodie up to her chin and pulled the hood over her auburn hair. As she stood between the granite pillars that supported the portico, the January wind whipped a dead leaf across the hotel steps.

Shoving her hands into her pockets, Barbara hunched her shoulders. When she'd arrived yesterday and seen the grounds unchanged, she'd half hoped and half feared that Luke had left Castlehill. Her plan had been to find him if he was still around, but now she wasn't sure she trusted herself to follow it through. She'd been shaken the previous night when Máire had mentioned him at dinner, and again when Henrietta had thrown out his name over breakfast. So was she really in the right state of mind to go looking for him? What was required was a calm, cool front. What if she couldn't summon it? Leaning against a pillar, Barbara struggled to decide. Fear of making a fool of herself nearly conquered her resolution and she almost turned tail and retreated through the revolving door. Then a voice at the back of her mind called her a coward so, squaring her shoulders, she ran down the steps.

Chapter 9

Barbara's feather-light hoodie designed for Scandinavian winters kept her snug as she crossed the windswept lawns. She made her way down the terraces to the stone-flagged riverside path where occasional stands of trees provided windbreaks. The peat-brown water was in winter spate and clumps of broken reed and twigs, looking like banshees' hair, streamed away from rocks and roots. On the path, the wind pushed her along, making her stride out and breathe deeply. At first, she simply revelled in the fresh air, thinking of nothing. Then a flock of crows rose from a tree ahead, Luke stepped on to the path, and her heart seemed to leap straight to her throat.

By the time she reached him she'd pulled herself together. 'Hi. Máire said you were still here.'

Luke leaned comfortably against the tree. Barbara stood and waited, her arms tightly folded across her chest. After a moment he held up one hand to shield his eyes from the winter sunlight. 'So, what's the story?'

'Sorry?'

'Did you come out into the wind to find me?'

Thrown by his apparent calm, she snapped, 'Talk about ego!' He didn't respond and, in the uncomfortable silence that followed, she became aware that her folded arms appeared defensive. Since neither aggression nor defensiveness had been part of her plan, she dropped her arms to her sides, and met his eyes. 'Look, it's far too cold to stand here. It's ridiculous. Can we go somewhere and talk?'

'There's my cottage.'

As this had been the scene of their last encounter, Barbara stiffened. Then she shrugged. 'Sure. Why not?'

He fell into step beside her and they walked on together. They were almost equal in height, his long stride matched hers, and it felt so familiar that, for a mad moment, she almost took his hand. Flicking a sideways glance at him, she saw he hadn't changed much since the previous year. Though his curling hair was a little longer, he still looked tanned and fit, and his plaid shirt, jeans and quilted jacket were exactly what he'd been wearing the last time they'd met; she recognised the work boots, the frayed shirt collar and the heavy pair of gloves that made his jacket pocket sag. Suddenly she remembered laughing up at him and saying, 'The received wisdom in business is that you dress to reflect your status. I'd recommend something more management and less gardener's boy.'

'By which you mean less Lady Chatterley's lover.'

'Yeah, right. Don't flatter yourself.'

She'd been lying in his bed watching him dress when she said it, and he'd laughed as he'd sat on the edge of it to lace his boots. 'Is this really the right moment to give me career advice?'

'You certainly need it.'

'Wanting and needing are two different things, Barbara. What I wanted was what we've just had.' Leaning over, he'd kissed her. 'Thank you for it. Now I should get back to work.' Returning the kiss, Barbara had pushed back the duvet. 'I'll grab a shower. I'm expected in the hotel.'

He'd gone and she'd showered in his tidy bathroom, astonished by what she'd just allowed to happen and hearing through the falling water the sound of his voice saying that wanting and needing were two different things.

Over the next three days, she'd repeatedly slipped away to meet him and, for Barbara, though that first encounter had been pure chance, both it and a love affair had felt inevitable. It was as if she'd been walking towards him all her life and had finally reached the place where she belonged.

Now, walking beside him, she still felt that sense of completion. But it wasn't a love affair, she told herself fiercely. It was a one-night stand a year ago that happened to last for a weekend. *That may not have been how it felt to me, but that's the fact of the matter. And the problem is that I've no idea how it felt to Luke.* Sliding her eyes sideways, she looked at him again, thinking that if she'd had any sense, she'd have stayed indoors this morning. Things had ended badly the last time, so why stir them up again?

By now she was as tense as a fiddle string, but Luke didn't seem to notice. When his cottage came into view at a bend in the river, he remarked that it would be good to get in out of the cold. There was no sign that he was remembering, as she was, the look they'd exchanged the first time they'd crossed that threshold together, or how quickly they'd stopped pretending that they weren't going to end up in bed. Now, determined not to give in to an urge to turn and run, Barbara said, 'Your garden's looking well.'

Luke raised an eyebrow. 'Thanks. There's not much to see at this time of year.'

'Well, no, but … everything's so well trimmed back. I mean … I mean, with acres to care for, you could be forgiven for leaving your own plot till last.' This sounded so lame that she wished she'd said nothing.

Luke grinned. 'Ah, but it's in my contract of employment. I've a requirement to *keep the tied cottage and its associated plot in good order, ready for inspection at all times.*'

Startled out of her embarrassment, Barbara stopped walking and stared at him. 'God, that's antediluvian.'

'I doubt if anyone's checked the wording since somewhere round 1911.'

'But there is such a thing as employment law. The indoor staff must have sane contracts.'

'They probably have. I've never asked. Anyway, as you once told me, I'm management, not staff.'

She searched his face but neither it nor his tone told her what he was thinking. Then he said, 'It's bloody cold out here, Barbara. Are we going indoors or not?'

Nothing indoors had changed since the previous January, when Barbara had slammed the door and left in a rage. Luke's housekeeping seemed to consist of keeping the cottage exactly as he'd found it – spotlessly clean and with no more personality than a show house. Like the older parts of the hotel, it was stone-built, and after Matty's retirement it had been rewired, replumbed and redecorated. Barbara could remember it from her childhood, when Matty had cooked on a battered range, and each of the four rooms had smelt strongly of dogs and fish. Matty's first love had been angling. Castlehill's land, which he'd ruthlessly subdued with a ride-on mower, had taken a poor second place. Occasionally, he'd allowed the girls to drive the mower, and leaned on a stick shouting instructions as they careered out of sight with his dog in pursuit. In her teens, Barbara had suggested the grounds could be more than just lawns to be crossed on the way to the river but, sensing the danger of being pensioned off, Matty had been derisive. That, plus her family's lack of interest in her suggestion, had stung, and she'd gone to study in Dublin with the vague idea that she might come back and prove them wrong. But more exciting possibilities had taken over. Then, when Matty retired and she heard Máire was interviewing for his replacement, she'd assumed it would be some brawny school-leaver from Killmoy, who'd fished since childhood and knew how to handle the mower. So, her initial encounter with Luke had surprised her in more ways than one.

It had happened the previous year, when she'd arrived for the get-together feeling energised and on top of the world. She loved her studio flat with its bird's-eye view of Dublin, and was sure she'd been right not to follow her boyfriend to New York. From the first day in her new job she'd loved the team she was working with too, so the move from Oslo had been an unqualified success. Having got to Castlehill and unpacked, she'd gone for a walk before dinner and caught her first sight of Luke, who'd been hunkered down on the riverside path, mending the boathouse door. He'd stood up as she approached, and smiled as she came closer. 'Nice day.'

'Isn't it? Amazing for January.'

'It'll get colder now the sun's down. The forecast's good, though.'

'Great. I hate being stuck indoors.'

'Are you here for a few days?'

'Yes. Sorry, my name's Barbara. I'm a Sullivan ... well, my grandmother's Nora Sullivan, and I'm here for a family shindig.'

'Luke Ryan. I look after the hotel grounds.'

'You're Matty's replacement?'

'So they tell me. You look surprised.'

'No ... I mean, no, it's none of my business. I didn't know who Máire had hired, that's all.'

'Apparently I'm part of a restructuring thing the hotel's got going on. I'm the grounds maintenance manager. I gather Matty was more a slash-and-burn kind of guy.'

'Have you been here long?'

He'd been packing away his drill, and had sat back on his heels to look up at her. 'Only a month, but I'm working on long-term planning. I arrived with a five-year development plan.'

'Definitely a change from Matty.'

Getting to his feet, he'd leaned against the boathouse. 'I suppose so. My background's landscape gardening, then a degree in water conservation and management.'

'Sounds like Castlehill's lucky to get you. Good luck with the plan. I'd like to see something made of these grounds. We've never done them justice.'

Raising an eyebrow, he'd asked if she was part of the family business.

'No, I work in Dublin. I sort of didn't fit in here. Look, I ought to get back. Nice to meet you.'

He'd held out his hand and, as soon as Barbara grasped it, she'd felt the shock of attraction that had sent her back to the river the following morning, where she'd found him hanging about, and had known he'd been waiting for her to appear.

After that, they'd dropped the fiction that they were meeting by chance and, by Sunday, she'd known for certain where they'd been heading. And now, she thought, here we are again in the bare, spotless cottage that I foolishly stormed out of last year.

'Tea?'

Jerked back to the present, Barbara looked at Luke blankly before realising he'd pulled out a chair from the table. 'Tea? Yes, I suppose so. Thanks.' She sat down, watched him disappear into the kitchen, and heard the sound of running water and the clatter of mugs.

The last time they'd been here together, it was she who'd made tea while he'd gone out to the shed to fetch fuel for the wood-burning stove. The living room had grown chilly when they'd been upstairs in the bedroom, but the fire had flared again when he'd added logs and adjusted the airflow while she'd boiled the kettle and put mugs on a tray. There was only one armchair so they'd sat on the sheepskin hearthrug and drunk tea in front of the leaping flames.

Now, sitting on an upright chair at the scrubbed wooden table, Barbara tried to stop her mind drifting to the past. She needed to concentrate on what was happening now. The kettle was boiling and, at any minute, Luke would emerge from the kitchen. And what then? She'd announced that she wanted to talk but, having got here, she'd no idea what she wanted to say. All she knew was that, for a year, she'd tried and failed to forget him. And that nothing, so far, suggested that he felt the same about her.

Luke came in carrying two blue-rimmed mugs, which he put on the table. 'I can light the stove if you're cold.'

'No, don't bother just for me.'

'Okay. I've assumed it's still milk, no sugar.'

'Yes. Thanks.' To buy time, Barbara made a play of finding the tea too hot, and carefully set her mug back on the table.

Luke had tilted his chair till it was balanced on two legs. 'So. What are we talking about? Presumably not my career path.'

Scarlet with shame, Barbara remembered the row she'd provoked last year, when she'd gone to the cottage to say goodbye before returning to Dublin. Halfway along the river path, the realisation of how she felt about Luke had overwhelmed her. How was it possible that in a few days of stolen meetings her organised world had been overturned? Scared by the intensity of her feelings, she'd arrived at the cottage in a jangled state and had pushed Luke away when he'd kissed her. Then, vulnerable and confused, she'd tried to assume an air of detachment. 'Listen, I've got to get on the road, but I've been thinking. Honestly, Luke, you really ought to consider how you present yourself at management meetings.'

'What?'

'It's just, if you want to be taken seriously, you should look the part.'

'O-*kay*.' He'd moved away and when he'd turned back his face had been inscrutable. 'And this is why you've come here this morning? To tell me that?'

Miserably aware that it wasn't, she'd said, 'It's what you need to hear.'

'Wanting and needing are two different things, Barbara.'

'Oh, I know you don't *want* to hear it.'

'I didn't say so.'

'Yes, you did!'

His quiet denial had fanned Barbara's nervous irritation into the blaze of anger that had allowed her to turn and storm out. She couldn't remember all she'd said, but she knew she'd behaved like a bullying boss who'd summoned a junior employee, and the understandable look of surprise on Luke's face had made matters worse.

He was looking at her now with distant reserve, his chair still tilted back and his tea mug in his hand. Barbara leaned forward. 'Look, about that stupid row. I owe you a huge apology. Your career is none of my business. What I said was intolerable, Luke. I've wanted to say I'm sorry ever since.'

'Sorry you left? Or sorry you told me I'm not up to my job?'

The first part of this question was much too close to the bone for Barbara. Unable to answer it, she repeated herself. 'I was way out of line to say what I did. It was arrogant. And it wasn't true.'

'It was true.'

Honestly surprised, she frowned. 'No, it wasn't.'

His reserve fell away, like a discarded mask, revealing painful bitterness. 'Oh, for God's sake, Barbara, I haven't made the slightest difference here. Me with my brilliant five-year plan and my rake of qualifications. I spent all last year going to management meeting after meeting. I even took your advice once and wore a suit. But, whatever I try, the same thing happens. I arrive with my PowerPoint, and I'm last on the agenda, and before I even stand up, they're all shuffling their papers together. They know there's no point in listening because they know your sister doesn't. And that's because she can't see what's right under her nose.' The front legs of Luke's chair hit the floor with a crash as he thumped the table. 'It isn't the loss of potential income that bothers me – it's not my money. It's the acres of sterile land that could be alive and useful. Nobody ought to own land and treat it as it's been treated here. And the way the river's been managed is practically nineteenth century. It shouldn't be hard to demonstrate that, if people would only listen.' He stopped abruptly, took a swig of tea, and shrugged his shoulders. 'But, clearly, I haven't got what it takes to do the job I'm paid for.'

'That's ridiculous.'

'No, I'm ridiculous. I should have asked more questions when I was interviewed for the post. Instead, I saw a blank canvas and assumed it was mine to work on. I honestly thought no one could look at what's here and not want to change it.'

To her surprise, Barbara found herself defending Máire. 'She's taken on a hell of a lot of work. Well, it was dumped on her. I reckon she's struggling to keep her head above water.'

'This doesn't involve her taking on more work. All she needs to do is approve it.'

'There are investment issues.'

'Of course there are and, obviously, I've worked out a budget. But she's got no grasp of government-grant schemes, or integration with national initiatives, or the extent to which this kind of project requires long-term planning. I don't think she even understands coordinated teamwork. But, look, I'm sorry. She's your sister. I don't mean to rant.' Relaxing, Luke caught Barbara's eye and gave her a rueful smile. 'The truth is I seldom get to talk to someone who knows what I'm on about.'

For months, Barbara had lain awake remembering his casual grace, his laugh, his strength, and his sense of humour. What she'd never seen before was this vulnerability. Instinctively, she reached her hand across the table, then checked herself when she saw Luke draw back. Mortified, she reverted to her apology. 'No need to say sorry to me. Not after how I behaved.' With an effort, she managed to assume an air of politely concealed distraction. 'And I really ought to go now. I have a lunch date.'

Luke's look of vulnerability changed to a blank expression. 'A lunch date? Right. Fine. I won't keep you.' He was on his feet, as if longing for Barbara to leave, so she stood up too and, with tears pricking her eyes, ducked her head to zip up her hoodie. When he held out his hand to shake hers she took it and felt the same shock of connection she'd had when she'd first touched his fingers. But, startled into meeting his eyes, she saw no response but polite indifference.

She was on the doorstep when Luke spoke behind her. 'Barbara?'

'What?'

'Why did you pick that fight with me?'

Having almost escaped, she turned back to face him, feeling wretched but managing a laugh. 'Oh, don't! I'm just naturally bossy. And, to be fair, Castlehill's grounds have mattered to me since I was teenager. If I'm honest, I think I've felt guilty about turning my back on them. Which is no excuse for lecturing you and storming off in a temper.'

'I see. Well, you're forgiven. If you'll forgive me for my rant.'

'Quits, then.'

Luke's expression was still unfathomable. 'Quits. Of course. Enjoy your lunch date.'

As Barbara made her way back to the hotel she told herself firmly that what she had to do now was move on. Luke's withdrawal when she'd reached out her hand across the table, and his apparent lack of response to the touch of their fingers later, had told her all she felt she needed to know. Summoning her mantra that God never closed a door without opening a window, she assured herself that a closed door was a good thing. It meant the uncertainty of the past year was behind her, and she could get back to enjoying life. It won't be easy, she thought, but I can do it. Last year was just a casual fling for Luke. That's perfectly clear. He can't be blamed for that. And it's not his fault that I fell in love with him. It's not mine either. It's just what happened. I mustn't allow the life I've built for myself to be undermined by stupid obsession. Now that I know the truth, I've got to accept it.

Raising her chin, she strode on, enjoying the crisp air and telling herself that this was freedom. She'd reached the bench near the boathouse when she stopped and sat down, trying to grasp a thought that had flashed through her mind. For a moment it eluded her. Then she pinned it down. For months, Máire had been expecting Luke's resignation, and Luke's disillusionment with his job suggested that that made sense. He was over-qualified, under-valued and justifiably angry. So why, instead of cutting his losses and getting on with his own life, had he chosen to stay at Castlehill?

Chapter 10

Raymond was sitting on the sofa when Máire came into the room. Pushing his legs out of the way, she sprawled beside him and kicked off her shoes. 'I've a dozen things to do but, God, I need a breather.' Raymond repositioned her so that her feet lay across his knees and her head was pillowed against the arm of the sofa. He wiggled her toes gently and she closed her eyes with a smile. 'That's nice.'

'Better than what's on offer in the spa?'

'A hundred per cent. Who needs fancy argan-oil treatments when they've got a husband with magic fingers?'

'What did the girls say when you showed them around?'

'Actually, they were rather nice about it.'

'Why shouldn't they be?'

'I don't know. Anyway, they were. We're meeting for lunch in the bar in about half an hour. Meanwhile, I've managed to find slots for them around my guest bookings, which, I can tell you, is close to miraculous. The Second Chance Club crowd has been texting requests for extra slots. They're on their way down from Dublin this morning, clearly in riotous form.' She interrupted herself with a yelp of pain. 'Ray! Take it easy!'

'This is a proper sports massage. None of your namby-pamby luxury treatments.'

'When can I expect to get feeling back in my toes?'

'These things take time, but they're worth it.' After a few minutes, he turned his attention to flexing her knee, then moved along the sofa to kiss her. Máire laughed. 'I told you, I'm due downstairs.'

'You're always due downstairs. Can't the girls have a drink while they're waiting?'

'They could, but I might get too comfortable and forget them.' Gently pushing him away, she swung her feet to the floor. 'Thanks, love, that made a big difference.'

'That was a drop in the ocean. What you and I need is some proper time together. Holiday dates carved in stone, not just pencilled and cancelled.'

'We'll get a holiday this year. I promise.'

She had tensed up again and, to lighten the atmosphere, Raymond laughed. 'I give you fair warning I won't settle for less than a full fortnight. Tell you what, we could relive our honeymoon. Croissants and *café au lait* at Parisian pavement tables. Bookstall browsing by the Seine and that trip we took to Versailles when flowers were blooming and you had a sneaky paddle in a fountain.'

'Hoteliers can't take time off in high season.'

'Or at Christmas. Or New Year. Or Easter. Or Mother's Day. Or any other feast day or festival you can disguise as a bumper getaway package.'

'That's just how the business is.'

'So you always tell me. But the way you run this place, you've no downtime at all, Máire, and you'll do Castlehill no favours by working yourself into the ground.'

'I'll clear a space in my diary, I promise.'

Raymond had bent to peer under the sofa, where one of her shoes had rolled when she'd kicked them off. He was aware that she was growing defensive, but lately they'd had so little time to sit down and talk that he felt he had to keep going. 'You've assembled a good team, love. I think you should start to trust them.'

'I do.'

'Then it's time you let them get on with things without you.'

'Raymond, stop. Please. You need to back off, okay? It's early days, and I'm trying to restructure while simultaneously keeping the boat steady. I can't take my eye off the detail. It's too soon.'

'Have you thought of hiring someone to take a look at long-term planning?'

'You're the one who always calls consultants a waste of space.'

'Well, how about talking things through with Nora?'

'Oh, right. "You've got one foot in the grave, Granny. Let's discuss the future"?'

'It might be better than treating her as if she's gone already.'

'Raymond! I don't!'

He had rolled off the sofa in his search for the missing shoe. 'You're right. I'm sorry. There's no one kinder to Nora than you are.

But it's still her hotel. She worked all her life to build it and she's seen the lot. Massive development. Boom. Bust. Changes in fashions and guests' expectations.'

'That's the point. Expectations do change. Things are different from how they were in her day.'

'My point is that things are always changing. Nora's seen plenty over the years. She's still sharp as a tack. She won't have forgotten what she learned. You could ask for her input.'

'She gave me the job, Ray. It's down to me to do it.'

'Well, like you keep saying, she won't be around for ever. There's succession-planning to consider, and I don't believe someone as savvy as Nora hasn't thought about it.'

'So, are you saying you want me to ask about her will?'

Raymond sat back on his heels, holding the shoe he'd fished from under the sofa. 'I'm saying she's someone who understands the concept of forward-thinking. She couldn't have built this empire if she wasn't.' He was choosing his words carefully but could see Máire had grown irritated.

Snatching the shoe, she put it on, snapping, 'Spoken like a banker.'

'Oh, Máire, love, don't be silly, and please don't let's fight about it. The building and the business are worth a lot, but that's not what I'm on about. You've said yourself that Nora could be feeling sidelined. I think you're right, so what I'm suggesting is that you sit down and talk to her.' Getting to his feet, Raymond held out a hand to help her up. 'You won't want to do it this weekend, but perhaps when the others have gone?'

Ignoring the hand, Máire stood up, straightened her skirt and reached for her phone, which had pinged with a text message. 'I'll have to deal with this.'

Raymond stood and looked at her for a moment before bending to straighten the sofa cushions. 'Okay. I'll be pottering in the garage today. See you later.'

'Okay.'

At the door, she turned and, biting her lip, spoke half apologetically. 'I know you mean well, and I don't want to sound ungrateful. But, honestly, Ray, what I needed just now was a breather, not a lecture.'

After the poolside session, Henrietta had cornered Sheila and suggested a walk round Killmoy before lunch. 'Jane wants to look at the shops. Why don't you come along?' Evidently in the mood for family reminiscence, she'd turned enthusiastically to Jane. 'Mum had a flat in the town once. I'm not sure where it was. We could get her to show us.'

This was more than Sheila had felt she could bear. Killmoy was on the up, so the shabby house where she'd rented was probably now a bijou residence, but she'd no desire to exclaim at that, or recall her memories of it. Hastily, she'd told Henrietta she fancied a rest before lunch. 'I'm not used to Buck's Fizz before midday. You two go on. I'll see you in the bar later.'

Now, sitting at her bedroom window with a novel, she felt a mixture of guilt and relief. It would have been good to spend time

118

with Henrietta, especially as she'd gone off looking apprehensive, as if she wasn't sure she could entertain Jane. On the other hand, it was lovely to sit in a comfortable yellow armchair and retreat into fiction with a guaranteed happy ending. She'd bought the book as a Christmas read and had tucked it into her suitcase because she was only a chapter or so from the end. Having finished the last page, she stretched, wondering lazily where Barbara had gone. Henrietta and Jane were presumably browsing gift shops, Nora was resting, and Máire was sure to be catching up on work. But Barbara had slipped away with no explanation.

She's never been gregarious, thought Sheila. And, heaven knows, those rooms I brought her home to when she was born were cramped enough to make anyone grow up yearning for privacy. The thought provoked a memory of the day of Barbara's birth when, yet again, Finbar had been away. Sheila's waters had broken prematurely, and, with no other option, she'd sent Máire to Nora at Castlehill. Afterwards, Finbar had claimed he'd booked to arrive in time for her due date, and couldn't have known that, with Barbara, things would 'go wrong'. In fact, his absence had been a relief to Sheila. So much had changed since she'd had Máire that the last thing she'd wanted was Finbar by her side at the hospital. He'd phoned a few times after the birth but hadn't turned up for a month, leaving her to cope with a colicky baby and an aggressively jealous four year old.

Those weeks were exhausting. Having flatly refused to have Nora with her for Barbara's birth, Sheila had brought the baby home in a taxi, rejecting Martin's offer of a lift. She'd known it would be sensible to leave her parents a key, so her heating could be turned on and there'd be fresh food in her fridge to come home to. But, determined to manage alone, she'd returned to comfortless rooms and frozen pizza, and had looked daggers at Nora who'd arrived with Máire by the hand. The baby had screamed, Máire had sulked and spat at her, and Nora's evident effort not to mention Finbar had ratcheted up the tension by several notches. When Nora was gone and the children were finally sleeping, Sheila had sat on the floor and cried her eyes out, more miserable than she'd ever felt in her life. Now she pushed aside her book and got up to stand at the window, thinking this was precisely why she loathed coming back to Killmoy. It was far too full of memories, regrets and unresolved conflict, and being here brought them all back to the surface.

Even the view from the window recalled the times she'd paced the hotel grounds, feeling ridiculous or miserable and not wanting to take the lift to the flat to pick up the girls. After Barbara's birth, it had been harder to keep Nora and Martin at arm's length and, to a large extent, Castlehill had become the children's crèche. Sheila would take them there in the mornings, before going to work, and they'd spend the day happy in their grandparents' company. It was Nora who'd found a way round four-year-old Máire's disapproval of baby Barbara's arrival. 'Would you look at her, pet, she's a real, live baby dolly! She's your own baba. You'll have to take care of her now, while your mam's at work.' After considering the idea, Máire had embraced it, and Barbara, who'd soon outgrown her colic, had placidly accepted being treated as a possession. As time passed, they'd formed a more equal relationship, though Máire always guarded her place in the family pecking-order, and used the name 'Baba' as a reminder whenever she felt Barbara was out of line.

People don't change, thought Sheila. Not really. Especially if they don't recognise their own patterns of behaviour. It's taken me years to understand why I put up with Finbar so long. Maybe I don't even understand now. Maybe that's why I hate coming here, where I'm forced to look back at the past. Pride is such a stupid, destructive emotion, and when it's mixed with guilt it leads to such stupid choices. And guilt is pointless too. It means you never escape the past. Sighing, she looked out of the window and saw Barbara, her hood up, making her way from the river path towards the hotel. A glance at the clock by the bed had told Sheila she ought to get ready for lunch but, somehow, she couldn't turn away from the sight of her daughter. We really are two of a kind, she thought. Not just in personality. Barbara's looks are pure Sullivan, just as mine are, and like me, though she ought to feel she belongs here, she seems to have no attachment to Castlehill.

Raymond tapped on Nora's door, looked in and asked, 'How's it going?'

'I'm grand, love, come in. I was just watching this silly morning programme.' Nora turned off the TV and gestured to a chair. 'Have a seat.'

'I won't stay. I know you're going down to have lunch with the girls.'

'Ah, I've time yet. Take the weight off your feet for a minute.'

'Fair enough.' Dropping into the chair, he said he'd stopped in on his way to town. 'I've a tin of polish to pick up. Do you need anything yourself?'

'Not a thing. What are you polishing now? Hubcaps?'

'The seats. It's a leather treatment I read about online.'

'And you'll pay through the nose for it too. Would you not use shoe polish?'

'On my lovely soft-top Saab? God forgive you!'

'Oh, they see you vintage-car enthusiasts coming, with all your notions.' Nora bent forward and tapped his wrist. 'I tell you what, though, love, I wouldn't mind a packet of fig rolls.'

'No problem.' Raymond gave her an affectionate smile. 'I hear the girls' spa appointments are all organised.'

'And we had a grand time earlier, by the pool. It's lovely to see them here again, and little Jane as well.' Removing the glasses she wore when watching TV, Nora stood up. 'I suppose I'd better shift myself and get down to the bar for lunch.'

'Right, I'll go and buy my polish.' Raymond hesitated, then made a decision. 'I've been trying to get Máire to let me whisk her off to France sometime this year. I want us to take the car over, like we did for our honeymoon. Stay in Paris, drive around. Feel the wind in our hair.'

'That sounds like an offer no woman could refuse. Are you telling me she's resisting?'

'No. Well, a bit. You know Máire's work ethic.'

Nora looked at him shrewdly. 'I was cross with you on Christmas

Day, did you notice? When you told me off for making too many demands on your wife.'

'I didn't say that.'

'Nonsense. For all you came at it sideways, you were marking my cards for me, and, once I'd taken a few deep breaths, it could be I saw you were right.'

'That's a carefully worded admission.'

Nora laughed. 'It's all you're getting, so make the best of it! Seriously, though, love, I'd say Máire does need a holiday. I was looking at her down at the pool this morning, and she didn't relax for a single minute. Have you suggested this trip to France?'

'I've planted the seed, but I haven't much hope of it taking.' Raymond looked down at his feet. 'The thing is, I know sod-all about running a hotel. I mean, I can see it's hard work, but I know nothing about the nitty-gritty. I just have a feeling that Máire's micromanaging. Not stepping back and taking the long view.'

Nora pursed her lips, then spoke slowly. 'And if you say that to her, she'll say you don't know what you're talking about.'

'The thing is ...' Raymond's voice trailed off ruefully '... it's horrible to sit watching, knowing what's wrong and not being allowed to help.'

In Killmoy, Henrietta backed away from the clocktower that surmounted the little town's corn exchange. The Victorian building's central hall was used for a Saturday market, where she and Jane had been browsing craft stalls. Now Jane was posed on the steps holding a patchwork cushion, like a model in a lifestyle magazine. Its pink floral design matched the décor of her bedroom, and Henrietta, who'd bought it for her, was taking a photo to send to Stuart's mother. 'That looks great. Hold it out a bit. Perfect. Now give me a smile. Gan-Gan will love this.' Having taken the shot, she glanced up at the tower's clock. 'Wow, look at the time. We'd better get moving.'

Returning the cushion to its carrier bag, Jane came down the steps. 'Do we need to change for lunch?'

'No, I'd say we're grand. We might want to dump our bags, though. I don't know how I ended up buying so much.'

'There were nice things on the stalls.'

'Did you like them?'

'They were nice.'

Shooting her a sidelong glance, Henrietta wondered sadly if she'd ever get past her stepdaughter's veneer of politeness. When they'd strolled around town, Jane had looked at shop windows, read tourist information boards, and leaned over the bridge to peer at the carved curlicues enclosing the date on which it had been built. Eager to keep her engaged and happy, Henrietta had made several purchases simply because Jane had held them up for a closer look. She strongly suspected this had been noticed because, after a while, Jane had kept her hands in her pockets. Whether she really liked the cushion, or anything else they'd seen on the market stalls, remained an open question. Sometimes, thought Henrietta, it's as if she says things to reassure me – as if I'm the child and she's a kindly adult eager not to discourage me when I'm trying hard to be good.

They walked back through streets crowded with Saturday shoppers and, reaching the gates, made their way up Castlehill's curving drive. At the foot of the hotel steps, a group of guests had arrived in taxis and were milling about, struggling with luggage and calling to each other. They were all middle-aged women, loud-voiced and evidently ready to have a great time. The concierge appeared with several of the reception staff, who stacked cases on trolleys and wheeled them to a ramp by the steps. As Jane and Henrietta stood by the lifts, waiting to go upstairs, the women surged towards them escorted by the duty manager, who flicked a smile at Henrietta. 'I'd say some of us might have to wait for one of the lifts to come back. Do you two need to go to your room? You could leave your shopping at the desk and collect it after lunch, if you'd prefer to.'

A cheery woman with perfect hair and makeup interrupted. 'We don't want to monopolise the lifts. Just give me a wall to lean against while I'm waiting, and I'll be fine.' There was a burst of laughter, and one of the others nudged Henrietta. 'We started last night with dinner in Dublin and didn't stop dancing till dawn. She's dead on her feet, that one. You've no stamina, have you, Cathleen? Here's the lift now. Go on, you two. You were first in the queue anyway.'

Having grown up accustomed to making way for the hotel's guests, Henrietta shook her head. 'No, you're grand, we can leave our things down here. We're due in the bar for lunch, anyway. If we go upstairs, we'll probably be late.'

'Well, okay. If you're sure.'

125

'Of course I am. I'd say you'll want to fall into your beds and have a rest.'

The cheerful woman gave another shout of laughter, causing all the others to join in. 'Well, you've got that wrong, for starters, hasn't she, girls? No, we're the Second Chance Club, here for the Castlehill Spa Experience and, believe me, we plan to experience the lot.'

Chapter 11

After buying his tin of polish, Raymond bumped into a friend and went to a pub for a pint and a sandwich lunch. They settled in the snug and chatted, replaying every match in the previous year's county minor league. Raymond had coached three of the young players, and his friend was the proud uncle of a right-wing forward who, against all odds, had scored a winning goal. Having swapped stories of recent leagues, they went back further and recalled games played when they'd been at school. 'God, Raymond, you were fast. We don't get the likes of you, these days.'

'You should see the kids I'm working with now. You couldn't beat them for speed.'

'I wish I could give a hand down at the club now and again but, the fact of the matter is, I haven't the time. Between driving my own kids to matches and pottery classes and God knows what else, I don't get so much as an hour to spare.'

'Well, I've got the time and, anyway, I enjoy it.' Finishing his pint, Raymond stood up. 'I'd better be going. I've a car at home wanting its seats polished.'

'Is it still the old Saab? That's a beautiful car. Wouldn't do for me, though. Not with the crowd of ruffians I'd have to ferry round in the back. They'd have it destroyed in no time and, besides, it wouldn't hold them.'

'No. Well, I'll see you again, Jim.'

'You will, of course. Cheers, Raymond.'

Walking back to the hotel, Raymond reminded himself that Jim had married at twenty and gone for fatherhood like a bull at a gate: two sets of twin boys in five years, a daughter a few years later, and a wife who was now happily pregnant again. Máire and I have never wanted that kind of life, he thought. There's no comparison to be made. Not really. And Máire's only in her mid-thirties so there's plenty of time for us to have a baby. Instinctively, his mind shied away from the obvious next question, which was whether Máire would ever have time to stop and consider the matter. He'd never felt that raising the subject himself was on the cards, because of the years he'd spent patiently waiting, fearful of saying the wrong thing at the wrong moment. Anyway, so much had changed since the day she'd slid him a sideways glance and asked, 'How about getting married?'.

'What? Máire, you devil! You must know I've been wanting to ask you for ages! So, what's the story now? You're saying you love me?'

'Of course I love you. Who else have I ever looked at seriously?'

'I seem to remember a guy called Brad. And that hunk you brought home from Limerick, what was his name? Richard? And Jürgen, the sous-chef from Baden-Baden. And – hang on – there was that weirdo you met at Lisdoonvarna, the lad with the teeth and the fake Fender guitar.'

'You knew as well as I did that they were just ships that passed in the night.'

'How was I supposed to know that?'

'Because it should've been obvious. Anyone with half an eye could have seen that I fell for you like a ton of bricks in my teens.'

'Well, you've wasted a helluva lot of time between then and now, haven't you?'

'Yes, I have. It was dumb. Let's get married immediately.'

After all his years of patience, it had been that simple, and for Raymond the takeaway seemed to be that waiting and keeping his mouth shut had done the trick.

On their honeymoon, when they'd stopped overnight somewhere between Caen and Rouen, Máire had turned her head on the pillow and whispered, 'I'm sorry.'

'What for?'

'Being so awful for so long. I don't know why you waited.'

'Don't you?'

'The truth is, I don't deserve you.'

'Bollocks. You've made me the happiest man in the world.'

They'd driven on to Paris with the Saab's top rolled down, raucously singing 'The Westmeath Bachelor' and waving at strangers. After the honeymoon, Máire went back to her job at Castlehill, where Nora was still at the helm, and Martin still spent lazy days chatting to anglers in the hotel bar. The house Raymond and Máire bought in Killmoy before the wedding was one he'd long had his eye on. He would have been happy if Máire had wanted to start a family at once, but the question hadn't arisen and, back then, it had felt like early days.

Now, reaching the top of the drive, he turned down a path that led round to the rear of the hotel. Still musing on the past, he remembered how Máire had thrown herself into renovating their house. It was a handsome Georgian property backing on to fields, with well-proportioned rooms, a garden full of roses, and a double garage for the Saab and their ordinary workaday car. One of the rooms had evidently been designed as a child's bedroom. Behind a sheet of plywood, Máire had found a little fireplace tiled with a pattern of storybook galleons in full sail and, under the windows, lids lifted on roomy toy-boxes lined with paper collages of figures from Grimms' fairytales. Though the old-fashioned effect was charming, Raymond had expected to see it all swept away. Instead, Máire had polished the fireplace, left the toy-box collages untouched and, having painted the walls, had moved on to the other bedrooms, and to modernising the rooms downstairs.

Two years later, when Martin died and Nora made her sudden decision to abdicate, everything had had to be done in haste. Máire's elevation to general manager was a big leap from her former role in the hotel's hierarchy, and all her energy had become focused on not letting Nora down. As the flat was smaller than the house, and the house was let unfurnished, most of the carefully chosen furniture went into storage, while other possessions were packed into the loft. The long-term implications of this simply didn't arise and, concentrating on being supportive, Raymond hadn't raised the subject. And since then, he thought, everything's sort of retreated. When we bought the house, the future felt full of exciting potential. Now it just feels uncertain, and the present is constant stress.

There was guest parking close to the hotel entrance, but the family's cars were garaged at the rear in a stone building that had started life as stables and a coach house. The stalls, tack room and hayloft had been dismantled, and some of the space gained was now fitted as a workshop. Unlocking the door, Raymond went in and opened the window shutters, revealing his Saab in all its vintage glory. Beyond a few trips to Athlone, to check it was still running, he hadn't taken it on the road for ages. Not that the engine's condition ever gave him cause to worry; if anything, it was over-cared-for, and the car's sleek exterior was in showroom condition. Reaching for a pair of overalls, Raymond pulled them on and went to let down the car's soft top. Seeing an online advertisement for the polish, he'd given in to temptation, telling himself that leather could always do with conditioning. Nevertheless, there was no point in denying that he was running out of reasons to spend time in the garage. I can't increase my hours coaching kids at the club, he thought. I do far too much of that already. And I hate sitting around in a flat that Máire treats as a crash-pad and I've no reason to think of as my home.

Shocked, because he'd never before expressed this thought so clearly, Raymond raised his head and saw a slight figure in the doorway. Collecting himself, he called, 'Hi. Are you looking for someone?'

Looking hesitant, Jane took her hand from the door and stepped inside. 'No. I just wanted to see what was in here.'

'Come and look round. You're Jane, aren't you?'

'You're Henrietta's sister Máire's husband.'

'Raymond. That's right. I didn't think you'd remember me. We met when your dad and Henrietta were married.'

'Everyone here seems to think I've forgotten the people I met at the wedding. I don't know why. It wasn't that long ago and, anyway, you all remember me.'

'You had a starring role, though. We were like extras in the background.'

'All I had to do was hold flowers and smile when they took photos. It was a bit boring, actually.' Jane looked at the Saab. 'Is this your car?'

'Yep. A 1993 Saab 900 Turbo Convertible. Do you like it?'

'It's very cool.' She came further into the garage. 'When did you get it?'

'About seven years ago. Do cars interest you?'

'I like STEM stuff. Engines and things come under that, don't they? Me and a couple of friends want to go in for Young Scientist of the Year.'

'Aren't you a bit young at this stage?'

'There's a junior level. Anyway, it takes time to come up with an idea.' Jane walked round the car, inspecting it from all angles. 'What are these dials on the dashboard for?'

'They provide information. Pretty much what you get these days on a digital display.'

'That's cool. How do you pull up the hood when it's raining?' Raymond demonstrated how to raise and lower it. She watched, then asked, 'What were you doing when I interrupted?'

'I was about to use this on the seats.' When he showed her the tin of polish, she touched the pale grey upholstery with one finger. 'My dad has a Lexus with leather seats. These are way nicer. Could I have a go with the polish, do you think?'

'Sure. But shouldn't you be somewhere else?'

Jane shook her head. 'I've a nail appointment at four. Gel art and glitter tips. Hen said I could explore the grounds till then, and it's only two thirty.'

Taking the tin from Raymond, she sniffed at it appreciatively. 'Should I start on the front seats or the back ones?'

'Whichever you prefer. It's up to yourself.'

Beaming at him, Jane scrambled happily into the car. An hour and a half doing what she'd prefer would be way better than nothing and, actually, far more than she was used to.

At lunch in the bar, where Nora had presided under Martin's portrait, they'd all talked and laughed over ham and cheese toasties. Having come directly from Luke's cottage, Barbara had found it a strain, but she'd joined in and found that having to rise to the occasion provided a distraction from her confusion. The hour between lunch and her spa appointment had proved more difficult. Not wanting to go up to the flat, she'd wandered into the hotel lounge with her mind in turmoil, always coming back to the fact that, whatever he'd said, and however he'd looked when they'd spoken, Luke was still at Castlehill for no apparent reason. In the lounge, she'd sat down unaware that two of the Second Chance Club ladies were drinking coffee on a sofa next to the armchair she'd chosen. Delighted to have company, they'd immediately introduced themselves and, since it would have been rude to stand up and walk away, Barbara had stayed, torn between misery and boredom, as the two of them told her in great detail about their club.

'It's not formal or anything. It's just a bunch of us who decided we ought to get out and do things, now our kids are reared and off our hands.'

'Most of us live round Howth Hill way – the far side if you're coming out from Dublin. We were going to call ourselves the Over the Hill Club, but that's a bit close to the bone, so we thought we wouldn't.'

'Did you get that, Barbara? Did you? The Over the Hill Club. I mean, what kind of eejits were we to come up with that?'

It had taken half an hour to escape and, by the time Barbara got to the spa, the last thing she wanted was company. But Henrietta had an appointment at the same time as hers, and Shawna met them with a confiding smile. 'I love that Mrs Sullivan established this tradition! It's so nice for you all to have family time together. Now, as you've both chosen massages for your first treatments, I've booked you into our double massage suite.' Henrietta beamed and, taking a firm grip on herself, Barbara did her best not to look apprehensive.

When they emerged from the changing rooms wearing flip-flops and towelling robes, Shawna introduced them to a blonde girl in a tailored smock. 'This is Stacey. Her colleague's already in the suite. Stacey will take you down there.' The corridor was bathed in the gentle ambient sound of water played through speakers. The massage suite had two couches, side by side. Stacey's colleague, Gemma, helped Barbara on to one, and covered her with a deliciously warm towel. Lying face-down, Barbara heard Henrietta settle on the other couch, and Gemma's voice above them, sounding hushed and professional. 'After the twenty-minute massage, Stacey and I will leave you to yourselves, for a slow, gentle wind-down: this space is yours for the entire session, so you're welcome either to stay here or to move to the relaxation area, where you'll find herbal teas to assist the process. So, let your tensions slip away and give yourselves to the Castlehill Spa experience.'

Barbara was trying to trace an elusive memory. As Gemma smoothed oil across her shoulders, she recalled lying, face-down, on a beach-towel next to Henrietta, and hearing their mum's voice above them, sounding fussed.

'I packed factor fifty, I know I did. Where is it? You'll be burned to a crisp without it, Barbara.'

'What about Hen? She gets burned too.'

'You've got a redhead's skin, Barbara, and you know what happens. In five minutes, you'll look like a boiled lobster.'

Henrietta's giggle, and the sound of Sheila rummaging in a beach-bag, echoed back to Barbara through the years. That was probably the last time Hen and I were this physically close, she thought. I don't think I could've been more than ten, which means Hen was five. It's weird to think she now has a stepdaughter older than we were then.

The lights dimmed. The subtle scent of Barbara's random choice of massage oil mingled with whatever Henrietta had ticked when she'd filled in her preference card. Neither smelt anything like the cheap bottle of factor fifty that Sheila had eventually found in the beach bag. Barbara wondered what her dad had been doing during that holiday. Probably sipping cocktails in the Bahamas, she thought, while Mum had to cope with us in a Donegal bed-and-breakfast.

The massage suite was beginning to fill with the recorded sound of waves interspersed with the distant cries of seabirds. Taking a deep breath, Barbara chased another memory. Sea buckthorn, she told herself. That's the base of this oil. I don't know why I chose it, and I've no idea what Hen's is, but they go really well together. I wonder if that's just chance. Perhaps Hen saw what I ticked, and matched her choice to mine. Maybe she heard Máire say we'd be booked for a session together. Maybe she even told me so. The truth is that, when we were by the pool, most of my mind was on Luke, and whether I ought to go and find him. Which was crazy. What made me think definitive action was the answer? And where did it get me? When I did find him, I couldn't find words, so I walked away again, and despite my bravado as I trudged back from the riverside, the truth is that I can't forget him.

The deep sound of whale song was interrupted by Stacey asking Henrietta if she was comfortable. 'Yes, thank you, I'm fine. Isn't this fantastic, Barbara? It's like drifting off into a dream.' Closing her eyes, Barbara attempted to blank Luke out of her mind. It would help, she thought, if the sea buckthorn oil didn't have overtones of woodsmoke. Because the last time I smelt woodsmoke was last year in Luke's cottage, when we sat on the sheepskin rug in front of his stove. She could feel her muscles tensing at the painful association, and disapproval flowing through Gemma's fingers. Oh, God, she thought, I don't need relaxation. I want a knotty problem at work, a battle to fight or a disaster to deal with. Something that demands total focus, and leaves no time or space for anything else. I have no dreams to drift off to. What I have is a life that needs putting back together, and all I want is to get back home and get on with it.

From the other couch, Henrietta whispered, 'She's fallen asleep.'

Opening her eyes, Barbara snapped, 'No, I haven't.'

Surprised, Henrietta raised her head, and Gemma bent forward solicitously. 'Everything okay, Barbara?'

'Of course. Sorry. I'm fine.'

'Are you finding the pressure painful?'

For a mad moment, Barbara was tempted to say that the pressure of keeping from screaming was tearing her heart out. But, consciously relaxing her muscles, she shook her head. 'Not at all. That's a beautiful oil you're using.'

'Have you noticed your sister's oil picks up similar woody notes? We often find that when siblings are close there's an affinity in their choices.'

This left Barbara feeling worse than ever. All these soothing sounds and scents were supposed to end in sisterly conversation, and evidently Hen, who'd settled comfortably back on her couch, was all for it. Barbara tried to imagine the two of them in their fluffy white robes, sharing confidences over cups of herbal tea. The scenario was unlikely but perhaps she shouldn't fight it. Perhaps she could even turn it to her advantage. Keeping Henrietta at bay wouldn't be difficult, but might it be better to tell her the whole story? Henrietta knew Luke. Not well, but they had had a chat when she arrived with Jane. Something he'd said then might throw light on why he was still around. Or, if that's too far-fetched, thought Barbara, Hen might give me some advice. She's not a golden-haired kid anymore and, despite all the wide-eyed stuff, she's never been stupid. But what advice could she possibly give that would make the slightest difference? The bottom line is that I look and feel ridiculous. I set out today to find answers, and came back with another question. No amount of herbal tea and sympathy can change that.

Chapter 12

Nora lay on her bed with the counterpane drawn over her knees. Traipsing round the spa in the morning and then having lunch with the girls had brought home the fact that she'd lost some pep since the last get-together. There was dinner tonight to get through as well, and all tomorrow's palaver, which included a champagne brunch, so a few hours' rest were definitely in order. Monday would be less strenuous, as they'd all have left by lunchtime, and after that, if she wanted to, she could stay in bed till noon every day for a week. Besides, she told herself, I'm a survivor. Reaching under the counterpane, she eased an aching knee, and realised she was older now than either of her parents had been when they died. Older than my brothers and sisters out in the States, she thought, who were all dead and buried before I had Sheila. Older than all those Sullivan men who sat around puffing their pipes, blaming me for not being able to keep a son alive. Despite her aches and pains, it seemed cause for celebration and, with a smile, she looked forward to having a fig roll with her tea.

She had slipped off the dress she'd worn at lunch and was wrapped in her paisley dressing gown, which she'd bought when she and Martin had taken their last jaunt together. They'd chosen a Rhine cruise, which had been fine by Martin, who loved boats, and because she'd fancied seeing several countries along the way. Martin's life had always been one extended holiday, but she'd never travelled before the first year of their marriage, when she'd taken herself off to England for a hotel trade show. She remembered her mother's amazement when she'd told them she'd booked a hotel room in London, and how her father had disappeared into the bedroom and returned with a sealed envelope. 'Put that somewhere safe now, girl, and don't go spending what's in it unless you have to. I won't have you off in a strange place with nothing to fall back on.' Nora had been about to say Martin never kept her short of money, but the look on her mother's face had kept her silent.

There were many levels of pride involved when dealing with her father and, when things went wrong, it was always her mother who had to patch them up. Thinking about it afterwards, Nora had realised that the envelope contained some of the windfall cash her dad would make now and then, at cards or on a lucky deal at the mart. Hoarded in a locked box, it was kept under the bed, as insurance against what her mother had called their dotage. It felt strange to look back now and remember how fearful people in those days had felt about getting older. She'd tried to talk to her mother about it once, and had got nowhere.

'You'll never go hungry, Mam, you know that. You've got me here, and the lads in the States, and all of us ready and able to help if ever you need a hand.' Her mother's only response had been a glance at the door, to check that her father hadn't overheard, and to whisper, 'You're a good girl, Nora, but we didn't raise you to have you fretting about us. We've got our health and our strength, thank God, and your father has the future well in hand.'

In England, Nora had carried the sealed envelope with her everywhere, terrified it might be lost or stolen, and checking on it so often that it almost became the focus of her trip. She'd driven out to the farm the day she'd got back to Killmoy, and placed it, unopened, on the kitchen table. Though nothing was said, then or later, she'd known that if she'd come back empty-handed, her father wouldn't have asked how she'd spent the money: the extent of the loss would have been visible in her mother's face, but neither would have questioned whether her need had been greater than theirs. And, as it happened, both had died while there was still money under the bed, so her father, who'd never trusted Martin to take proper care of her, had been spared the humiliation of ending his life dependent on his Sullivan son-in-law.

She'd made other business trips after that first one to London, as well as the jaunts with Martin, which had started years later, after Sheila's marriage. Nora wished they could have brought Sheila along on those or taken the girls to give Sheila a bit of a break. We went to plenty of places the children would have enjoyed, she thought, but even letting them play up here went against the grain with Sheila: she'd have been a happier woman if she'd inherited Martin's laziness instead of my grit and my father's pride. That said, she made a fine job of raising those girls single-handed. I wish I could tell her so, but she's got no interest in my opinion. I saw that when she was hardly older than little Jane is now.

Restlessly, Nora tugged at the pillows behind her, wondering when this fad for piling hotel beds with them would go out of fashion. It had started when people had taken to twisting towels into swans, and leaving chocolates on bits of slate in the bedrooms. Given her way, Nora would have had none of that kind of thing. Picking pillows up off the floor only added to Housekeeping's work and, nine times out of ten, you got chocolate stains on the sheets. Daft as it might seem, those kinds of decisions mattered. It's never about looks, she thought. It's about vision. You have to make what you've got into something better, but you've got to know how to cut out the dead wood without destroying the tree. You can't replace good judgement with nothing but energy and action. Which is why Máire's out of her depth and struggling. Raymond's seen that and, if the truth be told, so have I. God knows, it's been evident for months. Máire has the drive to build things up, like I had, but building is more than bricks and mortar expansion. What's needed now is commitment to a new kind of vision, or things will stagnate, the business will fail, and poor Máire will feel she's let me and Castlehill down. Perhaps I shouldn't have thrust such responsibility on her so suddenly. But what else was there to do, with nobody else to take it?

Petulance fed by helplessness gripped Nora. Reaching back, she dislodged one of the pillows piled behind her, and pushed it sideways till it slipped to the floor. I don't know why Raymond came bothering me, she thought. If he can't get his wife to listen to him, what makes him think I can? Frowning, she fixed her eyes on the fallen pillow, which was now humped on the floor beside her like a fat white cat. Something ought to be done or said to help Máire, but Máire, too, was a chip off the old block. She had Sheila's stubborn pride and determination, along with a wayward streak that was all her own. Look at how she'd played Raymond along, and kept him guessing. Look at her fierce reaction as a child, when Barbara was born. She could never be driven, always had to be given a long halter, and allowed to come to conclusions for herself. Offering advice was never the answer. And God knows why I'm congratulating myself on being a survivor, thought Nora. I'm a peevish old woman not even able to go out and buy her own biscuits. The fact is that you're useless when you're old.

As Jane came into the spa, Shawna stood up behind the desk. 'Hello, there. You're here for your manicure?'

'Is this not the right time?'

'It is, come along in. You're Jane, aren't you? Now look, I know the idea was that you and your stepmum would have a fun session together. The thing is, we didn't have a double appointment slot available. There's a ladies' club booked in this weekend, and all our staff manicurists are doing a group session with them.'

'Yes, Hen said. But if you're busy I could just skip the appointment.'

'Not at all, there's no need for that. We've a single booth all set up, and Carolyn, who works Saturdays, is ready and waiting for you.'

Though she'd have been just as happy to skip the appointment, Jane smiled and said, 'Oh? Okay. Thank you.'

Taking her arm, Shawna led her to the booth. 'So, Jane, this is Carolyn. She's going to make you look like a million dollars.'

'Okay. Thanks. Hi, Carolyn.'

Shawna left and Carolyn gestured Jane towards a chair. She had a cheerful face and, in a local accent, explained that she was at Castlehill on work experience. 'Right. Gels are on your card, but I'll run you through everything that's on offer. There's Gel, Powder Dip, Acrylics, Regular Polish, and Shellac.'

'Hen talked about glitter tips.'

'We wouldn't do tips and a gel together. The gel is a polish that's cured under a UV lamp. Your tips would be glued on, so that's not a mix-and-match option. I could do you tips with a powder dip, if tips are what you're after. Or gel in any one of these colours on the chart.'

'Oh. Okay.'

'You'll need to choose what you're going for. Who's Hen?'

'My stepmother. Mrs Sullivan – the one who owns the hotel? – she's her granny. Hen married my dad. She brought me here for the Sullivan Girls' Get-together.'

Abandoning the colour chart, Carolyn bent forward and leaned on her folded arms. 'Shawna was telling me all about that. It's a great idea, isn't it? Mind you, there's been a huge fuss about getting you booked in for treatments. We've other guests, and locals in. Plus there's a big group of ladies from some club up in Dublin here this weekend as well.'

'I know. I saw them.'

'Gas, aren't they? Ladies who lunch leppin' around like two-year-olds. Fair play to them, though. I hope I have their energy when I'm their age.'

'Does this gel stuff get chipped easily? Like, does it come off?'

'No, the way it hardens and adheres, it can last a few weeks. Actually, it's the most robust option we offer. To get it off, you have to soak the nails in acetone.'

'Isn't that bad for them?'

'We have remedial preparations.'

Jane sat on her hands. 'The thing is, I might be messing around with a car engine tomorrow.'

'Really?'

'Máire, the hotel manager, my stepmum's sister? She's got a husband called Raymond, and he's got this vintage Saab.'

'Is that a car?'

'Yeah. A totally cool one. It's in a garage around the back of the hotel. Anyway, I was there just now, talking to him about it. Sometimes he takes the engine apart, and he says, if I come back tomorrow, I can help him. It's got a turbocharger. I don't know how they work, and I'd like to.'

'Jesus, girl, if I were you, I'd think twice about that. I mean, gel's really strong but I wouldn't recommend it to a mechanic.'

'And tips could fall off, couldn't they?'

'Bound to. They'd probably damage the engine.'

'But I'm not going to miss the chance of getting a proper look at a turbocharger. And I'll have to get something done here. You said it's a big deal that I've even got this appointment. I wouldn't want them to think I'm ungrateful.'

Carolyn screwed up her face, then looked inspired. 'I could do you the trim, shape and buff option. That doesn't use polish. It's not what's on your preference card, but that shouldn't be a problem.'

'Would you get into trouble if you didn't do what's on the card?'

'I might if you were an ordinary client, but you're royalty, aren't you?'

Surprised, Jane said she wasn't.

'I don't mean actual royalty. I mean, you're a Sullivan. Well, you are and you aren't, but you know what I mean. It's a big once-a-year thing when the family arrives. Shawna said so. The staff's supposed to pull out all the stops and make sure you're happy.'

'Okay. Maybe the buff thing is the answer. It wouldn't be spoiled if I got oil and stuff on my hands from the engine?'

'Well, I've products I could recommend but, to tell you the truth, you ought to be grand with a pair of gloves and some Vaseline. There's boxes of gloves here. I could give you a pair.'

Carolyn removed the colour chart and substituted a nail drill and an electric buffer. Jane was looking at the displays on screens around the booth. 'How do people even pick things up if they've got those pointy ones? And doesn't having jewels stuck to your nails weigh your fingers down?'

'You're not supposed to be picking things up. It's Queen for a Day stuff. People get them for weddings.'

'Hen didn't. She did have a Swarovski crystal tiara, though.'

'That's what I mean. Fantasy fashion.' Carolyn, who had assembled what she needed, began to work on Jane's nails. 'What did you wear at the wedding?'

'I was the bridesmaid. It was a shepherdess dress. You know, like the ornaments people have on their living-room mantelpiece? Well, my gran has them, other people mightn't.'

'I like the top you're wearing now. That's a lovely chain too.'

With her free hand, Jane lifted the chain to show the little heart that hung from it. 'My dad gave it to me. It belonged to my mum who died.'

'Isn't that gorgeous? How did she die, if you don't mind me asking?'

'I don't mind. She had a heart attack when I was a baby.'

'That's so sad.'

'I suppose so. I don't remember her. People don't talk about her much.'

As Carolyn concentrated on the cuticle she was trimming, Jane tried to remember what was scheduled for the next day. There was the champagne brunch, more spa appointments, and Nora had said that, in the afternoon, there'd be music in the bar. She knew she could give the music a miss because, when Nora had mentioned it, Barbara had murmured, 'Poor Jane! I bet she isn't into dyedly-eyedly stuff. Concertinas and fiddles. Are you a trad fan, Jane?'

Hen had said, 'Don't tease her. You can make up your own mind, Jane. Maybe you'd like a swim in the pool instead?' Jane hadn't answered one way or the other, and the rest of them had gone on chatting. So that meant, if she skipped the music, she could go round to the garage without anyone wanting to know where she was.

Looking at Carolyn's bent head, Jane realised that today she'd talked more about herself than she'd ever done before. At home, everyone always needed her to be happy – whether it was Dad expecting her to sparkle and be a princess, Gan-Gan eager to make her accept Henrietta's arrival, or Hen desperate to be her best friend. But Carolyn was just a girl being friendly, while Raymond had seemed glad to find somebody interested in his car. It's restful here, she thought. Like it says on the hotel website, it's a retreat from the ordinary stresses of life. Admittedly, Hen's family seem to have plenty of tensions to deal with but, when I'm doing stuff on my own, this isn't a bad place to be.

Carolyn had switched her attention to Jane's left hand. 'So, what other treatments are you having this weekend?'

'Well, Hen and her mum and sisters have things booked for tomorrow morning. And we're all gathering in the rasul place before our last dinner.'

'The rasul chamber is just amazing. I would SO love a session there.'

'What actually happens?'

'Okay, so Rasul's a traditional Arabic body treatment that involves steam and mud. And the muds are all different colours, and they've got mineral properties, and you know the way the chamber has tiled seating? All done in silver and turquoise mosaic?'

'Yeah.'

'Well, that's because it fills up with herb-infused steam. You sit there and talk and relax. It's, like, a detox? But first you've applied the muds, and it's self-application.'

'What – everyone chooses their own?'

'Like at a salad bar in a burger place. You put the mud on yourself, or you can do it for each other. The steam opens your pores, lets in the healing properties, and there's ambient sound and music. Did you get to see the lighting?'

'No, we just looked round the door.'

'It's so cool. So, the roof of the chamber is a dome, and it's got little pinprick lights in it, like stars. And when you've had the steam bit, there's this tropical rain thing happens, like it's from a night sky. The mud gets washed away by the warm water, and you're left with skin that's silky-smooth and polished.'

'Like a conditioned car seat.'

'What?'

'Sorry. Probably not like that. I was polishing leather in the garage.'

Carolyn looked nonplussed. 'Okay. Anyway, that's the rasul chamber.'

'It sounds wild. You haven't tried it yourself?'

'God, no. It costs a fortune. I saw a video when I was at college.' Reaching the last of Jane's nails, Carolyn smiled at her. 'Okay, another five minutes or so and you're done. Don't let me forget to give you the gloves.'

'That's really kind of you.'

'No problem. You're welcome. Nobody here's going to miss them. And, look, if your hands end up grubby even though you've used protection, my mum always swears by lemon juice on a pot-scrub.'

149

Chapter 13

Máire clicked on a group of addresses to which she was sending an email. Third from the top was Castlehill's head housekeeper, a woman she'd always struggled to like. I know why she annoys me, she thought. It's because she's super-good at suggesting I need her more than she needs me. Nothing overt, nothing any reasonable person could possibly take offence at. Just quiet smugness that gets under my skin. And, dammit, I shouldn't let that happen. She only arrived at Castlehill the year before Granny retired. Plenty of people who now work for me started here twenty years ago, and none of them insinuates that I only got this position because Granny lost her marbles when Granddad died.

She was staring at her screen, brooding, when Sheila looked into the office. 'I don't want to interrupt.'

'No, you're okay, what can I do for you?'

'Oh, darling, I'm not here to add to your troubles.'

The concern with which this was said irritated Máire, who scowled. 'I'm not troubled. Why would you think so?'

Laughing, Sheila sat down by the desk. 'I don't know who's getting under your skin, but don't take it out on me.'

For a moment Máire looked belligerent. Then she laughed. 'I'm literally sitting here cursing myself because I've let one of my team get under my skin. How could you know that?'

'Because I know you.'

'You've always been a mind-reader. Once, Baba and I nearly convinced Henrietta that you were a witch.'

'No! The poor little thing!'

'She didn't sleep for a week.' Decisively, Máire closed her laptop and leaned back in her chair. 'Anyway, that's enough of that. How are you and the girls getting on?'

'Hen and Barbara had a massage this morning. Jane's got something this afternoon, and I'm supposed to be foil-wrapped before dinner. Which makes me feel I'm going to be served up like a side of salmon.'

'Nonsense. You'll enjoy it.'

'I expect I will.' Sheila shot her another concerned glance. 'You've been run ragged trying to arrange this weekend, haven't you?'

'No, it's fine.'

'It isn't, though. I can see you're overworked.'

'Oh, Lord, not you too! You're sounding exactly like Raymond.'

The warning note in her voice made Sheila back off. 'My magical powers are limited. Who's been annoying you?'

Máire hesitated, shrugged and said, 'She's on my management

team. Housekeeping tsar. Actually, I bet that's exactly how she sees herself.'

'Striding along the corridors in highly polished boots?'

'With a riding-crop and a waxed moustache.' Máire gave a snort of laughter. 'Her name's Dymphna McDonnell. Honestly, Mum, she'd drive you to drink. I just have to think of her smarmy voice, and that unconvincing obsequiousness, and I want to do something utterly childish, like stick out my tongue.'

'That would make for an interesting management meeting.'

'And I can't believe I'm wasting time I can't spare, thinking about her.'

'Why not give yourself a break and come and have coffee with me?'

'Because I don't have time to spare! Besides, this is just an ongoing niggle. I shouldn't let it bother me.'

'It sounds like a personality clash. You won't solve that by ignoring it. Maybe, if it bothers you, you should confront it.'

'It *doesn't* bother me.' There was a long pause before Máire shrugged and reopened her laptop. 'Okay. Obviously, that's a lie. Let's just move on to whatever you came in here for.'

'Nothing, really. I thought you might like a coffee break, but I'll see you at dinner, okay?'

'Sure. Enjoy your foil wrap.'

As Sheila got up, Máire saw a Post-it note on her desk. 'Hang on, Mum, if you see Hen, can you tell her Granny asked if Jane would come up to her suite for a chat sometime? Or, no, don't bother, I'll text Hen myself. That way, I can cross her off my list.'

'Okay. See you later.'

When Sheila left, Máire sat staring at her screen. That was unfortunate phrasing, she thought, and Mum thought so too, though she didn't say so. This weekend is supposed to be about quality family time, and I'm behaving as if it amounts to yet another to-do list. Glancing at the clock, she decided she'd better talk to Henrietta, rather than just shoot off a text. At least it's a gesture, she thought, as she sat with the phone to her ear. I ought to make time to get to know Jane as well. She seems like a nice kid, and I've hardly said two words to her. It's so weird to think that Hen's become a mum before me and Barbara. She was always the baby, tagging along and showing zero signs of ambition, but when you think about it, choosing to take on a child is huge.

It took several rings for Henrietta to answer her phone. 'Hi. Sorry, I'm in the bar, having hot chocolate with Jane.'

'No problem. It's just that Granny says she'd love Jane to come up for a chat in the suite sometime. If she'd like to, that is.'

'That's so nice. I'll pass on the message.'

'Thanks. How are the spa treatments going?'

'Fab. Jane's had her manicure, and Barbara and I had a wonderful massage.'

'I'm sorry I couldn't fit you and Jane in for a joint manicure.'

'No, you're grand. Arranging things must be massively complicated. I'm just impressed by how you're coping with organising us lot, on top of your work.'

To Máire's surprise, this got under her guard and brought tears to her eyes. There's no pleasing me, she thought crossly. I make enemies of people I think aren't being supportive and, if people are kind, I turn into a water spout. Steadying her voice, she said, 'Well, thanks, but, honestly, it's not a problem. The get-together's important. Not just to Granny. To all of us.'

'I didn't know you thought that.'

I didn't either, thought Máire. But I suppose it is what I think. Granny's been amazing at holding this family together. It feels like an awful lot's gone unsaid for an awfully long time. But she's kept the lines of communication open. We're literally here for each other, and that's what matters, even if we only demonstrate it once a year.

In her bedroom, Sheila opened the minibar in the wardrobe, and poured herself a gin and tonic. Well, that bright idea didn't work, she told her reflection in the mirror. Máire's got far too much on her plate already. I can't expect her to help me to tell Henrietta about my divorce. And, clearly, Barbara's preoccupied with something in her own life. So, what now? Closing the wardrobe, she frowned at the glass in her hand, thinking she could have been wrong to choose this weekend to share her news. Was it really fair to chuck a bombshell into the middle of Nora's get-together? Might it be better to keep her mouth shut, take part in what had obviously been an effort for Máire to organise, and compose a round-robin email when she got home? But wouldn't that be a cowardly solution? If hearing about the divorce was going to upset Henrietta, she ought to be told in person. There'd be things to say that couldn't be put in an email and, anyway, this was something they needed to process as a family.

Though God knows what I mean by that, thought Sheila, slumping into the chair by the window. We've never processed things, just kept going. All I did when the girls were young was put one foot in front of the other. It's the only available option when you've no control over your life, and no idea what's going to happen next.

In the four years before Barbara was born, Finbar had hardly been home. Throughout them, Sheila had done her best to hide her misery and humiliation from Máire, but she'd never been sure she'd succeeded. And when Barbara arrived, she'd worried about the effect on both children of her own accumulated stress. According to the visiting nurse, Máire's reaction to Barbara had been textbook stuff. 'You mustn't worry. Sibling rivalry happens. Máire's had her mum to herself long enough to see Barbara as an intruder.'

'She seems really resentful, though.'

'It's just something to be navigated. You'll be fine. And it's helpful to show a united front in a case of sibling rivalry, so do let their dad take some of the slack. You don't want Máire playing one parent off against the other.'

The conversation had ended there. The overworked nurse, who'd been based in Athlone, not Killmoy, hadn't grasped the extent of Finbar's absence and, wary of questions, Sheila had kept it to herself. When a few months had passed and Máire had begun to behave well for Nora, she'd still been difficult at home, and on the few occasions when Finbar was around she'd resisted Sheila's efforts to play happy families, making it clear she preferred her grandparents' company to her dad's. For the sake of peace and quiet, Sheila hadn't argued. Their rented rooms were overcrowded at the best of times, and Finbar's flamboyant presence had made them feel smaller. Looking back, those years seemed like a jumble of panic, worry and exhaustion. Sipping her gin, Sheila told herself grimly that it was amazing she hadn't taken to drink. After Barbara's arrival, Finbar had appeared, flat-broke with a suitcase full of dirty laundry. In her mind's eye, Sheila could see him waggling his fingers at Barbara, who was lying in her cot. I felt like a fly trapped in a spider's web, she thought sadly. I knew by then – how could I not? – that nothing was right about the marriage, but I was bound up in sticky threads that held me in place until he chose to come back to me. I kept telling myself things might change but, deep down, I knew they wouldn't and, all the while, I was trying to decide what was right for the girls. Because, whatever that stupid nurse thought, there was nothing planned about any of my pregnancies and, God knows, the poor little things hadn't asked to be born. I was the one who'd made the dumb decision to marry Finbar and, as I saw it then, everything that followed was my fault.

Tossing back the last of her gin and tonic, she reminded herself that the nightmare was over. Cheers to me, she thought, because I didn't take to drink or have a breakdown. I hung on and did all I could to keep my girls safe and give them security. I love them to bits, and I've always loved them equally. But I think that, of the three, I know Máire best. Barbara's like me in so many ways that I know her from the inside, but I learned to know Máire in those four years we had alone together, when I was still fending off everyone's offers of help. I learned who she was by watching each expression that crossed her face, fearful that she might fall, or be unhappy, or starve, or die. Which sounds very caring and laudable, but wasn't. The truth is that, mostly, I was waiting for a look that would tell me she thought I was a useless mother. It was something I'd already concluded about myself so, back then, it seemed logical that, sooner or later, my beloved, resentful little girl would think so too.

In the bar, Jane was looking at a poster. 'Does this group play here every week?'

Henrietta swivelled round to read the names. 'I don't know about these particular players, but weekend sessions in the bar are a Castlehill tradition. It's a big local thing to come here for lunch and stay for the music afterwards and, generally, it's local groups that play.'

'Barbara said it's dyedly-eyedly.'

'Well, this group is definitely trad. A concertina, two fiddles and a bodhrán. You can't get more traditional than that.'

Jane pushed marshmallows into her hot chocolate with a spoon. 'Was that the kind of music your dad played?'

'No, he's a bass guitarist. He tours with bands. Big stadium stuff, all over the world. That was why he couldn't be there when your dad and I got married.'

'And he sent you those flowers.'

'Forget-me-nots and rosemary. For remembrance.'

'Well, he's your dad. You weren't going to forget him.'

'Of course not. He wanted me to know he'd remembered me.'

Jane stirred the pink and white marshmallows in her tall glass. 'Did you miss him when he was away? When you were growing up, I mean.' This wasn't a comfortable conversation for Henrietta but since, for once, Jane seemed ready to chat, she didn't want to shut it down. 'I think we just got used to it. We never knew exactly when he'd be back.'

'But don't tours have schedules?'

'Well, yes, but he did studio sessions too. And tours can get extended.'

'I thought big stadiums scheduled things years in advance. Like *Disney on Ice* at Wembley. Gan-Gan got tickets for it months ahead. Six or seven. By the time we went, I'd nearly forgotten she'd booked for it.'

'I suppose if a tour's a huge success, somebody juggles the logistics. And there were other things as well. I remember he had to go somewhere for a TV documentary and, once, when we were expecting him home for Christmas, he had to play at a birthday party for Elton John.'

'Cool.'

'Or for one of the guys in Elton's band. I can't remember what Mum said. Anyway, it was a disappointment. But it was always exciting when he did come home.'

'Would we have another hot chocolate?'

Henrietta grinned, and signalled to the barman. 'Though, if this one has any more sugar, she'll probably take off and orbit the moon.'

Jane grinned back. 'I can handle any quantity of marshmallows.'

'Okay. Just don't blame me if you can't eat your dinner.'

'Will there be apple cake again?'

'Did you like it?'

'It was good.'

'I doubt if Granny will have ordered the same thing two nights running. There'll definitely be a pudding, though. She's very big on those.'

'She's nice, isn't she?'

Henrietta smiled. 'We think so. Máire says she's invited you up to the suite for a chat sometime. No pressure, but if you fancy it.'

'I could go up after this.'

'Or tomorrow. There's no rush.'

'But there's all sorts of stuff happening tomorrow. The champagne brunch, and the music, and the rasul thing later on.'

Henrietta beamed. 'You're really getting into the swing of the weekend, aren't you? I'm glad.'

Lowering her eyelids, Jane said she wasn't sure what she'd do tomorrow. 'I might go for a swim, like you said. Maybe give some of the other stuff a miss.'

'It's up to yourself. It'd be good to see Granny today, though, in case the other things take over tomorrow.'

'That's no problem. I can give her a call.'

'Cool.'

The barman arrived with the order, and leaned over to drop an extra spoonful of marshmallows into Jane's glass. She gave him a grateful smile and turned back to Henrietta. 'Do you miss Dad when he's away?'

This was taking the conversation to a new level, and Henrietta blinked in surprise. 'Yes. I do. A lot. You miss him too, don't you, when he's off on a trip?'

Jane nodded. 'I like it better when he's home. I always know when he'll be coming back, though. Even when I was little, he used to leave me flight details. Where he was staying. How to get in touch, if I wanted to. If I needed him, I wouldn't even have to tell Gan-Gan. I've always had my own phone and been able to call him wherever he is.'

Unsure of how to respond to this, Henrietta said nothing. Jane licked her spoon again, and seemed to be pondering. When she spoke, it was more to herself than to Henrietta. 'It can't have been nice for you, not knowing when you'd see your dad.'

'Being a musician is different from being a businessman. My dad always used to say it was harder for him than for us. We did have wonderful times with him, though. That's what he meant when he sent me those flowers.'

'I guess that was fine, if you were happy. I'm just saying that, if it was me, I don't think I could get used to it.'

Henrietta was rummaging in her bag to find her phone to call Nora. 'I wouldn't worry, pet. It's never going to happen in your case.'

'I'm not worried. I just think it's kind of sad that it happened to you.'

Heartened though she was by Jane's willingness to chat, this view of her own childhood came as a shock to Henrietta. Finding her phone, she hit Nora's number, her mind still playing on what Jane had said. Of course I was happy at her age, she thought, and it wasn't Dad's fault that he couldn't be with us. All the same, it must have been hard for Mum. I can't imagine how I'd feel if life with Stuart was like that. I guess I'd be as upbeat as I could, for Jane's sake. I suppose that's what Mum did with us, though it didn't feel like that at the time. It's never struck me till now that she might have been putting on a brave face.

Chapter 14

It seemed to Barbara that, wherever she found to sit in the hotel's lounge or foyer, other guests, seeing she was alone, would try to catch her eye. With the exception of a beery man, who attempted to pick her up, most people were interesting and friendly and, had she been more relaxed, she'd have been happy to sit and chat. But explaining who she was and why she was there felt fraught with complications, and avoiding people's eyes was wearing her down. Eventually, certain that if she went into the grounds she'd encounter Luke, she decided to go upstairs to the flat. With luck, she thought, I might have the place to myself. Máire said Raymond had plans to work in the garage this afternoon. I can flop on the sofa for a bit, watching mindless telly. And when Ray and Máire come up, it'll likely be time to get ready for dinner.

But when she went into the flat, Raymond was there, watching a match on TV with his feet up. He swung his legs off the sofa as she came in. 'Hi. How're you doing?'

'Fine. I just thought I'd come and crash before dinner. I'll be in my room.'

'No, don't feel you have to retreat. This is a re-run. I'm just killing time watching it. Do you want a coffee?'

'Well – let me make some for the two of us.'

'Okay. You know where things are. There are KitKats in the tin. I got them earlier, in Killmoy.'

'Máire said you needed to pick up something there for the Saab. I didn't know you still had it.'

'It doesn't get too many outings now, more's the pity. Henrietta's Jane found me messing about with it in the garage. She gave me a hand polishing the leather.'

'Wasn't she supposed to be having a manicure in the spa?'

'That's what she said. I had to remind her about the appointment. Once she began on the car, she really got stuck into the job.'

Barbara went through to the kitchen to switch on the kettle. When she'd made the coffee, she carried it back to the living room on a tray. Setting it down, she said, 'Don't stop watching your match for me.'

'I told you, I've seen it already. It's not that interesting anyway.' He was reaching for the remote when Barbara's phone rang.

'Sorry, I'd better take this. It's Hen.'

'No problem.' Hitting mute on the remote, he politely kept his eyes on the TV screen while she took the call.

'Hi, Hen. What's the story?'

'Nothing. I've just been hanging out with Jane. She's really opening up this weekend. Up to now, if the truth be told, she's been scarily self-contained. Sweet, but not forthcoming. You know? But we've just had an actual chat.'

'Good for you. Raymond says she was chatting to him earlier, round in the garage.'

'With Raymond? She didn't say.'

'Did you ask her?'

'No. I mean I had no idea. She just said she was going for a walk in the grounds. Then she had her spa session – on her own, as it turned out, because they couldn't book us one together, but it sounds like she got on fine with the girl who did her manicure. And, after that, she and I had a chat over hot chocolate in the bar.'

'Hasn't it occurred to you that those three facts might be connected?'

'How do you mean?'

'Two interactions on her own, with people she seems to have liked spending time with, followed by a relaxed chat with you. When I was her age, I hated the thought of adults checking up on me obsessively. I would've been far more likely to chat if I felt I'd been given a bit of space to myself.'

There was a pause in which Henrietta appeared to absorb this. 'Okay. That makes sense. I don't check up on her obsessively, though.'

'Oh, come on, Hen. You go around like a human Geiger-counter, constantly monitoring people's reactions and feelings. Jane seems like a bright kid. I bet she can hear you buzzing in the background all the time.'

'Thanks for that.'

'Don't get huffy. I'm pleased for you, really I am. I'm also kind of touched that you chose to call and tell me.'

'Well, you needn't get cocky, because, actually, that wasn't why I called. I wanted to mark your cards about this rasul-chamber session.'

'What about it?'

'You're planning to give it a miss, aren't you?'

'Why would you think so?'

'Because of what you said when we talked on the phone before Christmas. You didn't fancy it, and you hoped it was optional. Remember?'

'You do know this is top Geiger-counter behaviour?'

'Are you going to be there?'

'I haven't decided one way or the other. Granny said it was up to ourselves.'

'Don't be horrible, Barbara. It won't hurt you to join in. Granny wants us to experience the full luxury package.'

As the full luxury package sounded like optimum touchy-feely, Barbara hedged, trying to avoid commitment. 'You're seriously saying Granny's going to turn up and get covered in mud?'

'Well, maybe she'll watch from the sidelines. I don't know. But she says she'll come.'

'I'll think about it. Good for you on the Jane thing, though. Congratulations.'

When she put down the phone, Raymond flashed his eyebrows at her. 'Look at you, going all child psychologist in your old age.'

'Was I wrong, though?'

Dunking his KitKat in his coffee, Raymond shrugged. 'Don't ask me. I'm not a parent.'

'That's dodging the question.'

'It's the truth.'

'Yes, but you must have had masses of training to coach juniors.'

'Fair point. I think you're probably right about Jane. Most kids need emotional space, and it sounds like the poor child was overprotected from way before Hen arrived.'

When Jane left the bar, she reminded herself that any visit to Gan-Gan required a dress. So should she nip upstairs and put one on? But her jeans were clean and she was wearing one of her favourite tops. So, since dinner was only a few hours away and she'd have to change for that, she decided that Nora, who seemed less fussy than Gan-Gan, wouldn't be bothered if she turned up as she was. It felt weird to be setting out for another chat with a stranger. On the other hand, she thought, meeting Henrietta's people is interesting. If I really am an onlooker, like Nora said last night, there's plenty of unexpected stuff here for me to look at.

In the lift lobby, she found a swarm of Second Chance Club ladies, going back to their rooms after their spa treatments. Several, who recognised her, explained to the others that they'd met at the lifts before, when they'd arrived.

'Are you having a lovely time, dear?'

'Yes, thank you.'

'We're all sleek and gorgeous. Aren't we, girls? We've had our facials.'

'And deep hand massages, and we've all got fabulous over-the-top nails.'

'Speak for yourself! Some of us went for understated French manicures.'

'What's the point of that, when you can push the boat out and get bling?'

It was all a bit over-the-top for Jane, who put her hands into her pockets in case they'd ask to see her own manicure. Henrietta had seemed surprised by what she'd chosen but, unusually, she hadn't wanted to know if Jane was sure she was happy with it. She hadn't asked how she'd passed the time before her spa appointment either, which had almost led Jane to tell her how she'd been helping Raymond. But her time in the garage, which, so far, had been the best part of her weekend, definitely wasn't on the laminated Sullivan Girls' Get-together agenda. So, she'd stuck to her rule about not offering unasked-for information.

Sticking to it now, she smiled and gave monosyllabic answers to the cheerfully inquisitive group of ladies.

'You're here with your mum, aren't you?'

'My stepmum.'

'Isn't that lovely? I thought she looked awfully young to have had a great girl like yourself.'

One of the women laughed loudly. 'Honestly, Emer! Talk about pass-remarkable!'

'Ah, she knows what I mean. Don't you, love? I hope, now, you're not offended?'

'No.'

'And do you have a room to yourself, or are you in a family one? I saw those on the website. They're lovely, aren't they?'

'Yes.'

The lift arrived, and the ladies swept her into it, announcing there was plenty of room if they all squished up. 'You're only a slip of a thing. Come on in! What floor is your room on?'

Jane said, 'Second,' and prayed they'd be getting off before her. If they discovered she was on her way up to Nora's suite, their questions were likely to turn into full-on interrogation. Fortunately, they all surged off when the lift reached the first floor, waving goodbye and still chattering loudly. Jane watched the numbers on the display change as the lift climbed higher, and found herself thinking that sharing a room with Henrietta had turned out to be fine.

Maybe because the practical crisis left her no time for fussing, Henrietta had sort of taken charge and got on with things quietly. Actually, thought Jane, she's fussed a lot less since we've got here. I suppose that's not surprising. After all, this is her place. At home, she's more like a visitor. Which is not so surprising either. Our house has always been mine and Dad's and, before that, Dad's and my mum's, and it probably hasn't changed much since I was born. According to Gan-Gan, Henrietta landed on her feet when Dad married her, because all the furniture and stuff was there when she arrived. But was that really so great? Might she not have preferred to pick out things like that for herself? Frowning at the lift's digital display, Jane remembered what Suzy had said about brides designing their own weddings. Perhaps it hadn't been much fun being made to carry pink roses if the kind of flowers you preferred were forget-me-nots and rosemary. Or did Henrietta just like those flowers because they'd been chosen by her father? She wasn't someone who seemed to have many preferences of her own. Which, when you thought about it, was both interesting and strange.

Though it was late afternoon, Nora's curtains were still open, and the lights flanking the hotel's drive and entry porch below made patterns on the ceilings of her suite. In the living room, the lamps on the sofa's end tables were lit. When Jane knocked on the door and came in, Nora turned and smiled. 'There you are, come here and we'll sit on the sofa. There's a Coke in the fridge for you, and I'll have a cup of tea.'

'I've just had hot chocolate with Henrietta.'

'And will that stop you having something with me now?'

Jane grinned. 'Not if you're offering.'

'I've everything there on the side for my tea. Boil the kettle, love, will you?'

The dining-table they'd eaten at the previous evening was gone, leaving the room feeling much more informal. Jane organised the drinks while Nora produced a packet of fig rolls. 'Will we have a biscuit?'

'Okay.'

'Raymond picked them up for me this morning, in Killmoy.'

Jane joined her on the sofa. Spreading her handkerchief on her knee as a napkin, Nora asked how the day had gone.

'Good. You have a nice hotel.'

'D'you think so?'

'Hen said it was built in the nineteenth century. This middle part, I mean, and that you added the other bits?'

'Not the nineteenth century, love. The house was built around 1911 on the foundations of another. The Sullivans bought it in 1920 when the English owners left.'

'Actually, Hen said she wasn't certain, but you'd be sure to know.'

'The wings on either side were added before I got here. We extended at the back in my time, though. D'you know what it is – I have something here that I thought might interest you.' Reaching into a drawer in one of the tables, Nora produced a slim, hard-backed book. 'We did this potted history in 1970, to commemorate the hotel's fiftieth anniversary. The Sullivan family had all the photos and Martin, my husband, got a local newspaper man to write the text.' While Jane took the book on her lap and turned its pages, Nora bit into a fig roll and blew on her tea. 'Cassidy's Print Place below in the town produced it and, of course, the family insisted on far too many copies. I've had boxes of them stored away for years.'

The title page showed a sepia photo of the original house with ivy climbing up the porch and a horse-drawn carriage at the foot of the steps. Jane bent to look, and Nora set down her teacup. 'That would have been taken before the English owners left. It was my husband's family that turned it into a hotel.' Flicking the pages, Jane saw the house change as if in a jerky silent movie. Ladies in Bond Street dresses dancing with men in tail-coats. Girls wearing big hats posing with shooting parties and dogs. A group of young men, who seemed no older than schoolboys, looking self-conscious in military uniform. Then different curtains at the windows, and the hotel sign appearing above the door. Men with fishing rods and ladies with tennis rackets, like those in the photos she'd seen downstairs in the bar. Builders at work on the new wings. Bunting, and a banner saying 'Grand Ballroom Opening'. The ivy growing and covering the whole façade until, between one photo and another, it disappeared. Nora leaned to look over her shoulder. 'I had the ivy taken off when I came here. Though, mind you, there were plenty of changes before then. I mean look at that.' She pointed to a shot of a car drawn up at the foot of the steps, where hotel staff were unloading heavy-looking leather suitcases. 'It's hard to believe how quickly people took to motoring holidays when, up to then, hardly a soul had a car.'

'That one's so cool.'

'It's an Austin saloon. I half remember them on the roads when I was your age. It was mostly horses and carts where I grew up, though.'

'Like in the first photo?'

Pleased by Jane's interest, Nora shook her head. 'Not at all, love. I'm talking farm horses. Things change fast, though. This place was built with stables and a coach house round the back, but there's photos of one of the English crowd that lived here sitting up proud as Punch in a motor-car. He was an only son, poor boy, and he died in the First World War.'

171

'That's sad.'

'Ah, a lot of them did, love, in that generation. Lads from the farms and the town, as well as the house. What I'm saying is, he'd have been driving round in a car when his parents would still have been taking the air in a carriage.'

The open touring car, which took pride of place in several photos, had huge headlamps and a spare wheel strapped to its running board. Jane bent closer. 'Wow. Look at his goggles, and the huge leather gloves.' Taking a mouthful of Coke and a bite of biscuit, she looked at Nora. 'Do you know how to drive a horse and cart?'

'Me? Many's the one I drove in the past, but I haven't seen a horse's tail from the seat of a cart for a long time. My father still worked with a horse into the 1970s, and I gave a hand on the farm right up to my marriage.'

'Then you stopped?'

'I had more than enough to do here, love. And, mark you, my dad was set in his ways. You wouldn't have found too many farmers working the land with a horse by that time.'

'I never knew things in history overlapped like that.'

'Have that book, if you want to read it.'

'Can I? I'll give it back before we go home on Monday.'

'Not a bit of it, love. You can have it to keep, if you'd like it. I told you, I've dozens that never came out of their boxes.'

'How come so many were printed?'

'Vanity. Sheer waste of money. I can tell you the Sullivan family was damn lucky the day I decided to marry in.' Nora shot a look at her. 'There now! I've shocked you.'

'I'm not shocked.'

Nora looked at her squarely. 'You're not, are you? Well, fair play to you, child, you've a head on your shoulders.'

'I'm interested in people.'

'I can see that.'

'Could I ask you a question?'

'Work away, girl.'

'Does marrying in mean moving into a house that's already furnished?'

'Oh, believe me, that's not the half of it. It means stepping into dead women's shoes. Generations of them that belonged to the house before you. It's going from your own place, where you matter, into a place where you're lucky if you're not looked on as an intruder. It means having to justify the choice your husband made when he married you.'

'But if he wanted to marry you, why would you have to justify it?'

'You might feel you had to.' Apparently confused by this, Jane fell silent. After a moment, Nora spoke abruptly. 'I was very fond of my mother. I never wanted to give her a moment's worry.'

'I don't really know about mothers.'

'Well, I'll tell you what I learned when mine was dead, and I'd had my own daughter. You can worry your mother far more by trying to hide your troubles from her than ever you might by allowing her to help you deal with them.' Taking another biscuit, Nora deliberately broke it in two. 'And, by the same token, you can do more harm than good by holding back when people you love make it clear they don't want your advice.'

Jane nodded thoughtfully. 'But people fuss, don't they? And if you say too much you give them more to fuss about.'

Nora's eyes were kind. 'Is that how it is for you at home?'

'Sort of. I think Dad worries about me.'

'I'd say Hen's a bit of a fusser too, isn't she?'

'Sometimes.' Jane shrugged. 'Most of the time, actually. I do like her, though. And she's awfully good for Dad.'

Chapter 15

As happened each year on the second night of the Sullivan Girls' Get-together, Nora encouraged everyone to go for a bit of glitz. A table was booked in the hotel's restaurant so, when Henrietta finished her phone conversation with Barbara, she made up her mind to get ready for dinner while Jane was in Nora's suite. Jane's been awfully good about having to share a bedroom with me, she thought, so if I get organised in advance I'll be out of her way later, when she'll be wanting to shower and dress.

Going up to the room, she laid her chosen dress on the bed, spent a leisurely half-hour in the bathroom, and sat at the dressing-table to do her hair. The dress was another favourite of Stuart's, apple-green with a high neck and mid-length circular skirt. He had bought Henrietta a pair of gold earrings that complemented its classic cut, and she'd packed a pair of gold high heels, to complete the 1950s film-star effect. Whistling through her teeth, she swept her hair into an updo, which, for once, stayed in place without having to be repinned. With her makeup completed, she clipped on the earrings and, deciding she looked rather good, took a selfie and pinged it to Stuart. A minute or two later, he replied from his Turin hotel room.

Gorgeous, but has Castlehill moved to a different time zone?

😄 It's an Early Bird dinner. Suitable timing for my granny and your daughter

Jane having fun?

Seems to be. Everyone thinks she's a pet

Got to finish these emails. Enjoy your dinner

Love you darling

You too x

Propping her elbows on the dressing-table, Henrietta remembered the first time they'd met. She'd been working at a Dublin jeweller's and he'd come in, just before closing time, to buy a replacement battery for his watch. He was very handsome, confident and charming. As she'd found and fitted the battery for him, he'd told her he was on his way to pre-theatre drinks. 'Not my kind of show at all. But I drew the short straw. I'm hosting a client.'

'What is your kind of show, then?'

'Truth is, I'm not really into theatre.'

'Me neither.'

'Give me a good, noisy concert and beer in a bar afterwards.'

That hadn't sounded great to Henrietta, but he was a customer so she'd smiled and said, 'Me too.'

With the battery installed, he'd glanced at the watch, said, 'Christ, I'd better be going,' then stopped at the door and looked back. 'You hate beer and noisy concerts, don't you?'

'Well …'

'So, does a quiet table for two in a restaurant sound better?'

She'd never imagined she'd let herself be picked up like that by a stranger, especially one so much older than herself. But three days later, there she'd been, getting ready to be taken out to dinner. Her flatmate, from whom she'd borrowed a silk jacket, sat on the bed and offered a stream of advice. 'I'll keep my phone on and, if there's a problem, let it ring twice and cut off. I won't even take your call. I'll get straight on to the guards.'

'What could possibly happen to me in the Dún Laoghaire Yacht Club restaurant?'

'He could put something dodgy in your drink.'

'Well, if he did, and I saw it, I'd call the guards myself, wouldn't I? And if I didn't see it and the nefarious knock-out pill kicked in, I'd be in no state call anyone.'

But she'd known for certain that nothing bad would happen. Weeks later, Stuart had told her he'd fallen in love at first sight. 'Literally from the moment I saw you in the shop. I don't know what came over me. I behaved like some guy in a cheesy movie.'

'No, you didn't.'

'Well, that's how it felt. And when I turned back to ask you out, I was sure you'd duck under the counter to avoid me.'

By the time they'd had that conversation, she'd known Stuart well enough to doubt that. But she'd never doubted that he'd fallen for her hook, line and sinker just as, when she'd sat at the restaurant table, she'd known instantly that she'd found the love of her life. After that, there was no looking back. For as long as she could remember, Henrietta had dreamed of a fairytale wedding, a husband, and a home of her own to look after, so Nora's warning that second wives were always in the ha'penny place hadn't bothered her any more than she'd cared about Barbara's raised eyebrows, or Máire's scathing look when she'd produced her engagement ring. Six months wasn't long to know someone before you got married, and taking on a stepchild hadn't been part of the dream. But I wasn't a fool, thought Henrietta, smoothing the folds of her apple-green chiffon skirt. I knew the difference between a fairytale wedding and a marriage. I may get nervous about stupid stuff, like whether or not to buy an organic turkey, but I've always known that, with things that matter, you have to follow your heart.

Barbara was still on the sofa in front of the muted television when Máire came in and saw what was on the screen. 'Please tell me Raymond hasn't converted you to hurling.'

Barbara chuckled. 'He was watching, I interrupted, and we had coffee and talked. He's just gone out and, actually, I'd forgotten the telly was on.' Finding the remote, she hit the off button. 'What time is it?'

Máire sank on to the sofa beside her. 'We're fine. There's a good three-quarters of an hour to go before dinner.'

'I'm going to need time to wash and dry my hair. The massage I had in the spa was great, but the hairline at the back of my neck got a bit oily.'

Máire frowned. 'That shouldn't happen.'

'Don't be daft. It's probably just me. I should wash my hair anyway. Granny expects us to glam up tonight.'

'What are you wearing?'

'Little black dress. Comes out of a suitcase looking great, and I just throw accessories at it.'

'I could do without having to change.'

'Will I pour us a glass of wine? It might put a spring in your step.'

'I think it'd put me to sleep.'

Barbara stood up. 'Tell you what, I'll make some more coffee. We can take twenty minutes before transforming ourselves into style icons.'

'Okay. Wake me if I drop off before the kettle boils.'

She perked up when handed a mug of fresh coffee. Barbara sat down beside her and said, 'So, listen, tell me. What are you going to be wearing tonight yourself?'

'PJs for preference. D'you think Granny would settle for a pyjama party next year?'

'Everyone up on her double bed in the junior suite?'

'Hen looking like Sandy in *Grease*, and you and me channelling a couple of Pink Ladies.'

'I see you as Rizzo. No, maybe Frenchie. Or Marty. What d'you think?'

Máire laughed. 'The truth is we're both a bit long in the tooth to be high-school kids.'

'Yeah, but let's face it, so were the cast in the film. Seriously, though, what are you planning to wear at dinner?'

'You didn't happen to bring your silver belt with you, did you? The one you wore in the evening at Hen's wedding?'

'It's in my case.'

'And is it what you're going to throw at your little black dress?'

Recognising an approach to a favour when she heard one, Barbara said, 'It doesn't have to be.'

'Truly? Because what I've got in mind to wear will be way too plain for Granny unless I have something to jazz it up. I know it's late in the day to ask ...'

'No, you're okay. You can borrow the belt, if you want to.'

'Baba, you're a star!'

'I rescind my offer.'

'No, stop! I'm sorry, I didn't mean to call you that. I'm just tired. I slipped into old habits.'

'Okay. You do look like chewed string, so I forgive you.'

'Charming. Still, at least now I'll look like chewed string in a snazzy silver belt.'

Barbara threw her a sympathetic glance. 'Hen said this year's dates aren't great for you.'

'I guess, originally, it was about having a family get-together in the downtime after Christmas. Problem is, these days, there is no downtime.'

'When did the tradition start? Do you know?'

'Nope. I did ask Granny once, but she was vague.'

'It was before Mum's time, I do know that.'

Putting down her coffee mug, Máire sighed. 'I wish I didn't have so much going on here this weekend. It's nice that we're all here together, and I feel I'm not joining in.'

Barbara cocked an eye at her. 'Are you seriously going to do this rasul-chamber thing tomorrow? Hen says you are, and that Granny's going to be hurt if I'm not there too.'

'Honest answer? I was going to skip it. Then I had second thoughts, and I've decided to turn up.'

Barbara groaned. 'Well, I suppose I will, if you will. It's not my thing at all but I've been feeling bad since Hen jogged my conscience.'

'I just want Granny to be happy. In a way, I feel I owe her. She was pretty amazing when we were kids. Before Mum decided to move to Athlone, you and I spent huge chunks of our time at Castlehill. And before you were born, I spent most of my days right here in this flat.'

'Can you remember that far back?'

'Kind of. I was four when you were born and I suspect I'd been spoiled rotten. I remember being really pissed off when Mum arrived home with you from the hospital. Big-time aggression from me, and Granny being a rock.'

'I just remember coming here to play when Mum was working. And Granny making us chocolate cake, and Mum waiting down at the gate to take us home.'

'She hardly ever came up, did she? What kind of weird thing was going on between her and Granny? Did you ever ask?'

'No. Well, it never felt safe to, did it? I can't remember a time when I didn't know that Granny couldn't stand Dad.'

'So many cans of worms.'

Barbara put down her coffee mug and turned to face Máire. 'So, here's a thing. Mum and Dad got divorced.'

'What?'

'No. Clarification. She divorced him.'

Máire was wide-eyed. 'Mum did? When?'

'It was finalised this year. She told me on the way here that she's freaked about breaking the news.'

'I can't see why.'

'Well, of course not. It doesn't bother you any more than it does me. But Mum thinks Hen's going to get all upset.'

Máire considered this idea. 'Okay. Yeah, I see that. But surely, by this stage, even Hen has seen through Dad.'

'Well, but look at the evidence. Think about how she reacted to his flowers at her wedding.'

Having thought, Máire nodded. 'Okay. Point taken.'

'It was hellish for Mum. She'd assumed he wouldn't send anything, so she'd ordered a mass of lilies and got the florist to put a card on them saying they were from Dad.'

'Wow! I did not know that. But, hang on, Dad did send flowers. What happened to the lilies?'

'By sheer chance, I intercepted the florist before they got to Hen. Mum found me in a corridor, sticking them in a bin. Meanwhile, Hen was raving over Dad's pathetic attempt to steal the limelight. Forget-me-nots pinned to her bosom, remember? She even stood up during the speeches and told the guests about them. With poor Mum sitting there at the top table pretending we hadn't been minutes from disaster.'

'God, she's well rid of him.'

'I'll drink to that.'

Máire settled herself more comfortably against the cushions. 'Dad was different with Hen, wasn't he?'

'Well, she was his little mini-me, wasn't she? Daddy's golden girl. Anyway, most things were different when we moved to Athlone. Like, when Hen was little, she was never as close to Granny as you and I had been.'

'I suppose that was inevitable. The hotel was only a walk away when we lived here in Killmoy, but bringing Hen back and forth from Athlone would've been a trek – and, like you said, Mum was weird about coming here, anyway. Mind you, I do understand that, if Granny was so iffy about Dad.'

'It wasn't just that, though,' Barbara said. 'Apparently, Mum hated living here when she was growing up. People she was at school with called the flat groovy and retro. She just thought it was dreary, and she'd no interest in the business.'

'She told you she hated living here?'

'The word she used was "loathed". It's why you've ended up with me as your get-together houseguest. Mum didn't fancy spending the weekend up here.' Feeling this might have sounded rude, Barbara hastily added, 'Because of all that emotional baggage, I mean. But she loves what you've done with the hotel bedrooms, so she's delighted to be where she is.'

Máire hardly seemed to have heard. Staring into her coffee mug, she said, 'Poor Granny.'

After a moment's thought, Barbara pulled a face. 'I hadn't looked at it like that, but you're right. Granny was building an empire so I suppose the plan was that Mum would take over.'

'Well, there wasn't anyone else, was there?'

'Was that why you went into the hotel business?'

'You mean did I spot a chance to inherit the empire?'

'Jesus, Máire! No, of course not. I mean did it feel like you didn't have a choice?'

Máire shrugged. 'I like hotel work. No, I love it. I always have, right from my school-holiday job here.'

'I remember that job. You wanted to spend your first wages on a present for Granny.'

'And she told me to have a bit of sense.'

'She must have started work at much the same age as you were then. Wasn't that what she told us last night? It was in a baker's. I'd never heard about that before. Had you?'

'No, but I wasn't surprised. She's got an incredible work ethic. Like you said yesterday: when you and I were little, she was cooking our dinners and wiping our noses as well as building this business.'

'I know. She's always been amazing. Which is why I felt bad when Hen went on at me about the rasul thing.'

'Don't worry, once I'd decided I had to be there, I'd've come down on you like a ton of bricks if you'd tried to shirk.' Catching a glimpse of her watch, Máire scrambled to her feet. 'Is that the time? We'd better get moving. Can I really borrow the belt?'

Barbara looked at her, poker-faced. 'Maybe you should have thought more about that before you decided to call your sister a shirker.'

'I never said …'

'Oh, shut up. I know you didn't. Of course you can have it.'

'D'you want a hair drier? You can have mine. There isn't one in your room.'

'Thanks.' Barbara stood up to go, then hesitated. 'You're not bothered that I'm the one Mum's talked to about the divorce?'

'God, no. Totally the opposite. I've enough on my plate this weekend trying to do things right for Granny without having to find time to hold Mum's hand as well.'

'Oh, come on, Máire, we've never had to hold Mum's hand.'

'No, we've just had to live with the consequences of her life choices.'

A rushed twenty minutes later, Barbara took a last look at her makeup. Although one part of her mind was on her eyeliner, another was replaying the conversation she'd had with Máire. That was the closest we've ever come to a cosy chat, she thought. The kind of conversation Sullivans, and especially Máire and I, don't go in for. I've never liked the way she strung poor Raymond along for years, and it's seemed to me that, as soon as she married, she got judgemental about how I live my life. And, in our different ways, we're both workaholics, so there's always been the excuse of having no time. This thought prompted a glance at her watch and, realising she ought to be going, she checked her appearance in the wardrobe mirror. She'd intended to wear the silver belt she'd lent Máire, but the silk shawl thrown around her shoulders looked just as good. Its embroidery was glitzy enough to please Nora, even though the dress was plain. Bless Granny, thought Barbara, she was always impeccably stylish. Heaven knows what kind of start in life Máire and I would have had if she hadn't been there to cook our dinners and wipe our snotty noses, and she did it all in heels and a business suit.

Picking up a clutch bag that matched the embroidered shawl, she was halfway to the door when a new idea made her pause. How odd, she thought, that it's never occurred to me that Máire and I have a history Hen doesn't share. Was that what made it easier for me to chat to Máire this evening than to talk to Hen this morning in the spa? The massage session, with its scented oils and gentle rhythms, was supposed to be conducive to gossip and shared confidences. The setting was perfect and Hen was totally up for it, but I couldn't bring myself to relax. Yet here in the flat, sitting on Granny's chintz-covered sofa, Máire and I shared more in one snatched conversation than I've shared with anyone in the family for years. I guess that's what swapping memories in a familiar setting does to you. We went through a lot together in the years before Hen was born. And, to be fair, there's plenty to admire about Máire despite her annoying need to control the world.

Chapter 16

For hours, Barbara's bedroom window had framed blackness relieved by a single star. Then the black had become grey, and each time she'd opened her eyes, the star had been less luminous. Dawn was breaking and she felt as if she'd hardly slept, though she knew she must have, because she'd been woken by dreams. In one, she'd been searching desperately for something to wear at yesterday's dinner, knowing she was late and that the family was waiting. In another she'd run through a wasteland of burned trees and fleeing animals, trying to scream and unable to make a sound. Repeatedly, she'd known that Luke was just around a corner but, no matter where she went, she couldn't find him. Once, she'd woken to find herself struggling to get out of bed, possessed by the conviction that there was something she had to do. But the window had still been dark and, as she'd stared out at the star, the conviction had faded, leaving her shivering.

Now, though the sun had yet to rise, the sky was pale silver. Giving up hope of returning to sleep, Barbara got out of bed, wrapped herself in the shawl she'd worn the previous evening, and went to look out at the Sunday-morning landscape where grass crisped by frost was exhaling mist. The trees by the river path were rigid lines within moving air, and the river, glimpsed beyond them, was a series of points of light. Nothing seemed fixed except the dark trunks and branches, top-heavy in places where untidy bundles of twigs were last year's crows' nests. Barbara glanced back at her luxurious duck-down duvet and the cosy candlewick bedspread that had slid, rumpled, to the floor. Tempted by the thought of returning to their warmth, she felt too wound up to lie in bed till she could reasonably go to the kitchen and make coffee. It seemed unfair to risk disturbing Raymond who, she'd been told, always slept late on Sundays but, after her own disturbed night, the confines of the room felt intolerable. Irresolute, she stood huddled in the embroidered shawl until, dropping it, she wriggled out of her nightgown and pulled on track pants, a sweater and her down jacket. Then, grabbing her boots and socks, she tiptoed barefoot through the flat and, stooping to put on her footwear in the empty corridor, made her way along it to the lifts.

It was too early for the front door to have been unlocked. Tapping into childhood memories, Barbara went through a door marked STAFF and navigated a maze of passages. No one she'd known back then still worked in the kitchen, but she was recognised by a yawning kitchen porter and her exit via the bin-store wasn't questioned. It was far too chilly and damp for a walk to be pleasant. Circling the building, Barbara reached a series of steps that led down the terraces to the riverside. The low-swirling wreaths of mist grew thick as she neared the water, and the cold made her pull a scarf from her jacket pocket. Looping it so that it drew her hood tighter around her neck, she clapped her arms across her chest and wondered why she'd abandoned her warm bed and plunged out of the building without so much as a cup of coffee. Somehow, her nightmares, and the sense of being stifled indoors, had overcome her disinclination to risk meeting Luke again. But it's not just that, she thought. I need to see him. Unless I do, I'll be dogged by uncertainty when I leave here tomorrow, and forgetting him will be hard enough without that.

By now she had reached the riverside path and exercise had begun to make her feel warmer. Despite her new conviction that she had to see Luke again, instinct made her choose to walk downstream, away from the boathouse and his cottage. I need time to think this through properly, she thought. I mustn't just go blundering in, like I did yesterday. Luke's spent the last twelve months in a job he feels he should never have taken. Was that because he knew I'd come back to Castlehill this year? I can't drive off to Dublin tomorrow leaving that question unanswered. But how the hell can I ask it? And what if the answer is no? Surely if he'd stayed here for me he'd have said so. Or – hang on a minute – did something I said to him yesterday make him decide not to? By now, she was walking so fast that she was breathless. Slowing down, she tried to recall all that had happened when she'd encountered Luke the previous day. There'd been the moment he'd held up his hand to shield his eyes from the winter sunlight, and asked if she'd come out in the wind to find him. How had he sounded then? She couldn't recall. Had she even noticed? And how had she responded? Horrified, she remembered the crack she'd made about his ego. Oh, God, she thought, he shut up like a clam when I said that. Did he mean he'd been hoping that I'd come and find him? He'd already seen Hen. He knew this was the get-together weekend. What if he's spent a whole year waiting to see me and, when he tried to say so, I slapped him down?

The idea was so dreadful that she felt her knees shaking. Leaning against a tree trunk, she tried to collect her thoughts. The previous year he'd seemed as relaxed and confident as she was, laughing at what she'd said about his appearance and capping it with his own joke about being Lady Chatterley's lover. So, until yesterday, when he'd gone into that rant about his work, she'd seen him as completely self-assured. But I was wrong, she thought. I wasn't aware of the vulnerability under his assurance. Which means I could have been equally wrong yesterday. Could his coolness then have been a shield to cover his disappointment? Did that rant about Máire erupt because he was furious with himself for wasting time hanging on here for me?

'Barbara?'

The sound of Luke's voice behind her made her turn so suddenly she almost lost her balance and fell. He grasped her elbow to steady her. 'Sorry. Are you okay?'

'Fine.'

'I didn't mean to startle you.'

'You didn't.' Trying to regain her composure, Barbara pointed at a root that had pushed through the tarmac by the tree. 'I stumbled on that root when I turned. I didn't hear you coming.'

'You looked like you were miles away.'

'Isn't it early for you to be up and working?'

'Isn't it early for you to be out for a walk?'

He'd released her elbow and she stepped back, avoiding the root. 'Ridiculously early, but I had a ghastly night. Couldn't sleep. Weird dreams. I woke feeling desperate for fresh air.' Aware that she was gabbling, she made herself look at him and smile. 'We'd had a big, glitzy get-together dinner, and my granny's choice of menus leans heavily on carbs.'

'Are you cold?'

By now, Barbara's shaking knees had gone into overdrive, so she groped for a convincing explanation. 'I came out without eating. I've a room up in Máire's flat, you see, and I didn't want to go crashing round in the kitchen. But, yes, I'm cold too. I ought to go back. The hotel breakfast room will have opened by now.'

'The first sitting's not for twenty minutes. Tell you what, I've a kettle in the boathouse. Come and I'll make you a brew before your full Irish.'

'It definitely won't be a full Irish. Granny's throwing a prosecco brunch later.'

'Doesn't change the fact that you need a hot drink or you'll keel over. Though I warn you that boathouse coffee means instant granules.'

I've got to let this happen, thought Barbara. I can't control it. There's no point in wondering whether or not this is a chance meeting, or trying to second-guess his feelings. Last year, whenever I came to the river, I knew he'd be waiting for me. This year feels like a living nightmare in which, though I'm desperate to find him, he's always out of reach. Aware that he was waiting for a response to his invitation, she looked him in the eye and said instant coffee would be fine. His expression suggested nothing more than casual friendliness, but she thought when she spoke that she detected a flicker of relief.

They entered the boathouse through the door he'd been mending the previous year. Stepping into the shadowy space and hearing the plash of water against a hull, Barbara was transported to her childhood, when Martin had sometimes taken her and Máire on the river. She recalled running down to the boathouse swinging the picnic basket, filled with an excitement that would soon become irritation. Ostensibly a family day out, the excursions had usually ended in hours spent wrapped in plaid rugs, kicking their heels in the bilge of a boat, while their granddad made yet another cast and told them that if they talked they'd disturb the fish.

The boathouse smells of river water, fuel, and damp wood and stone were unchanged. Luke took a blanket from a stack on a shelf in a bank of lockers. 'There are cushions in there as well. Stick a few on the bench before you sit down. I'll get the kettle going.' Barbara pulled a couple of long cushions from the locker, put them on the bench and sat with the blanket round her shoulders. It was disconcertingly reminiscent of the plaid rugs of her childhood but, immediately, she felt less chilly and, by telling herself that a tête-à-tête was exactly what she'd wanted, she managed to check the nervousness that had made her knees shake. It didn't look likely that Luke was about to declare undying passion. He was rapidly making coffee and, when he brought the mugs to the bench, he just said, 'Budge up, and mind your fingers. These are hot. There isn't any milk.'

Taking a mug, she moved along to make room for him on the bench. For several minutes, neither spoke. Then Barbara said, 'Those boats are new.'

'Which ones?'

'All of them. I mean new since I was a child. I've got memories of wooden ones and outboard motors. I don't think I've been on the river since then.'

'These will have been upgrades. I gather your granddad was heavily into boat shows.'

'I can believe it. Angling was the only bit of the business that interested him. He and Matty were always off buying gear.'

'Shame he didn't pay more attention to managing his stretch of river.'

This was something Barbara hadn't thought about before. 'Was it not efficient management? I'd say he just did whatever his father had done.'

'Yeah. That would be my diagnosis.' Luke blew on his scalding coffee, to cool it. 'Didn't you tell me once that you wanted to make changes here?'

'To the grounds, yes. I don't know much about waterway management. Anyway, that was ages ago, before I went to college. None of the family was interested, though, so I just moved on.'

He shot her a look before staring out across the shadowed water.

'That makes sense. When things don't go your way, moving on is a valid coping mechanism.'

Another silence fell, and Barbara felt the need to fill it. 'I don't know where I picked up the idea of doing environmental science. Television, I guess, or something I read at school. How did you make your career choice?'

'I started from the premise that I *didn't* want to do what my father had done. He took your granddad's approach. Stuck with what he knew, and assumed his sons would do the same.'

'You've got brothers?'

'One older, one younger. My dad's retired. If I'd stayed, we could all have made a comfortable living. I couldn't have stood it, though. My elder brother sticks to the same old trajectory: pull out walls to make fields big enough for bigger machinery, then pour in whatever chemicals produce the greatest yield. The farm has a bit of river and some wetlands he's had his eye on. He hasn't a clue about what his run-off is doing to the water, or what the effect of draining the wetlands would be. But he'll crash on and tell himself he's an efficient manager.' Still looking past the moored boats, Luke shrugged. 'There's a lot to be said for being the middle son in a family.'

'You mean nobody notices when you walk?'

'Well, it doesn't feel irresponsible, like it might if you were the eldest, and you're not your mammy's baby, so there's less chance you'll be missed.'

Barbara chuckled. 'Believe me, it's no different when there's three girls in a family.'

'I suppose, to begin with, I thought I might go back.'

'Snap.'

Somehow, the conversation felt even more intimate than the times they'd spent together in Luke's bed and, as they sat side by side not touching each other, Barbara felt closer to him than she had when he'd held her in his arms. Suddenly, she heard herself articulating something that, up to now, she had hardly realised. 'The truth is, I didn't just move on. I was pretty angry. I had a lot to offer to Castlehill, but no one was interested.' Though her head was down, she could feel him glance at her, and prayed he'd ask no questions. She needed to process this discovery and, for that to happen, she needed time. To her relief, Luke seemed to feel her withdrawal, and continued talking about himself.

'In my case, it was a non-starter. I didn't want to fall out with my elder brother and, anyway, I'm the last person he'd choose to listen to.'

'What about the younger one?'

'He's twenty-four and still his mammy's baby, and my mother thinks my father knows all there is to know about farming. So, even if the young fella agreed with me, he wouldn't be one to rock the boat.'

'Do you feel bad about it?'

'Weirdly, no. Land is land, whoever happens to lay claim to it. The boundaries humans invent mean nothing at all. I've come to the view that it doesn't matter which piece of the earth you care for. So long as you're doing the right things in one place, there'll be a knock-on in the next.'

Barbara pulled the fleecy blanket tighter around her shoulders. 'I know Máire's being an idiot about everything you've proposed but, seeing her this weekend, I think I understand what's happened. A business the size of Castlehill needs super-effective teamwork. But, like you said yourself, Máire's completely the wrong person to put in charge of running a management team. She's desperate not to let Granny down, but when she gets stressed she turns into a control freak. Which means that, given her nature, she's been handed a poisoned chalice.'

'It's certainly poisoned as far as this stretch of river is concerned.'

'Seriously?'

'In the sense that your fish stock's getting weaker all the time. The land round here would have been a callow in the past, a meadow that the river flooded annually. The flooding's been inhibited for generations, which affects the water quality as well as the land's fertility. That means depleted habitat, both in the grounds and the river, and managing things by chucking in imported fish stocks each year makes matters worse.'

'And you've said all this in your presentations?'

'The ones no one pays attention to? Yes, I have.'

Suddenly, Barbara realised this was her chance. Without any nudging from her, the conversation had arrived at a natural point for her to ask her question. She could go for something like 'What's your hope for the future?' which would be suitably vague. But why be a coward? If it was now or never, why not go straight for the jugular? She could put it to him directly: 'You haven't been able to change things here, so why haven't you moved on?'

She had opened her mouth to speak when Luke bent forward and set his empty mug on the decking. Without looking up, he asked, 'Your granny was born on a farm, wasn't she?'

'What? Yes, yes, she was. She grew up there. Somewhere outside Killmoy, I don't know where exactly.'

'You didn't spend time there?'

'Gosh, no. Her parents were dead before I came along.' Feeling she'd been interrupted while poised to jump off a precipice, Barbara swallowed her question and looked down at the top of Luke's head. It felt insane to be sitting chatting when all she wanted was to reach out and touch him. She could almost feel the crisp curls that grew on the nape of his neck, the smooth skin on his temples and the hard line of his jaw. Their last kiss last year had been on the threshold of his cottage. He'd grasped her by the elbows and drawn her close for a final hug, then held her hand at arm's length before she'd broken free and run back to join her family. Even then, thought Barbara. Even then I hadn't admitted how I felt. It wasn't until the following day that it hit me. I'd truly had no idea that I was in love. And when I went back the following day, I started a stupid row instead of having the guts to admit my feelings.

Now Luke looked up and, for an endless moment, it felt as if a spark had been reignited. Holding her breath, Barbara waited for him to make the first move. She could hear the lapping of the water and, beyond the half-open boathouse door, the cawing of crows whirling from their roosts in search of food. Streaks of pale sunlight were dispersing the shadows, and Luke's eyes were as close to hers as they'd been when he'd first bent over her in bed. She closed her own eyes and waited, but nothing happened. Then she opened them and found he'd stood up and moved away. He'd set his back against the stone wall and, as she looked, Barbara saw him retreat behind a shield of aloofness. Though her mind was screaming, 'What just happened?' she gritted her teeth and said nothing. What's the point of asking, she thought, if it's going to get me nowhere? I still don't know how he feels, but the message couldn't be clearer. It's okay to chat about subjects of mutual interest, but there's no way he's going to let me past that shield.

Chapter 17

When Nora had made her move from the flat to her junior suite, someone had decided she'd like a photo of Martin by her bed. It was still there, expensively framed, on her bedside cabinet, partly because Nora hadn't had the heart to move it and partly because she knew that its absence would cause gossip. And that would never do, she thought, sitting up in bed and looking at the photo. However good or bad things might have been between me and Martin, it's nobody's business but mine, and that's the way it's going to stay. I didn't even talk about it to my own mother, so I'm having no gossip or speculation now he's gone.

Contemplating the programme for the day ahead, she wondered what Martin would think if he saw her in a rasul chamber where people took off their clothes and got plastered in mud from head to heels. There had been a time when he might have found it funny, but that side of him had soon calcified. Turning the photo to look at his face, Nora told herself dispassionately that his lack of character had become marked on it as he'd grown older. It was strange to think that she wouldn't have started the Sullivan Girls' Get-togethers if Martin had been a different kind of man. But what else could I do, she thought, when my own husband didn't stand up and support me? I had too much pride and sense to go running to my parents.

Restlessly, she lifted the frame from the cabinet and propped it against her up-drawn knees. Three babies I lost, she reminded Martin. Three sons whose existence nobody left alive remembers. Each of them hoped for and wanted and carried under my heart. And when I was grieving, what did the men in your family do? They called me a failure. They puffed their pipes and shook their heads and muttered to each other, saying you'd brought home a wife who couldn't produce a male heir. And you never said a single word to stop their mouths. You could have stood up to them, and spoken up for me, but you didn't. The Sullivan Girls' Get-togethers were my only defence.

It was stranger still to think that there was no one left but herself who remembered how she'd set out to build an inner, female, family circle as a bulwark against those disapproving men. The growth of the get-togethers had mirrored her own determination to grow the business and prove her worth as Martin Sullivan's wife. Tea and cakes in the flat had become five-course dinners in the Riverview dining room, extending over the years to an overnight stay for far-flung cousins, and morphing into girls-only weekends of food, wine, squash games and poolside partying. As the older generation died off, and their negative comments were forgotten, the invitation lists had shrunk to immediate family members. By then, the gatherings had become an annual affirmation of female family solidarity, and only Nora remembered their painful, defiant roots.

She'd first met Martin at a charity whist drive in the hotel's function room, which, in those days, had been the library of the old house. In the empty spaces on the shelves, between books discarded by Castlehill's former owners, the Sullivans had placed angling trophies and, for the occasion, the room was dotted with card tables and chairs. Nora had come with a group of girls who'd recently left school and found jobs with good wages, and had dressed with every intention of turning heads. She was wearing a cocktail dress sent home from the States by one of her sisters. The brocade sheath knocked spots off the other girls' full skirts and sweetheart necklines, and had made her mother clasp her hands in delight. 'Ah the little bolero jacket is only gorgeous! You look straight out of a magazine! Doesn't she, Joe?' Nora's father had only grunted, but he'd told her he'd bring round her bike so she wouldn't get mud on her shoes in the yard. 'Though God knows how high you'll have to hitch up that skirt to get yourself on to it.' It wasn't easy to mount the bike, but she'd managed, and had cycled the six miles of country lanes and roads to Killmoy. She'd met the girls at the bridge, where they'd left their bikes chained together, and carefully checked their appearance before walking up through the town to the hotel. Appearance mattered. You wouldn't want the townie crowd spotting cow shit on stockings or grease from a bicycle chain on a skirt.

Martin was circling the room, topping up people's drinks and emptying ashtrays. In those days, his parents had played host and done the hand-shaking: he was just the son who'd come home after working in Tullamore. Gossip said he'd had an easy berth in an uncle's business and returned under a cloud, having failed to make the grade. During the evening, he followed Nora from one table to another, constantly in attendance and filling her glass. If she'd drunk all he brought, her back teeth would have been floating in red lemonade. Still, she'd had to admit she'd enjoyed the attention. Then, a few days later, he'd seen her in town and asked her to a hop.

They went in his car, which made a change from pedalling dark lanes, and when he came to the farm to collect her, he produced a corsage he'd brought for her dress. It was a rose and a fern held together with silver paper, a silver ribbon bow, and a pin at the back. When Nora came home from the dance, she pressed the rose petals in a book, not because the gift had come from Martin, but because she'd never been given flowers before. Her mother was enchanted, and her dad had muttered darkly that the Sullivans had ever had more money than sense.

The dress Nora wore that night had been red with a black lace overskirt and, as it happened, Martin's rose had been white. Which was lucky, she thought, still staring at the photo she had propped against her knees. If he'd brought one that clashed with my outfit, I might have gone off him there and then. I might have taken the emigrant boat in the end, like my brothers and sisters. Instead, I set out in Martin's car impressed by his choice and chivalry and, simply because in those days he had a sense of humour, by the end of the evening I felt as if I'd found a friend.

The dance was held in Killmoy parish hall. There were benches around the walls and a bar at the back selling minerals. The ladies' room was up a staircase off the entrance lobby. As soon as they got there, Nora went upstairs to powder her nose. The shoes she was wearing were two-tone stilettos and – like everyone did in those days – she'd stuffed the pointed toes with crumpled paper to keep their shape. When she came back down the stairs, Martin was waiting in the lobby. The first few steps were fine but then her ankle twisted and, as she grabbed the banister, one of her shoes fell off. Bouncing from step to step, it careered down the stairs ahead of her and, just as it landed, the tissue paper she'd stuffed into the toe fell out. Scarlet, Nora had limped down towards Martin, arriving as he picked up her stylish shoe in one hand and the pointed wad of tissue in the other. That was when they'd found they shared a sense of humour. Having neatly restored the paper, Martin sat on the bottom step to slip the shoe on to her foot, caught her eye, and they both burst out laughing. For the rest of the evening they chatted as if they'd always known one another, and Nora, who was used to escorts treating her as a trophy, discovered what it was like to dance with someone who focused on her, not his watching mates.

So, although neither of their families had really approved of the union, she'd decided that marriage to Martin was the right choice. She could tell that, when his parents died, he'd be useless at running the business, but that was fine because she fancied running it herself. Martin was good-humoured, healthy, easy-going and generous. He was also the best prospect she had if she didn't want to emigrate. What she hadn't bargained for was how quickly he'd age. By thirty, his youthful good looks had gone the way of his sense of humour, and indolence had caused him to put on weight. It was then she'd discovered how deeply the indolence was ingrained. She'd known that standing and fighting wasn't in his nature, but his failure even to speak up on her behalf made her feel betrayed.

When the pain of each lost baby was compounded by the pipe-puffers' reactions, she'd longed to run home to her mother for support, but she knew that if her dad heard what Martin's relations were saying about her, he'd most likely wade in on her behalf. Things were bad enough without a civil war with her in-laws, so she decided to let time solve the problem. And, eventually, time did just that. But you were my husband, Martin, she thought, looking at his photo. You were my husband. The Sullivan Girls' Get-together was born from the deaths of my babies. I'd never have had to cosy up to the women in your family, if you'd had the guts to square up to the men.

With the prospect of a mid-morning Sunday brunch ahead of them, everyone was giving breakfast a miss. Still in her pyjamas, Jane lay on her bed reading, the book propped on the pillow and her chin in her cupped hands. Looking up, she spoke to Henrietta who was lounging on her own bed, having just taken a shower. 'The house *wasn't* built in the nineteenth century. Not this one, anyway. There was an older house that got knocked down in 1911. Actually, it sounds like there's always been some kind of house here. This says the site was probably first used in the Bronze Age, as a fortified dwelling.'

'What are you reading?'

'A book Nora gave me. It was written for one of the hotel's anniversaries. There's lots of photos. See?'

Leaning across the narrow gap between the two beds, Henrietta looked at a page of photos. 'There are prints of some of these in frames downstairs in the bar.'

Jane took a chocolate from the box she'd found in their welcome basket. 'D'you want one of these? This one's filled with orange mousse.'

'You'll ruin your appetite.'

'People always say that. I literally don't know what it means.' Turning the page, Jane pointed at a photo. 'Wow, look at this one. It's the old stables. The people who lived here used to go driving in a horse-drawn coach.'

'That building's the family garage now.'

'I know.' Jane murmured this absently, her focus still on the book, but after a moment she glanced at Henrietta, apparently having made up her mind to say something more. 'Actually, I was round there when I went for my walk yesterday.'

Her eyes returned to the page and, looking at her covertly, Henrietta wondered how to reply. Ever since her phone conversation with Barbara, she'd mentally been rejecting the accusation that her eagerness to please other people was stifling. It was painful to think that in trying to do the right thing by Stuart's daughter she could be doing exactly the opposite. But honesty and the fact that Jane hadn't mentioned her chat with Raymond suggested that Barbara could be right. Stuart and his mum constantly fussed about Jane's welfare, so how must it feel to have yet another adult breathing down her neck?

But it's different in her case, thought Henrietta. It's all very well for Barbara to make comparisons with our childhood. She doesn't understand how things are for Stuart. He never talks about it, but I know that, each time he's abroad, he has nightmares about what happened when Jane's mother died. It must have been hell to pick up a phone in a hotel bedroom and be told the guards had been called to your house by a neighbour who'd heard your baby screaming for hours in her cot. He'd left home a happily married man on an ordinary business trip and flown home to cope with devastation. No wonder he's so protective of Jane, and that she's always been cosseted. He lives with the thought of what might have happened if no one had heard her crying. And what would he say if he knew I'd allowed her to wander off on her own? Okay, she was perfectly safe with Raymond, but the hotel grounds are public space. I've been given the role of responsible adult this weekend: what if something happened to her on my watch?

Jane had wriggled to the edge of her bed and was sitting cross-legged. She looked younger than ever in the pink flowery pyjamas Stuart's mum had given her for Christmas, but her face wore the inscrutable look that always worried Henrietta. I mustn't pester her, she thought. I know where she was and who she was with, so there's no reason to question her about it. On the other hand, I know Stuart would freak at the thought of her being secretive. But, dammit, Barbara's right, the child has to have her own life. It's potentially dangerous for her to go round keeping secrets, and isn't she more likely to be forthcoming if Stuart and his mum start to trust her a bit? Having swung from one side of the argument to another, Henrietta came to a sudden decision. If she wants to tell me how she spent her afternoon, she will. But I won't push her. I'm going to give her the space I think she needs. Slightly surprised by her own firmness, she bent forward to look at the book on Jane's knees. 'The old coach house hasn't changed much. When was that picture taken?'

'It says 1896.'

'It's older than this house, then. I didn't realise.'

'I went into it, actually. The door was open.'

'Did you?'

'Máire's husband Raymond was there. He's got a cool car.'

Rolling on to her back, Jane lay with her knees bent, holding the book at arm's length above her head. 'I might go back there this afternoon. Like, instead of swimming? He said he'd show me how the engine works.'

With an effort, Henrietta managed to answer casually. 'Sounds interesting. Why not do it, if it's what you'd prefer?'

'Okay. Cool. Maybe I will.'

Don't ask for certainty, Henrietta warned herself fiercely. Just say nothing, and let her leave it at that. To fill what felt like an ominous void, she stood up and said, 'I'm going to make coffee. Want some?' As soon as the words left her mouth, she was certain she'd sounded like Stuart's mother, who was always urging Jane to eat or drink. I've got the same impulse, she thought. It feels like nurturing but, in fact, it's demanding, and I know it annoys the hell out of Jane. Convinced she'd spoiled things, she waited, feeling her heart sink to her toes.

But, this time, instead of a stilted refusal, Jane gave her a brilliant smile. 'Is there any hot chocolate?'

'I think there's a sachet over there. Wait, yes, there is. Would you like some?'

'Please.'

'To go with your chocolates?'

'Yep.'

Now shut up, Henrietta told herself. Don't start fussing about sucrose levels. Take yourself into the bathroom, fill the kettle and make the drinks.

She'd come back and plugged in the kettle when Jane spoke casually from behind the book. 'Have you ever read this?'

'No, I haven't.' Praying she wasn't pushing her luck, Henrietta added, 'I'd like to, though.'

'Okay, that's no problem. You can borrow it when I'm done.'

Sheila was sitting in the yellow armchair when Máire tapped on her bedroom door and asked, 'Am I disturbing you?'

'Not at all. I was watching those gallant women doing yoga in the mist.'

Máire went to look out the window. 'The Second Chance Club. They're terribly present this weekend, but very sweet. And the bar takings have definitely seen an uplift.'

'Have they been here before?'

'I think they target recently opened spas around the country.

The woman who made their booking said they live in pursuit of the cutting edge.'

'Well, I hope they've got thermals on under those Sweaty Betty ensembles.'

'Ah, they've all had full Irish breakfasts, they ought to survive a bit of damp.'

'Far too energetic for me. I'm perfectly happy being pampered in the spa.'

'How was the foil-wrap?'

'Amazing. I think I'm hooked.'

'I just thought I'd put my head in and check that you're happy with this room.'

'Of course I am. It's charming, and so comfortable.' Alerted by something in Máire's voice, Sheila raised her eyebrows. 'Why the concern? Has Barbara said something?'

'She mentioned you weren't too keen on having your old bedroom up in the flat. You would have been very welcome, you know.'

'Oh, darling, of course I know that. Barbara shouldn't have said anything.'

'She said something else too.'

'Did she?'

'That you and Dad are divorced.'

'Oh.' Sheila sat down abruptly. 'I've been trying to find a suitable moment to tell you.'

'I imagine that's why you turned up in the office yesterday. I'm sorry I didn't realise. I was having a bit of a moment.'

'I know. You're busy. And, darling, I only told Barbara first because—'

'Oh, Mum! You don't owe me an explanation. Your marriage is your business, after all.'

'Yes, but Finbar's your father.'

'Well, the fact that you've divorced him doesn't change that. More's the pity. And, honestly, it's no big deal that I happened to hear it from Barbara. I'd far rather that than being summoned to a big family announcement.'

Sheila pulled a face. 'I think that's what I had in mind to begin with. Some idea of breaking the news when we were all here together. But then Henrietta had to bring Jane ... and it was a ludicrous notion, anyway. Besides ...'

'Besides, you think Hen's going to take it badly.'

'Barbara's really been talking, hasn't she?'

Máire laughed. 'We did have a bit of a natter before last night's dinner. Unusual, but I was exhausted, and she'd plied me with strong drink.'

'You seemed perfectly sober at the meal.'

'I'm exaggerating. We chatted a bit and she told me about the divorce, and that you were worried about how Hen might react. To be honest, I didn't see why, but I've thought about it since.'

'You don't think I'm being silly?'

'No. I see your point. Hen's always been besotted with Dad.'

Sheila leaned back in the armchair. 'I just don't know how to handle this. Which is silly because I've handled so many other potential disasters provoked by Finbar.'

'Jane's the spanner in the works this weekend. If you tell Hen and she gets upset, you don't want Stuart's kid picking up the vibes.'

'Exactly.'

'Have you told Granny?'

Sheila groaned. 'No, and that's another problem. She's sure to crow, and I'll probably lose my temper. I lay awake half the night wondering if I should just go home and send her a letter. The truth is, whatever I choose to do is going to make me feel either irresponsible or a coward.'

Máire threw up a hand in a gesture of frustration. 'Even when Dad's out of your life, you're left carrying the can! Everything to do with him always turns out to be toxic. I don't know how you put up with him so long.'

'I had you three to consider.'

'We'd have been better off without him.'

'Oh, darling, you say that, but would you? And think of Hen.' Sheila pressed her hands to her lips. 'Please don't look like that. I don't mean that Hen was more important than you and Baba. But she was younger and – I don't know – I thought it was better not to upset the apple cart.'

She looked hopefully at Máire, who spoke slowly. 'I do understand. Truly. It can't have been easy, and God knows I can't comment. I don't suppose anyone can who isn't a mother.'

'I've always thought you blamed me.'

'What for?'

Sheila's response was somewhere between a giggle and a sob.

212

'The decisions I made. Not making decisions. Not knowing what to decide.'

'That's comprehensive.'

'Baba was always independent. Hen was always a baby. You're the one I worried about the most.'

'Seriously?'

'But I never can tell whether or not you're happy. It's always seemed to me that I know you well, but I've never known that.'

Máire went and straightened the rug at the bedside. 'Are you happy now you've got rid of Dad?'

It's always been this way, thought Sheila. You've never wanted to talk to me about your emotions, and I'm always on the outside trying to second-guess what you feel. Knowing that pressure was likely to make Máire fly off the handle, she accepted the rebuff by answering the question. 'I'm glad I divorced him, if that's what you mean. I just don't want it to make Henrietta unhappy.'

Máire looked at her ring finger, where Raymond's sapphire sparkled beside her platinum wedding band. 'I want Granny to be happy. I don't want her to die thinking everything she's achieved here will just dissipate.' Sitting down on the bed, she thrust her hand into her jacket pocket.

The tense pose made Sheila choose her words carefully. 'A job shouldn't be a burden, though, and it shouldn't dominate your life.'

Máire bristled. 'Are you saying I can't make a go of it?'

'Of course not. I'm saying I saw at first-hand what Castlehill does if you let it take hold of you. I don't know what drove your granny, but her commitment to the business was relentless.'

'What's your point?'

'Are you happy living in the flat?'

'Why shouldn't I be?'

Already regretting having started down this dangerous road, Sheila decided she had to keep going. 'Because you have a home of your own, Máire. A place you poured your heart into. You have your own achievements. You have your marriage.'

Máire pushed herself to her feet. 'Oh, please! You're going to lecture me about marriage?'

'I'm not lecturing you.'

'Good. Because you're hardly a role-model, are you?'

'Darling, please. I just want to help. I'm your mother.'

'And, in fairness, you weren't too expert at that either.' Máire flushed and seemed about to apologise. Then she hunched her shoulders, set her teeth and glowered.

Sheila nodded. 'You're right. That's fair. I probably wasn't the best of mothers. But the point, since you ask, is that there isn't anyone in the world who cares more than I do about your happiness.' She had stood up and taken a step towards Máire, but now she retreated and gripped the back of the yellow armchair, determined to finish what she'd accidentally begun. 'Actually, that's not true. Raymond cares as much as I do. Don't take him for granted, Máire. Even saints have breaking points. I'll always be your mother, so I'm going nowhere. That's a given. Don't assume the same applies to your husband.'

Chapter 18

In remodelling Castlehill, Nora had struck a balance between creating a modern hotel and leisure centre and retaining the charm of a country house. Though she'd knocked several rooms together to make the spacious foyer with its revolving door from the old entrance porch, she'd kept other areas on the ground floor virtually unchanged. One of these, still called the ladies' parlour, was a square, panelled corner room lit from two sides by tall, graceful windows. Today, a sign on an easel outside the door read PRIVATE FUNCTION. Inside, the pale wood seemed gilded in the low winter sunlight. Surmounted by an oval mirror, a fire burned in the cream-painted fireplace, and brunch was laid out on a long buffet table to which the staff were still carrying trays of glasses and plates. Nora's customary armchair stood at the fireside, and the rest of the seating was grouped to allow for separate conversations between two or three people.

Barbara arrived first and settled on a window seat. After leaving the boathouse, she'd retreated to her room in the flat, telling herself that now she had to accept that Luke didn't love her and desperately tried to muffle sobs by burying her face in her pillow. This was precisely the scenario she'd imagined half jokingly when she'd told herself she might regret insisting that Sheila took the hotel bedroom. Eventually, exhausted by stress and her broken night, she'd fallen asleep and woken to find it was almost time for brunch. Scrambling to find something to wear, she'd caught sight of herself in a mirror and realised no amount of makeup would disguise her swollen eyes and blotchy skin. With no time to spare, she'd pulled on a pair of trousers and a sweater, slammed on foundation, combed her hair forward, and decided her best hope lay in getting down to the parlour before the others, so that she wouldn't have to make an entrance. As she sat down, she told herself that, with luck, she could keep a low profile. The honeysuckle-patterned curtains shadowed her face and she could stay on the window seat while she ate.

Even when the house was built, the parlour would have had an old-fashioned air, its décor more suitable for the elder ladies of the household than the younger set who'd danced the Charleston, drunk cocktails, and driven the cars that had ousted the horses and carriage from the coach house. Now it was one of the most photographed rooms at Castlehill, a testament both to Nora's sense of what the public wanted and her inherent dislike of waste. When she'd married Martin the parlour had been in perfect condition, so, except for some reupholstering and burnishing of brasses, she'd announced it would be daft to spoil what didn't need changing. Looking around her, Barbara supposed Máire took the same view.

Which isn't surprising, she thought, remembering the house Máire and Raymond had bought in Killmoy: it's so easy to modernise an old building unsympathetically, but Máire didn't put a foot wrong there.

The door opened, making Barbara shrink back behind the curtain, but the girl who came in was one of the staff, carrying a tray. She was followed by another, wheeling a trolley of chafing dishes, which they put on the buffet along with serving spoons and a stack of plates. There were already cups and saucers next to a coffee pot and, before leaving, one of the girls offered to pour some for Barbara. 'We'll be bringing tea in a moment, but would you like some of this now? Or a glass of prosecco? It's there in the ice-bucket.' Barbara stood up, accepted coffee and returned to the window seat. The girls were leaving when Máire walked in with a face like thunder, raked the room with a professional eye and went to make up the fire. Having rattled the poker violently, she curtly refused coffee and set about straightening chairs. When the door closed behind the trolley, Barbara set down her cup. 'Has something happened?'

Máire swung round. 'I didn't see you there. Nothing's happened. Why would you think so?'

'Why else would you be slamming round like the Antichrist?'

'Oh, shut up, Baba. I'm fine.'

'Well, that's a big, fat, whopping lie.'

'Come to that, you're not looking great yourself.'

Barbara hunched a shoulder. 'Don't change the subject.'

Suddenly Máire sat heavily on the sofa. 'If you must know, I've just had a flaming row with Mum.'

217

'What about? Not the divorce?'

'No, of course not. Well, yes, in a way. At least, that's where it started. I mean, we were talking about it and, somehow, we got on to me and Raymond. And Mum went into a lecture about my marriage, which was rich, coming from her.'

'It doesn't sound like Mum to lecture.'

'All right, it wasn't a lecture. I suppose she thought she was being helpful.'

'What did she say?'

'She's always hated Granny, you know.'

'Máire! That's just bollocks.'

'Okay. I know it is. I'm overstating. But she does hate Castlehill. You said so yourself.'

'What did she say about you and Raymond?'

'She told me I've been taking him for granted.'

Unable to repress a chuckle, Barbara said, 'That's not news. You've been taking Raymond for granted since you were twelve.'

'Shut up, Baba.'

'You have, you know. I've even heard you and Raymond joke about it. How come it's a big deal when Mum says it now?'

'Because ...' Máire bit her lip and stared hard at the flames in the fireplace. 'Because Mum reckons Castlehill is going to destroy our marriage.'

Barbara came and sat on the sofa beside her. 'She said that?'

'Stop cross-questioning me. No, she didn't say so. She didn't need to.'

'What you mean is, as soon as she tried to say anything you went into a strop.'

Suddenly, Máire's voice trembled. 'Okay, yes, I did, and I feel dreadful. I went to her room intending to be supportive about the divorce. I'd thought about it since you and I talked, and I do see why Mum worries about telling Hen. I was there to be the positive, helpful elder daughter. But, somehow we flipped from her divorce to talking about my marriage. What she actually said was that even saints like Raymond have a breaking point.' Still focused on the fire, Máire's eyes filled with tears. 'And the thing is, Baba, she could well be right. He keeps trying to be helpful and I keep holding him at arm's length.' Brushing away the tears, she muttered, 'Damn. Look at the time. They'll all be swarming down in a few minutes.'

'How did you leave things with Mum?'

'How do you think? I stormed out in a huff.'

'Oh, great. Recipe for a cheerful family occasion.'

'Back off, okay? By the look of your face, you won't be the life and soul of the party either.'

Henrietta and Jane, who'd been distracted by Nora's book, were having to dress for brunch in a hurry. As Jane came out of the shower, a text pinged on Henrietta's phone. Shooting back a smiley face emoji, she called, 'That was your dad, saying good morning.'

'Cool. What do you think I should wear? Brunch in a parlour sounds posh.'

Unaccustomed to being consulted, Henrietta put down her phone. 'It's a pretty room, but no one's expected to turn up in frills and flounces. Maybe a skirt, rather than jeans? Granny likes people to make an effort.'

'Okay.' Jane held up a blue skirt and a white angora jumper. 'What about these?'

'Perfect.' As Henrietta spoke, her phone pinged again. 'It's Granny. She wants someone to help her come downstairs.'

'I can do that, if you like.'

'Would you? I've got to finish my makeup. You're not dressed, though. Let me call one of the others.'

Jane shook her head. 'I dress at the speed of light. It's one of my super-powers.' She proved her claim by getting ready in minutes, and disappearing while Henrietta was still applying eyeliner. Left alone, Henrietta considered this transformation from introverted child to cheerful companion. It's amazing, she thought. All Jane needed was a bit of time and space to herself, and all I had to do was step back and let her take it. This validation of her judgement seemed so miraculous that when her phone rang, and she saw it was Stuart, she answered the call bubbling with excitement. 'Hi. Didn't you get my text?'

'The brush-off emoji?'

'Don't be daft! We got up late, and we're rushing.'

'Okay. You're forgiven.'

'It's lovely to hear your voice, though. Darling, we're having such a good time.'

'Jane too?'

'Jane especially. Well, I think so. She's really blossoming, Stuart. I've never told you, but I've been worried about my relationship with her. She's always sweet and polite, but we haven't been close, not really. I said at the start that I wouldn't know how to be her mum, remember? I've never wanted to. It would be weird. But I've wanted to be her friend, and I've felt sort of shut out, and now it's different.'

'Darling, slow down. Are you sure you haven't hit the prosecco early?'

'Don't laugh. I'm serious. Things have really turned a corner. And all she needed was a bit of space to herself!'

'I thought you said you were crammed into a titchy room together.'

'Not actually titchy but, yes, it's a twin room.' Henrietta stopped and thought for a moment. 'Perhaps that's part of what's made the difference.'

Stuart gave a hoot of laughter. 'Honestly, gorgeous girl! You're talking in contradictions.'

'I'm not. Well, I know it sounds that way ...'

'I'm beginning to think you've downed the prosecco and moved on to Manhattans.'

'Stop it, Stuart. I'm still dressing. We haven't gone down to brunch yet.'

'Well, take it easy when you do. Listen, I've a call coming in. Let me say hi to Jane before I take it.'

'Jane's not here.'

Stuart's voice sharpened. 'Why? Where is she?'

'She's fine. She's gone up to Granny.'

'I'm not sure I like the thought of her wandering corridors alone.'

'She's perfectly safe. She knows her way. She's just taken the lift to the flat.'

'All right. But keep an eye on her, won't you?'

'Of course I will. I always do.' Henrietta hesitated, trying to find the right words to suggest that they might discuss this when she was home again.

But before she could speak, Stuart said, 'Damn. Incoming call. I must go.'

Thrown off balance, she blurted out, 'Hang on a minute, I really think Jane's been feeling a bit smothered.'

'Nonsense. Of course she hasn't. Sweetheart, I have to take this call. Give my princess my love. I'll see you both tomorrow.' The call cut off leaving Henrietta aware of her half-finished eyes reflected in the dressing-table mirror. As so often since her marriage, they were wide and anxious. Before that phone call, she thought, I was feeling so sure of myself. Now I look like a hare caught in headlights. It's ridiculous. I'm here. Stuart isn't. I can see the change in Jane's behaviour and he can't, so why should he doubt me? And, more to the point, why on earth am I sitting here doubting myself?

The lift doors opened on a group of Second Chance Club ladies huddled in fleeces and dryrobes after their yoga session in the mist. They bunched together to make room for Jane but, to her relief, they didn't include the chatty woman who'd quizzed her about Henrietta, so she squeezed into a corner and said nothing as they swished upwards.

Having reached her destination, she knocked on the door of the suite, and when she went in, found Nora sitting on the sofa.

'Hi. Hen said you wanted someone to help you downstairs.'

'Did she, now?' Nora was smartly dressed in a pink suit and high-necked blouse, and was holding a two-strand pearl necklace. Jane came further into the room. 'Would you like a hand with the clasp?'

Nora threw her a wink. 'It could be that's the help I really wanted.'

'I did think the text was odd.'

'Why was that?'

'Well, because you use the lift, not the staircase, don't you?'

'Didn't I say the other night that you've a sharp eye in your head?'

Jane took the necklace and went to the back of the sofa to fasten the pearls round Nora's neck from behind. 'It's fiddly to manage if you're old. Do your hands hurt? My gran's do.'

'At my age, love, something's always hurting. There's no rhyme or reason to it, either. It's whatever happens to ache when you wake in the morning. And that'll change twenty times during the day.'

'Gan-Gan's doctor says she has osteoarthritis.'

'Isn't that a baby name you have for your granny!'

'Baba's a baby name too, but that's what Máire calls Barbara.'

Nora laughed. 'There's nothing wrong with your ears either, is there? Now! You've done it. You're a good girl.' She stood up stiffly, smoothed her skirt and looked approvingly at Jane. 'You're looking nice and tidy too. That's a smart outfit.'

'Hen said you like people to make an effort.'

'Did Hen send you up to me or did you offer to come yourself?'

'I offered. She'd have come if I hadn't, though. They're all very fond of you, aren't they?'

'They're three good girls. I'm a lucky woman.'

Jane picked up Nora's handbag, which was on the floor by the sofa. 'Did you have sisters?'

'I did, love. Five of them, and three brothers. That surprises you, doesn't it? But it's how things were in those days. Women had big families. It was what the men expected.'

'You only had Sheila, though.'

'That's true.' Taking the handbag, Nora checked its contents. 'Look at that, now! I haven't a tissue. Run and get me one – there's a box by the bed.' Obediently, Jane went to the bedroom and came back with a paper handkerchief. She was vaguely conscious that something she'd said was unwelcome, but the number of Nora's siblings had caught her imagination. 'What happened to them? All your brothers and sisters?'

'They went to America. That was a thing in those days too. There was no money to be made on a farm. Not for three lads on a place the size of my father's.'

'What about your sisters?'

'You wouldn't find women farming then, or many that went into business. Each of them went away in their turn, and sent back the price of the passage to the next one. Some of my brothers flew, but my sisters all crossed on a ship. They got work in Boston. Factory work. And secretarial, there in the Irish Club. Most of the lads worked on the sites. Construction was big at that time.'

'Did they come back?'

'Only for funerals. The farm went to my eldest brother when my mother died, but, sure, he was settled over there, so he sold it. They're all dead now, of course. They were older than I am.'

'Did nobody send you the price of the passage?'

'Ah, they would have done, love, they were never slow to send money. Parcels too. Shoes and bags, and lovely dresses. I had a red frock with a black lace overskirt. Boston Maid was the label. It was the height of fashion. I'd say my sister had hardly worn it before it came to me. And one of them sent me a brocade sheath with shoes dyed to match it. Girls used to cycle to hops back in those days. They'd hang their high-heels round their necks while they were riding the bike. Little strappy sandals too. I had a pair of gold ones. We all got parcels from Merica. Half the crowd I was at school with couldn't wait to get out there. I never wanted to go, though.'

'Why didn't you?'

'I wanted to be here for my mother, when she'd get old and need me.'

Jane frowned. 'But you said women didn't go into business. How come you ran a hotel?'

'You'd want to listen more carefully. I didn't say that. I said not many women.'

'Yes, but how come you did?'

'I fell on my feet, love, that's the long and the short of it. I married a lazy man, you see. That's how I built my empire.'

'Wow. Did you actually plan it? Like, work it out beforehand?'

'Life's not that simple. Mostly, it's more about making compromises than making choices.'

They had reached the lift lobby when Jane asked, 'Do pains in their joints make people tired?'

'They do, love. Sometimes I think the worst part of getting old is how it exhausts you.' Reclaiming the handbag Jane was carrying, Nora stepped into the empty lift. 'What made you think of asking?'

'I just wondered. You looked awfully tired after that first-night dinner we had in your flat.'

Chapter 19

Raymond's Sunday morning lie-in had been interrupted, first by the sound of Barbara tiptoeing through the flat at daybreak and then by her stealthy return. He'd managed to drop off comfortably the first time but, waking again when she'd closed a door, he'd drifted in and out of sleep for hours before deciding he might as well get up. On his way to the kitchen, he'd hesitated outside Barbara's bedroom, wondering if she'd like a cup of tea. Máire had already gone down to her office, having had toast and coffee, and he'd thought that, after an early walk, Barbara might appreciate something warming. But her door was shut and, hearing no sound, he'd decided not to disturb her. Instead, he'd showered, had something to eat and, in tracksuit and beanie, set off for a run by the river with a towel around his neck.

By then, the Second Chance Club ladies were doing downward-facing dogs in the mist so to give them a wide berth he took a diagonal route. Reaching the river path, he settled into a steady rhythm, jogging along beside the foam-flecked water and feeling the welcome warmth of the sun as the mist began to lift. The previous night, he and Máire had sat up later than usual, talking about her mum's divorce. 'Can you believe it, Ray? Barbara broke the news to me before dinner. Apparently, Mum only told her when the whole thing was done and dusted.'

'How do you feel about it?'

'Glad, if it's what she wanted. Baba says Mum's in a state about making the announcement, though. Mum told her she's worried that Hen's going to be upset.'

'Is she going to announce it this weekend?'

'By the sound of it, she's bottled it. And I do see her point. It could turn out like something in a TV soap.'

'I wonder why she said nothing while the divorce was going on?'

'It doesn't surprise me. She's spent most of our lives trying to paint Dad as the ever-so-slightly-absent-but-absolutely-perfect father. In fact, he's erratic and utterly irresponsible, so I bet getting rid of him took a hell of an effort. Mum wouldn't have wanted comments from the sidelines.'

They'd been sitting up in bed, and Raymond had turned on his side to look at Máire. 'You've never sounded so aggressive about your dad before.'

'I suppose I haven't. Perhaps I've been released.'

'By the divorce?'

'By the fact that Mum's dropped the pretence.'

'Was it always pretence, though? I mean things might have been different once.'

'Trust me, they weren't. Dad was unreliable but we were never allowed to say so, and Mum was on a mission to cope with everything on her own. I remember those horrible rooms we had down in Killmoy. It was totally weird. Like living in a hovel while your grandparents lived in a castle. People at school used to say things.'

'Not in front of me. Why didn't you tell me? I'd have stopped their mouths for them if I'd known.'

'Oh, Ray, that's so sweet. I know you would.' Reaching out, she'd touched his face. 'You'd have taken on the lot of them in the school yard, and ended up in detention, dripping blood. Then it wouldn't just have been kids talking. The whole town would have gossiped about it for weeks.'

'True enough.'

'It wasn't a big deal anyway. Plenty of other kids used to come asking for Dad's autograph. Which also felt weird, by the way.'

'Didn't he turn up in town once wearing snakeskin trousers? I seem to remember girls at the school gate getting all overcome.'

'I must have blotted that one out. It'd be just like him, though.' Máire had pushed herself upright against the bedhead. 'The thing is, I always knew Mum was worried sick about money.'

'But surely your grandparents wouldn't have seen her stuck?'

'Of course not, and she knew it. But she was stubborn. I reckon Granny said from the start that Dad was a useless con-man, and I bet Mum realised what he was like soon after they married. She just wouldn't admit she'd made a mistake.'

'I definitely remember you and Barbara spending a lot of time here. Nora used to mind you after school.'

'That was the crazy compromise they arrived at. It freaked me out when I was younger. I mean, Mum could've had a job here if she'd wanted one, and we'd have got out of those ghastly rooms in town.'

'Maybe she thought your dad would settle down as time went on. Things change. So do people. And she did get you out of the rooms and off to Athlone, eventually.'

'Oh, I know it wasn't straightforward. Marriages never are. That's why I don't blame her.'

Now, jogging along the path, Raymond saw movement by the boathouse. The door swung open and Luke came out, his chin sunk into the upturned collar of his jacket: hearing feet on the tarmac, he turned his head, saw who was coming and raised his hand in a perfunctory wave. Raymond waved back without breaking his stride, and by the time he reached the boathouse, Luke was walking away towards his cottage. Idly wondering why he appeared to be working on a Sunday, Raymond continued along the path behind him, expecting to pass him with a cheerful word. But, as the distance between them shortened, Luke veered sideways into a stand of trees, as if intentionally avoiding a meeting. Something about the set of his shoulders made Raymond wonder if all was well. God, I hope so, he thought. If something's gone wrong with the grounds or the fishing, it's likely to freak Máire out.

Approaching a bench, he slowed down and jogged on the spot, mentally re-running the previous night's conversation. The news of Sheila's divorce wasn't bothering him. Máire was fine with the break-up and, apparently, Sheila was too. It sounded as if it wasn't going to be easy to tell the others but, presumably, once that was done, they'd all move on. No, what was bothering him was what had been said last night when the light was off and the conversation about the divorce was over. Or, rather, what wasn't said. That was the issue. Máire had switched off the bedside light and they'd settled down to sleep when he'd felt her breath warm on his cheek and her mouth close to his ear. 'It might have been interesting to let you go full Sir Galahad on those kids.'

Drowsy, he'd answered, 'Could never have happened. You're too like your mum. Determined to do things on your own terms, to your own satisfaction.'

'You love me for it, though, don't you?'

For a split-second Raymond had hesitated before answering. Now he remembered how a rustle of bedclothes in the darkness had given the impression that Máire had drawn back to stare at him. 'Ray? Tell me you love me.'

'Don't be an ass. Of course I do.'

'Then say so. You've never not said so.'

'I love you. It's late. Go to sleep. You've a million things on tomorrow's schedule.'

Troubled by the memory, Raymond stopped jogging on the spot and went to sit on the bench. Leaning back against damp wood, he looked up at the sky, where crows were circling above last year's disintegrating nests. From the moment he'd first met Máire, he'd known they were made for each other and, ever since, that certainty had been the bedrock of his existence. No vacillation or apparent lack of interest from Máire had changed his conviction that, ultimately, they'd marry and spend the rest of their lives together. So what had happened to cause that split-second of hesitation? As his eyes followed the circling crows, his mind shrank from his train of thought's direction. Did he really doubt his love for her? How could that be possible?

I spooked her, thought Raymond, and now that's spooking me. His thoughts crowded faster now that he'd asked the unthinkable question. Have we changed? Has something happened to make me feel different about our relationship? The truth is that, though we're married, Máire and I have been living apart. Okay, we share a flat, but you can't call it living together. We've moved out of the marital home, we've no shared plans for the future, and she's set up so many barriers that we hardly talk any more. Can you actually call that a marriage? It struck him that Máire's mind, which had always moved faster than his, might already have analysed his split-second of hesitation and reached a conclusion he was still groping towards. When he'd told her to go to sleep, she'd rolled to the other side of the bed, drawing up her legs and pressing her elbows against her sides, so that not an inch of their bodies touched under the tightly stretched duvet. It astonished him now to remember how quickly he'd drifted into sleep, and how his waking sensation had been no more than resentment at the interruption of his Sunday lie-in. Something's gone badly wrong, he thought, and we've both realised it. I don't understand how it's happened, or why, but it mustn't be ignored.

Half an hour later, on his way back to the hotel entrance, Raymond passed the parlour window. He could see Barbara sitting well back behind a curtain, and figures moving in the room beyond, where Nora and Jane sat by the fire and staff were filling glasses and plates at the buffet. Instinctively, he slowed down, seeing Sheila join Barbara on the window seat and Máire briefly framed between them, crossing to Nora's chair with a glass of prosecco. She was wearing one of the dark, well-cut jackets she kept for work, but had paired it with relaxed white trousers and a camisole top. From where Raymond stood concealed by a laurel that grew next to the window, he caught only a glimpse of her before she moved on. It recalled the first time he'd seen her as a teenager and known in an instant that his heart was lost. Looking ten times better than most girls managed to look in the school's lumpy uniform, she'd been moving purposefully away from Barbara and Sheila who'd stood side by side in the schoolyard. Raymond couldn't remember why all three had been there together but, then as now, Máire had exuded such self-sufficiency that, even as a teenager, he'd recognised it as an act. There's never been a time, he thought, when I couldn't see past her bristles and bumptiousness, so I've never felt we've needed to talk to each other about how we feel. But now it's like we're living on opposite sides of a pane of glass. I can see her, but I can't make out what she's thinking any longer, and every day she's moving further out of my line of sight.

At the fireside, Nora took the glass of prosecco from Máire's hand. 'That's grand, dear. I won't have anything to eat.'

'Are you sure?'

'I am, of course. I had my usual breakfast before we came down. I'd say Jane would like a pain au chocolat or something. Would you, love?'

Jane, who was sitting on the hearthrug, got to her feet eagerly. 'I can get it myself, if you'd like to sit down, Máire.'

'No, you're fine.'

Nora shook her head at Máire. 'Sit down and don't be ridiculous, the child's legs are younger than yours. And you might as well get me a pastry too, Jane. They're not what I'd normally have but, sure, this is a special occasion. Sit down, there, Máire, and take the weight off your feet.'

As Jane went to the buffet, Máire laughed and took a seat. 'There's no need to make me feel ancient!'

Nora threw her a shrewd glance. 'Well, you look like you haven't slept.'

'I had a restless night, that's all. It sounds like you were up early. Didn't you sleep yourself?'

'Trust me, you wouldn't ask that question if you really were ancient. Sound sleep is for youngsters. Old ladies like me spend half the night awake, waiting for morning.'

'That can't be right. Should you have a word with your doctor?'

'I've never been one for running to doctors, you know that. I'm grand in my perfectly comfortable bed.'

Máire looked at her anxiously. 'I don't like to think of you lying awake worrying.'

'Who said I worry? I haven't a thing in the world to worry about. You're in charge now, and signs on it, if you're having restless nights.' Deliberately, Nora looked at Máire, meeting her eyes over the rim of her tall glass. 'I don't want you working yourself into the ground, you know, love.'

'Don't be silly, Granny.'

'And I didn't come down in the last shower either. No one knows better than me how hard a place like this is to run.'

Aware that her reaction had been defensive, Máire tried to assume a professional tone. 'Things have changed since your day, though. I'm installing modern systems.'

'It's people that make the difference in business. Not systems.'

'And I've got professional qualifications.' An edge came into Máire's voice. 'I thought that was what you valued when you offered me the job.'

'If that's what you thought, you were wrong. Oh, I've nothing against qualifications. I dare say you learned plenty at your college that I had to work out for myself. But the bottom line is I gave you the job because I thought you wanted it, and you'd be good at it. If I hadn't thought so, I wouldn't have offered it to you.'

'I did want it. And I do. Granny, is this leading up to something?'

Before Nora could reply, Jane arrived with a plate of pastries and several paper napkins. Sitting down, she held out the plate to Máire. 'I thought you might like one.'

'What? No. Thank you, I'm fine.' Thrown by Jane's arrival, Máire stood up and forced a grin. 'I'd better go and check people's drinks. You stay and talk to Granny. Don't try giving her croissants, though. She doesn't go in for them.'

She had turned away when Nora, who'd been looking at her shrewdly, laid a firm hand on her arm. 'We ought to talk more. After the weekend?'

'Sure. Of course.'

As Máire moved away, Nora smiled at Jane. 'I might have one of those mini-croissants. To soak up the wine. Give me one of those napkins, now, and I'll tuck it here under my chin. It's not the fashionable way, but I don't want bits of crumbs on my pearls.' She took the napkin and, tucking it into her high-necked blouse, smoothed it carefully over the pearl necklace.

Biting into a pastry, Jane asked, 'Are the pearls old?'

'They're not antique, love. My husband gave the necklace to me on Sheila's first birthday.' Nora gestured with the croissant, and called across the room to Sheila. 'I'm taking your name in vain over here. Telling Jane that your father gave me my pearl necklace on

236

your birthday.' Sheila smiled and waved to her from the window seat, and Jane watched Nora bite into the croissant, from which a drift of pastry flakes floated on to the napkin. Having brushed them neatly on to the hearth, Nora held up her hand to display the bracelet on her wrist. 'Marking occasions with bits of jewellery was a Sullivan habit. My husband gave me this for our ruby wedding anniversary.'

'Is that what the stones are? Rubies?'

'Set in gold. It's Victorian. He got it from an antique shop up in Dublin.'

'It's cool.'

'Ah, it's nice enough. It's another one with a fiddly fastening, though. But, sure, my hands have got thin. I can push it on to my wrist without opening the clasp.'

'My dad buys jewellery all the time for Hen. Not for special occasions, though. More like random presents.' Jane unfastened the chain she wore round her own neck and showed it to Nora. 'He gave me this pendant ages ago. It's a little gold heart, see? It was my mum's, so I guess that means it counts as antique.'

'It's a pretty piece.'

Splaying her fingers, Jane dangled the heart so that it caught the firelight. 'He bought it for Mum just after they married.'

'Well, that sounds right.' Nora took another bite of croissant. 'Once they're married, men always like to hang chains around their wives' necks.'

Jane's attention was on the glinting pendant in her hand.

Over her head, Nora saw Máire choose a chair that put her at a distance from the others, and turn it as if to repel any approach. The edginess she'd shown at the point when their conversation was interrupted had hardened into such tension that it made Nora frown. Raymond's right, she thought, the child's tired. But everyone in this business is tired after Christmas. It's more than tiredness with Máire. I suspect that the bottom line is she's simply not up to her job.

Chapter 20

When Sheila had come downstairs from her bedroom, she'd chosen to sit on the window seat partly because she'd noticed Barbara seemed upset. But, having thrown her a tight smile, Barbara had turned her face away so, balked, Sheila had balanced her plate of food on her knee and surveyed the room from the shelter of the curtains. Nora and Jane were by the fire. Máire was circulating. Henrietta was at the buffet, where baskets of pastries and bowls of fruit salad stood between dishes of scrambled eggs, grilled mushrooms and tomatoes, and long platters of thinly sliced smoked salmon decorated with watercress and lemon wedges. Next to the fruit bowls were yoghurts sourced from a local farm, a cheese board and baskets of crackers; and alongside the flaky, golden pastries was a loaf of Castlehill's famous home-baked bread.

Troubled by Barbara's tense presence beside her, Sheila made up her mind to reach out and lay a hand on her arm. 'I can get you a plate of food, if you'd like something, love.'

With her head still averted, Barbara said no. 'I'm fine with this coffee. Anyway, aren't you lurking here to avoid Máire?'

Despite how she'd felt only seconds before, Sheila found herself irritated. Her voice sharpened. 'You and Máire seem to be doing a lot of talking this weekend.'

'Sorry?'

'Apparently, you had a long chat about my divorce from your father, and now she seems to have rushed to you with the next juicy titbit.'

'She was in a bit of a state when she came to check the buffet. I was here, I asked what was wrong and she told me, that's all.'

'Oh.'

Barbara set down her coffee cup and turned to face her. 'Look, I gather your row wouldn't have happened if I hadn't told Máire about the divorce. I'm sorry. I probably should've kept my mouth shut. It's just we were talking and it came out.'

Shocked by Barbara's appearance now that she saw her full-on, Sheila shook her head vehemently. 'I'm the one who ought to be sorry, not you, love. I should have spoken up by now and broken the news myself. But, listen, are you okay? You look wretched.'

'I had a bad night, that's all. Nothing black coffee won't cure.'

Sheila felt she had to accept the brush-off. I can hardly demand to be treated as a confidante, she thought, when I've just accused her of tittle-tattle. She was casting about for something uncontroversial to say, when the sight of Máire at the other side of the room made her revert to her own trouble. 'Did Máire tell you what our row was about?'

'Not in any detail. There were staff coming in and out.'

Sheila sighed. 'Like I always seem to, I said completely the wrong thing. I'd been worrying about what you'd said to me about her and Raymond.'

'What I said? When?'

'On the way down here. I realised I'd been so obsessed with my own marriage that I hadn't given a moment's thought to whether or not Máire and Raymond were happy at Castlehill.'

'Well, that throws light on what she said to me.'

'What did she say?'

'That you told her even the likes of Raymond have their breaking points.'

'Did I? Yes, I did. No wonder she blew up at me! She said I'd no business lecturing her about marriage, and God knows that's true. It's not the same, though, is it, Barbara? I mean, I've actively dumped a useless shyster. What if Máire carelessly loses a saint?'

'Isn't that a bit over the top? Okay, Raymond's remarkable, but he's human.'

'That's exactly what I'm saying. She's always tended to take him for granted. What if he gets fed up?' Sighing again, Sheila put goat's cheese on a sliver of soda bread. 'I'm probably being silly. Pay no attention. I'll corner Máire this afternoon and make my peace with her.'

To her surprise, instead of accepting this, Barbara lowered her voice and moved further behind the curtain. 'The thing is, Mum ...'

'What? What is it?'

'I have a feeling you hit a nerve.'

Sheila put down the soda bread untasted. 'What do you mean?'

'The staff were in and out, like I told you, so Máire didn't say much. But she did get a bit weepy and admit that you might be right.'

By the time Henrietta joined the others in the parlour, the defiance she'd felt before talking to Stuart had totally dissipated, leaving her in her usual state of nervous anxiety. Now, pensively eating strawberry yoghurt by the buffet, she was sure that, almost as soon as she'd entered the room, she'd made a major error and upset Máire. Well, possibly not major. Not on a scale of one to nuclear warfare. And not really an error at all, more like a moment's lack of concentration. In fact, it shouldn't be that big a deal, she told herself resentfully. Máire's being dreadfully touchy this weekend. Frowning, she replayed the moment when Jane, who'd been by the fire with Nora and Máire, had come to the buffet, chosen a plateful of pastries and, uncharacteristically, asked for her advice. 'I came over to get these for me and your granny.' With most of her mind still on Stuart, Henrietta had nodded. 'That's nice. I'm sure she'd like one.'

'I know she would. She said so. But the thing is, she and Máire are talking now, so I might be in the way if I brought them over.'

'Not if Granny told you to fetch them.'

'Okay.'

But the set of Máire's shoulders as she'd got up to make way for Jane had shown beyond doubt that it *had* been an interruption and, though Máire had made what looked like a cheerful remark when moving away, Henrietta wished she'd thought twice before sending Jane to join them. Granny looked sort of thrown as well, she thought. I should have had more sense. I ought to have seen that they weren't just exchanging chit-chat. Máire's cross, I know she is, so I'd better apologise.

Pouring a cup of coffee, she crossed to where Máire was sitting alone, in an armchair by a small table. 'I thought you'd like this.' It looked as if Máire was going to refuse but, instead, she took the cup. 'Thanks. You don't want it yourself?'

'I've just had some.' Henrietta sat on a chair next to her. 'And the food's gorgeous. You've gone to a lot of trouble.'

Looking abstracted, Máire shrugged. 'Option Two on the Private Brunch menu, that's all. Plus a few touches for Granny, like the flowers and the cut-glass champagne flutes. Generally, they're reserved for Option One.'

'Still, you've been working flat-out this weekend. And, Máire, listen, I haven't properly thanked you for having Jane.'

'Don't be daft. She's more than welcome. She's a nice little thing.'

'I know, but that's not the point. She interrupted you just now, when you were talking to Granny. I should have kept an eye on her but I'd just been talking to Stuart, and I got sort of distracted, so I wanted to say I'm sorry.'

Losing her distant air, Máire snapped, 'Oh, honestly, Hen …!'

'What? Don't pretend she wasn't a bother. I saw what happened.'

'You're making a mountain out of a molehill. Granny and I were just chatting.'

'I'm not thick, Máire.'

'Nobody said you were. I'm saying you're mistaken.'

The dismissiveness in Máire's voice was so like Stuart's that, to her horror, Henrietta felt a lump rise in her throat. Mortified, she groped for a paper napkin, hoping Máire wouldn't comment. Instead, Máire asked crossly, 'What's the matter? It's bloody Stuart, isn't it? He's said something to upset you.'

'No, he hasn't. Well, yes, he has, but he was probably right.'

'For Heaven's sake, Henrietta!'

'Don't keep snapping at me. I said something about Jane, and, well ... But he's her father, he knows best. You can't deny that.'

'I'm not denying that he's her father.'

'The point is, it stands to reason that he'd know what's best for his daughter.'

Máire snorted. 'If you don't mind my saying so, you've always had a weird view of fatherhood.'

'I do mind you saying so. What do you mean?'

'Nothing. I'm sorry. Forget it. You're right, I'm having a heavy weekend.' There was a pause in which Máire sipped coffee before she put down her cup with a clink and said, 'Seriously, though, Hen ...'

'What?'

'You've got to stop letting Stuart undermine your confidence.'

'I don't.'

With a quick glance, Máire checked that Jane was out of earshot. 'Look, I've no idea what you and Stuart said, and it's none of my business. But I know you and I wouldn't be having this conversation if talking to him hadn't left you feeling you always do everything wrong.'

Blinking away tears, Henrietta muttered, 'It did a bit.'

'It's what I've said before. You let him walk all over you.'

'But Jane …'

'Not just where Jane's concerned. It's everything. Take those parties you had over Christmas. By the sound of things, you had to play the perfect hostess from dawn to dusk.'

'But Stuart …'

'Stuart loves entertaining. So you always say. But it's not Stuart who has to do the donkey work. It's you. He plays host while you scuttle round doing catering with one hand and putting on makeup with the other. I bet he hasn't a clue about what it takes to run things that smoothly. And he never even considers pulling his weight when it comes to Jane.'

'That's just not true. He adores her.'

'Of course he does. He adores you both. He showers you with love, and you all play house together. It's just a shame that he can't see how he's grinding you down in the process.'

Henrietta sniffed. 'He doesn't mean to.'

'Of course not. And he's not stupid, but clearly he hasn't the sense to see what he's doing. It's going to be up to you to tell him, Hen.'

'Do you really think so?'

Máire shrugged. 'You've already said you don't need marriage counselling from me and, God knows, I'm the least qualified person around here to give it. But, yes, that's exactly what I think. You need to grow a spine, and, if you're planning to stay with him, Hen, you need to start laying down boundaries.'

Amazed, Henrietta lowered the napkin from her eyes. 'Of course I'm going to stay with him. He's my husband.'

'Well, that's no guarantee of anything, these days, is it?'

On the window seat, Barbara had lapsed into silence, leaving Sheila twice as disturbed as she'd been when she'd come down to brunch. It was shocking to find that Máire had been distressed by the row in the bedroom. It's so unlike her, thought Sheila. I'd have expected anger and indignation, not tears, and certainly not an admission that she might have been wrong to turn on me. And now I'm not sure how I ought to feel. I can't be pleased that I seem to have won the argument because, if Barbara's right to think Máire feels Raymond may not be happy, things could be worse in that marriage than I'd imagined. Looking at the room from the shelter of the curtain, she could see Máire in animated conversation with Henrietta. It didn't look like a cheerful chat, though. Whatever it is they're discussing, thought Sheila, poor Hen is feeling cornered, and it's evident that Máire's no calmer than she was this morning. So, with Barbara in some kind of state and me tense as a fiddle-string, this is not turning out to be a relaxing Sullivan family occasion.

Turning away from the room, she rested her forehead on a windowpane and thought about the tensions of her childhood. Days when Nora hadn't a moment to stop working and play with her and Martin was holding court in the bar or fishing on the river.

Bad-tempered teenage hours spent in her bedroom, bored stiff, with nobody to talk to. Long summer holidays lounging pointlessly in the hotel grounds, where there was nothing to do and she wasn't supposed to bother the guests.

Perhaps if I'd had siblings, she thought, I mightn't have rushed into marriage. I hated being an only child. It was miserable. Everyone I knew at school seemed to have people their own age at home to hang out with. All I had were parents who seemed to take no interest in me, a gaggle of Dad's elderly aunts, and his dreadful sporty sister, who was always playing golf and going to horse shows. Oh, and Mam's mother, who we hardly saw except at Christmas and funerals, and who was very sweet but felt ancient. I was so little when she died I can hardly remember her, and the grand-aunts were gone by the time I was in my teens. I do remember them turning up each year for Mam's get-together, and me being expected to join in, just as poor Jane is now. Though Jane certainly seems to be coping far better than I did, and she's definitely made a big hit with Mam.

Glancing across to the fireside, Sheila watched Nora laughing with Jane, and wondered, half enviously, what they were talking about. The warm room, full of light and conversation, suddenly seemed to exclude her, as the hotel always had in the past.

Turning back to the chilly view beyond the window, she saw Luke carrying a file of papers, climbing the terrace steps towards a side door. At first she couldn't think who he was. Then she remembered he was old Matty's replacement about whom there'd been a kind of spat at the first-night dinner. As Luke disappeared around a corner, her mind strayed to the days when Matty had ruled Castlehill's grounds. God, Matty was a chancer, she thought. He can't have been more than middle-aged when he started insisting on help. Those drive-on mowers that kept needing upgrading, and assistants in high season to give him a hand with the heavy work. I don't know why Dad never saw through him. Mam certainly did. Maybe Dad did too, and just didn't know how to stand up to him. Dad would do anything for a quiet life.

Beyond the laurel tree outside the window, the bleak terraced lawns sloped down to the river, reminding Sheila of the hours she'd spent loitering in the grounds when Máire was a toddler. I suppose, she thought, I preferred it to seeing how well Mam coped with Máire when she was minding her, and feeling that, in comparison, I was a useless mother. That was how it began, anyway. Pointless wandering by the river just so there'd be no time to sit down when I came to collect Máire. Things might have been so different if I'd had a bit of sense. But back then I was so confused and conflicted. All I knew was that I was lost and angry, and had no one I could confide in about my marriage. If I couldn't admit my mistake to my parents, I sure as hell couldn't tell my friends or talk about it at work. All I could do was trudge along beside that blasted river, miserable and longing to escape. And yet, if I'd run upstairs, grabbed Máire and made a dash for freedom, Barbara and Hen would never have been born. Two beautiful children who've grown to be women any mother could be proud of. No, whatever mistakes I may have made for whatever dumb reasons, bringing my girls into the world wasn't one of them.

By now, Luke had reached the house and disappeared through the side door. Still hunched at the far end of the window seat, Barbara was staring out at the barren view. I wish I knew what's bothering her, thought Sheila. Only yesterday I was telling myself that I know her from the inside, but she's so good at shutting people out that, while I can sense she's unhappy, I can do nothing to help unless she chooses to tell me what's happened.

Chapter 21

The first time Nora found she was pregnant she'd hardly been married a year. She left the doctor's surgery and walked slowly up through the town, her heart beating so loudly she feared the people she passed might hear it. When she climbed the hotel steps and pushed the revolving door to Reception, she saw Martin on his way to the bar with a group of guests. He waved and she gestured to show she wanted to talk to him so he dropped back, saying he'd join the guests in a little while. It would have made sense to go up to the flat and tell him her news there but, unable to wait, she took his arm and drew him into the parlour. Though trees were budding down by the river, a little fire was dancing in the polished steel grate. The room was warm. The chairs were upholstered in chintz patterned with blush roses, and the hearthrug took up the same design in pale green. Nora closed the door and leaned against it, feeling the handle pressing into her back. Looking at her, Martin said, 'What?'

'I've been down to the doctor.'

'Why? Is something the matter with you?'

'Not at all.' She held his eyes until she saw realisation dawn in them, and burst out laughing when he gasped and gathered her up in a hug.

'Truly? What did the doctor say? When are you going to have it?'

'Don't say "it". You're talking about a baby. He said you'll have a son or a daughter to bounce on your knee before Christmas.'

'How far are you gone? Should you sit down? Come and sit by the fire.'

'I've probably six months to go, and I'm not an invalid, Martin.'

'Six months? He'll be born long before Christmas.'

'I know, but imagine how great it'll be to have all the family over, and a big tree in here, and everyone sitting around a roaring fire.'

'And people raising their glasses, saying, "God bless us every one"?'

'Don't laugh at me.'

'I wasn't.'

'Yes, you were, but it doesn't matter.' She let him lead her to the fireside, and sat down bubbling with excitement. 'Dr Logue says I'm grand. Better not to tell anyone yet, though.'

Perplexed, Martin said, 'Why?'

'Ah, it's probably just superstition. You know Dr Logue.'

'Does he say it to everyone?'

'Don't you know he does? My mother's the same. She'd be drinking tea with a neighbour who was just about to drop, and not a word said about the baby for fear of bringing bad luck.'

'So I can't tell my mam and dad?'

'"Give it a while yet." That's what the doctor said. Anyway, I wouldn't mind it being our secret for a bit.'

Martin sat on the hearthrug, leaned forward and put his arms round her waist. 'You women are daft, d'you know that?'

'Don't you think it's nice for you and me to keep it between us?'

'No. I want to go up to the roof and shout it to the world.'

When Nora woke the following day, there was a jeweller's box on her pillow. Sitting up in bed, she saw Martin by the door. 'What's this?'

'Something to mark the occasion.'

She opened the box and gently touched its contents with one finger. 'It's beautiful, but you shouldn't have, Martin.'

He came to the bed and fastened the fine gold chain around her neck. 'Why? Do you think it's bad luck?'

'Of course not. I don't believe in pishogues. I just think ... Oh, I don't know. It's beautiful. Really. Thank you.'

'You're welcome.'

'You didn't go telling them all down in Crotty's Jewellers why you were buying it?'

'I said it was for my lovely wife. I didn't mention my son.'

'Ah, Martin ...'

'Don't fuss. I was the soul of discretion.' Sitting on the side of the bed, he bent to kiss her. 'So, what are we going to call him? Martin junior?'

'Or Martina.'

'That won't happen. The eldest Sullivan's always a strapping boy. Another Martin's too obvious, though. What about something modern? How about Bing?'

'Are you out of your mind?'

'As in Bing Crosby. We could all sit around, like you said, and sing "White Christmas" under your tree.'

But despite the doctor's assurance that she was grand, Nora lost the baby, and her misery was made worse by the fact that it had, indeed, been a boy. When she was pregnant again a year later, Martin bought her a locket, a silver heart in which he'd got the jeweller to put one of their wedding photos. She carried that baby almost to term and they grieved his loss together, but when she conceived the third time there was no box from Crotty's Jewellers, Martin had stopped coming up with names, and the Sullivan pipe-puffers were out in force, muttering at family gatherings and giving Nora sideways looks. Nora guarded her tongue when she went to the farm to visit her parents, though she longed for her mother's sympathy and comfort more than ever, having lost yet another son. Stillborn, and seen by the Sullivan men as evidence of her failure, the baby was buried with little ceremony. Nora was still in bed, on Dr Logue's orders, and Martin, who'd gone to the graveyard, came home looking sullen, and said nothing except that it had rained.

Then, Martin was called in by the doctor and told that another pregnancy might well be the death of Nora. 'Some women are built that way, so I'm giving you fair warning. Take to the prayers now, if you're determined. You married her as God made her, and if you try again and things go wrong, I won't be held responsible. Mark that.' Shaken, Martin ordered twin beds from a shop in Athlone, and told Nora their private life was nobody else's business. 'So don't go round discussing it. We don't want any talk in the town. You know what people are like.' But the pipe-puffers' sideways looks and muttering continued, and at every family gathering in the parlour, Nora came into the room with the feeling that her sleeping arrangements had been discussed behind her back.

Then one night, on her narrow mattress, she conceived again. Martin's first reaction when she told him the news was anger. 'Jesus Christ, Nora, you know what the doctor told us!'

'I do, and it wasn't me came creeping over into your bed.'

'Do you feel all right? Did you have your blood pressure taken?'

'I'm fine.'

This time it was he who insisted on keeping it a secret. 'We won't say a word about you falling pregnant. Mind you don't go talking to your mother.'

'I never do.'

'We'll say nothing. You could get yourself one of those caftan things the film stars wear.'

'Oh, that'd keep people from talking all right.'

'What? Okay, fair enough. Bad idea.'

It shocked her to think he hadn't noticed the talk in his own family. It was later that resentment at his failure to confront it began to grow, and then to fester. This time she carried to term; and Sheila was born healthy and strong after a labour so short that the doctor almost missed the event. The idea of holding a Sullivan Girls' Get-together came to Nora as soon as the baby was placed in her arms. She knew the fact that she'd had a girl would disappoint Martin's male relations and, though all had gone well, she had no intention of risking her life again to produce a boy. So she made her plan. She'd gather a bulwark of Sullivan women around herself and her baby and, building on what she'd already done for the business, show the world she could take Castlehill to heights her lackadaisical husband hadn't the gumption to envisage.

The second part of that plan wasn't something she and Martin talked about but, from then, it was she who took the reins and drove the business forward. If Martin wasn't prepared to stand up for her when she needed his support, she didn't consider she needed his permission to make decisions; and, whether or not the Sullivans liked it, Sheila was heir to Castlehill. A combination of Nora's success and the friendships she forged with Martin's female relations made her feel less emotionally vulnerable. Martin, who was content to let her get on with running things, had shown no disappointment when he'd heard the baby was a girl. Though just as uninvolved with Sheila as he was with the business, he was a kind, responsible father, eager to see his daughter happy. But it was clear that, to begin with, he'd had no faith in the likelihood of her survival, and he'd waited until her first birthday before going down to Crotty's to buy Nora's pearls.

Now, sitting by the parlour fire, Nora looked around the room at her family. It was hard to believe that the stylish middle-aged woman by the window was the longed-for baby she'd held in her arms that day. Harder to cope with, given the work it had taken to build the business, was Sheila's lack of interest in the hotel. She was sitting now, as she'd always sat, slightly apart from the company, and Barbara, beside her, seemed equally withdrawn. In an armchair by a small table Henrietta was sipping coffee, a shaft of light from the window emphasising the curve of her cheek and her golden hair. It's no fault of hers, thought Nora, that she's the image of her father, and I dare say I ought to be pleased that at least he gave one of Sheila's children his good looks. God knows he's given this family nothing else. Turning her head, she looked across at Máire, who was at the buffet watching the staff gather and stack plates. It's odd, thought Nora, how looks reappear in different generations. Sheila's got Martin's colouring and height, and so has Barbara. Máire's small-boned like me, and dark-haired like my mother. She's got my father's contrariness too, and all his stiff-necked pride. That's something that came down to Sheila, and I've plenty of it myself. Maybe that explains a lot. Two of a kind don't always sit well together. I'd say Martin and I rubbed along all those years partly because we had so little in common. These days, people would call that counter-intuitive. I call it good sense. Still looking at Máire, Nora's expression softened. Every rule has an exception, she thought. However contrary Máire was, she and I got on together. Maybe that was because she spoke out, whereas Sheila was always reticent.

Straightening the hearthrug with her foot, Nora wondered in passing what had become of the old green rug she remembered.

Then she recalled Sheila tripping and spilling coffee on it, at a Sullivan Girls' Get-together when she was in her teens. Everyone had gathered round and dabbed the stain with napkins, except Sheila who'd just stood glowering. It was something that could have happened to anyone, so it wasn't her fault, and later Nora had tried to say so. 'It's been in my mind to spruce up the parlour, anyway. It makes commercial sense to keep it feeling traditional, but you've always got to keep two steps ahead of your guests' expectations.' Now she frowned at the memory. I suppose, she thought, I'd have done better to reassure her without mentioning the business, but I always imagined that, as Sheila grew up, she'd get interested in it. Anyway, there's no use trying to analyse things at this stage. All a mother ever wants is for her child to be happy, and Sheila did well for herself in the end, and has three lovely girls to her credit. The chances are that I'll never know why she went off and married that waster but, at least, I managed to keep her close to home so I could help her with the girls.

The firelight glowed on Jane's swinging pendant and, unconsciously, Nora reached to touch the pearls around her own neck. The armchairs with their cross-stitched cushions, the gleaming brass fender, and the polished steel fire-irons all spoke of generations of conscientious housekeeping, heads bent over embroidery frames, family secrets revealed and concealed. God alone knew how many joys and sorrows the room had seen, intensely important at the time and now mostly forgotten. Nora had always wondered how the English owners had felt when they'd sold Castlehill to the Sullivans. They'd only just knocked down their old house and built a new one, she thought. They must have had such hopes for the future when they sat down and designed it. Someone planned the rooms back then, chose the chintzes, furnished the bedrooms, greeted friends on the steps and welcomed them into firelit gatherings. They can't have imagined that, in a few years, they'd be selling it off and leaving. By all accounts, they'd been decent enough landlords. Did they think there was no place for them in an independent Ireland? Were they frightened of being burned out in the lawless days? Or did they just lose heart and leave a house that must have felt haunted when their only child, who had danced in it, died in a trench up to his knees in Flanders mud? Parents build for their children, she thought. We plan and work in the present for the future. That's what I did for Sheila. It's what Sheila did for her girls. You sweat to prepare the ground, like a farmer who dreams of a golden harvest. Then life steps in and knocks your dreams sideways, and there's nothing to do but make your peace with what's left.

Jane looked up and asked, 'Are you going to the spa this afternoon?' Jerked out of her reverie, Nora shook her head. 'I've said I would, love, but I'm not sure now. I'm a bit tired. I'll see how I feel after I've had a rest.'

'I'm going round to the garage. Hen says I can if I want to. I met Máire's husband yesterday. He's going to show me the engine of his car.'

'Well, if that's what interests you, love, it's kind of Raymond. But you can't go messing with engines in those clean clothes.'

Jane looked down at her white angora jumper and gauzy skirt. 'I only packed respectable clothes to come here. Actually, all the clothes I've got are respectable. New, I mean, or expensive. I'd better change into my jeans.'

'If your jeans are new or expensive you'd better do nothing of the sort.' Rapping on the table beside her, Nora called to Máire. 'Come over here for a minute. Let the staff get on with those plates.'

As Máire approached, Jane spoke under her breath to Nora. 'I don't want to be any trouble.'

'Not a bit of it. Come here to me, Máire. Would you have some kind of a coverall the child could wear in the garage?'

'The garage?'

'Raymond's going to show her the innards of his car.'

It was so evident that this was news to Máire that Jane felt she needed to explain. 'I'm interested in engines. Well, STEM stuff generally. The car has a turbocharger. It's a vintage Saab.'

'I know.'

'Of course. It's yours too, isn't it? Or don't you drive it? Hen doesn't drive my dad's car. She's got her own.'

'I've driven it now and again, but, no, it's Raymond's baby. And you certainly can't mess with the engine in that jumper and skirt.'

'I can wear my jeans.'

Nora rapped the table again. 'Don't be silly. Máire will lend you something. Won't you, Máire?'

'There's an ancient pair of dungarees somewhere upstairs that might fit her.'

'There now! Didn't I say so? Take her up to the flat when we're finished here, Máire. She can change in one of the bedrooms and collect her own things later.'

'Okay. Will that suit you, Jane?'

Jane nodded and said a subdued thank-you. She was pretty sure that, earlier, she'd annoyed Máire by interrupting her conversation with Nora, so the thought of going up to the flat with her was daunting. On the other hand, the thought of a pair of ancient dungarees was rather exciting. In her own clothes, she'd probably just have to watch while Raymond showed her the engine. In something that didn't matter, he might let her help him to take it apart.

When the plates were gathered, the staff went round offering more coffee but, by common consent, the party was breaking up. Joined by Jane, Henrietta was surprised to hear Nora's proposal. 'Granny asked Máire to lend you a pair of dungarees? Are you certain?'

Jane was assuring her that she was when Máire appeared beside them. 'Everyone's drifting off. Will we go upstairs, Jane?'

Henrietta put out her hand. 'Hang on, Máire, I don't want Jane to be a bother.'

Máire smiled at Jane. 'She's a fusser, our Henrietta. You're no bother at all. Come on up to the flat and we'll see what we can find for you. Catch you later in the spa, Hen.'

In the lift, Jane wondered if she should make conversation, but Máire took out her phone, saying, 'I need to check a rota,' so nothing needed to be said as they made their way to the flat. With no idea what to expect, Jane was struck by the contrast between its old-fashioned appearance and the modern, streamlined look of the hotel. Seeing her reaction, Máire laughed. 'Not my décor. This was Granny's flat before she moved down to the suite. Most of what's here wasn't her choice either. My granddad's parents lived up here before he and Granny moved in.'

'And you and Raymond live here now?'

'Yes, since my granddad died. It makes life easy when you're in charge of running the hotel.'

'Where did you live before that?'

'We had a house of our own in Killmoy.' Máire steered Jane to the sofa. 'I think I know where those dungarees are. Hang on here while I look. You'll be swimming in them, but I'll find you a belt.' She was back within minutes, carrying a worn pair of denim dungarees, a sweater and a leather belt with a buckle. 'This'll probably go round you twice but, at least, it'll hold them on.' It turned out not to be quite as bad as predicted. The sweater was chunky, so it bulked out the denim, and, pulled to its last hole, the belt kept everything in place. Standing back to look at her, Máire said, 'Those were mine. It's ages since I wore them.'

'I'll try to keep them clean.'

'Don't bother. I can't imagine I'll ever wear them again.' Her phone rang and she took the call with a brief word of apology, turning away and frowning when she heard the voice in her ear. 'Slow down. What's the problem? ... No, that's perfectly fine. As long as the bunting's fixed to their own stalls ... Well, find whoever's organising them, and say they mustn't. Well ... What? ... Okay, grab her and put her on to me.' When the call ended, she smiled at Jane, who'd edged to the end of the sofa so it wouldn't seem like she was listening. 'Sorry about that. It's this Seedsavers thing in Reception. Someone was trying to string bunting from the chandeliers.'

'Do you need to rush down?'

'No, crisis averted. The woman who's organising the exhibition has things in hand.' Putting her phone in her pocket, Máire added, 'Raymond's not here. He must be down at the garage already. Are you okay to find it on your own?'

'Sure. I was there yesterday.'

'Were you? Oh, of course you were. I knew that. Run along, then. Have a good time.'

Chapter 22

Left alone, Máire stood still for a minute. Then she went to the kitchen, looked into each of the bedrooms, and put her head round both bathroom doors before going back and sitting on the sofa. It felt idiotic to double-check when she knew Raymond was out, but she badly needed to talk to him and was longing for a hug. All the same, having confirmed his absence, she felt a perverse surge of relief. There was so much to process.

The strangeness of what had happened last night when he'd paused before saying he loved her, the row with her mum, which had seemed to erupt out of nowhere, and the half-finished conversation in the parlour with Nora. It's all happening at once, she thought. Mum coming out with dire warnings about the state of my marriage the very morning after that strange hesitation of Ray's. Granny saying out of the blue that she wants me to be happy, as if there's some reason why I shouldn't be. Has Ray been talking to them? But why should he? If there's something the matter, why not discuss it with me?

Having asked herself the question, she realised she knew the answer. I'm busy all the time, she thought. Too busy to talk to Ray. Too busy even to think about whether or not I'm happy. Or perhaps I'm not thinking about that or talking to him because I'm afraid to. I know that I'm on a slippery slope, and the truth is that I'm exhausted. I'm qualified to do this job but Granny's right: it takes more than qualifications. Ray's been trying to tell me that too, but I haven't been listening to him. I keep thinking I'll reach a point at which there'll be time to stop and think. But instead I'm constantly fire-fighting, and feeling inadequate, and having to hide how I'm feeling. Mum's right too. I've allowed the stress of work to affect my relationship with Ray. And, as if that weren't enough, now I'm worried about Hen's marriage. She's a grown woman but she's still my little sister, and I can't bear to watch her confidence sapped by someone who loves her but just doesn't see what he's doing.

Groaning, Máire lay back against the sofa cushions and pressed the heels of her hands against her temples. She remembered driving past her own house on Christmas Eve and seeing the door swing open to let in a group of visitors. Beyond them in the hallway, glowing against the paintwork, a tall Christmas tree had been wreathed in strings of lights. Briefly, she'd glimpsed a little boy running downstairs to greet the arrivals, and now, with a lump in her throat, she recalled the storybook fireplace and the toy-box seats she'd preserved in the bedroom above the porch. She'd driven on, stabbed by a pang of envy, and now found herself overwhelmed by a longing to be back in her own home with Ray, coming in from work in the evenings, eating in the kitchen, and putting a child to bed in the room where storybook galleons sailed across the tiles on the cast-iron fireplace. Envy of her tenants' lifestyle was followed by such a wave of exhaustion that she was tempted to grab a break. But before she could put her feet up another text pinged in on her phone so she roused herself and went downstairs.

Reception was full of cheerful people repositioning green bunting. Making her way to her office, Máire saw Luke talking to a woman who was riffling through a pack of papers. The woman, who was wearing a Seedsavers badge, came forward with her hand out. 'I'm terribly sorry about the bunting on the chandeliers. I hope we've reorganised things as they should be.'

'Yes, they're fine. Sorry to fuss.'

'Not at all. Some of the volunteers can get over-enthusiastic. We should be ready for kick-off on time. Thank you for having us. There's huge public interest in environmental issues, so exhibiting somewhere with footfall like yours is important.' She held up the pack of papers. 'And, obviously, it's brilliant to showcase what's being done here too.'

Luke intervened quietly: 'It's what's been planned, rather than done. I just thought it might chime with your theme of investing in the future.'

Squinting at the pack's contents, Máire recognised graphics she'd repeatedly seen in Luke's management-meeting presentations. The fact that he'd chosen to share them with this comparative stranger felt like revenge for her own refusal to give them any attention, and though they weren't in any way commercially sensitive, Máire had an urge to snatch them from the woman's hand. Controlling it, she met Luke's eyes, asked, 'Do you have a minute?' and, having murmured good wishes for the success of the exhibition, steered him away towards her office.

Inside, with the door closed, she turned to face him. 'Did I know you were planning to share that information beyond the team?'

'If you did, it wasn't I who told you.'

Fresh from a morning of family tensions, Máire was finding it hard to relocate her work persona. She couldn't tell whether Luke's response was sarcastic, bored or deliberately offensive so, playing for time, she went and sat behind her desk, gesturing him to the chair that faced it. In recent management meetings, his style, which had been defensive, had begun to change to barely concealed anger. Now his manner was different, and she couldn't gauge how he was feeling. At the back of her mind, she'd known for months that she hadn't been treating him fairly and that, sooner or later, things would come to a head. But, oh, God, she thought, why did it have to be this particular weekend? I'm tired and confused about every damn aspect of my life, and the last thing I need is a professional blow-up.

Slumped in his chair, Luke looked as if he was past caring and, for a mad moment, she was tempted to tell him she felt much the same. The problem was that she'd got things wrong from the outset, and been too overwhelmed by other work pressures to put them right. Accustomed to her granddad's absolute confidence in Matty, she'd thought Castlehill's river and grounds must have been expertly managed and, determined not to ask for help, she'd conducted the interviews for Matty's replacement without seeking experienced advice. So she'd had no idea that someone as well-qualified as Luke would see Castlehill much as a doctor might view a patient suffering from decades of reckless misdiagnosis. She'd realised her mistake the first time he spoke at a management meeting, but the pressure of everything else to be done had allowed her to ignore it.

Now, distracted by her fears about Raymond, the row with her mum, and her interrupted conversation with Nora, she was in the worst possible state of mind to cope with work. But I must, she thought. I can't neglect my job because of the ghastly state of my personal life, especially when, as a manager, I've behaved disgracefully. Instead of addressing the consequences of my professional failure, I've been wishing one of my team would lose patience and go away. Well, unless I can come up with something to mend matters quickly, it looks like my wish is about to come true. And, oh, God, if it does, it'll only add to my problems. I can't run a hotel renowned for angling with no one to manage the river, and it stands to reason that if things were bad when Luke took over from Matty they won't have improved in the interim when nothing's been done to change them.

Luke was still expressionless at the other side of the desk. Having brought him to the office on a wave of unjustified indignation, Máire wondered if she ought to apologise for her tone, and suggest they have a formal meeting tomorrow. Prolonging the current conversation wasn't likely to help things, especially as he seemed as tired as she was. Or was it just tiredness? He looked drained, almost defeated, as if something had happened since she'd last seen him. Perhaps he'd reached breaking point and, if so, it was her fault. Or maybe he'd had a personal blow, in which case, as his employer, ought she to ask if he needed her support? Flinching at the thought of what his answer might be, Máire decided she had to say something, if only to break a silence, which, by now, felt unnaturally long.

'I didn't mean to sound snappy just now. I'm sorry if I did.'

'You didn't. It's fine.'

'Okay. Well, look. I've been thinking we ought to discuss your proposal.'

With a faint smile, Luke asked, 'Which of them had you in mind?'

'I mean your vision. For Castlehill. How you see things progressing in the future.'

'You want to discuss that now?'

'No. Well, obviously not. It's Sunday and, anyway, we should have a proper planning meeting. Say in a few days? How does that sound?'

Luke got to his feet abruptly. 'I'm afraid things have moved on.'

'How?'

'I'm not sure I have a vision for the future anymore.'

Confused, Máire said, 'Look, I know I've been less than receptive.'

'It's not about you.'

This response was so flat that Máire started to panic. 'Honestly, Luke, Castlehill's lucky to have you on board. I'd really like to sit down and understand what you've got in mind. I'm sure you feel you've been wasting your time …'

'Yeah, I reckon I have been.'

'And that's been my fault.'

'No, it's been mine. I should have had more sense than to stay here.'

Dismayed, Máire said, 'You're not thinking of leaving?'

'Yes, I am. As soon as I can. I was going to talk to you tomorrow but, since we're here, you might as well know now.'

'No, please, we need to discuss this ...'

'There's nothing to discuss. I've faced the fact that I've made an ass of myself, and this is the end of it.'

'But you haven't made an ass of yourself. I'm the one ...'

Luke's jaw clenched. 'Look, I'm sorry, I don't want to talk now. We can take this forward tomorrow, or whenever you want next week. Obviously, I'm not going to walk out and leave you in the lurch. But I've made up my mind, and I'm not going to change it, Máire. I won't be staying at Castlehill.'

The gloves Carolyn had given Jane were in a drawer in Jane's bedroom, so she went to pick them up before going to the garage. When she stepped out of the lift into Reception, the Second Chance Club group was milling around the Seedsavers stalls. Emer, the bouncy woman she'd encountered the previous day, gave a squeal when she recognised her. 'Well, look at you, all dressed up for the winter weather! Are you off for a walk?' One of the others poked Emer in the ribs. 'Leave the poor child alone, and don't be nosy.'

'I'm not nosy. I'm friendly. The child knows the difference. Don't you, love?'

A volunteer offered Jane a leaflet. She was about to refuse it when, seeing the headline, she stopped and asked, 'What's a seed bank?'

The volunteer, who was in his teens, leaned across the stall enthusiastically. 'It's absolutely brilliant. There's a seed-drying tunnel, and sorting and threshing areas. Seeds are dehumidified, packed and sealed, and there's a freezing facility and a lab.'

The thought that such things might happen hadn't occurred to Jane before. 'Where do the seeds come from?'

'They're gathered from native habitats. I think some other crowd do wildflowers, but I volunteer for this lot, and they're apple trees and veg.'

'And you give the seeds away?'

'It's to preserve endangered species.'

'Cool.'

One of the Second Chance ladies interrupted them to ask if he had any poinsettias. 'Mine always die after Christmas, but you keep buying them, don't you? It feels like a waste but Christmas wouldn't be Christmas without them.' The rest of her group turned on her in chorus.

'He does apples and vegetables. Poinsettias are flowers, aren't they?'

'Poinsettias aren't native to Ireland.'

'The whole poinsettias-at-Christmas thing is just makey-uppy. It began with a marketing campaign in America.'

Under cover of the cacophony, Jane nodded goodbye to the boy and slipped away through groups of guests that were chattering at the stalls. When she reached the main door, she saw Luke leave Máire's office. With his head bent and a set expression, he looked older and sterner than he'd appeared when Henrietta had introduced Jane to him on their arrival. Wondering if he'd recognise her, Jane hesitated, and before she could make up her mind to wave he was gone.

The temperature outside had dipped again. As Jane came out of the front door, she turned to look back at the hotel. Frost was gleaming on the granite walls of the main house, making it stand out from the newer wings that flanked it. Crows called loudly in the trees down by the river and, looking up, Jane remembered the ivy she'd seen in the photos in Nora's book. She wondered if small birds had nested against the speckled grey walls among dark green leaves and black berries. Birds that wove nests from wisps of grass and wool instead of the crows' lofty bundles of sticks. The kind that lived on insects you'd find in ivy. Maybe they kept away now that they'd lost its shelter. She'd asked Nora why she'd had the ivy removed from the walls, and been told the hotel looked smarter without it. 'It was shaggy, dirty-looking stuff, love. My father always cut it back if it started climbing the cowshed. Mind you, that was because my mother hated spiders.'

'Did cutting it back get rid of them?'

'I don't know if it did or it didn't. It made her feel better anyway.'

'Where would the spiders go if they couldn't live in the ivy?'

After a moment, Nora had thrown her head back and chortled. 'Into the cowshed, maybe. It had plenty of nooks and crannies.'

'But wouldn't that make matters worse for your mum?'

'I suppose it would have, if she'd thought about it.'

Now, thinking about it herself, it struck Jane as odd that, indoors, there was a big event about planting and growing while in the hotel grounds everything looked so barren.

Luke made for the side door and took the steps down the terraces, hardly noticing where he was going. That's it, he thought. It's all over, and I can't think why I ever thought things could possibly end differently. Anybody with sense would have known in his first few months in this job that taking it was a bad decision. And anyone but a lovesick ass would have faced up to the fact that Barbara didn't love him. But that was something I couldn't face, and there was so much I wanted to do here that badly needed doing. His own voice came back to him from a year ago, when he'd sat on the side of his bed in his cottage lacing his boots with Barbara lying beside him. *Wanting and needing are two different things, Barbara*, he'd told her. Now, standing on the terrace steps, he came to a realisation. I wasn't shutting down a discussion of my career, he thought. I'd found myself in love with her and was trying not to show it. I think that, from the moment we met, Barbara and I knew we'd end up in bed together. But she'd made it clear from the start that this was a weekend fling, so what must have kicked in as I laced my boots was self-preservation. I had no idea how she felt, and had hardly begun to realise my own feelings. All I knew was that I was going to get hurt or look stupid unless I kept things light and kept my distance. *Wanting and needing are two different things, Barbara.* I trotted out the same flippant line when she came to the cottage last year to say goodbye to me. It sparked the row that sent her off to Dublin in a rage, and left me even more bewildered. *Wanting and needing are two different things.* Not in my case. Not where she's concerned. I'd realised it then, and it freaked me so much that I couldn't handle it. I sure as hell know it now after a year of waiting and hoping, and failing in a job I should never have taken. And this weekend has proved that, though I can tell Barbara still wants me, it's evident she doesn't need me the way I need her. So, since Castlehill doesn't need me either, it's way past time I faced facts and moved on.

Chapter 23

Raymond was in the garage tinkering aimlessly with the Saab. He'd known Jane wouldn't appear until brunch was over, but hadn't wanted to be in the flat when Máire came upstairs. The idea that they were living on different sides of a pane of glass had taken hold of his mind and now troubled him almost as much as the memory of how she'd drawn away the previous night. Walking round the car to lift the bonnet, he told himself he had to snap out of this mood before Jane arrived. She was a child to whom he'd made a promise so, however little he felt like demonstrating the works of a turbocharger, that was where his focus needed to be this afternoon. Plus, for a while at least, it gave him a valid excuse for avoiding Máire – though the thought that he needed one made him feel sick.

Jane appeared round the door looking younger than yesterday because of her oversized sweater and dungarees. Automatically assuming coaching mode, Raymond smiled. 'Come on in, it's freezing out there.'

'Is it still okay to have a look at the engine? Máire lent me these things to wear so I wouldn't get mine dirty. Do you think I could give you a hand taking the turbocharger apart? If you have time, I mean. I don't want to be any trouble.'

'Of course I have time. You're not expected anywhere else, though?'

'No, I said this was what I wanted to do and Hen was fine about it. Mostly, we don't talk a lot. She fusses. But she's being different this weekend. Much less Percy Pig. I told her I was coming to look at the engine.'

Accustomed to talking to kids, Raymond ignored the Percy Pig reference and concentrated on the substance of what Jane had said. Good for Hen, he thought. She's actually listened to Barbara. He wondered if being away from home had made Henrietta and Jane more relaxed in each other's company. Maybe it all came down to balance. Jane had been physically distanced from her overprotective father and housed in circumstances that brought her closer to Henrietta, and, like tweaking an engine, the process had made everything work more smoothly.

Jane peered under the Saab's bonnet. 'What's the actual point of a turbocharger?'

'Efficiency. It increases the density of the air the engine draws in, so you get more power per engine cycle.'

'Cool.'

'I'll get it on to the bench and show you how it works. Then you can help me put it back together.'

'This is vintage, right? So are modern ones even more efficient?'

'Way more. There are always better versions of what you've got and, at the same time, new technologies take over. Sooner or later, I'm going to convert this car to electric.'

'How come you haven't done it yet?'

'Because, like I said, things are developing all the time. So I keep waiting for the right moment.'

Jane thought about this and said, 'But if things are constantly changing, there'll never be a right moment, will there? I mean, if you're waiting for the right moment, won't you just wait for ever?'

Bent double, with a wrench in his hand, Raymond hardly heard the question. 'Do you want to see this or not? Because, if you do, you need to stop talking.'

'Mostly, I don't talk much to grown-ups generally, not just Hen.'

'I'm flattered. Now, shut up while I lift this out.'

'Do we take it to the bench?'

'We do, and we'll be using oil degreaser when I get it there, so keep your distance.'

'I don't need to. My manicurist gave me plastic gloves, and Máire said she can't see herself wearing these dungarees again, so I'm totally sorted.'

For the next hour or so Raymond was focused on freeing recalcitrant bolts, replying to Jane's questions, and ensuring that her unpractised use of a hammer resulted neither in bruised fingers nor in damage to what she was hitting. When everything had been taken apart, discussed and reassembled, he returned the turbocharger to the car and reinstalled it. 'Thanks for your help.'

Bright-eyed and grubby, Jane flashed him a smile. 'I probably wasn't helpful. Thanks for showing me, though. That was brilliant.'

'No bother.'

'Do you know anything about dehumidifying seeds?'

'Seeds?'

'Heritage seeds. Of plants that might disappear if other kinds take over. There are stalls about it in Reception this morning. Have you seen them? It's a crowd called Seedsavers. They preserve native apple trees. Vegetables too. A volunteer told me. He says they dehumidify seeds, and freeze them, and they've a lab, so I guess they must analyse them.'

'I'm a bank manager, Jane. I don't know much about agriculture.'

'No, but it's interesting. The technology.' Jane removed her plastic gloves and inspected her manicure.

Wiping his own hands on a rag, Raymond asked, 'Did that survive?'

'Yup. Still silky-smooth and polished.'

'Would you like a cup of tea? I'd say I could rustle up a KitKat.'

'Here?'

'There's a kettle there behind the bench.'

'Okay. That'd be cool.'

Jane was perched on a stool drinking tea when she looked at him thoughtfully. 'On Friday, after we arrived, we had dinner in Nora's suite.'

'The first-night meal's a traditional part of the Sullivan Girls' Get-together.'

'I know. Hen told me. But the thing is, Nora said that if she had her time again, she'd make proper use of the land around the hotel. She'd raise animals and grow food and save a fortune in the kitchen.'

'Did she?'

'And it turned into a weird quiet fuss I didn't understand. Barbara wanted to talk about growing things and Máire didn't. Hen got worried, and everybody got iffy.'

Jane didn't seem troubled but, since she appeared eager to chat, Raymond asked, 'What happened then?'

'They realised I was there and changed the subject.'

'Sounds tricky.'

'Actually, I kind of staged a diversion. I don't like rows. Growing things here sounds like a good idea, though, doesn't it? I mean, they're your family, so I don't want to be rude, but it's all a bit empty.'

'It is a bit.'

'Nora's nice, isn't she?'

'She's a great old girl. I like her.'

'Me too.' Jane was picking up fallen flakes of chocolate with a licked finger. Concentrating on balancing them, she transferred them to her mouth. 'Yesterday, she told me she married into Castlehill. You did too, didn't you?'

'I suppose I did.'

'Hen married into my dad's house. Gan-Gan says she was lucky. I think it might have been more fun for her to have a new house, one she could do what she liked with. You and Máire had a house of your own, didn't you?'

'Did Hen tell you that?'

'Máire did. When we were up in the flat finding something for me to wear. She said you had a house in Killmoy. Did you sell it?'

Lifting his mug, Raymond swallowed his tea in a single gulp. 'No, it's still ours.'

'Will you go back and live there again?'

'To be honest, I don't know, Jane. We've been waiting for the right moment but, like you said, that's not sensible. Not when that could well mean waiting for ever.'

Having finished her tea, Jane asked if anything else needed doing. 'We probably got hand-prints all over the car. I could wash it if you like.'

'It doesn't need washing and, even if it did, it's far too cold for you to be outdoors sloshing water around.'

'I could clean up in here, if you've got a broom.'

Like the car, the garage was in spotless order but, seeing her eager face, Raymond said, 'If you want a job, you could take out the car mats and hoover the inside.'

'Okay.'

'You're sure you wouldn't prefer to be getting pampered up in the spa?'

'I'm not really into girly stuff like pampering.'

'I thought Hen told Máire you were looking forward to it.'

Jane shrugged. 'Well, you can't be rude, can you? Not when people are trying to be nice. Anyway, Hen couldn't come here this weekend without me, and she was all for coming.'

Throwing her a friendly grin Raymond went for the vacuum cleaner. 'You looked fairly girly at Hen's wedding.'

'That's how bridesmaids are supposed to look.'

'I know. I'm only teasing.'

'Anyway, sometimes it's easiest to wear whatever they give you.'

Leaving her to work out for herself how to remove the car mats, Raymond returned to the bench to gather the tools he'd used on the engine. The sound of the vacuum made further talk impossible so, once he'd tidied up, he poured himself more tea and watched Jane set about her task. Her borrowed dungarees had been bought for a trip he and Máire had made to Lisbon. They'd taken the Saab to Cherbourg and driven on through France and Spain, stopping along the way wherever they fancied. It was back in the day, before Martin's death, and they'd both saved up enough leave to take off a full week in high summer. In a way, Raymond thought, it was almost better than our honeymoon trip to Paris because we'd moved into our house by then and were full of plans for it. Everywhere we drove, Máire saw colours she wanted to capture and bring home to Killmoy. In fields full of wildflowers, and on glazed pots stacked by roadside stalls. On mosaics that inspired her choice of tiles for the kitchen. In yellow sunflowers, pink rosé, green jalapeño peppers, and that intense blue she used for the skirting boards in our stairwell because she'd admired it in some Portuguese guesthouse.

The depression that had lifted while he'd been showing the engine to Jane descended again on Raymond, like a blanket. I found the house, he thought, but it took Máire to make it a home. Looking back, he could see her eagle-eyed in a Spanish market, discovering precisely the right doorknob for a cupboard, and burrowing into piles of vibrant cotton in search of something perfect for cushion covers.

'Ray, look! The very thing! And, wow, that's a stunning platter!'

'We'll never fit all this into the boot.'

'Don't laugh. Of course we will. Let's have that tall jar as well. It's a brilliant match for the jug I got yesterday.'

She'd been so determined to travel light and make purchases on the way that they'd set out with almost no luggage. Raymond remembered her leaning in to snatch things out of his suitcase while he was packing.

'Nobody needs jackets and ties on a Mediterranean jaunt!'

'One jacket and one tie. What if we go to a restaurant?'

'Restaurants don't give a toss what you wear if you're bums on seats at a quiet time in the evening.'

So I spent the week in golf shirts and nondescript chinos, thought Raymond, while she contrived to look like a million dollars in those dungarees. Stripy T-shirts on sunny days, a hoodie on top when it rained. And, in the evenings, that filmy shirt with trailing sleeves and embroidery that made her look as if she'd stepped out of the latest issue of *Vogue*. On the last night of the trip, they'd booked dinner at a hotel restaurant where double doors next to their table had opened onto a little balcony. Máire's shirt, which was muslin, had a drawstring neck. He remembered how, when she'd leaned across the table to kiss him, a string of citrine beads had swung away from her tanned collarbone. Her hair had been piled on her head, and she'd smelt of sea-salt and honey. Looking at her, Raymond had felt his breath catch in his throat. It had still seemed almost impossible that at last he was sharing his life with someone he'd waited for doggedly since his teens. The meal had ended with cherry sorbet and coffee, and they'd taken glasses of local brandy on to the balcony. Leaning on the rail, Máire had looked out at the view of a shimmering lake and raised her glass in a toast. 'To the future.'

'And whatever it may bring.'

Laughing, she'd said, 'Oh, I think we know what that is. I'll be back at work next week. Shuffling rotas, smiling at guests, and stepping in at the last minute if somebody's cut their finger in the kitchen.'

'So much for romance.'

'Were you trying to be romantic? Oh, love, I'm sorry. It's been a brilliant trip and, actually, I can't wait to get home. I've a car jammed full of fabulous things, and a house waiting for them.'

'And there's more to the future than work.'

'Isn't that what I'm saying? You can rush home from arranging loans, I'll abandon the rotas, and we'll sit in empty rooms and imagine how we're going to fill them.'

And then Martin had died, Nora had handed her the hotel and all that might have happened didn't.

Now, with half an eye on Jane, Raymond remembered the nursery fireplace he and Máire had found in the house shortly after their trip. Tapping on the boxing, she'd said, 'Give me a hand,' and together they'd pulled away the plywood from the tarnished cast-iron surround and dusty tiles patterned with storybook galleons.

'Wow! Treasure trove, Ray! It's original, I think. This must have been a child's room for generations.'

Over the vacuum cleaner's whine, Jane called, 'Nearly finished.' It's weird, thought Raymond. Finding a bedroom used by generations of children felt huge yet when she'd restored it Máire moved on to finish the rest of the house, and we hardly mentioned the fireplace or the toy-boxes again. But, then, we didn't have time to. Martin died and our world turned upside down. Jane switched off the vacuum cleaner and called to him again: 'That leather polish we put on the seats yesterday works, doesn't it? It's like we gave them a luxury spa treatment.'

'It's certainly all looking shipshape now.'

'It didn't really need hoovering. I wish I could have washed it. A friend of mine at school does his mum's car for pocket money.'

'I'm sorry you couldn't, but I don't think I'd be forgiven if you ended this weekend with double pneumonia.'

Jane unplugged the vacuum cleaner and perched on her stool again. 'Time's gone really quickly. I want to take some photos in the grounds before it gets dark. Hen says we're having a final dinner with Nora tonight. And tomorrow I'll be in Dublin again.'

'Maybe, when you go home, you can be your family's official car-washer.'

'Dad has a service. Anyway, he'd be worse than you about me getting cold.'

'I meant you could do it when the weather's warmer.'

Jane shrugged. The resigned gesture made Raymond want to reach for his phone and call Henrietta. But giving unwanted advice was unlikely to help matters. Anyway, he thought, who am I to offer it? I may have had years of coaching kids but that's not the same as being a parent.

Sliding off the stool, Jane dusted her knees. 'Bye, then. I suppose I'll see you again this time next year.' She held out her hand and, as Raymond shook it, his thoughts went into overdrive. Was it possible that, this time next year, he'd still be messing about in this blasted garage? A coach, not a parent, a loser doing pointless things to the Saab, not facing up to the state of his life or his marriage? Why had he and Máire never talked about having kids? Was it something to do with how she'd grown up with an irresponsible father? The pressures of running Castlehill? A fear of not living up to Nora's expectations of her? Or could it be that what Máire feared was being tied to him for ever? For ages, she'd been reluctant to commit to marriage, and with no children to hold her it would be simple to walk away. Was that it? Did that explain why they'd never even discussed having a baby?

About to go, Jane turned back, oblivious to Raymond's panic. Her eyes were shining. 'No one would let me near Dad's car but you know something? Hen might let me clean hers when he's away on business. She's got one of her own, you know, like Máire has.'

'Máire?'

'Hasn't Máire got one? I thought she said so when we talked.' Wholly focused on summoning an accurate recollection, Jane gave him a brilliant smile. 'No, I know she did. She was chatting to me up in the flat when she looked for these clothes I'm wearing. I asked her if she drives the Saab, and she said she used to, but now she doesn't. She said she has her own car. She told me the Saab is your baby.'

Chapter 24

Barbara arrived for the rasul session to find Máire ahead of her, organising the choice of ambient music. 'God, Máire, do you never take a break?'

'If I hadn't checked, we'd be relaxing to "I Will Survive" played at full volume. The Second Chance crowd were in here this morning.'

'How are you feeling now?'

'Feeling? I'm fine.'

In fact, Máire was looking even more wretched than she'd been when they'd talked before brunch, and it seemed that by now she was regretting that hasty conversation. She hates to be seen to be vulnerable, thought Barbara. The more pressure she's under, the more she needs to keep people at arm's length. And I do understand that, maybe better than anyone. We've both got Mum's independent streak. Still, Máire can't go on like this much longer. Professionally, she needs to recalibrate her workload, and personally she's got to sit down and talk things through with Raymond. At that moment the door opened and one of the Second Chance ladies looked in. She was wrapped in one of the spa's towelling robes and carrying a huge straw beach-bag. 'Sorry to interrupt. I've a head on me like a sieve! We were just in there now, the lot of us, being pampered up to the hilt, and I think I left a scrunchie in the rasul chamber. It's no big deal, really, only my granddaughter made it for me. You wouldn't have seen it, would you?'

Máire gave her a bland, professional smile. 'The rasul chamber's been set up for the next session. If you see Shawna at the desk she'll have a look in lost property for you.'

'Ah, thanks a million. I'll do that. It matters when it's family, doesn't it? And come here to me now, I've seen your photo up on the board in Reception.' She beamed at Máire. 'You run the hotel, don't you? It's a gorgeous place you've got here. You must be very proud of it.'

'Thank you. I'm glad you're enjoying your stay.'

'And this must be your sister? I hear you've all come for your annual family weekend jaunt?'

The woman slung her bag on a bench and was evidently about to sit down for a gossip when, seeing Máire's face, Barbara intervened. 'Let me take you out and we'll see if Shawna can find your scrunchie.'

'What? Oh, right. Thanks very much. Do you work here too?'

'The desk's just through here. I'll be back in a minute, Máire.'

Impressed, the woman picked up her bag and clasped it to

her chest. 'Talk about service! I'm telling you, girls, you've a great place here altogether. Team work makes the dream work, doesn't it?'

When Barbara came back a few minutes later, Máire looked up from her playlist and said thanks.

'No problem. We found the scrunchie. In her bag.'

'Oh, God! Of course you did.' Though Máire still looked harassed, they exchanged a genuine grin and, feeling the moment for possibly unwelcome conversation had passed, Barbara returned to the subject of ambient music. 'What have you chosen?'

'Generic medieval flute. It's all I've got strength for.'

'That sounds a bit restrained for Granny.'

'Granny's decided not to come down.'

Having made the effort to attend specifically so as not to disappoint Nora, Barbara was taken aback. 'Is she okay?'

'She's feeling tired after brunch, so she's having a nap in her suite.'

'That's not like her.'

'You said you were tired yourself. How are you feeling now?'

Since Nora wouldn't be with them, Barbara was half inclined to double back on her own decision and sneak upstairs to her room. But that felt both cowardly and unkind to the others, so she said, 'Grand. Absolutely up for the mud-wrestling.'

'It's a relaxation chamber, Baba.'

'And that was a joke, Máire. Okay, I'm off to the lockers. It's no jewellery, no makeup, quick shower, then bathing suit under a robe. Is that right?'

'Yep. Mum and Hen are on their way down, and the session starts in ten minutes.'

They gathered in the chamber in their fluffy white robes and sat on padded cushions on the turquoise and silver benches. It was evident to Barbara that Máire and Sheila were doing their best to paper over the cracks of the row they'd had earlier. At least, she thought, I can be helpful by diluting the mix. In the determined atmosphere of goodwill, Sheila was being over-enthusiastic about the lighting when Henrietta's phone bleeped in her pocket. She reached for it guiltily. 'Sorry, everybody, I meant to put it on vibrate.' This produced an irritated chorus.

'Darling, there's a huge sign outside saying no mobile phones in the chamber.'

'I just thought Jane might need me.'

'Don't fuss. Raymond's looking after her.'

'I know, but ...'

Barbara rolled her eyes. 'Oh, Hen! Turn it off and put it out in your locker.'

Máire interrupted. 'No, don't. We need to get mud on before the steam starts. Just turn off the phone, Hen, and stick it somewhere in here.'

At that moment, the chamber filled with the sounds of parakeets and humming insects. Leaving her robe on her cushioned seat, Barbara went to where pottery bowls containing coloured muds were laid out on a bench. 'Come on, then, since Máire has us on a schedule.'

Máire bristled. 'I didn't say that.'

Sheila stood up authoritatively. 'She didn't, Baba. And stop squabbling, the lot of you. What's the grey mud for, Máire?'

'Exfoliation. You use it on your back, arms and legs. There's sea salt there to add to it, if you want to. The white mud's for the face and bust. There's a scalp one too. You massage it on with your fingers.'

'Okay. Bundle your phone up in your robe, Hen, and come and help me. I'm going to mix some salt in with my grey stuff.'

The jungle sounds dipped to a background murmur and, feeling shamefaced, Barbara called to Máire, 'I'll do your back if you'll do mine. We can cope with our busts individually.' With a reluctant laugh, Máire came to help her, while Henrietta and Sheila smoothed mud on the backs of each other's legs. The chamber was warm and the cool mud felt surprisingly soothing. Applying a silky grey layer to Máire's tense shoulders, Barbara told herself fiercely that she needed to treat the session as a new beginning. If she'd no choice but to move on, she might as well embrace the rasul idea of shedding the past and washing away toxins. Time to forget Luke since, clearly, he didn't want her. Time to re-embrace herself as an independent woman with a challenging job and a stunning home overlooking a vibrant city. And time to stop all the childish sparring with Máire, because if she and Ray were having difficulties in their marriage, she was going to need her sisters' support, not sarky comments. I feel as if I'll never get over Luke, she thought, but I must. It's pure indulgence to sit about making a fetish of my feelings. Broken hearts mend eventually and, even if they don't, people get on with life because they have to.

Up in her bedroom, Nora took off her pink skirt and jacket, eased her feet out of her shoes and went to lie down for a little. She needed to think. Sitting on the edge of the bed, she reached up to undo her pearls, then muttered an unladylike curse when the clasp proved too much for her arthritic fingers. Defeated, she fell back against her pillows, wincing at the sharp pain that shot through her hip. Her doctor, who was young and kind, had recently prescribed new doses of anti-inflammatories and told her she mustn't hesitate to use painkillers if she needed to. 'I bet you hold back and think you can soldier on without them. My grandmother's just the same – I'm always having to scold her. We can't cure old age or arthritis, I say, but there's no need for you to be in pain. Take those paracetamols, now, if you find you're not comfortable. I don't want you overdosing on them, but the odd time won't hurt if you're having an arthritis flare.' Nora had wondered grimly what his granny thought of that. No doubt, like herself, the poor woman kept her mouth shut and preserved her energy to battle her constant state of discomfort, which, at any minute, might turn from a few aches and twinges to agony.

The jagged pain in Nora's hip had subsided, but the pillows against which she'd fallen were now bunched behind her back, making her neck and left shoulder ache. She lay still, trying to work out how to reposition herself. I'm like a beached porpoise, she thought. A porpoise in a string of expensive pearls. Knowing better than to risk taking her weight on her hands, she rocked to and fro on her back, inching her way across the bed, until her shoulders and pelvis were better aligned. Once settled, she realised how exhausted the effort had made her. The trouble with having a gathering once a year, she thought, is the way it demonstrates how time has moved on. This time last year, I wouldn't have needed a lie-down after eating brunch in a fireside chair. I had better health twelve months ago, and I slept eight hours a night. I didn't realise then that, despite medicine doing its best for me, I'd increasingly be fighting a losing battle. I think the most exhausting thing is fending off enquiries when there's nothing to do but say I'm fine, or grand but could be better, and change the subject as briskly as I can. It comes to us all, I suppose, if we're still overground at my age, but that doesn't change the fact that it takes you by surprise.

Closing her eyes, she wondered about having a paracetamol, but the effort of getting back on her feet and into the bathroom to find one felt too great. Anyway, the warmth of the duvet she'd pulled across her legs was soothing. Better to stay where she was, let her ageing body recover and, in the meantime, face up to something she'd been refusing to face for far too long.

Martin had died without leaving a will, which, as Nora had told herself later, was absolutely typical of his laziness. When she'd found out how things stood, she could almost hear him say, 'Ah, what matter? If I die first, all I have will come to you anyway, will or no will.' Which was true. Though Martin was lazy, he'd been no fool.

He'd known that, if he did nothing, she'd be his heir by default, as his widow. What she hadn't known was how much his estate would be worth. There wasn't a penny that came in or out of the business that she couldn't account for without even looking at her books. But the capital value of Castlehill was beyond her expectations, and she hadn't known the extent of Martin's family's investments, or what he'd inherited from his unmarried sister and his aunts. When probate was granted and she'd paid the costs of his lavish funeral, she'd looked in amazement at the sum she was left with, and told herself she needed advice before making a will of her own. So she'd turned to Raymond.

He'd dropped in to see her one morning not long after he and Máire had moved to the flat. 'How are you doing today? Can I get you something in town?'

'Not at all. I'm grand. I'll walk down there myself later.'

'And you're really sure you're comfortable here in the suite?'

'I'm sound as a pound. Come here to me, Raymond, do you have a minute? I want to ask you something.'

'Of course.' He'd sat on the sofa and looked at her kindly. 'What can I do for you?' But then, when she'd talked to him, his expression had stiffened. 'God, Nora, I'm sorry, but I'm not the one to help you.'

'Why not? Don't you spend your whole life dealing with people's money? And you're family, Raymond. Who better to give me advice?'

'That's the thing, though. It wouldn't be appropriate.'

'What wouldn't?'

'You need a solicitor, Nora.'

'Don't I know I do? I'm not stupid. It's because I'm not stupid I'm making no appointment with a lawyer till I've got things straight in my own mind first.'

'But you must see that I can't advise you. Máire's your granddaughter so, if you're making a will, she'll presumably be a beneficiary and, if that's the case, as her husband, so will I. Don't you see the problem, Nora? I'm a bank manager with professional standards to think about. What would be said, in the circumstances, if word got around that I talked to you about how to leave your money?'

'Ah, for God's sake! It's me that's sat you down and started the conversation.'

Leaning back, he'd shaken his head at her. 'But you can see yourself that it won't do, can't you, Nora?'

She could. She was even slightly shocked that she hadn't seen it sooner. Raymond had gone away saying she'd do well to take her time, have a think, and call the Sullivan family solicitor when she'd a mind to. But she'd never liked old James Carney, who was pompous and patronising, and she'd no idea which of Killmoy's other law firms to approach. She'd known that Raymond with his sense of professional probity wouldn't mention their conversation to anyone, even Máire. So, unsure of what to do next, she'd done nothing. Now, lying in bed, she told herself sardonically that the failure to act she'd felt guilty about had saved her a heap of money. James Carney wasn't a man to redraw a will without charging a pretty penny, and, back then, she'd have drafted hers based on a set of assumptions that this weekend was rapidly overturning.

I've never been one to dodge a painful fact, she thought, and I'm not going to start now. If handing the reins to Máire has been the wrong decision, I'll have to revise my plans for the future of Castlehill.

The jungle sounds had changed to flute music, and Máire was holding out a bowl of mud to Henrietta. 'This is the facial kind. The scent is nectarine and honey.' A waft of fragrance rose from the bowl, and Sheila called from a nearby bench, 'Try it, Hen. There's a version here for a scalp massage too, the same scent but a different texture.'

Henrietta, whose arms, legs and back were now charcoal grey, shot a glance at the robe she'd bundled up round her mobile phone. Noticing it, Máire gave her a push. 'See, this is why guests are asked not to bring phones into the chamber.'

'I'm sorry. I'm just worried about Jane.'

'It's that call you had with Stuart this morning, isn't it? Honestly, Hen, the man's obsessed with surveillance.'

'That's not fair.' Henrietta stood up, grabbed the robe and clutched it to her chest. 'It's not surveillance. He just wouldn't like the thought that Jane can't reach me. And I don't like it either so, I'm sorry, but I'm going outside to call her.'

'But you can't ...'

'Darling, don't be silly ...'

'Wait until after the steam bath and the rain shower happen. You can't walk out now, covered in mud.'

'I can. I'll shower out at the lockers. Jane might have been texting me. I can't relax till I know.'

The chorus began again, but Máire took the robe and held it ready for Henrietta to put her arms into the sleeves. 'All right, then. Get a move on or you'll be dripping as well as dark grey.'

'I don't want the robe to get covered in mud.'

'Well, you can't go wandering round the spa without it.'

'But ...'

'Forget the robe, they go straight into the laundry after a session. Come on, Hen, get it on and get out, if you're going.' Henrietta looked around at her family's mud-covered faces, sure they were all cross with her but unable to see their expressions. Stifling a sob, she let Máire hustle into the robe and, wrapping it round herself, checked to be sure that her phone was in the pocket. 'I didn't mean to spoil things ...'

Another chorus answered her.

'Oh, Hen, stop.'

'Don't worry.'

'Go on, we'll see you later.'

Feeling like Eve ejected from a turquoise and silver paradise, Henrietta stumbled out, heard the door close behind her, and fled down the corridor to the lockers. Several Second Chance Club ladies turned their heads as she passed, and an elderly guest being taken to a massage room in a wheelchair tutted at the sight of her charcoal-coloured legs and feet. Luckily, the locker room was deserted so, once in the shower, she calmed down and found she could easily wash the mud off her body. For a panicky moment, she feared it would form a layer of dark grit in the shower tray, but it swirled away in seconds and she stepped out in relief, furling herself in a towel and reaching for her phone. A passing member of staff murmured, 'Could you wait till you're outside, please?' so she had to struggle into her clothes and go through to Reception.

She found a quiet corner where she leaned against a wall and, as soon as the screen lit up, saw a missed text from Jane. Without waiting to read it, she called the number. 'Jane? It's me. Are you okay? Has something happened?'

'No. Nothing. Where are you calling from? They don't allow phones in the spa, do they?'

Feeling foolish, Henrietta sat down on a red velvet banquette. 'No. I'm not in the spa. The others are. I left early.'

'Didn't you like the rasul chamber?'

'It was fine. It was lovely. No, I just ... Why did you text me?'

'I thought you'd like to know where I am.'

'What do you mean? Where are you? Aren't you with Raymond?'

'I was. It was brilliant. Hen, is everything okay?'

Aware that she must sound hyper, Henrietta said, 'Everything's grand.' Then, having controlled her voice, she asked, 'But where are you now?'

'I wanted to get some photos in the grounds while it's still light. Shots of how things are now, to compare with the photos I showed you in Nora's book. Remember?'

Henrietta's heart, which had been thumping, began to slow down.

'Yes, of course. Of course I remember you showing me. That's a good idea.'

'So I'll be a while. Is that okay?'

'As long as you're indoors before dark.'

'That's what Raymond said too. I would have come in anyway without either of you fussing.'

'Okay. Good. Enjoy yourself. I'll see you later. And, Jane ...'

'Yes?'

'Sorry I interrupted you. I should have read your text before I called.'

'That's okay. Bye.'

Henrietta slumped against the banquette, wishing she'd stayed with the others and not made a mountain out of a molehill. Obviously, Raymond would have made sure that Jane was okay, and Jane had even had the sense to text her. On the other hand, she thought, my phone *was* off, so if anything bad *had* happened I might not have known till it was too late. This is what comes of being too tense to think things through properly. Máire's right. When it comes to Jane, I let Stuart make me too anxious.

Putting her phone into her bag, Henrietta got to her feet realising she now had time to kill and nothing to fill it. Over near the reception desk, the Seedsavers exhibition was thronged with hotel guests and locals. She was going to wander over to a stall and have a look, when it struck her that what she really wanted was recovery time with a large vodka and tonic. Jane was safe, Stuart was focused on his work in Turin, and tomorrow she'd be back in her Dublin kitchen, facing the frozen remnants of her Christmas turkey. But now, hitching her bag on to her shoulder, she threaded her way through the milling crowds around the stalls in Reception towards the double doors that led to Castlehill's welcoming bar.

In the rasul chamber the steam had produced a dreamy ambience, and Sheila, Barbara and Máire were feeling mellow. Alone together for the first time that weekend without either Henrietta or Nora, their conversation turned to Sheila's divorce.

'It's crazy to think you went through it all without saying a word to us.'

'If I'm honest, I hadn't the energy, darling. Your dad made things so difficult that all I could do was plod on, putting one weary foot in front of the other.'

'We could have been supportive.'

'You'd have wanted to be, Barbara, but I couldn't count on it. And there just wasn't room on my camel's back for yet another straw.'

'Wow. That's a bit harsh.'

'She's right, though, isn't she, Baba? You'd have been full of pompous advice, and I'd have wanted to find Dad and strangle him.'

'I'm never pompous.'

'Oh, please! You're always being the sophisticated, high-flying, eco-supremo.'

Barbara glared. 'I'm so not.'

'You so are. With your jobs abroad and your laid-back sexy relationships. Isn't she, Mum?'

Sheila laughed. 'And this, m'lud, is why I felt I had to conserve my energy.'

Chuckling, Barbara said, 'Fair comment. Plus, I guess you couldn't have told us and not Granny.'

'That didn't necessarily follow.' Sheila ran her hands through her hair, and breathed in the scent of honey. 'I do still have to tell her, though, and I'm absolutely dreading it.'

'So who are you going to break it to first? Granny or Henrietta?'

'Darling, I don't know. I can't bear to think of it. Couldn't we just sit here in steamy laziness for ever?'

Barbara stretched out her foot and gave her a reassuring push. 'You've just got to go for it, Mum, and get it over with. You'll survive.'

At that moment the flute music switched back to jungle sounds, the domed roof of the chamber glittered with pinprick stars, and warm water descended, like a sudden tropical shower. The pleasurable shock was so great that all three of them burst out laughing. It was the first completely stress-free moment they'd had together in years, and, suddenly, as the water continued to rain down from above, Sheila gathered them all into a spontaneous hug. 'I survived your dad, didn't I? Just call me Gloria Sullivan Gaynor!'

'You've changed your name back to Sullivan?'

'It felt like the final step. You don't mind, do you, darlings?'

Unable to hear above the jungle noises, Barbara yelled, 'What?' Then, as they mouthed at each other, she shook her head, laughing. 'I can't hear a damn thing! Never mind, Mum, it doesn't matter.'

The partially dried coloured muds had begun to liquefy and, freed from their masks, they could see each other's expressions. Elated, Sheila loosened her grip on her daughters' slippery shoulders and, still laughing, they joined hands and formed a circle. With mud streaming down their bodies, they raised their faces to the stars and, to their amazement, found themselves stamping on the glittering tiles, shouting, 'Hey, hey,' and singing Gloria Gaynor's defiant chorus.

Chapter 25

The lunchtime crowd had left the bar, a waiter was clearing tables and the musicians in the corner had begun their final medley of polkas and reels. Henrietta chose a stool at the long, polished mahogany counter, dropped her bag on to the floor and smiled at the barman. 'How's it going, Des?'

'Game ball. We had a full house for lunch. It's the music brings them in. Are you here for a bite yourself? I'd say there's soup left.'

'Nope. I'm here for a vodka and tonic. Plenty of ice and lemon.'

'No marshmallows?'

'Just the hard stuff.'

'That's a grand little girl you have there. It was nice to meet her.'

'You've certainly made her welcome.'

'Ah, you can't give a child hot chocolate without adding extra marshmallows.'

'I remember you saying that to me when I was her age.'

Des put the drink on a coaster and Henrietta sipped it gratefully. 'God, that's good.'

'I thought you were all due to be down in the spa this afternoon.'

'We were. Well, Jane wasn't. I went down for a while but I've left the others to it. Granny wasn't there either. She said she was tired.'

'She's a ball of energy, is Mrs Sullivan. In fairness, though, she's getting on. I'd say she might want a lie-down after having prosecco with brunch.'

'I'm not sure she drank that much.' Henrietta sighed. 'She is getting older, isn't she, Des? It hits home when you haven't seen her for a while.'

'Ah, sure, we're none of us getting any younger. There's times I look at your sister and think, That woman's my employer and I remember her first day washing glasses behind this bar.'

'Do you really?'

'Sure, I was working at Castlehill before you were even born, girl. When your sisters would be above in the flat, being minded.'

'Were you here when my mum lived here?'

'Ah, I wouldn't go back that far. I'd see her out in the grounds, though, waiting to come and pick up your sisters.' Putting down the cloth he was using to polish the taps, Des leaned on the bar. 'You were never here as much as they were.'

'I was born after Mum moved to Athlone. That's the difference. I've always loved visiting, though.'

'But you never fancied a job here.'

'I never thought of it, really. I don't think I'm cut out for hotel work.'

'Not everyone is. Mind you, it takes all sorts of skills to make a place as big as this turn a profit. Take for example, we'd have great-quality food here but, like I say, it's the music that brings the lunchtime crowd in on Sundays.'

Henrietta looked across to where the group of musicians was seated around a table under her grandfather's portrait. Having played their medley, they were now finishing pints and cups of tea, putting instruments back into cases, and considering sandwiches. One of the waiters hovered, waiting to take their order, while people who'd stayed to hear the last of the music had begun to leave. Unaccustomed to vodka on top of prosecco, Henrietta decided to have a sandwich too. Des served it to her at a table by a window, where she sat looking out at the view, feeling the morning's tensions recede.

Jane appeared on the terrace below, bundled up in Máire's chunky sweater and dungarees, looking the picture of concentration as she lined up shots on her phone. Henrietta watched her fondly. At her age, I loved coming here, she thought, but visits were all about party frocks, attention and extra marshmallows. I hardly noticed the building or the photos on the walls. Granny's right about Jane being an onlooker. And there's a stillness about her she definitely didn't get from Stuart. I wonder if she inherited it from her mother. Perhaps that relationship was an attraction of opposite types. This train of thought felt almost like eavesdropping on Stuart's first marriage. I can't help it, though, thought Henrietta, because this is stuff I should have considered before. When Stuart proposed, I imagined I could be a big sister to Jane. I suppose I liked the idea because I rather fancied the role. Anyone might, after being the baby of her own family. But the role of a parent is different. I ought to have known that. So should Stuart.

On the terrace, childish in the adult outfit that swamped her, Jane hunkered down to change her perspective on the façade of the house. A cold feeling gripped Henrietta, deeper and more penetrating than her usual state of nervous anxiety. She looks so alone, she thought. A tiny figure in a huge landscape that might swallow her if I blinked or glanced away. I wish she wasn't so clever. I wish I could make Stuart shut up and listen. I wish I knew why at times I feel I understand her completely when, at others, I feel I've nothing to offer that she could need.

Taking a large gulp of vodka and tonic, Henrietta stared out of the huge picture window, realising none of this would have occurred to her if Stuart hadn't insisted that Jane come with her to Castlehill. When I get home we're going to have to make changes, she thought, and it'll be difficult and complicated. Jane needs the freedom to be a child in her childhood but, equally, Stuart has to back off and give her space to grow up. It won't be long before she spreads her wings as an adolescent and, if he tries to clip them, she'll resent it. The trouble is he's so used to living in fear that he thinks it's normal. He may even feel he deserves the nightmares he has when he goes abroad and, if that's how he feels, he's got to face and get past it. He shouldn't feel he has to atone for what happened when his wife died. It's harming Jane, and burying his trauma isn't good for him either. I've always felt it's not my place to trespass on their past but, for all our sakes, I'm going to have to start the conversation. Turning from the window, Henrietta picked up her sandwich. Máire's wrong about one thing, though, she thought decisively. I don't just need to grow a spine if I'm going to stand up to Stuart. I also need to step up to the mark and be a real mum to Jane.

Boosted by the chorus of 'I Will Survive', Sheila walked down the corridor to Nora's suite. The girls are right, she thought. All I need to do is focus. In the door, tell her about the divorce and get back out again. Keep it civil and light-hearted, just like Barbara said, and remember Máire's advice about not getting sidetracked. Reaching the door, she took a deep breath and knocked. Belted tightly into her paisley dressing-gown, Nora was sitting on the sofa. She still had her pearls around her neck.

'Will it disturb you if I come in? Máire said you were feeling tired.'

'Not in the least. I was lying down, but I fancied a cup of tea, so I got up. There's a second cup over there if you'd like to join me.'

Accepting the tea, Sheila sat down and said they'd missed her in the rasul chamber.

'I doubt that.'

Determined not to be sidetracked, Sheila laughed. 'I was a bit unsure about it, but it turned out to be fun. The truth is, I haven't seen enough of the girls for the past while. That's why I'm glad you keep having the get-togethers.'

Nora put down the *RTÉ Guide* she'd been holding on her knee, and looked at Sheila over her glasses. 'I've often wondered why you keep turning up to them yourself.'

'Come on, Mam, that's not fair.'

'No, I suppose it isn't.' Getting no response to this, Nora indicated the biscuit barrel that stood on the console table with the tea-making paraphernalia. 'There's fig-rolls there, if you want one.'

'Gosh, I remember that biscuit barrel. It was Dad's mum's, wasn't it?'

'I'd say it probably was. It was in the flat when I married him.'

This wasn't the conversation Sheila had come for, but she felt she'd been given an opening it would be cowardly to miss. 'It's strange to think Máire's living there now. Actually, Mam, I've been wondering about that.'

'Have you, now?'

'Yes. Well, I've been asking myself how she felt about moving in. I mean, when Dad died, she and Raymond had just got their own home completed. I know it makes sense to live here when you're running the place. But still ...' Glancing sideways at Nora's rigid figure, Sheila thought miserably, *This is getting me nowhere*, and then *Shit, why didn't I focus? I keep starting down the wrong roads this weekend.*

To her surprise, Nora set down her teacup and turned to face her. 'Your dad spent money like water when it suited him, you know. When he and I married, I had the notion I'd redesign the flat, but he'd grown up there and he was happy with it. I put my foot down about the kitchen but, otherwise, I was snookered. After all, I was the one who was always preaching economy.'

'Didn't you like it as it was?'

'Nobody asked my opinion. There was nothing wrong with it, anyway. Everything was well-made and expensive.' Grim-faced, Nora added. 'You never liked it. But it was you I was saving money for.'

Looking down at her hands, Sheila said, 'I do know that. I didn't at the time, but I realised it after I'd had Máire. The thing is, I don't think I've got much imagination. I have to live through something myself before I understand it.'

'Aye, well. We're all as God makes us.'

'I don't think he made me much use as a mother.'

'Ah, sure I spent years being told I was a useless wife.'

Surprised, Sheila said, 'Really? Who said so?'

'I wasn't good enough for your father's family. Mind you, my family didn't think much of his either. It wasn't an easy row to hoe.'

'But what did Dad's family have against you?'

Nora made a dismissive gesture and, when Sheila persisted, said she supposed she hadn't come from good enough stock.

'But that's pathetic, Mam! Who the hell were the Sullivans, anyway?'

'That's what my father said. Leave it be, now. I don't want to go raking up the past.'

'It was a good marriage, though. I remember the two of you as a team.'

'Do you? That's what Martin used to call us. I can't say I remember him pulling his weight.'

In the awkward silence that followed, Sheila decided it was time to get the conversation back on track. 'I didn't know what marriage to Finbar was going to be like.'

'I did.'

'I know you did. You made that abundantly clear, both before and after the event.'

Here was the opening Sheila needed to lead to the divorce. She opened her mouth again but, taking off her glasses, Nora forestalled her. 'I've been thinking about your father a lot this weekend. He was lazy, you know, and he wasn't always the easiest man to live with. But now and again, when he'd see me about to make a stupid mistake, he'd take the trouble to step in and stop me.'

'I didn't know that.'

'Well, you wouldn't. I'm not in the habit of admitting I make stupid mistakes.' Lifting her teacup, Nora emitted a faint chuckle. 'I'm not in the habit of making them either. But speaking my mind too loudly about your Finbar wasn't clever.'

Sidetracked again, Sheila asked, 'Did Dad say you shouldn't?'

'Do you know what it is, I can't recall. If he did, I wasn't listening. He stopped me making the same mistake with Máire, though, when I was scared to death that she'd miss her chance of marrying Raymond.'

'Is that how you felt? Me too. I was dreadfully worried. But I knew if I opened my mouth she'd bolt or do something equally stupid.'

'Like you did?'

Right, thought Sheila, this is where we focus on what I've come for. 'Are you asking me to admit that I was a fool to marry Finbar? We both know it's true, so I might as well give you the satisfaction.'

Nora raised an eyebrow. 'How well you've kept your beak shut till I'd make my own admission.'

'Well, I've said it now.'

'You haven't.'

'God, Mam, you're a hard woman.' Abandoning all idea of focus, Sheila put down her teacup. 'Look, there's something far more important that I ought to have said years ago. I don't think I was ever going to want to inherit the business, but I should have had the grace to sit down and talk to you about it. Maybe it was lack of imagination again. I don't know. Anyway, I'm sorry.' In the silence that followed, her mind screamed, *Christ! What kind of can of worms have I opened?* Nothing happened for what felt like hours.

Then, turning her head away, Nora reached out her hand. 'It's all right, child. Isn't it history at this stage?'

This was the last thing Sheila had expected but, unable to let the elusive cue pass, she heard herself saying, 'So's my marriage.'

'What?' Nora's head jerked around and her eyebrows flew up to her hairline.

Grasping the outstretched hand, Sheila said, 'I'm divorced, Mam.' Inside her, decades of anger, regret and resentment were dissolving, and astonished relief was expanding like a watered flower. At the same time – because nothing in life is ever simple – the forefront of her mind was taking unholy pleasure in the look of amazement on Nora's face.

In the bar, Henrietta had moved back to her seat at the counter where Des was deep in reminiscence again. 'I'd say, now, I'd be around the same age as your mother. Maybe a few years older – my retirement's coming up soon. I've seen a fair few changes here over the years, I can tell you. Back in Mrs Sullivan's time, we didn't have different departments. A management system, you know? Or all the rotas up on computers. Basically, it used to be indoor staff, outdoor staff, kitchen, bar and restaurant, Housekeeping and Reception. And all the rotas in Mrs Sullivan's head. She was a wonder. It was flowers on every table, leap to your feet when she entered a room, and God help the poor bar staff if the glasses weren't polished.' Holding one up, he revolved a tea-towel inside it briskly. 'I'm not saying standards have fallen. Not a bit of it. Your sister's as much of a stickler as your granny ever was. And, of course, in those days, it was your granddad looked after the angling side. We'd have fewer fishing parties now, and more coming into the spa. When you girls were young, there used to be lads hired in to give Matty a hand in the grounds and on the river.'

'I don't remember much about Matty.'

'No? Well, you wouldn't have seen a lot of him, I imagine.'

'I think he used to let Máire and Barbara drive the ride-on mower.'

'He had that cottage down by the river. The one Luke Ryan, the grounds manager fellow, has now. There's an example for you. We've a crowd of managers, these days.'

'So, are you the bar manager now?'

'I am not. I'm a barman, plain and simple. I don't need a fancy title. I'm not complaining either, I'm just saying things change and move on.' Returning the glass to its place on a shelf, he winked at Henrietta. 'And that's a sign of old age, if you like. Looking back through rose-tinted specs.'

He moved away to polish a tap, and, swivelling on her stool, Henrietta looked round the room, which was now nearly empty. An elderly local was reading a newspaper at a distant table, a coffee cup at his elbow and Sunday supplements scattered on the floor around him. Kneeling on an upholstered bench, a Second Chance Club member was trying to read the caption of a photo that hung on the wall. There were still coats and instrument cases on the chairs at the musicians' table, but the players had disappeared, presumably to go to the loo before leaving.

As Henrietta watched, a man came through the double doors, letting them swing to behind him. He took in the instrument cases and, wandering over to the table, idly reached a violin that lay between a glass and an empty plate. Hearing the twang as he plucked a string, Henrietta winced, wondering how the musician would feel at the thought of a stranger picking up his fiddle. The man, who was wearing an anorak, laid the instrument down carelessly, and made for the bar, unzipping his jacket and pushing back its hood. Under the lights above the bar, his thinning hair gleamed as, hitching himself on to a stool, he leaned forward and clapped Des on the shoulder. 'I see you've still got the old dyedly-eyedly shit on a Sunday? Throw me out a pint, there, Des. My stomach thinks my throat's cut.'

Hardly able to believe her eyes, Henrietta stood up and walked towards him. 'Dad?'

He turned, his blue eyes widening in recognition, and his face broke into a charming smile. 'If it isn't my golden girl! Talk about timing! Make that pint a whiskey, Des. She can buy a drink for her daddy.'

Chapter 26

Before leaving the garage, Jane had explained to Raymond why she wanted photos of the hotel. 'You know all those things in frames that are up on the walls in the bar? Posters and old pictures and photographs? Well, Nora gave me a book that's a kind of history of Castlehill. Some of the pictures in it are the same as the ones in the frames. You can see how things changed as time went on. Like people using cars instead of horses. And how the old house got extended. Nora did some of that.'

'So did Máire.'

'Really?'

'She did the new spa building. I don't mean she designed it, but she oversaw the project. It's almost entirely carbon-neutral.'

'See, I think all that's really interesting. So, I thought if I took photos of how the place looks now, my dad and I could compare them with the pictures in the book.'

'Is your dad into history, then?'

'He's never talked about it. But anyone would be interested, don't you think, if they saw a kind of Then and Now exhibition? I was thinking I could print out the photos and mount them on boards, like you'd see in a museum.'

'He takes you to museums?'

'No, mostly to artisan restaurants. But I went with my class at school to a brilliant place called the Dead Museum – all stuffed animals, and insects pinned to boards. I mean, there's got to be better ways of studying nature than killing things, but this was all done in the old days when they were into taxidermy. I wouldn't mind going again. And I want to go back to London. There's a science museum over there that's world-class. Have you ever been? '

'Not to the science museum. I've been to London, though.'

'Gan-Gan took me there to see *Disney On Ice*.'

'Was it good?'

'It was okay.' Jane had produced her phone and held it out to him. 'This is new. I've hardly used the camera. Dad buys my phones. He's always upgrading them.'

'That's a pretty high-end phone, the camera should be fine. But you'd better run if you don't want to lose the daylight.'

'Do you know about photography?'

'A bit. Go on, get moving, or you'll end up with half an exhibition. And make sure you're indoors before it gets dark, okay? No hanging round to experiment with flash photography.'

'As if I would.'

'I bet you would.'

'Would my phone be up to it?'

'Do as you're told, and no messing.'

She'd flashed him a grin, said, 'Okay, I will,' and disappeared round the door before looking back to thank him again for showing her the engine.

Left alone, Raymond had put the car-cover over the Saab, which, being indoors, it didn't need. He'd only met Stuart once, at Henrietta's wedding, when he'd registered him as a nice enough guy who was clearly smitten by Hen. Now his depression, which had lifted while Jane was in the garage, came back with a new focus. How could a man with a daughter like that fail to appreciate her? Couldn't Stuart see how stupid it was to take a child over to London without asking what she'd like to do there? And how could he not realise she'd be happier cleaning his car than being taken for meals in artisan restaurants?

Slumping on a stool by his workbench, Raymond gritted his teeth. Ever since Máire had turned her back on him the previous night, he'd felt that his world was steadily unravelling. Now he remembered a noisy GAA party held in a pub in Killmoy to celebrate the birth of his friend Jim's first set of twins. They'd all been waving pints and singing 'The Westmeath Bachelor', and someone had roared, 'You're rearing a team there, Jim-boy! They'll be playing for the county before you know it.' Lurching across the bar, Jim had hooked his arm cheerfully round Raymond's neck. 'If they're coached by Raymond, they won't stop at that! They'll be off playing internationals!' This had produced cheers and a round of raucous toasts to Raymond.

'They will, by God! No better man for getting the very best out of a lad.'

'Or a girl, either. We'd have no minor girls playing for Killmoy if it wasn't for Raymond.'

'It's a talent. A rare talent. Bringing up the next generation.'

The chorus had been interrupted by a group of younger men attempting to hoist Jim on to their shoulders. Recalling the good-natured scuffle, Raymond remembered looking on and punching his fist in the air with the others. The twins were now in one of the groups he coached on Wednesday evenings, clumsy, bullet-headed lads with feet already almost as big as their father's. They'd never play for the county, much less for Ireland. But Jim doesn't give a damn about that, thought Raymond. He's unstoppable. He'll drive them halfway across Ireland to watch some match they're excited about, just as he'll make a big fuss about his other kids' wonky pottery, and work himself into the ground to pay for the clay and the paint and the overpriced official jerseys, and all the shoes for all those growing feet. That's what I want.

I want to watch my own kids grow, and throw themselves into things and make mistakes and discoveries. I don't want to rear a team, like Jim, but I do want to be a father. And not a distant one, like Stuart. I want to be involved. People go on about how, if you're a woman, your biological clock is always ticking. Nobody seems to think that a man might feel the same. But it's how I feel. Knowing that, theoretically, you could still have kids when you're ninety isn't the point. Not if you want to be part of a child's life when they're growing up. I know the energy kids demand. I want to be there for mine.

With his eyes on the car shrouded in its protective cover, he remembered Jane recounting the conversation she'd had with Máire. *We were chatting when I was up in the flat. She told me the Saab is your baby.* It was only a turn of phrase, he thought. Máire doesn't do irony. Or maybe it wasn't a turn of phrase. Perhaps it's how she sees things. She may believe I'm happy to pour my energy and my time into a geekish choice of car, rather than have a family. That might even be fine with her. But it isn't with me. Or, if it has been, it isn't any longer. The clock's ticking. I love Máire, but I can't go on like this. I don't want to. With the best will in the world, I don't see how we can save this marriage.

Henrietta and Finbar had moved from their bar stools to a table, where he was eating a sandwich and fries and she was having a coffee. Pushing away his plate, he said, 'That was good. I suppose Des would kick off if I lit up a ciggie?'

'I'd say he would. I mean, I know there's no one around ...'

'Hey, no panic. Better to stay on the right side of the law.' Giving her an urbane smile, Finbar held up his glass. 'I could do with another one of these, though. Castlehill's always kept a good cellar.'

Henrietta called across to Des for a second whiskey, and watched as Finbar threw back the drink in one swallow. 'It's fantastic to see you, Dad. I'd no idea you were coming.'

317

'Yeah, well I took a chance. I hoped I might hit the get-together. It's fantastic to see you too. I've missed you like crazy.'

'Máire and Barbara are here as well.'

'Of course, and I'll see them later. Happening to catch you first is something special, though. We've always had something special, you and I.' Leaning forward, he looked into Henrietta's eyes. 'I was gutted to miss your wedding. You do know that?'

'Of course I do. The flowers were amazing.'

'What did you think of the present?'

This made no sense to Henrietta. 'Present?'

He smacked the table with his hand. 'Ah, for feck's sake! It didn't arrive? I sent it to you from Melbourne.'

Confused, she said, 'I thought you were in Hawaii when I married.'

'What? Yes. But you know how it is. One place and then another. No, actually, I waited till we got as far as Australia. There's a little guy there who sets opals in gold. They're amazing. I got him to make you a necklace. I can't believe it went astray.'

'That's awful.'

'You must have been thinking of me as a terrible dad.'

'Of course I wasn't. The flowers were stunning anyway, and I loved what you wrote on the card.'

'Oh, yeah. Those words said it all.' Hitching his lip in an imitation of Elvis, Finbar raised his empty glass and hummed the tune of 'Always On My Mind'.

'I think you wrote "Never forget me, always remember", because the flowers were forget-me-nots and rosemary, for remembrance.'

Looking slightly irritated, Finbar said, 'Sure. I know.' Then, recovering himself, he smiled into her eyes again. 'The point is, you're always on my mind. Wherever I go, whoever I'm with, you're always in my heart. Actually …' he waved a hand '… that's how I designed the necklace. Two hearts intertwined. I had him cut the opals specially. I wish you could have seen it, but it's the thought that counts, isn't it?'

'Of course.'

'Anyway, here you are, and you look like a million dollars.'

'It's probably the spa treatments. We've been having a great get-together weekend.'

'When are you off home?'

'Tomorrow. Dad, are you around for a while? You haven't met Stuart. I'd love you to come and stay with us in Dublin.'

'Well, obviously, I want to meet the man who stole my daughter. But, sweetheart, I couldn't intrude. I mean, would you have room for a guest?'

'Of course. There's bags of room. You can have your own en-suite. Oh, Dad, I'd love you to come. Stuart would too, and you could meet Jane. She's here with me, in fact. Stuart's away so I brought her with me.'

'Travels a lot, does he?'

'Yes. For business. He'll be home this week, though. You could come back to Dublin with me tomorrow. Do you have a car?'

'Actually, no. I haven't got round to hiring one. I flew in to Shannon from LA and made do with public transport.'

'I'll drive you. Will we do it? I'll call Stuart. Hang on, let me pay

319

for this first. Then I'll give him a shout and text Annaliese to ask her to make up the guest bedroom.'

'Who's Annaliese?'

'Our au-pair. Come on, Dad, say you're up for it. I know you'll probably have to shoot off somewhere soon, but this would be so great.'

Eyeing the platinum credit card she'd taken from her bag, Finbar said that, in fact, he hadn't any new dates in his diary. 'You know how it is, when the phone rings I'll have to get back on the road again. But, as of right now, I'm yours. It's a fantastic idea, sweetheart. Let's have another drink to celebrate!'

'Really? You'll come home with me?'

'Absolutely.' Finbar signalled to Des, who looked at Henrietta.

She nodded and said, 'Okay. Not for me, though. I'm not sure I could take it. Not on top of vodka.'

Finbar leaned back in his chair. 'Well, you've grown up, haven't you? And, obviously, you fell on your feet when you married. Those rings you're wearing didn't come cheap.'

Slightly taken aback, Henrietta said Stuart was wildly generous.

'That's good to hear.'

Knocking back his third whiskey, Finbar leaned his elbows on the table and fixed her with his huge, slightly unfocused, blue eyes. 'You know something, golden girl? I am so damn lucky to have you. I mean, it's cold out there and I've genuinely been wondering where the hell I was going to sleep tonight. Well, no, not tonight. I could have found a bed-and-breakfast. But God knows how long

I'll be here in Ireland before the phone rings, and finding Sheila had changed the bloody locks was a low blow.'

'Mum had? What locks?'

'In Athlone. My keys wouldn't let me into the house. I mean, talk about vindictive! But she was always the same, Hen. She's a bitter woman, just like her mother. No sensitivity. No understanding. I mean, I'm an artist. I'm a musician. Life on the road is hard, you know? A man needs comfort sometimes. And I sure as hell didn't get it at home, with three bloody kids underfoot.' Half aware of Henrietta's startled reaction, Finbar reached out and grabbed her hand. 'Not you. Not you, obviously. Not my golden girl. But kids are bloody demanding, Henrietta. Well, you know yourself, you've got Stuart's brat. They suck your soul out, don't they? Okay, no, no, maybe not. But they cost a fortune. And then, when you split up, your wife wipes you out. I mean, fair enough, she was pissed off at the time. I do understand that. And maybe bringing a girlfriend home was a bit iffy, but why should it bother a woman who, let's face it, is way past her sell-by date? I mean, over the hill and right down the other side.'

Staring in disbelief, Henrietta snatched her hand away. The weakly handsome face creased in amazement and, standing up, Finbar came round the table and tried to hug her. She pushed him off and, as he stood there swaying, she tried to speak and found her voice wouldn't come. She was dimly aware of Des in the background, looking concerned, and a couple of guests hovering in the doorway, evidently wondering if they should come in. When her voice came, it sounded weird, as if she'd been half strangled and only just managed to free herself. 'You've divorced Mum?'

'Of course not. Isn't that what I'm trying to tell you? She's divorced me and she's changed the bloody locks!'

Still trying to digest her conversation in Nora's suite, Sheila was on her way down to the bar. When the lift doors opened at Reception, she found Jane waiting outside to go up to her room.

'How was your afternoon with Raymond?'

'Brilliant. I helped him strip down the turbocharger. And I've just been out taking photos in the grounds.'

'That's nice. You're not cold?'

'It did get chilly when it got dark, but I'm going up to have a hot shower before dinner.'

'It'll just be the five of us. Nora's having an early night.'

'Is she okay?'

'She's fine. Just tired. If Henrietta's up in your room, will you tell her?'

'Sure.'

But as the lift closed and Sheila turned away, she saw the bar doors open on Henrietta, who came storming towards her like a bat out of hell.

'Hen, darling, what's the matter?'

The bar doors, which had swung to, were pushed open again from inside, revealing an all-too-familiar figure. Horrified, Sheila stepped backwards. 'Dear God! Is that your father? What's he doing here? What's happened?'

'Apparently, you've divorced him.'

'What? Oh, darling! I was going to tell you. I've been wanting to. I was trying to find the right moment.'

'Don't worry. He's done it for you.'

'Hen, I'm so sorry. I can explain.'

'Forget it, Mum. It doesn't matter. We're way past that point now.' Swinging round, Henrietta looked daggers at Finbar, who was hesitating beyond the Seedsavers stalls. She jabbed her finger at the exit and, when he didn't move, drew in her breath and strode threateningly towards him. Mesmerised, Sheila watched and, despite the wide expanse of Reception, saw the colour drain from Finbar's cheeks. An ingratiating smile she recognised flicked for a moment. Then his face sagged and, before Henrietta could reach him, he bolted like a rabbit and disappeared through the revolving door.

Chapter 27

If her conversation with Nora had sent Sheila in search of alcohol, she was twice as much in need of a drink after the scene in Reception. In the circumstances, a titchy minibar screw-top seemed inadequate but, as Henrietta had overturned several chairs when she left the bar, Sheila decided it would be wise to give Des time to recover. So, going to her bedroom, she seized the corkscrew and opened the bottle of wine, which, up to now, had remained untouched in her welcome basket. She drank most of the first glass with the bottle in her hand, then delved into the basket to find the box of chocolates. Though each was an exquisite work of art filled with raspberry mousse and caramel, she wolfed three without noticing their appearance and, taking a fourth, closed her eyes and washed it down with another gulp of Rioja.

Moments later, when she opened her eyes, she saw that her glass was almost empty, and recoiled at the smears of chocolate on its rim. Okay, she thought, sitting down in her yellow armchair.

First of all, I seem to have knocked back half a bottle as well as several kilos of fat and sugar. Secondly, if I don't drop dead or succumb to palpitations, I may come to see what's happened as the best possible outcome. Because, if I'd told Hen about the divorce myself, I would have presented it as a sensible conclusion reached by a responsible couple who'd happened to drift apart. Why did it never cross my mind that Finbar would try to prey on her? I should have seen that only the truth would protect her. Trying to keep it from her would have been a disastrous mistake.

Remembering Henrietta's flushed indignation in Reception, Sheila sat marvelling at the fiercely protective lioness who seemed to have taken the place of her youngest daughter. Hen had been less upset about Finbar's feet of clay than by the thought that she'd nearly opened her door to a feckless parasite who'd certainly have tried to ingratiate himself with Jane. Which means, thought Sheila, that if nothing else I managed to raise a daughter whose instincts as a mother are less messed up than my own. Jane seems to have more sense than the lot of us, but she's a pleaser, like Hen's always been, so God knows what damage might have been done if Finbar had got his feet under that table. But he met his match today, and it was glorious to see it. As for Hen, I doubt that the lioness she's become will ever revert to his fluffy little kitten.

The combination of red wine, raspberry mousse and chocolate was beginning to make Sheila feel dizzy. You've got to get your head together, she told herself severely. In only a few hours, we'll be having our last-night dinner. Mam's not coming down, you're supposed to be doing duty as the hostess, and here you are, half-cut, with way too much to process. Way too much, and no idea how you're going to manage.

Struggling to concentrate, she recalled her scene with Nora. The surge of optimism with which she'd approached the door of the suite. The mixture of relief and anticlimax when Nora had reached out her hand and they'd let the past fall away behind them. Her glee at Nora's reaction to the news of the divorce. And Nora's own bombshell, only moments later: it had blown everything that had gone before completely out of the water. The scene with Henrietta had driven it out of Sheila's mind. Now Nora's voice came back to her, making her reach again for the wineglass.

'What you said about Máire and Raymond not being happy in the flat? You're right, Sheila. I've seen it too. But you've missed the real point.'

'What point?'

'Máire's not happy because she's not up to managing Castlehill. My fault entirely. I made a bad decision. I don't blame myself. I'd just been widowed, and Martin had died unexpectedly. Still, it was my mistake, and it's up to me to correct it.'

'Correct it?'

'Put things right. She can't go on as general manager, that's perfectly clear. She'll fail, and that'll break her heart as well as destroying the business.'

'But, Mam, you can't sack her.'

'Of course not.'

'So, what are you going to do?'

'Sell Castlehill. Let it to go to the highest bidder, and divide the proceeds equally between you, me and the girls. I built the business for you. You didn't want it. I thought Máire had what it takes, but she doesn't. She won't back down, but I'm the one who made her position impossible. I've thought about it, Sheila. I've thought of little else over the weekend. This way, everyone gets a slice, and Máire doesn't lose face. So that's my decision.'

Groping for another chocolate and finding an empty box, Sheila sat back and clutched her head. It's logical, she thought. It does make sense. Or does it? It's evident Máire's overstretched, and that she isn't happy. But how will she feel if her job is whipped out from under her, like a rug? And what if her marriage to Raymond does fall to pieces? Where will she go? Okay, she'll have money, but how could she bear to live in Killmoy if the home she created goes, and Castlehill's sold off to the highest bidder? It's all very well for Mam to say the business has run its course. That's how she's always seen Castlehill, but it isn't the whole story. How will the girls cope if a hotel that's been the hub of their lives loses its identity to some faceless chain or conglomerate? God knows the thought's shaken me, and I've always hated the damn place.

Standing up, Sheila went to the window and stood looking out at the river. Hen loves it here, she thought, and it's obvious Jane's falling for it too. And what about Barbara? Something's gone awfully wrong in her life. I don't know what it is, but I know that more disruption's not going to help her. And I know Mam. Once she's made a decision, she'll go into action. She'll be down to the family solicitor as soon as we leave tomorrow, and make the announcement afterwards, as a fait accompli. There'll be no discussion. No talk of options. Not that there is any option I can think of. But how can I think, with all that's going on? It's as if I've spent the entire weekend on a runaway train that picks up speed again each time it starts to slow down. And now there's this on top of all the rest. Mam doesn't want a word said about the sale till she's set things up, and I can see why. But is that fair to the girls? Ought I to tell them over dinner? Or maybe just Barbara. Or Hen, now she seems to have turned into an adult. I can't very well tell Máire but, if I don't, wouldn't it be wrong to tell the others? And, dammit, it can't be over dinner. Not with Jane there. If only there was time to think, but there isn't. We're all leaving tomorrow, so I've got to come up with an answer, but it feels like every choice will lead to disaster.

In his cottage, Luke turned on a lamp and looked round his living room. Outside, the light was fading fast, the room felt chilly, and he hadn't yet lit the stove or cleared his breakfast things from the table. Moving automatically, he took the dishes through to the kitchen, ran the tap and left them to soak in the sink. The top of the iron stove was cold to the touch. Kneeling down, he riddled ashes from charred remnants of logs, took out the tray and tipped it into the ash-bucket by the hearth. Then, having replaced the empty tray, he systematically went round the room, dusting ash from surfaces, sweeping crumbs from the table, and straightening the sheepskin on the floor and the cushion on his armchair. Well, that's that, he thought. Tomorrow, I'll give my notice in writing. If all Máire wants is a handyman gardener who'll keep an eye on the boats, it won't be hard for her to find my replacement. Or, if she's seriously seen the light, there'll be plenty of qualified people who'll repeat exactly what I've tried to tell her, and might get a hearing.

Sitting on his heels, he began to construct the makings of a fire, crumpling paper and positioning new sticks on the charred remnants. I wish I could just walk away, he thought, but obviously I can't. It wouldn't be fair and, as Barbara would doubtless tell me, it would be suicidal as a career move. The reminder of Barbara struck him like a blow but, resolutely, he continued assembling kindling. There was no good in dwelling on what he'd lost, but no point in denying it either. Besides, he thought, she was never mine to lose. That was wishful thinking. And, to do her justice, she'd made her position clear to him from the beginning. He could see her now, cross-legged in the armchair by the stove, her auburn hair lit by a shaft of last year's sunlight. He'd looked up at her as he'd set a coffee pot by the hearth. 'So, I'm bedding a rootless, ruthless career-woman, is that the story?'

'That's one way of putting it. I prefer to think I travel light.'

'Comes to the same thing, though, doesn't it?'

'Yes, if you like. How about you?' She'd thrown a glance round the sparely furnished room with its few contents. 'It looks like you travel pretty light yourself.'

'I suppose it does.'

'So, we're two of a kind. Perfectly matched, you might say.'

He'd turned and encircled her with one hand on each arm of the chair, then pulled back, fearing the gesture was too possessive. Keep it light, he'd thought. She's laid her cards on the table. Anyway, nobody falls in love in a couple of days' snatched meetings. Now, as he balanced one stick of kindling against another, he told himself he'd known nothing about love. By then, it was far too late for me to save myself, he thought, and, as time went on, I let myself think that perhaps we *were* two of a kind. That maybe the same thing had happened to her and, like me, she'd been too scared to trust it. The fact is, though my pride is hurt, I didn't make an ass of myself by staying here, waiting and hoping. I could have been right. It was worth a chance, but I've had my answer this weekend. She made things plain again yesterday, when she left saying she had a lunch date. She must have met someone up at the hotel and made a date with him. And why not? Last year I was the man she met, so I'm in no position to be judgemental.

Lifting a basket from the hearth, he hefted it on to his shoulder and went outside to get logs from the woodshed. In the darkening garden he could hear the sound of river water and, closer to hand, the creak of wings as crows made for their roosts. If the river were properly managed, he thought, there could be a whole different kind of angling. In summer, these grounds could be full of wildflowers, and bees making honey. The hotel could graze cattle and horses, have hay to harvest, grow food for its kitchen. None of this land is barren. It's just waiting to come to life. Barbara sensed that once, but no one listened to her either.

The gravel path crunched underfoot as he made his way down to the shed. Nearby, on the lawn, movement in a pile of leaves revealed that he'd raked a shelter for a mouse or, perhaps, a hedgehog. A patch of snowdrops glimmered at the base of a sycamore. When he hunkered down, he could even see their spear-shaped leaves, dark green against the black roots that sheltered them. He'd planted the bulbs himself in his first months at Castlehill, one of the few personal touches he'd added to his living space. Yesterday, Barbara had told him his garden was looking well, and, facetiously, he'd quoted his contract of employment: 'A requirement to keep the tied cottage and its associated plot in good order.' Now, when he touched one of the snowdrops with his finger, its white petals were cold as the iron stove indoors. I didn't plant them because it was required of me, he thought. It was because I can't be happy without putting down roots. I never thought I'd be here for ever, but when I planted these, they were a token of commitment to all I wanted to do at Castlehill. Now, though they'll come back year after year, I won't be here to see them. I don't even know where I'm going to be in a few months' time, or how to live without hope of a life with Barbara. I can't wish that I'd never met her, but I wish things could have been different. If only they had, we might have been a team and put down roots here together. Instead, we'll both be packing our baggage and going our separate ways.

Máire was in her office mentally cursing her situation. If it hadn't been for the last-minute block-booking, she could have given Barbara a hotel bedroom and, right now, having a houseguest up in the flat felt unbearable. Her scene with Luke had been the last straw. All I want, she thought, is to go upstairs and howl, but how can I? If Barbara's there, I'll have to make conversation and, if she's not, I'll be constantly on the alert for her arrival. Staying here in the office will be just as bad. Serves me right for having an open-door policy that lets any one of the staff come barging in with hardly a knock.

The office, to the rear of the reception desk, was poky and had no window. Leaning on her elbows, Máire remembered her work room in Killmoy. It was at the back of the house and had a French door that opened directly on to the garden. A winter jasmine grew next to it, tied back to a trellis. At this time of year, she thought, the wall's starred with yellow flowers and, when the door's open, the scent is glorious. It's one of the nicest rooms in the house. So much so that it felt selfish to claim it. But Raymond insisted that it was made for me.

'It's obviously yours. We'll find you the perfect desk, and an armchair where you can loll while you're having ideas. Or a chaise-longue, like in a Jane Austen novel. I can dash in and make mad love to you on it when you ought to be at your desk going through budgets.'

She hadn't really needed a work room at home but, back then, her job didn't require her to be in the hotel twenty-four seven. Granny was still at the helm, thought Máire, and I still had a life. There was time to be creative, and have ideas, and smell the jasmine. I loved our first year in the house, when everything indoors was still chaotic, and flowers we hadn't known were there had begun to appear outside. Soon it'll be springtime again, and the family who rent the house will be opening the doors of my work room, wandering out into the garden, and watching birds swooping round with straws to build nests. Dismally, she sat back and looked at the strip light above her, her imagination working overtime. If

Raymond and I don't get our act together, I'll never open that work-room door again. All our stuff is in storage so, if our marriage breaks up, it'll make sense just to put the house on the market. Maybe we won't even need to bother. The tenants would probably leap at the chance to buy it. Who wouldn't? Anyone with a grain of sense would see how special it is. More to the point, anybody with sense wouldn't risk losing Raymond.

As she stared at the strip light, despair began to become determination. Luke's just shown me how dangerous it is to let things slide, she thought. If I'd listened to what he was trying to tell me, I wouldn't be sitting here now, faced with the prospect of having to cope without him. That's not going to change. It's clear that Luke's made his mind up. But surely it isn't too late for me to make things right with Raymond? He can't have fallen out of love with me completely. Or can he? Mum's right. Everyone has a breaking point. But I won't give him up without a fight. I mustn't. It's always been Raymond in pursuit. Now it's my turn to run to him.

She'd stood up and made for the door when it opened without a knock and Dymphna, her Housekeeping tsar swept in, bubbling with indignation. 'Sorry to disturb on a Sunday but, really, I can't be doing with this! I've been looking at next week's management-meeting agenda. What's this item about reviewing our laundry-service contract?'

Stopped in her tracks, Máire blinked at her. 'What item?'

'Oh, for goodness' sake! I assume it was you who drew up the agenda?'

'Yes. It was. What's the problem?'

'Well, I haven't wanted to say so before, but in my previous employment, it's always been the case that contentious agenda items were issued in draft in advance to the heads of relevant departments. I know your experience hasn't been wide, but it is the industry norm.'

'Look, Dymphna ...'

'I'm sorry but, really, the line has to be drawn somewhere. I do understand that the staff who've known you from childhood want to support you, but if you can't even recall an agenda item you've written yourself ...'

At that moment, something snapped in Máire. Sidestepping Dymphna, she snarled, 'I'll deal with you tomorrow,' and, squaring her shoulders, strode out of the office. As the lift carried her up to the flat, it struck her that tomorrow she might be facing the loss of not one but two of her management team. But, bursting through the door, she found Raymond making tea in the kitchen and, heedless of Barbara, who was there too, holding a tin of biscuits, she charged at him and grabbed him round the neck. 'Ray, I'm sorry. Honestly. I'm an absolute idiot. I should have listened to you. I got everything arseways.' Half aware of Barbara edging discreetly towards the door, Máire could feel Raymond's hands on hers, trying to free himself. She clung tighter and kept babbling. 'I want to go back to our house. I don't want to lose you, Ray. Please don't push me away. Please, let's talk. I don't want you to leave me.' He broke her hold and she burst out crying, sobbing so loudly she couldn't hear his reply.

'Raymond, listen, I want us to be a family. You and me. I want us to live in our own house and have a baby.'

He pushed her away again, and held her by the elbows. 'You do?'

'Yes. Really. I do. I mean, I do if you do. It's not too late, is it, Ray? I haven't ballsed the whole thing up? You do still want us to be married? Please say you do.'

Chapter 28

As substitute hostess, Sheila did her best at the last-night dinner. Some of the restaurant's tables were occupied by local diners who, seeing them troop in, raised their glasses in a friendly toast. Acknowledging the smiles and little bursts of clapping, Sheila made her way to their reserved corner, smiled at the waiter, appreciated the flowers on the table, and exclaimed at the menu Nora had chosen for them. There was a cheerful flurry as they found their seats but, what with Jane's presence and everyone's individual preoccupations, conversation when they sat down was limited, to say the least. By unspoken consent, they settled on Jane's photography as the safest subject for discussion. The shots she'd taken that afternoon were admired and commented on, and her phone passed around the table from hand to hand. But, though Henrietta and Barbara did their best to keep things buoyant, Máire seemed in a world of her own. So, eventually, when the talk was in danger of flagging, Sheila suggested sending Jane upstairs for Nora's book.

'I've always known it existed, but I don't think I've ever seen it. Have any of you?'

Picking up the cue, Henrietta shook her head. 'Not till Granny gave it to her. Did you know about it, Máire?'

Apparently lost in a reverie, Máire blinked and said, 'What? I don't think so.'

'Run up and get it, then, Jane. This is interesting, isn't it, girls?'

The book saw them through the rest of the meal, which broke up early with everyone saying they ought to go and pack. Still conscious of her role, Sheila moved to stand beside Barbara. 'We ought to mark the occasion. Let's get a group selfie. You'll take it, won't you, Jane? You're the expert.'

'Okay.'

'You can add it to your Then and Now exhibition.'

'Cool. Nora won't be in it, though.'

'We'll do another on the front steps tomorrow. She always comes out to wave us off.'

As Jane held up her phone for the shot, Sheila looked beyond her to where, among tables of tourists and Second Chance Club members, a doctor from Killmoy was dining with his wife, two women she'd been to school with were sipping Chardonnay as they chose their meal, and a farmer with a hearty voice was hosting a family party consisting of several generations. With Nora's decision to sell at the forefront of her mind, Sheila found herself seeing them with new eyes. Castlehill belongs to them more than to us, she thought. Long before we Sullivans turned the house into a hotel, members of these people's families would have worked here. They're the unnamed faces in the photos in the book that Mam gave Jane. Estate managers and stablemen, cooks, gardeners and nannies, coachmen, chauffeurs and parlourmaids, and boys who blacked the boots. People who, otherwise, might have had to leave home to find employment. Families who knew this place better than its owners. They would have been the men who dug the foundations and built the house. And, as time passed, the same local families became hotel patrons, or worked here in the holidays, or made a career here, like Des the barman. In a sense, they own this place as much as we do. The truth is, they'll continue to own it when we're gone. It's a strange thing to realise and, with the end in sight, I'm not certain whether or not I like the thought of it.

Twenty minutes later, Sheila was removing her makeup when Henrietta tapped on the door, came in and sat on the bed. 'I meant it, you know, when I said it didn't matter that you'd told Barbara and Máire ahead of me.'

Sheila could hardly bring herself to face her. 'Oh, Hen …'

'No, listen. I understand. You were worried about how I'd take it. Máire and Barbara were always offhand about Dad. I was the one who hadn't the sense to see through him.'

'I kept trying to hide the truth. I thought it was for the best.'

'Mum, you don't need to explain that either. I see it now. Truly.'

'I hate that you had to find everything out from your father.'

'Actually, that was something I found out from Jane.'

Astonished, Sheila turned from her seat at the dressing-table. 'From *Jane*?'

'Something she said sort of put things into context. And I got to thinking of how I'd cope if Stuart disappeared all the time, like Dad. I think I'd do exactly what you did. I'd cover his tracks because, if I didn't, Jane would be the one to suffer.'

'I'm still not sure it was the right thing to do.'

'Yeah, I'm starting to see that comes with territory when you're somebody's mother. But I promise you, Mum, I'm fine. There's no need to worry. I wanted to tell you before you lay awake all night in a state.'

'Thank you, darling.' Still troubled, Sheila gave her a shaky smile. 'There's a hell of a lot from the past for you to process, though.'

'I know. But we'll have plenty of time for it. I've been thinking it'd be good for you and Jane to get to know each other better, and I do have that spare room I was dumb enough to mention to Dad.'

'You mean I could visit? I'd like that.'

Henrietta smoothed the duvet cover. 'I'd like you to get to know Stuart too. And you know what? After this weekend, I think I'm going to be able to convince him that he needs to spend a lot more time at home with his family.'

Barbara and Máire had taken the lift back up to the flat. Alone together for the first time since Máire had burst in on Raymond, they avoided each other's eyes until Máire said, 'Sorry about that.'

'No good deed goes unpunished.'

'What?'

'Offer someone a room in your flat and they're sure to be making tea at the wrong moment.' Seeing Máire's blank look, Barbara gave her a push. 'That was a joke. I'm lightening the atmosphere.'

'Don't be daft. And don't push me. I'm a rotten hostess, though. I should've remembered you'd be there.'

'Oh, shut up, Máire. I take it that you and Raymond are okay now?'

Having contained herself through dinner, Máire suddenly glowed. 'Yes. Well … we will be. We're going to have a baby.'

'Woah. What? Wait! You're pregnant?'

'Of course not. Not yet. But that's the plan. Things are going to be different, Baba. I want to move back to the house. Change my priorities.'

'Give up your job?'

'Don't be silly. Obviously, I'm not going to leave Castlehill. We'll tweak things. It'll be fine.'

Beneath the glow of happiness there was a steely determination that Barbara recognised from the past. As the lift came to a stop, she put a hand on Máire's arm. 'This is going to take more than tweaks. What if it's not fine with Granny?'

'Don't be silly, Baba.'

'I'm no expert on babies, but I'm pretty sure they take a helluva lot of time and attention.'

'Things'll be fine. They have to be.'

The dogged note in Máire's voice told Barbara it was useless to press her point. 'Okay. Well, good luck.'

Though Máire had pulled her arm away, she said, 'Thanks. That means a lot.'

'Really?'

'You don't have to look so surprised.'

'Surprised? I'm gobsmacked. This is how Raymond must have felt when you charged in without warning and fell on his neck.'

The following morning they assembled on the hotel steps waiting for Nora to come and wave them goodbye. Having gone to bed relieved by her conversation with Henrietta, Sheila had spent half the night lying awake fretting about Nora's decision to put Castlehill on the market. Now she glanced at Máire, who was standing apart from the others, looking like a geyser about to explode. I ought to have told her, she thought. Whatever about the other two, I ought to have warned Máire. But there wasn't time and, anyway, the news isn't mine to tell her. It's Mam's hotel and I've accepted that she's going to make the announcement. It's too late to change my mind now.

There were two bright spots on Máire's cheeks, which intensified when Nora appeared in the doorway, and Sheila saw her hang back as the others surged forward. Linking Nora's arm, Henrietta drew her on to the steps. 'We'll never all fit in a selfie. Let's stand here, and Jane can take a group photo. No, hang on, she should be in it too. Could we ask one of the staff on Reception to take it?'

Nora, looking trim in a smart coat with a fur collar, laughed and gave her a cheery slap. 'Stop being bossy, that's my job, not yours! Jane, run in to Reception and find someone to take the shot. The rest of you, stand in line, get rid of your cases and straighten up. We'll have a proper formal family photo. Big smiles, and the hotel sign behind us.' Obediently, they started to put their bags behind the pillars, and Henrietta hugged Nora's arm. 'Another to frame and hang in the bar, Granny?'

'I'll have Cassidy's do prints and frame one for each of you. Get Reception to bring a chair out to me here, Jane. I'll sit in the middle and you can all stand around me.'

Sheila had a lurid vision of the last of the Romanovs standing and sitting in a formal line-up with no idea they were about to be shot. Oh, for feck's sake, she told herself. There's no need for melodrama. The sale is the sensible way forward. It's a clean break that means Máire won't have to lose face. And, much as I hate being marshalled into photos, it'll be nice to have a memento of our last get-together. Glancing along the line, she saw Barbara looking strained but composed. Máire, in her business suit, exuding pent-up energy. Henrietta, tucking Jane's hair behind her ears, then standing behind her with a radiant, maternal smile. Nora was in the centre with her fur collar turned up. I wonder how I look, thought Sheila. Probably just as I do in that photo of me on my eighteenth birthday, resentful and obviously longing to get away. How odd to know that, after all those years of longing, I'll never have to come here again.

When the photo was taken, the cars moved away in convoy towards the main gate. Nora stood on the steps waving till they were out of sight, then turned, tilted her chin, and went back indoors. Máire disappeared into her office.

In the passenger seat next to Barbara, Sheila loosened her scarf and said, 'That's that.'

Barbara shot her a glance in the rear-view mirror. 'I gather Hen knows about the divorce.'

'Did she say so?'

'There wasn't much time for detail, but yes.' They'd reached the gates and, in a resolute gesture, Barbara stepped on the accelerator. Then, as the hotel fell behind and the road stretched ahead, she shook herself and glanced at Sheila again. 'Did you get a chance to talk to Máire this morning?'

Sheila was still thinking about the sale, so her voice sharpened. 'Talk to her about what?'

'There was a big scene with Raymond last night before dinner.'

'Oh, God, no! What happened?'

'Calm down. Everything's fine. They're planning an idyllic future back in their own house.'

'They are?' Sheila's mind began to do somersaults again. 'They're moving out of the flat, then?'

'That's the idea. She's prioritising her marriage, just like you wanted. And not only that. Brace yourself. She's planning to make you a granny.'

'Hang on. Are you saying Máire wants to give up her job?'

'She definitely doesn't. She reckons things can be tweaked to allow her to keep the business suit and add a baby and roses round the door.'

'But how? There aren't enough hours in the day, and she's overstretched already. She can't have thought this through.'

'Of course she hasn't. She knows what she wants, though. It turns out she and Raymond have both been longing for a baby. But, from what Máire said to me last night, there's no way she's going to be happy unless she's still working at Castlehill.'

Henrietta's route to Dublin took her through Killmoy. Crossing the bridge, she turned left past the old corn exchange where, on Saturday, she and Jane had browsed the craft stalls. It seemed like an age since she'd found the pink floral patchwork cushion for Jane, and it struck her that she hadn't seen it since then. 'Do you know what happened to the bag we brought back from the craft market?' Jane, who was editing photos on her phone, gave a guilty start. 'My present? It's on the back seat. I didn't bring it into the hotel because … well, it wouldn't have fitted the décor. It's lovely, though. I mean, I like it. It'll go well in my room at home.'

'That's fine. I just hadn't seen it when we packed.'

Henrietta said no more till she'd cleared the town traffic and had settled into cruise on the motorway. Then she spoke without turning her head. 'You know something? There's no need to say you like things when you don't.'

'How d'you mean?'

'People who love you want to give you things that make you happy.'

'I know that.'

'If you're happy, they're happy too. But they wouldn't want you to pretend just to make them feel good.'

Jane side-eyed her. 'This isn't just about your cushion, is it?'

'No, it isn't. It's about Gan-Gan too. And your dad.'

'I don't hate frills and pink pom-poms. I've sort of moved on a bit, that's all.'

'I know. And Dad and Gan-Gan are just going to have to catch up.'

Jane stared at her phone. 'Do you think Dad's going to like my photos?'

'I know he will. Can I tell him about your Then and Now exhibition while you're assembling it? Or did you want to make it a surprise?'

With another sidelong look, Jane said, 'I don't mind if you tell him.'

'Okay. Leave it with me and I'll lay the ground.' With a surge of happy confidence, Henrietta hit the accelerator. 'Your dad and I have a lot of talking to do when we get home, anyway.'

Barbara's car drew in at the kerb outside Sheila's house. Still trying to take in the implications of what she'd been told about Máire, Sheila asked, 'D'you fancy a coffee before you press on for Dublin?'

'No, thanks, Mum. I'd better keep going.'

Hearing a catch in Barbara's voice, Sheila looked round and saw how tightly she was gripping the wheel. Frowning, she realised they'd been driving in total silence, and that Barbara was sitting stony-faced, with her jaw clenched. 'Darling, what's the matter?'

'Nothing's the matter. Look, I don't want to throw you out, but I need to keep moving.'

Suddenly something snapped in Sheila. 'All right, that's enough. We're not going to do this. I've been tiptoeing round you girls all weekend.'

'There's nothing to tiptoe round me for.'

'You've been in a state since yesterday.'

'No, I haven't.'

'Oh, for Heaven's sake, you were hiding behind a curtain during brunch!'

'Mum, please ...'

One of Sheila's hands had been on the door handle. Now she deliberately linked them on her lap. 'No chance, Barbara. I'm going nowhere.'

'What?'

'I'm not getting out of this car till you tell me what's happened. Which leaves us with three options. We sit here till the crack of doom, you take me with you to Dublin, or you talk to me and let me try to help.'

'There's no point in talking.'

'I warn you, if you take me with you to Dublin, I won't get out of the car there either.'

'Mum ...'

'And if we sit here long enough, someone's bound to call Social

Services or the guards. So, actually, you don't have any option. Tell me what's wrong.'

Barbara thumped the wheel with her fist. 'All right. My heart's broken. That's all.'

Sensing that a dam was breaking, Sheila kept her voice calm. 'Please, tell me about it, darling. Often things aren't as bad as you might think.'

'Actually, they're worse, because I haven't the faintest notion how to handle it. I've never felt out of control of my life before, and now I'm a mess.'

The story came out in clipped sentences punctuated by pauses in which Sheila held her breath for fear Barbara would clam up. When it ended, she said, 'So, this is what I'm hearing. Luke didn't kiss you, so you left.'

'No. That's not what happened at all.'

'That's what it sounds like.'

'Mum, it was so obvious I'd got the whole thing wrong. I'd thought that, since it seemed to me that I'd found my one and only, it was possible he might feel the same. But he didn't. And I know he still fancies me. We could have been there in the boathouse this morning, going at it like rabbits. Instead, he stonewalled me. He must have spotted how I felt, and decided the sex wasn't worth the aggravation.'

'Well, if that's the case, all I can say is you're well rid of him.'

'You know what, Mum? That remark really doesn't help.'

'Why should the poor man have to speak first? Why didn't you just tell him you love him?'

'Because …' Barbara's voice wobbled '… because I was afraid he'd say he didn't love me.'

'And if he *had* said that?'

'Then everything would've been over.'

'Oh, right. Like it isn't over now.'

Barbara raised her fists and thumped them against her temples. 'Shit!'

'You've driven away with no idea of how Luke actually feels. You'll never know unless you ask him.'

Barbara's voice was now so strained it was almost inaudible. 'And last night I heard Máire tell Raymond he's leaving.'

Something like an electric shock shot through Sheila, and all the kaleidoscope pieces of the weekend spun in her head. Gasping, she watched them reassemble themselves into a new picture. Reaching over her shoulder, she grabbed her seatbelt and rammed it home with a determined click. 'Okay, get this car started and do a U-turn. We're going back to Castlehill.'

The car came to a screeching halt just inside the hotel gates, and Barbara, who'd driven with ferocious intent, looked at Sheila. 'Hang on a minute, why have I brought you with me?'

'Because you're not the only one of us who's got something important to say. Go and find Luke. I need to talk to your granny.'

'Mum … I can't.'

'Of course you can. It's being in control of your life. That's your thing, remember? Just like never being on top of anything at all has been mine.'

'I really don't have time to stay here and tell you that's utter bollocks.'

'You don't need to. It's about to change.'

Hardly aware of what was being said, Barbara peered at herself in the mirror. 'What do I look like?'

'Death warmed up. Get out of this car, and get on.'

Sheila watched her till she disappeared down the riverside path. Then, turning away, she looked up at the hotel. It was a bright January morning with a sense of incipient spring, and sunlight glinted on the tall windows. Bracing herself, she walked up the curving drive. Cyclamen were flowering in the urns that flanked the doorway, patches of purple under the carefully clipped hollies. As she approached the revolving door, it spun to reveal an emerging group of Second Chance Club ladies. Talk about a merry-go-round, thought Sheila. It's not much more than an hour since I walked down these steps thinking I'd never go through that door again. Now I'm about to sweep in and make authoritative pronouncements with nothing to back them but a bizarre kaleidoscopic moment and a conviction that I'm right. The chattering group divided and flowed past on either side of her, exclaiming at the beauty of the morning. Lifting her chin at an angle that exactly matched her mother's, Sheila put both hands on the revolving door and pushed.

She was halfway to the lifts when she heard a voice behind her and turned to see Máire coming out of her office. 'Mum? What are you doing here? You left with Baba.'

'I'm going up to your granny's suite.'

'Why? No, but you can't. Not now. I'm on my way up to talk to her.'

'Máire …'

'Oh, Mum. This is important. I need to see Granny.' Lowering her voice, Máire stepped closer. 'Okay, look, you were right. I did push Raymond almost to breaking point. But we've talked, and we're fine, but there's going to have to be changes.'

Grasping her elbow, Sheila pulled her behind a potted palm and, shielded by foliage, said, 'Máire, *listen*. I'm going up to your grandmother's suite and you're staying down here till I've had a talk with her.'

'But I need to speak to her right away. It's important.'

'Stop this, Máire. I know you've spent your entire life refusing to take anybody's advice, especially mine. But I'm your mother and, this time, you're going to do as you're told.'

'But—'

'Stay down here. You can come upstairs when I've spoken to your granny.'

Chapter 29

'So, that's my proposal, Mam, and I'm certain it's going to work. I do see the logic of selling up in the circumstances you outlined. But not if circumstances have changed. And I think they have.'

Nora raised her eyebrow. 'You think they have?'

'I know they have where Máire's concerned. And I'm pretty certain Barbara's going to want to jump at it too.'

'I don't see why.'

'She's always been interested in the grounds. You know she has. When she was at school, she talked about it. We just didn't listen.'

'If you want me to listen to you now, you'd better sit down and stop looming over me.'

'Sorry.' Sheila sank on to the sofa next to Nora. 'We're not much good at listening in this family, that's been the problem. That and the fact that we're not much good at talking.'

'You've certainly found your voice.'

'It's not about me, Mam. It's about the girls. Remember me saying I'd always thought of myself as a useless mother? And you telling me you'd spent years thinking you were a useless wife?'

Nora bristled. 'It was how I was made to feel, and it was nonsense. I proved that. But, all right, yes, I did begin to think it. What are you saying?'

'I'm saying I didn't need anybody to tell me I was useless: I knew it. I should have left Finbar the moment I realised what kind of man I'd married. I could have taken Máire and come home to you. It would have been far better for her, but I hadn't the guts to do it. And then I got pregnant with Barbara and I didn't know what to do next. Oh, look, I don't want to start raking up the past again. All I'm saying is that, as a mother, I made a lot of dumb choices. Finbar's not here to blame anymore, so it's time to start making amends.'

Nora, who'd listened in silence, straightened the cuffs of her quilted dressing-gown. 'In my day, people were raised to mind their own business. But I've always wondered why you stayed with Finbar when you got pregnant with Barbara.'

Something in how this was said made Sheila turn her head sharply. 'What do you mean?'

'I mean I wondered what made you choose him instead of Barbara's father.'

'Her father? But ...'

'Ah, child, I've always known it wasn't Finbar. It was the lad who worked with Matty that summer, wasn't it?'

Stunned, Sheila asked, 'How did you know?'

'I used to watch you from the window when you were in the grounds. You hated coming up to the flat when Máire was here with me, so you used to be up and down the river path before you'd collect her. I saw you walking with that lad. I don't recall his name.'

'Owen.'

'That's right. He was a good worker. Martin wanted to keep him on, but he disappeared without even giving his notice.'

'I'd told him I wouldn't leave Finbar.' Sheila suddenly buried her face in her hands. 'Owen wanted me to come with him. I couldn't, because of Máire. He would have been happy for me to bring her, but he wasn't Máire's dad.'

'Did Owen know you were pregnant?'

'No. I didn't find out until he was gone. And later I thought, What have I done to Barbara? Because I'd sort of convinced myself Finbar might change as the girls grew older. But he didn't. And then I thought I could build a new life for the three of us in Athlone. I'd have a decent home for the two girls, and I could divorce Finbar. He was hardly there, anyway. I thought I could wait till the girls were settled and work was going well. But Finbar kept turning up out of the blue, and they seemed pleased to see him. It felt like we might make a go of being a family. And then, like a fool, I got pregnant with Henrietta. But he hadn't changed and, as time went on, I could see Máire and Barbara begin to despise him. But Hen was his golden girl, Mam. She adored him. If I'd left him then, she'd have been broken-hearted.' Dropping her hands, Sheila looked at Nora with tears streaming down her face. 'You knew all along? About Barbara?'

'I say I knew, I suppose I just guessed. If you didn't choose to tell me, I certainly wasn't going to ask you.'

Sheila gave her a watery smile. 'Well, that would have been the last straw. I don't think I could have coped.'

Nora responded with a country-woman's dig in the ribs with her elbow. 'D'you know what it is, girl? There's a pair of us in it. When things went wrong for me, I couldn't bring myself to talk to my mother either. I suppose you're right. We're no good at talking or at listening.' Cocking her eye at Sheila, she said, 'It must have been a relief when Barbara turned out to look like you. You're both the spit of that fancy portrait of Martin. I assume you've told her nothing?'

'No, but I will. One day, when she's found contentment and knows who she is in herself. By then where she came from won't matter.' Sheila took out a tissue, blew her nose and wiped her eyes. 'Does it matter to you, though? Given what I'm suggesting?'

'Let me get this straight. You're suggesting I split the general manager role in two, and give Máire responsibility for the hotel buildings while Barbara takes over the grounds?'

'That's the idea.'

'Two Sullivan Girls running the place, instead of one.'

Sheila laughed shakily. 'That's a broad definition of Sullivan Girl. Máire's taken Raymond's name and Barbara has no real right to Finbar's.'

'I'm the one that decides who's a Sullivan Girl and who isn't. Jane's been brought into the fold, remember. Besides, this sounds like a workable idea.' Getting up, Nora went to the window. Her voice, which had been businesslike, softened as she stood with her back to Sheila. 'Nobody knows better than me that being a mother's not easy.'

'Well, thanks for that!'

'Be quiet, child, and listen to what I'm saying. Whatever we got wrong in the past, the bottom line is that you and I kept going. You're a good mother. You always have been.'

Sheila found another tissue and blew her nose again. 'We're breaking the habits of a lifetime, are we? Okay, here's a thing that also needs saying. I haven't come up with this bright idea just for the sake of the girls. I don't want Castlehill sold, Mam. I've been thinking. It matters to me. I want the Sullivan family to stay rooted here.'

'Is that so? Here's a thought for you, then. We could split the general manager role three ways instead of two. After all, you made a fair fist of that business of yours in Athlone.' This was Nora in full negotiation mode, as poker-faced as she'd ever been when doing a deal with a builder.

With a genuine laugh, Sheila got up from the sofa. 'Nice try, Mam, but no, we couldn't. I'm no more a hotelier than Hen is.' Pushing the tissue into her pocket, she went and joined Nora by the window. 'You're right, though, we will need a third wheel. When Máire's not overstretched, she's good at what she does: she loves Castlehill and she's got the right qualifications. Barbara's experience means she'll know how to integrate the two sides of the business. But we'll want someone with a background in landscape gardening too, and a degree in water conservation and management.'

'That tripped off the tongue. I can tell you've got someone in mind.'

'Máire's been struggling for months, and she sort of cracked this weekend. She's managed to get her head straight, but it looks like she may have lost a vital team member.'

'I should have taken a grip on things sooner. Who's leaving?'

'Luke Ryan. Apparently, when we drove away this morning, he'd made up his mind that there was nothing to stay for.'

Nora absorbed this, met Sheila's eyes, and took her time replying. 'I see. But you've come back. With Barbara.'

Reaching out, Sheila put an arm around Nora's shoulders and moved her closer to the window. 'Look down there. No, to the left. By the river.' Standing side by side, they looked out together. Far below, on the river path, Barbara and Luke were leaning against a tree trunk, kissing. Beyond them, water gleamed like green silk, and crows called in the sycamore branches above them.

Nora stepped back, lest she be seen watching, gripped the curtain with one hand and held out the other to Sheila. 'That's exactly how you and her father looked when I saw you from the flat.'

Sheila took the outstretched hand. 'I imagine it was. It's how people look when they're in love. Perfectly happy to have no idea what might be coming next.'

'But this time we do know, don't we?'

'Yes. Yes, I think we do.'

'And you're sure about Máire? And Raymond?'

'Especially Raymond. He and Máire are planning to have a baby.'

Down by the river, the crows rose in an iridescent swirl of beating wings and stretched beaks. Barbara and Luke broke apart, looked up at them, and laughed in sheer exuberance. With a smile, Nora turned from the window and moved her grasp to Sheila's elbow. 'I haven't got much time left to me now, and I'm not going to waste any more of it picking bones out of the past. Let's get those children up here and start planning a better future.'

'Mum! Really?'

'Really. But I'd best get out of this dressing-gown first, and put a suit and some heels on. Come through to the bedroom with me, girl. I'll need you to give me a hand.'

Acknowledgements

My first thanks go to everybody who buys my books or borrows them from their local library, to book clubs, reviewers and bloggers, and to the tireless booksellers who organise events, set up gorgeous displays in their shops, and feature my novels on their websites and social media. That kind of exposure doesn't just increase sales, it forms human connections in empathetic, creative ways that algorithms will never manufacture. It's a network of support that always surprises and delights me, and I'd like you to know how much it's appreciated.

The seeds of different novels germinate in different conditions. With some, it's a case of diving head first into the writing, while others may need research and contemplation. I'm grateful to the beautiful, welcoming Falls Hotel and Spa in Ennistymon, where I spent time when researching *Once a Year*. Special thanks to sales and marketing manager Michelle McManus, and to her predecessor Sharon Malone, who generously gave her time and advice and arranged for me to talk to her colleagues about the running of a luxurious country-house hotel.

I'm grateful to Geraldine McGlynn, former owner of Golden Ireland, and to all the hospitality industry professionals I met over several years of writing about Irish tourism. Ireland's hoteliers' growing commitment to sustainability was part of the inspiration for Barbara and Luke's storyline, as were the numbers of people I met who, after working abroad, have chosen to bring their world-class experience and professionalism home to the rural areas where they grew up.

Once a Year was written on a West Kerry mountain and in central London. Huge thanks are owed to my neighbours in both places, for friendship, interest in progress reports, coffee breaks and laughs, as well as emergency access to printers and broadband, and fresh milk in the fridge when I'd stagger in after hours of travel.

I'm indebted to everyone at my publishers, Hachette Books Ireland, particularly Ciara Doorley who commissioned *Once a Year*, my editor Joanna Smyth, publishing assistant Stephen Riordan, and to my copyeditor Hazel Orme. I'd also like to say thank you to two Hachette legends – group managing director Breda Purdue and sales director Ruth Shern – for their support over the years, the crowded signing days with Ruth, who's known and loved in every bookshop in Ireland, and the fact that it was Breda whose response to a tentative pitch brought me from writing scripts to writing novels.

My husband Wilf is a rock without whom nothing at all would be written. And, as ever, my heartfelt thanks are due to my stellar agent Gaia Banks at Sheil Land Associates, London, and to all her colleagues, in particular Natalie Barracliffe and Lauren Coleman.

RAISING READERS
Books Build Bright Futures

Dear Reader,

We'd love your attention for one more page to tell you about the crisis in children's reading, and what we can all do.

Studies have shown that reading for fun is the **single biggest predictor of a child's future success** – more than family circumstance, parents' educational background or income. It improves academic results, mental health, wealth, communication skills and ambition.

The number of children reading for fun is in rapid decline. Young people have a lot of competition for their time, and a worryingly high number do not have a single book at home.

Our business works extensively with schools, libraries and literacy charities, but here are some ways we can all raise more readers:

- Reading to children for just 10 minutes a day makes a difference
- Don't give up if your children aren't regular readers – there will be books for them!
- Visit bookshops and libraries to get recommendations
- Encourage them to listen to audiobooks
- Support school libraries
- Give books as gifts

Thank you for reading.
www.JoinRaisingReaders.com